ONLY THE WIND

Then, as she stood there, it seemed that a deep, sweeping cloud came over the moon. And standing alone in the darkness outside the hospital, she felt vulnerable, as she never had before.

Stephanie . . . come!

It was the darkness, the strange shadows. She clamped her hands over her ears. She was letting her imagination play terrible tricks on her.

Stephanie . . .

She thought she heard throaty laughter.

It was only the sound of the wind, whispering through the trees.

She turned and ran back to the hospital.

Back to the blazing light that she knew, beyond a doubt, to be real.

Because she knew, deep in her heart, that she was being called.

Called . . .

Into the darkness.

Other books by Shannon Drake

The Awakening

Realm of Shadows

Deep Midnight

When Darkness Falls

Beneath a Blood Red Moon

Published by Zebra Books

SHANNON DRAKE

Dead by Dusk

ZEBRA BOOKS
KENSINGTON PUBLISHING CORP.
http://www.kensingtonbooks.com

ZEBRA BOOKS are published by

Kensington Publishing Corp.
850 Third Avenue
New York, NY 10022

All Kensington titles, imprints and distributed lines are available at special quantity discounts for bulk purchases for sales promotion, premiums, fund-raising, educational or institutional use.

Special book excerpts or customized printings can also be created to fit specific needs. For details, write or phone the office of the Kensington Special Sales Manager: Kensington Publishing Corp., 850 Third Avenue, New York, NY 10022. Attn. Special Sales Department. Phone: 1-800-221-2647.

Zebra and the Z logo Reg. U.S. Pat. & TM Off.

First Printing: January 2005
10 9 8 7 6 5 4 3 2 1

Printed in the United States of America

Prologue

Legend

Raoul Masson, squire to Conan de Burgh, burst in upon his master where the great Norman warlord sat at his desk, writing letters to his king in Paris.

Startled, Conan de Burgh looked up.

Raoul was in a rare state of anxiety.

"They're coming. The villagers, the people, from miles around. Knights who have long since surrendered have taken up their swords and shields again."

This area of fierce Calabrian tribesmen had certainly produced its share of excellent fighting men, and yet, it was difficult at first to understand Raoul's agitation. Fighting to subdue the populace had often been brutal and cost many lives, but the battles were long done. The townspeople were little able to make war now against the power of the Comte de Burgh's well horsed, trained, and steel-armed knights. Though de Burgh had reached his position of power through heated battle and tournament, time and time again, he was a man who had come to greatly love peace and the riches of posterity. He was known for the mercy he showed those who were conquered and brought under the Norman yoke. Though his men could easily smash a small rebellion of peasants bearing scythes and hoes, he did not want the slaughter it would cause. Even if a great number of trained soldiers had arisen again, they had been bested before and could be brought down again.

He was puzzled. The chain of command had been running smoothly. In the last year, he had proven to the people that they could live well beneath his rule. To many peasants it mattered little where the man had come from who called himself lord, just that he refrained from slicing their necks, raping their wives, and stealing their entire produce.

Conan frowned, rising, reaching for the heavy battle sword that never left his side.

"What is their grief?" he asked Raoul.

Raoul, a strapping young man, looked ill. "The slaughter, my lord. Sweet Jesu! The slaughter. I saw . . . I saw myself. They were strewn . . . in pieces . . . across the field. They say that it was the Lady Valeria, so they were told, and there have been the whispers . . . you must see yourself, you must see! The people . . . they are not rising against you. They are demanding that you act. You have refused to see the evil in Valeria and François, my lord, but now the people are rising against *you*. François intends conquest even here, and she is with him."

Conan felt ill. His heart sank.

Valeria.

He had come here, the great conqueror, proven, confident, and self-assured, but then found himself at a loss, shaken by his deep desire for the incredible daughter of the Italian magnate Paolo Ratini. Quick to see the power of the great waves of Normans, Paolo had astutely joined forces with the conquerors.

The first time Conan had ridden to the Palacio Ratini, Valeria had stood out upon the balcony, and he had seen her, ebony hair bared to the sun, eyes huge and deep blue, face sculpted like the finest porcelain. She had smiled, evidently fascinated by the sight of him—or his great party.

He hadn't known or cared.

The great passion of his life had been born. She was well bred, naturally, the daughter of such a man as Paolo. He had intended marriage from the moment he saw her, and it would have been right, natural, just like the nearly excruciating hunger that had grown between them. A vital man of tremendous strength, bred himself to conquest, power, courage, and the endless battle such a life required, he'd known innumerable women throughout his life, from the basest whores to the most refined nobility, and yet, he had never known anyone like Valeria. She had been widowed during one of the first battles between native lords and encroaching Normans, and was experienced, fully mature and beautiful in her form, the mother of a young daughter. Intimacy with her was as raw as the rugged cliffs and verdant earth of Calabria. It was something more as well, almost ethereal, a touch of heaven, thoughts that a man such as himself shared with no one, including the woman who so enthralled him. He had planned on marriage, a life of such never-ending fever and bliss.

But destiny had other plans for the lady in the form of François de Venue, an illegitimate cousin of the king in Paris. Thus far, Conan's great strength, and his natural ability to lead and draw others to him with absolute loyalty, had preserved his presence here, and he assumed that François would not dare to challenge him. But the bastard royal, François, had arrived upon the scene with a brutal and unnecessary violence. Those areas still in minor rebellion fell beneath his onslaught. Men who still might have ridden proudly beneath a Norman banner had been slaughtered. Somehow, François and his men had triumphed over larger forces, leaving battlefields with few of their own lost, while the enemy lay decimated.

The first conquest François had made upon his arrival

had been that of Valeria, as well as her father's holdings. Conan was stunned by the betrayal. Had Paolo turned his daughter over to François in pursuit of what he perceived as a greater power? Or had the man been threatened to such an extent that he'd felt he'd had no choice? The one tryst Conan had managed with Valeria after the arrival of his French counterpart had been deeply wrenching; he had been willing to fight any man for Valeria, including his own king. But while the beauty clung to him, in tears, holding tight as if she might forever memorize their time together, she denied him. She didn't want him to fight for her. He would never understand, but she was betrothed to François because she had to be, and any effort Conan made on her behalf would cause her nothing but harm. And so he had stepped aside. He had kept his fury leashed, watching François ravage the countryside, killing again and again. He had been stunned to hear that Valeria had often appeared on the battlefield at the side of her betrothed, and it was rumored that it was she who brought about such death and destruction. He had never thought, however, that an entire populace could believe the woman capable of such horror. And yet . . .

He heard again and again that indeed, it was she, Valeria, who brought about the anguish and bloodshed. The people had spoken of her as if she were a witch, a monster, the devil's own bride cloaked in beauty. As of late, he had even begun to fear for her.

"My lord, they will be upon us any minute," Raoul reminded him, urgency growing in his voice.

Conan strode for the door in the office of the magnificent fortress, built right into one of the cliffs and almost impregnable. A fine hallway with Roman marble columns brought him to the sweeping stairway; he descended to the great hall, where his knights were assembling. Well trained and attuned to his every move, men rushed forward with his armor, buckling chain and plate into place and proper position.

Hagar, his massive black war stallion, was brought to the entry, and he strode at the head of his men, readying to meet the hordes.

And they were coming. Just as Raoul had said. It was night, but then, he had heard that much slaughter had taken place at night, and de Venue and his company had often fallen upon the innocent during the very late hours, before the dawn. They rode with monsters, he had been told, great dogs that tore into the flesh of men and babes alike.

Now, torches burning in a sea so great it might have been day, the people were coming. Some were soldiers, some peasants, others were women and children.

Conan mounted Hagar at the head of his men; he motioned that the gate down the slope be opened, and he rode out from the walls with his most trusted knights at his side, his men-at-arms following in rank. Before the great field at the foot of the cliff, his fellows flanked him in a line; then he rode forward alone.

"Halt! Tell me, what is it that you seek from me?" he bellowed loudly to the crowd, his voice deep and rich with the confidence and authority he never failed to wield.

A fellow burst forth from the crowd, a man he knew: a fine Calabrian warrior who had lain down his arms and accepted a truce. He was Giovanni da Silva, young and intelligent, a man of God and of faith, and yet tonight, his eyes were as wild as those of a madman.

"Lord Conan!" he called. "We have accepted your rule—the peasants beneath you saw a kinder man than they had served before. But tonight, if you do not lead us against the devil horde of François de Venue, we will die to a man—indeed, the women and children among us as well!—if you do not take arms against the unholy butchery of your countrymen. Against him, the witch who commands the wind and fog, and the demon dogs that come before them. Lord Conan, you alone have the power to fight such unearthly demons, and you alone, blessed sire, must rid us of the monster queen who would slay us all."

"Good fellows, knights and peasants among you, surely you cannot believe that the woman is such a monster!" he called back.

"Make way!" da Silva called, and a woman, young and slender, work-worn at a tender age, burst through with the bloody, battered body of a young lad in her arms.

"She did this!" the woman cried brokenly to him. "I saw her. Saw her stand upon the hill, and the demon dogs rushed around her, and laid claim to our village. I saw her! Saw her lift her hand, saw the light of hell in her eyes. If you do not stop her, slay her, she will tear down everything. By gracious God, dear Lord Conan!" She fell to the earth, her tears mingling with the blood of her son. "You must help us!"

From the southeast, a bloodcurdling howl suddenly encompassed the night. The earth itself seemed to tremble. Conan was not a man who feared battle, pain, or even death. Yet at the sound of that howling, he felt as if his blood grew cold and congealed in his veins. Fear trickled in icy rivulets along his spine. Angrily, he ignored it, ignored the unholy unease that seemed to filter into his very being.

Wolves. Wolves crying to the moon by night, nothing more. Or wild dogs, perhaps, their one-time owners dead and decaying upon shorn fields where battle had taken place, now left to starve and rampage and ravage on their own.

"Wolves, or wild dogs," he said aloud.

"No! You don't understand, you've yet to see . . . you won't believe. You must come, now. You must lead us. They attack yet another village!" da Silva told him. "Lord Conan! For the love of God!"

He nodded. Best that he lead the forces against François and Valeria, who was surely forced to ride at his side, who must now have witnessed such horror that she stared upon it, her eyes glazed with dismay. If he were to conquer François, he would make himself an enemy of his own king. And yet he had earned his place here; the king would have to make war on him, and he doubted that, far away in Paris, the king could afford the men and arms he would need to roust Conan from his powerful hold. That mattered little. Seeing the horde before him, the tears, the blood, the strange majesty of the thousands of torches burning in the night, he knew there was no choice.

"Aye, then, we ride against François," he said.

"Wait!"

From the crowd, a cleric rushed forward. It was customary to pray before entering upon the field of battle and death. Yet this fire-eyed priest would demand that he dismount and kneel, were he not to do so of his own volition, and so he did. The priest burst into a spate of Latin so rushed that Conan could not follow, though he, like others of his status, was taught the language as a child. And when the words were done, the priest stepped forward, placing a huge silver cross around his neck. Even as he mounted, he felt himself doused with drops of holy water as the priest intoned more words he could not discern.

Mounted again, he lifted his hands, and his knights and men fell in beside him, the hordes of people behind them, Normans and natives of the Italian peninsula as well.

They rode.

The moon high above them, a strange, cold wind whipping at their mantles.

They approached Trincia, the village under attack. As they rode, the wind whipped higher, for there was a fog upon the ground, and the wind did not disperse it. They could hear screams and cries, and the unearthly howling of dogs. Riding into the mire at last, they saw the troops of François de Venue emerging through the fog, making a line before them.

François led.

Valeria was at his side.

Dark hair billowing down her shoulders, violet eyes dazed, and yet he thought that the strange glow came from tears. He had loved her so.

"Get from here, Conan!" François shouted angrily. "I have let you live—go, and be grateful."

"Eventually, you will come for me," Conan said. "But that matters not. You've become a warrior against life itself, against God and man, and I will stop you!"

The dark, handsome face of François de Venue darkened into a scowl of fury. Then he smiled. "Never," he said. "Tonight, Conan, is as good as any night for you to die!"

"We shall meet in hell then, François. If need be, we shall meet in hell," Conan told him.

"Valeria!" François roared suddenly.

She didn't move, but stared at Conan.

"Remember the child!" François said sharply to Valeria. And he leaned toward her, whispering.

The wind began to whip anew in an eerie, dark swirl of fog and night. The baying began.

And the demon dogs came rushing through the throngs of horsemen that flanked François and his troops. And Valeria.

Conan drew his sword. "For God and man!" he roared.

The first animal leapt upon him and Hagar. The great war horse staggered. The animal was a dog, and not a dog. It was huge in size, but not a wolf. Its teeth were more those of a great cat, a tiger in the night, than those of a canine. Its shoulder muscles were huge, and its massive paws held cat claws. The sight of the beast, bringing down both Hagar and himself, was so startling that Conan almost missed his instinctive reaction. But he brought his sword forth in powerful fury, and severed the animal's head from its shoulders before its teeth could tear into flesh.

All around him, he heard the screams of his men as they met the beasts. Slashed, cut, and stabbed, they rose again to attack men and horses. Unseated, Conan fought in a desperate fever himself, fighting in front and behind, striking fur and flesh and bone, only to have the creatures rise again. With a great blow, he severed the head of another creature and realized that death came to the demon dogs only then.

"The heads! Sever the heads!" he roared to his men.

And slowly, slowly, with screams of death and despair rising around him all the while, the demon dogs were brought low, and then they were left to battle the men who fell in line behind them.

Despite the wind, the dark swirl of eerie fog, the forces of Conan de Burgh began to push back the enemy.

François himself was upon him then, in a rage of energy, his sword swinging with such fever and strength that Conan was incredulous, battling desperately for his life. He had never encountered such power in a man. His men, engaged around him, could do nothing, and he feared that his great efforts would fail, for should he fall, his men would retreat, and the forces of his enemy would follow, and all would be slaughtered in this bloodbath.

He deflected a mighty blow from François, who was in such a berserk wrath that foam gushed through his thin lips. Down upon the ground, he feared the brutal weight and strength of his enemy would finish him at last. Yet as François lifted his arm to deliver the *coup de grâce*, Conan managed to lift his sword, and the tip of his weapon struck straight into the base of the man's throat, where no helmet or mail protected him. He caught hold of a vein, and the man wavered. Calling upon his last resources, Conan forced the sword deeper, finding his feet against the weight of his own chain and mail, and with a maddened pressure delivered by God or desperation, he pressed the sword with an ever greater fervor. Like the demon dogs, he knew somehow that François would perish if his head were severed.

And so it was. His enemy fell to his knees, gurgling

through the blood that spurted from his throat. Conan strained harder, and François was forced down on his back, and still his eyes were alive with fury and hatred, and some strange glint of knowing.

"Valeria! Valeria! Valeria!"

The chant had gone up from those around them, as great as the field of torches and lights that had filled the field of battle.

"They have her!" Conan heard, and saw that Raoul had never faltered, had fought at his side all along, while others had rushed forward.

François de Venue remained on the ground, fingers around his throat, choking on his blood.

"His head. Sever his head!" Conan commanded. He was already moving. He had to reach Valeria. They meant to kill her.

They had fought at the village in the valley at the base of great cliffs. And as he looked up now, he saw that the men had taken Valeria, that she was laden down with silver chains, and a large silver cross swung between the valley of her breasts. Giovanni da Silva had her high up on the tor of a cliff. She was being forced to her knees. Da Silva was ready to deliver an executioner's blow upon her neck.

"No!" Conan roared the word, casting off his helmet as he raced the distance to the cliffs, threw himself upon the rock, and began to climb.

"By God, she must die!" da Silva called back.

By some insane mercy, Conan reached the cliff and the outcrop of rock where Valeria had been taken. The little plateau might have been a strange, sacrificial altar, the way it protruded high above the ground and jutted out over the battle-field.

Da Silva drew his sword high, and Conan crawled atop the rock and found his footing just in time. He grasped the man's arm, with Valeria at his knees, and there they locked in a magnificent struggle.

Conan glanced down. And he saw her eyes.

And for a second, he was frozen in the midst of his very struggle.

"Conan de Burgh!" came a roar, and he was distracted to the edge of the tor, where he saw that François de Venue, incredibly, had crawled as well, his life's blood still streaming down his throat. By all rights of nature, the man should have been dead!

Da Silva screamed out, crying to God, and to the heavens, and to all that was holy.

A great sound suddenly filled the night, a rumbling of the earth, a schism in time and place and being, in the very world.

A cracking . . . fracturing . . .

And suddenly, the tor upon which they stood began to shake, and all were thrown to the earth. The rumbling continued until . . .

Strewn upon the ground, helpless against the explosion of the earth, Conan heard a whisper. "My love . . . !"

She crawled to him, violet eyes huge. Stunned, he felt the shattering of ground.

And one more thing.

Her tears upon his face.

Her lips . . . against his flesh.

The earth, the rock, the very ground upon which they stood began to break and crumble. It seemed that there was another howl in the night—the horrible, dying shriek of a demon dog.

And then the earth exploded, and the cliffs themselves tore apart and fell . . .

François, covered in blood and still at the edge of the precipice, toppled first. Down . . . down to the earth below them.

Then the rock shattered like glass, and all who had stood upon it came crashing down to earth.

People, shrubs, creatures, rocks, and trees . . . all crumbled and fell. And as dust and earth and bits and pieces of rock came tumbling after, the dawn came.

Streaked with gold, yet heavily laden with the crimson of spilled blood.

And beneath great piles, tons of rock, lay the bodies of those who had struggled.

The godly and determined Giovanni da Silva.

The beautiful Valeria.

And the great and powerful Conan de Burgh.

His men wept openly.

Had he only let da Silva behead the witch Valeria, as was right, he would have survived to enjoy the bounty of goodness and life left to those he had led.

But now . . .

Alas. He had loved the evil beauty far too deeply.

Yet she was his again.

For beneath the rock, they were entombed together forever.

Or, at the very least, centuries to come.

Chapter 1

"The others will certainly join you by tomorrow," Arturo Agnazzi said, eyes bright, words cheerful, smile exuberant.

Exhausted and exasperated, Stephanie Cahill stared at him blankly. "I'm sorry. Could you explain all this to me one more time, please?" It had been a ridiculously long day. The last thing that had gone right had been her flight from Chicago to Rome. Then, there had been a glitch in the flight from Rome to Naples. When she'd arrived in Naples, the car that was to pick her up and bring her to the southeast part of the country had failed to show up. Her international phone had failed to work. It had seemed that all the Italian she knew—and that was not at all what it should have been when she had agreed to accept this job—flew out of her head. When she tried to ask for help at the airport, words in other foreign languages would pop into her head. At last, she had gotten through to Bella Vista and Reggia Café, and discovered that her driver had arrived to get her at the airport, but hadn't found her, and after a few espressos at a coffee bar in Naples, had shrugged and headed on back.

He would return. She was grateful, of course, but after

her frustrating efforts to get through, she was weary and then had another two hours to sit around waiting.

She tried walking. After all, walking around would be good. She felt like a pretzel. The airlines might have added more room to economy, but it hadn't been enough. She was five-nine, and had to wonder how those over six feet actually survived the trans-Atlantic flights without their limbs becoming permanently entwined.

Had she waited a day, she might have been able to upgrade to first class on her airlines bonus miles.

But she hadn't waited a day, because she had been scheduled to meet with the entire cast of her show here, at the club, this night, at seven p.m.

Now she was discovering that her entire cast had somehow managed to vanish for the evening. Doug Wharton and Drew Cunningham had been delayed by a car breakdown over in Sorrento, Lena Miro and Suzette Croix had gone on a tour to the local ruins, where a rock slide on the return road had caused the guide to call in with the information that they'd be camping out for the evening, and Clay Barton had yet to check in. Gema Harris was around somewhere, according to Arturo, but since the others were AWOL, she'd decided to take the night off, too.

Fair enough, Stephanie thought. But she was still frustrated, sore, worn, and ready to kick herself for being such a stickler for punctuality that she hadn't taken the later flight, and arrived in a far more optimistic mood.

At the moment, she wanted to strangle Reggie—the woman responsible for her being here. The entire project was so off the wall, Stephanie doubted she should have accepted the task, even if she did adore Reggie. After all, was Reggie here? No, of course not; she was off pushing this latest project to military personnel in Germany somewhere, assuming that when she returned, all would be in perfect order. But that was Reggie, or Ms. Victoria Reggia, who had been like a windstorm many times in Stephanie's life, blowing in and out, and turning the world upside down like a modern-day Auntie Mame. She was actually Stephanie's mom's cousin, and since she was always traveling the world somewhere, Stephanie had rarely seen her until her parents' funeral. Then, Reggie had been a godsend.

But then again, she had to admit, despite this shaky start, Reggie's offer regarding this job had been something of a godsend, as well. At twenty-seven, Stephanie could be proud of both her talent and her business acumen. An automobile accident had left her orphaned at seventeen, and she had still managed to live on her own and acquire her master's degree in fine arts, with a minor in business. She had gone from acting with the Park Street Players in Chicago to managing the small but esteemed comedy club. Yet for all her education and life-enforced maturity, she hadn't foreseen her relationship with Grant Peterson, the club's owner. Grant had been an even greater power in her life—electric, vital; from the moment she had first seen him, she had felt compelled to come closer to him. Admittedly, she mocked herself—she had been compelled just to touch him. She had never wanted anyone as she had wanted Grant, and she had known that the minute she had walked into his playhouse and watched him speaking from center stage. She had met him, and in his eyes, she had seen an equal fascination. Sometimes, she wondered why. He had traveled the world with touring groups; he was far more knowledgeable and sophisticated. And yet, it had seemed that he was in love with her.

For a year it had been a passionate if volatile relationship, but her life had seemed set. He was assertive, fair, determined, but never cruel. He didn't patronize his cast or crews, but there was no question that he was in complete control. Theater and improv were his passions, but he loved jazz and the opera, and more than anything else, museums and art and ancient civilizations. His major, oddly enough, hadn't been fine arts, but history. He played a mean guitar, and enjoyed street fairs, budding artists, as well as collecting armor and movie paraphernalia.

Stephanie's life had been nearly perfect.

Her work was her life's dream and Grant was her heart's desire.

Then it had ended. Maybe it had been as much her fault as his. But it had been difficult to ignore his sudden state of distraction, though he had claimed he hadn't understood quite what was plaguing him himself. He'd been up at all hours of the night; he'd gone out at all hours of the night. They were both accustomed to working with ensembles, so she had first scoffed at the idea that she was suspicious or jealous. But then she had thought about Grant. He had everything he needed to succeed—in business, and in his personal life. He was six feet, two inches of lithe muscle and mobility, since his intrigue with the theater had taken him into any number of pastimes including fencing, kick-boxing, riding, and some stunt work. He also possessed more than a fair amount of charm and sensuality, which had been wonderful for the success of his business, and horrible on a personal level, once Stephanie had decided that there was something seriously wrong.

Then the dreams had started, or the nightmares, and they had been very strange. Sometimes he had tossed and turned. And sometimes, he had come to her with a volatile urgency that had been both exhilarating and terrifying, the latter because she wasn't sure when she came down whether he was actually awake during it all.

Then . . .

From the depths of sleep one night, he had cried out another woman's name.

Despite the fact that he was drop-dead gorgeous and incredible in bed, the last had been a slap that went into her soul. She felt that she wasn't what she wanted to be in his life, and never would be. They had argued bitterly because she couldn't tell him why she was leaving—he would have claimed that she had been mistaken, or worse, that the name didn't mean anything to him. Their last argument had been volatile.

But she had still worked for him.

To say it was a strained relationship was sadly understating the current of hostility that seemed to evolve around them. Worse. Anger could be volatile, and far too quickly turn into something else.

Still, not being independently wealthy, she had needed work. So, in a burst of spontaneity, Stephanie had jumped at Reggie's offer without really thinking it through. Ironically, immediately after her resignation, she heard from a mutual friend that Grant would be gone for some months as well, doing some kind of work somewhere else. If she'd stayed on, she could have managed the company in his absence.

Too late. She'd agreed to come here, and here she was.

Arturo, the club's general manager and ever the optimist, didn't even sigh as he began to explain the whereabouts of Stephanie's missing troop members once again. "You must understand where you are, and what is going on here, of course. The ladies, they meant to cause no trouble—they simply wanted to see the ruins. Everyone wants to see the ruins! The archeologists bring new things to light on an almost hourly basis! Ah, but then there was the rock slide, so the ladies were stuck. The gentlemen—the two of them, anyway—have had car trouble. Mr. Barton is lost in transit somewhere, which you must surely understand yourself. And so, the lovely Miss Gema thought that she would spend the evening at leisure, so she could come to you fresh and ready to work hard tomorrow!" His smile faded and he frowned suddenly. "My English is well spoken, isn't it?"

Stephanie waved a hand in the air, smiling, and ruing her own impatience. "I'm so sorry, Arturo. Your English is excellent. Better than mine, maybe! I just tried so hard to get here on time myself. I'm tired. Please forgive me."

He nodded brightly again. He was a small, balding man, compact, with a reserve of energy that seemed apparent in his every movement. Reggie had assured her that his English was far more than fluent, and that he would like her right off the bat. She might be taller than he, but he would fall all over himself to please her. He had a thing for women with dark hair and blue eyes, so Reggie said. He wasn't a lecher in the least, just a lover of women in general, especially those who were young, light-eyed, and dark-haired.

He was wonderful. Polite, concerned, and sweet. And he did speak English excellently. Stephanie was so glad, because she was so tired that trying to remember even the simple courtesies in Italian seemed absolutely daunting at the moment.

"You'll be happy to know that you'll have a full audience next Friday night. Reggie has arranged for a tour group of over fifty American military men and women and their spouses, if they choose, to come for a three-day vacation," Arturo informed her.

"Next Friday night!" The news snapped her back into full wakefulness. It was Sunday afternoon. "And will this place hold that many people? What about the fire laws?"

"*Sì.*" Arturo was beaming with pleasure to give such information. "This is—"

"Yes, yes, this is Italy."

"We'll easily get enough tables in here."

"Let's hope we're easily ready," she murmured. Stephanie felt ill. A week. One week to get together a cast of performers she had yet to meet.

"We'll have to start first thing in the morning," she said.

Arturo shook his head. "First thing in the afternoon!" he told her.

"But—"

"The campers will not be back until at least eleven—they have no choice but to wait for the road to be cleared. And the car over in Sorrento?" He shrugged. "It will take a bit. But you mustn't worry. This is Italy. All will be well."

Stephanie had already learned that the last two sentences Arturo had offered were his catchall comments, and part of his eternal optimism. *This is Italy. All will be well.*

She sure as hell hoped so. At the moment, she couldn't begin to see how, or why.

Her luggage was still strewn by the chair where she sat with Arturo in the club room where her troop would be performing. Nice room. The stage was ample, but intimate. Tables were arranged throughout, with a bar at the far rear of the room and chairs along either side, so that a good number of people could be accommodated. The basic skit for the troupe revolved around the fact that they were a group of world scientists who gathered together at The International Club to converse, share information—and brag. The comedy was built around the fact that none of them ever really had anything to brag about, and therefore, they most frequently had to make up their stories. Audience participation was an integral part of the fun. It was the kind of show that Stephanie loved, and despite the strange circumstances—doing a show in English in a small town in southern Italy that was just beginning to draw tourists—she had at once been enthused about the project.

But getting together a group of unknown variables—actors—in the time given was a bit daunting.

"Would you like to see your room?" Arturo asked brightly. "You must be very tired, traveling all night—and then all day."

"Yes, of course, thank you," Stephanie said, rising. She started to gather up her various bags, but he shook his head. "No, no, we have help! Leave your things, and Giovanni will come for them."

She smiled, but took her backpack anyway. She never left

her passport lying around. But she touched nothing else, determined that she wouldn't let these people think that she might even begin to imagine that something could come up missing.

"You are outside, in one of the beach houses—cottages, bungalows, whatever you'd like to call them. You have the best one, naturally, but since there are twenty-two of them and we're not at anything near capacity, we've got your cast in them as well." He winked. "Honestly, though. I chose them. Yours is the best! And closest to the back, or theater side entry to the club. Reggie thought you would like that," Arturo informed her.

"Whatever Reggie says," she murmured.

He grimaced ruefully. "Come this way. There is a door that leads to the beach, and your little cottage. It is delightful. And you can slip back into the theater area without having to go around or come through the rest of the club. You will love it."

He was so delighted with the arrangement that she nodded and forced a smile. "Sounds wonderful."

She followed him up the few steps to the stage and then into the backstage area. There was a loading dock, and a regular doorway. Arturo opened it and moved on out. A small, paved area gave way to the beach and, not fifty yards away, a scattering of small cottages that sat right on the water. The sea scent was strong on the air, but pleasant. The breeze was light, wafting, and felt magnificent against her cheeks.

A short walk brought them to the door where Arturo handed her a key. She accepted it, opened the door, and stepped into her little cottage.

Reggie had done well. It was delightful. There was a living room with a light Berber carpet and modern furnishings to match. The draperies were beige with soft blue sea patterns— mermaids, starfish, and other delicately drawn little creatures. Steps led to the loft—the bedroom, she assumed—while the living room went straight into a dining area, and back past that, a kitchen with doors that opened directly to the beach. She could faintly hear the fall of the waves against the shore.

She turned to Arturo. "Wow!"

He nodded, very satisfied. "Brilliant, yes? Not so much money into development as you might think, either! Of course, unlike the great structures in Rome, these little places will probably not stand for several thousand years. But! They are new, clean, clever, and very nice, yes?"

"Very, very nice." Stephanie made a mental note to quit damning Reggie in her mind. Her living quarters were beautiful.

"You must go up to the loft. You will like it even better," he told her.

"I'm pretty happy right now," she told him.

With a broad gesture, he indicated the stairs. "I'll leave you to that exploration alone," he told her. "Giovanni will bring your things, and I will certainly be here first thing in the morning. The kitchen has a few basic needs, but if you wake and wish to have a truly fine espresso, the morning room with its little coffee bar is open from six a.m." He gave her a modest shrug. "Your actors may not be together by then, but you need only ask, and I will be happy to join you."

"Thank you, Arturo. You are very kind."

"*Buonasera, e buonanotte!*" he told her, and with a deep smile and low bow, he left her.

Stephanie looked up at the painted wrought-iron steps that led to the loft, then hurried up them. The area was even better than the downstairs. The same light tones and decor had been used throughout the entire cottage, but here, there were more of the sea blues used in the carpet and bedspread. There were ample pine dresser drawers, the bed itself was queen-sized, a half-wall looked down to the living area below, and huge sliding glass doors opened to a wide, railed balcony that looked directly over the sea.

For several moments, she stood by the little whitewashed rail that surrounded the porch, just staring at the sea at night, hearing the lulling crash of the waves. Then she turned. To the west, she could also see the rise of the cliffs and hills and jagged, mountainous tors inland. The summer sky was not truly dark, but a deep, beautiful blue. The moon and stars cast the night into a magnificent frame around the darker rise of those cliffs, and the towns that sat upon the jagged, surreal landscape. Breathtaking. Here, the sea, and there, the mountains.

Haunting.

She was a beach person, herself. She loved water, and everything to do with it. Sun and sand, sailing, diving, fishing. All of it.

And yet . . .

As she stood there, just staring at the darkness and mystery of the inland area, she was surprised to feel a yearning to go toward the mountains. So lovely and fascinating. She knew that the towns upon the cliffs were old, very old, and charming. The history of the area went back . . . well, probably forever.

It was Italy.

Stephanie closed her eyes. The trials of the long day seemed to slip from her shoulders like a discarded cloak. The air seemed to stir around her, warm enough, yet pleasant and cooling. She looked to the mountains once again and smiled. How odd.

In the night, they seemed to beckon.

She gave herself a shake. Giovanni would be bringing her things. And she needed to get some sleep.

But still . . .

She found it difficult to tear herself away from the night, from the view, from the comfortable, encompassing touch of the sea breeze.

She wouldn't have to leave it, she reminded herself. After Giovanni brought her baggage, she'd take a quick shower, slide beneath the cool sheets, and sleep with the vast glass doors open to the night breeze.

She couldn't wait to rest, to fall deeply asleep in the soft bed, caressed by the gentle and lulling breeze.

Strange. She had been feeling so tired, frustrated, and aggravated. Then . . .

Well, now . . .

She felt almost seduced.

The night sky was magnificent. Since they were far from a town, much less a city, there were no lights, other than the dimly burning lanterns the workers had meted out at the campsite.

And that was a distance from him now.

The world, he reflected dryly, had changed. His world, at any rate.

The darkness was amazing. The night sky was broken only here and there by a star, and looking about the lush trees and foliage that seemed swamped in secrecy, it was possible to just faintly see the line where mountains, hills, and tors gave way to the heavens. The air was sweetly cool, and the breeze moved through the trees gently, seeming to whisper.

She would be here now.

Riveting. Just the knowledge was riveting . . .

And now, it was connecting; how or why, he wasn't certain.

But here, in the night, he, a man not at all prone to fantasy, felt that he was lifted. A dream world? Maybe. The call of the darkness? Perhaps. Simple weariness from backbreaking labor and time and distance? Most probably.

And still . . . he felt that he had moved. Covered time and distance and space from some bizarre mist that rode over the earth.

Dreaming?

Ah, yes, dreaming.

Simply that, and nothing more.

"God in heaven! But you are some man!" Gema Harris said lightly. She spoke beneath her breath, but she wasn't certain that it mattered.

She was pleased, definitely, to see the fellow at her side, having felt as if she had come to the ends of the earth where her great talents would be sadly wasted. Jewels cast before swine, or some such thing. She had been sitting at the small bar on the little seaside strip on the Adriatic, enjoying good, cheap wine here rather than spending her time at the more modern complex where she would soon be working. She had, albeit, almost been crying in her beer—except that it was wine, and she hadn't exactly been crying, just rueful of her lot in the world at the moment, and wondering if she couldn't improve it. She was a good actress, a good comedic actress, with a quick wit, which made her a natural for ensemble work that included a lot of improvisational theater. At last check, she was far more than average-looking, being a tall blonde with a *natural* hourglass figure and beautiful, long legs—if she did say so herself.

Lately, she hadn't needed to. Italian men were wonders in the flattery department—unfortunately, those she had met so far were either short and bald or tall and somewhat sexy with wives and dozens of little *bambini*!

She had just been considering breaking her contract and making a move to Rome—she had informed anyone who might listen that it was something she could very easily do—when she had turned to see the man at the bar.

Mamma mia!

Maybe he didn't speak English.

Didn't matter much. In her experience, men tended to be a lot better when they kept their mouths shut. Um. Not exactly, she thought whimsically. They were better when they didn't use their mouths for *speech*. Talk tended to be so much rubbish, and little more. She'd never wanted promises. She had a life to lead herself, a career to pursue. One day, wherever the hell she was—though she doubted if it was going to be at *this* little comedy club—the right person was going to see her. And she would be a star. Men—the right men—would be at her beck and call. But until then . . .

Damn, this one looked good.

"*Scusi. Parla Inglese?*" she asked.

He smiled, sitting at her side, and spoke in Italian to the bartender, ordering a Campari for himself and, she saw, though she didn't quite understand his words, another drink for her.

Whatever he spoke, they were going to get on fine.

"Thank you. *Grazie!*" she said.

He nodded.

"*Io parlo un poco Italiano, ma non parlo molto bene,*" she said, explaining, she hoped, that she spoke some Italian, but not very well.

His smile deepened.

"God, you're hot!" she whispered, finding it somewhat amusing that she could probably say whatever came to mind, and he wouldn't have the least idea.

"You're something of an inferno there, yourself, miss," he said, and once again, the grin deepened.

Gema was certain that she did resemble something of a blaze, for she blushed to the roots of her hair. Unusual for her. His English was perfect. She couldn't even tell if there was a trace of an accent in it, and she could usually peg people immediately regarding their background through their speech.

"Thanks," she said wryly.

"So, what are you doing in these parts?" he asked softly.

She slowly arched a delicate, flyaway brow. "Considering leaving them," she told him. "I'm an actress. I'm here to do a friend a favor." That wasn't really the truth. Close enough. The job had seemed a decent offer at the time. But now . . .

"Ah, but this is an up-and-coming area, you know," he told her.

"I want the action in my lifetime," she said.

He leaned closer. The man was pure magnetism. "Somehow, I get the impression that you create action wherever you go."

"We only live once," she said lightly.

"How true." He straightened and indicated a table in the corner. "There's some nice shadow over there. A cozy little place. It may look a bit dingy, but a hard-working family owns this place. It's always very clean. Why don't you come over and tell me more about yourself."

Gema quickly slid from her bar stool.

"With pleasure," she told him, the sound of her words something like a purr. The corner. Delightfully dark. Intimate. Like the man. Sensually charged.

A little shiver ripped through her.

Yes. Oh, Lord. He had an aura of pure sexuality . . .

And danger.

A half-hour later, she barely knew what she had said to him. And she definitely had no idea of what he had said to her. She knew that they had talked, that they had gone through several drinks, and that she was floating on air.

She was leaning closer and closer and was startled when he suddenly looked at his watch and frowned.

"What is it?" she asked.

"I—I have some business. Come, I'll walk you home. Or to wherever it is that you're staying."

"By the club." Gema wrinkled her nose slightly. "I have a

lovely little place. That, at least, is a boon to being here. My cottage is small, but really charming."

"I'll walk you," he said.

She smiled, pleased. Nothing like a protective man.

"Is there a large crime element around here?" she queried. "Actually, I hadn't thought there could be anything so exciting."

"It's a wonderful place," he assured her. "As to crime, you never know. So I will walk you."

They strolled through the streets. Gema didn't think that they passed anyone, but she wouldn't have known. She couldn't take her eyes from him. The arm he placed around her shoulder seemed more supportive and protective than affectionate, but that was all right. He could be a gentleman. She knew, through his eyes, through his voice, by the very way he had sat so near in the bar, that he could and would be a passionate and experienced lover.

But when they reached the downstairs door to the pleasant little cottage, he stepped back.

"You're not coming in at all?" she asked huskily. "I have a truly fine liquor cabinet. The views are gorgeous. And naturally, I've lots of my own music."

"Maybe I'll make it back," he said.

Gema was sure she could do a better job of enticing the man to stay. But she wasn't given the chance. He inclined his head with a secretive smile, then he was headed down the path that would take him around the club and back to the main road.

He stopped suddenly, though, looking back. "Keep that door locked. It may be a foreign country and a quaint town, but you should keep your door locked."

"But you're coming back."

"I'll knock loudly."

Gema watched him go. Watched the set of his broad shoulders, the long, easy stride with which he seemed to cover distance quickly. The scent of him seemed to linger.

She leaned against her door, smiling. She'd had a bit too much to drink, but . . .

Energy returned to her. He'd be back. And she'd be ready. She flew up the stairs where a hallway divided into three full rooms, all with access to the outer porch. The accommodations were nice enough. Even very nice. But she wasn't sure what the builders had been thinking, putting three bedrooms in such a charming little bungalow. Nor what she had been thinking when she hadn't insisted that she have really private quarters.

Ah, well—tonight, she was alone.

And waiting.

She hurried to her bathroom, started the water, and fantasized about the night to come as she stroked her flesh with scented soap.

Giovanni was between twenty-five and thirty, exceptionally tall. He had an easy appearance that made him seem almost lanky, but a look at his tightly worn knit shirt clearly showed that he was really incredibly well honed. He also had a smile Stephanie was sure had broken many a young female heart. He had a lazy, sensual look about him, and yet she had discovered that he had almost as much energy as Arturo, and was a worker who could move like the wind. He was cute, all right. Sexy.

But she felt far more mature, and not at all in the mood.

He arrived with her two heavy suitcases, coat, and garment bag, all carried at once. Stephanie wasn't quite sure how he had managed it all, but he stood at the front door, grinning, and not appearing at all burdened by the weight.

"Good evening, Miss Cahill. I will run these up to the loft for you?"

Stephanie arched a brow, wondering if even the young,

muscle-bound Giovanni was capable of *running* it all up the stairs.

"Sure, thanks, come in," she told him.

He nodded, and started up the stairs. He wasn't running, but he did move darned quickly. A second later, he was back.

"Is there anything else I may do for you?"

"Thank you very much, but no. I think I'm just going to get some sleep."

He nodded, but didn't move. "You like the cottage?"

"It's beautiful. The sea is wonderful. The mountains . . . are even better."

"Haunted," he said, and nodded sagely.

"Oh?"

He shrugged. "There were many battles in the cliffs and hills."

"World War Two?" she asked.

He grimaced. "A few. But years ago, the local people, kings of the region and Sicily, fought. Many Crusaders moved through here. Many did not want to leave. They are finding the remains of all kinds of old things up there. But the people have always said the hills cry by night. Pretty, yes? Oh—I haven't frightened you, have I?"

Stephanie laughed. "Not at all. I do have a few fears, but none that include warriors from the Crusades coming to burn down my house."

"Still, if you like, there are many lovely small towns to see, and I can show you. Of course, sometimes, it's not easy. Your actresses are stuck on the road, you know."

"Yes, I know."

"But the rock slides do not happen often."

"Just on the day I arrive," Stephanie murmured.

"It will be fine."

"Yes, I know. It's Italy."

"Pardon?"

Stephanie shook her head. "I know that it will all be fine."

He nodded and started to leave, then paused, turning back. "I could be a very good actor."

"Really? Well, we'll see—how's that?"

"Very, very good." Giovanni had what could be considered almost stereotypical good looks. Tall, dark, and well-muscled, he also possessed a finely sculpted face and two of the deepest, darkest eyes Stephanie had ever seen. He was pleased with her interest.

"I could be part of the troupe?" he asked.

"Giovanni, right now, I don't even remember what the troupe is supposed to be doing. We'll talk tomorrow, okay?"

"*Certo!*" His eyes lingered over her. She'd been warned that men here liked to pinch women. So far, she hadn't been pinched. She couldn't begin to imagine Giovanni walking over to pinch her. And still, there was a certain smouldering in his gaze that suggested he was a man finding a woman to be attractive. She wondered wryly if it had to do with the fact that she was an unmarried, hopefully attractive young woman, or if he felt that it would be a good thing to seduce the person who might give him his first break in show business—even if it would be a very strange break!

"Good night, Giovanni, thank you," she said.

"Truly a pleasure. Anytime you need anything, please, you need just to call on Giovanni."

"Thank you, again. I'll remember that."

"Tomorrow, *bella signorina*," he told her, and was gone.

Stephanie shut and locked the door. She couldn't help the smile that stayed in place as she shook her head and headed up the stairs, ready to unpack and call it a day.

Bless Reggie. Maybe this was going to be fun after all.

She took the time to unpack a few things and arrange her toiletries in the delightfully modern bathroom, then stepped into the shower. It, too, was almost thrilling. The water was hot, and the pressure was strong.

She lingered there, then stepped out, toweling dry, and slipping into her nightgown and light velvet robe. She pulled the coverlet from the bed, then hesitated, looking to the sliding glass doors that she had left open.

The air was so very good . . .

But there was a small flight of stairs that led from that second floor balcony area down to the beach.

She had no idea what the crime rate might be here—or if there was one. Exhausted, she decided that she didn't care. So what if it might be absurd that she had so carefully locked the front door after Giovanni's departure, only to leave the back wide open.

She was simply so weary.

And the breeze was so, so good.

She shimmied out of the robe, and into the bed, turning off the bedside lamp and snuggling low into the covers.

The sky outside remained a fascinating shade of deep blue. The air continued to waft around her on the softest movement of a breeze . . .

Strange that she had been so frustrated and worried when she had arrived. Travel was difficult. Building a new life was hard.

Trying not to remember what she had left behind was harder still. But it would be all right.

It was all so beautiful here. Truly, there was nothing like it. Her sense of well-being, derived just from the air and her view of the mountains, remained with her. She marveled at the feeling of . . . almost a dreamlike euphoria that seemed to have settled over her. Tomorrow, she was certain, all would be well. After all . . .

It was Italy.

She closed her eyes. And the sense of being enfolded and almost sensuously cradled by the air remained as she drifted . . .

Gema could hear the sound of knocks on the door when she turned off the water. For a moment, she stood dead still, never having expected him back so quickly. Then, she flew into action, afraid that he would think she had fallen asleep and go away.

She quickly slipped into a silk wrap and caught a glimpse of herself in the mirror as she rushed out. Um. Not so bad. The silk clung to every curve on her wet body, enhancing the fullness of her breasts and clearly delineating her nipples. Sexy, she determined. Her hair was damp, falling free around her shoulders. Not at all bad.

She raced down the stairs and threw the door open.

And stood there, her mouth forming into a round O shape.

She started to close the door.

But didn't.

Her limbs felt like lead. A state of excitement and anticipation like nothing she had ever known began to rush through her body. And yet . . .

She backed away as her visitor entered.

She wanted to speak, even scream. Her throat was frozen. Even the piece of gauze she was wearing suddenly seemed to be too much.

Soft, husky laughter sounded. The voice that spoke was deep and still, like air, with a raspy quality.

"Gema . . . how lovely. All this. For me."

She was vaguely aware that the door slammed, and they were shut in, together.

None of that mattered.

Darkness encompassed her. The silk drifted from her shoulders.

The touch . . .

Fingertips danced down upon her flesh, delicately breezed over her breasts.

They were long . . . the knuckles felt like fire as they brushed her nipples.

He was closer, and there was a whisper in her ear, and a burst of liquid heat. His mouth moved against her throat while his hands created a flow of lava, sliding down the length of her body, finding the center of her sex and the apex of the lava-like stream of arousal that didn't just fill her, but seared into every pore of her flesh.

The tongue.

Moving against her ear, her throat . . . her lips. Then moving . . . too . . . so great a blaze she was certain that she would collapse, but she would not, could not; she was frozen, cast into a stillness of total acquiescence, as if he had to be, and power her to his will.

Liquid fire.

The teeth . . . nibbled, played, promising . . . against her flesh.

Incredibly evocative . . .

Going down.

All the sensation she might have dreamed . . . fantasized.

The things that were done . . .

And done . . .

And her own body moved at last, as he willed it, until she was laid upon the floor, and the delirious rush of need and hunger was suddenly fulfilled and she was soaring . . . feeling so very much that it was a little like dying . . .

And then.

She could feel no more.

It was a lot like dying.

Chapter 2

Maria Britto shivered slightly as she stepped outside the little house where she lived with her mother.

It was morning, but early morning, and the sun had yet to so much as touch the horizon. And yet, if she was to make work by nine, she had to go now.

She smiled, and shivered again, but with anticipation. She felt a touch of guilt; she shared so much with her mama. But this . . . well, her mama would not understand.

Maria was usually a serious girl. She had made very good marks throughout her school years, but there wouldn't be any money for her to go to university, and she knew it. Since her father had been sick and died, money had been a struggle. Her brothers had gotten jobs in the States, and her mother was grateful. Maybe when they made money, they would send for her and her mother. Or maybe the area would pick up, as so many hoped, and the Americans would begin to come en masse, and they would be like Venice, surviving on well-off foreign visitors. That time had not come yet. Her mama struggled daily to take in laundry, to clean houses, to make them the money they needed to survive. She was lucky, so lucky, to have the job at the shop.

And she had Roberto.

They were the same age, they had grown up together on the same cliff. He was a good boy. He worked hard for his father, doing construction and repair. He was saving money. He wanted to get married, and everyone understood that they would do so. He was pleasant and young, and she felt a faint stirring when they shared their few kisses.

She would marry him. With more luck, she would continue working at the shop. She would cook and clean and have babies, go to church on Sundays, and maybe have a night out once a week because Mama, no matter how tired she was, would take a night to stay with the babies. That would be her life, and she was resigned, and happy, she thought, as one could be, because she did love her mama and if she didn't feel a wild elation and passion for Roberto, he was still good, and most importantly, as her mama said, Roberto loved her.

And so . . .

This was not an affair that would ever mean anything. It was just an affair, because she did want something wild and exciting before she settled down to have babies with Roberto and grow old and worn as her mother had.

She walked quickly along the path, praying he would come for her, because the walk to their place of assignation was long and hard. And yet . . .

Since they had met . . . since his eyes had touched hers . . . she had known. It was like a fever in her blood. She had dreamed about him, coming to her at night. Such a beautiful dream . . . white curtains blowing in the breeze, her flesh, naked, the feel of fiery lips upon her . . . her arms, trembling as they settled around the man. His lips upon hers, whispering words in her ears, settling upon her throat, her breasts . . .

The dream was strong. So strong. She had to be up, and she had to be walking along the path, because she must have it, if just once, in her life. Then in the years to come, she would have the memory.

She did wish, however, quite fervently, that the light would come. Just a few rays! But at this time of year . . . ah, well. She had lived here forever. She knew the path, despite the fact that not even the moon seemed to break through the clouds, and she could barely distinguish shapes in the darkness. Ah, at last! A cloud shifted. There was not really any illumination, but now, she could see the road, and the shadows that made up the trees, and where the trees broke, and the world became sky.

Hurry, hurry . . . there would be so little precious time.

Despite her sense of urgency to move quickly, she suddenly became aware of a cold that seemed to trickle along her spine, as if someone walked behind her.

Someone, or something.

She stopped, looking back the way she had come. The darkness had already swallowed her home. But she could see nothing.

She turned, thinking it ever more important that she reach her would-be lover in all haste.

She heard the labored sound of her breath. Then . . .

Something like laughter. No. It was her imagination. It was only the trees. But there wasn't really a wind that night.

She quickened her footsteps again. Her limbs felt heavily laden.

Maria . . . Maria . . . Maria . . .

Her name seemed to echo on the night air, not even aloud, just within her mind, and she thought that she heard the laughter again.

Was this her conscience talking to her? Was she going to go to hell for what she intended to do? No, if there was a

God in heaven, He understood. He knew that she would do all that would be expected of her. She would marry, and when she did, she would be a good wife. She was a good daughter, and she would be a good mother.

But the cold . . . that trickle of cold going down her neck . . .

She turned abruptly, thinking if there was something there behind her, she would see it now.

There was nothing, except . . .

It seemed as if the darkness itself was a great cape. As if it flowed in the air like a malignant shadow, coming after her.

She swallowed hard. It was just the darkness. She knew the darkness that could come. She had lived here all her life. She had heard the legends about demons, and laughed at them—when she had not sat with others her age in a car somewhere, and acted delightfully giddy and frightened. These woods . . . the fields, valleys, cliffs, and tors . . .

She had walked them all of her life.

Maria, Maria . . . you cannot run, Maria.

And again, the sense of laughter in her head, evil laughter, as if . . .

She stared behind her, at the darkness, the giant, sweeping shadows. Suddenly, more than anything in the world, she wanted to go home. But instinct warned her that she could not run that way, she couldn't run into the arms of the shadow.

And so she turned, and ran ahead hard.

She blinked as dust flew into her eyes. Then she slammed against something hard and warm. And she looked up.

Her mouth opened . . .

The laughter sounded in her mind again. The whisper of her name. She wanted to scream. But she saw the smile, then felt . . .

A wave of sheer, sweet eroticism. Dear God . . .

"There should have been more time," her lover said regretfully.

"I hurried. I ran to you," she whispered.

"Sweet one, my dear, sweet, naive one."

"There was something behind me. I thought . . . for a minute . . . it was you. And when I first saw you . . ."

"There, there, my love!"

His eyes caressed her first. She *felt* them, as if they were feathers streaking over her naked flesh, awaking, arousing . . .

"The day is coming too quickly," he murmured.

"The day?" she said foolishly.

"Never mind," he said, and his mouth found hers, and he drew her from the road, to a copse. Leaves had fallen, and they made the most delightful bed. She had never been with a man, and yet, she couldn't free herself of any form of modesty quickly enough. He drew her into his arms, seemed to taste her lips, and then her flesh, and she nearly shrieked with the sweet ecstasy of his touch. Everything bold; his hands, so powerful; his kiss, a fury . . .

And then . . .

It should have been painful. It was not. It was the most incredible glory.

She heard him . . . heard him, against her.

And listening . . . to the sound made . . . it should have been horrible.

It was not.

She clung to him.

Her body seemed to . . . erupt. It was the ecstasy within, about which she had only dared dream. It was hot, vivid, shocking, staggering . . . brilliant . . . climactic . . .

And then . . . icy. Icy, and dark. And yet . . . he had said that the day was coming too quickly. She was numbed . . .

It was that strange . . . chill.

A paralyzing cold that filled her, just as the fire had done.

She opened her eyes, and it was a terrible effort. And she saw.

And she would have screamed—oh, God, she would have screamed . . .

Except that life expired at that moment, and still staring, she collapsed.

The faint echo of laughter filled the hills, and the darkness.

It was still a few minutes before the dawn would actually break.

Stephanie was glad that Arturo had told her that she couldn't possibly expect to meet with her cast until the afternoon.

She had no idea why, but she'd slept later than she'd imagined possible. Of course, there was the natural adjustment caused by jet lag, but still . . .

She'd slept the night through, haunted by the strangest dreams.

At one point, she had awakened, certain that someone was in the room with her. She hadn't had nightmares—on the contrary, the dreams had left her again with a surreal sense of the world being well. More than well. She had the most absurd notion of being stroked throughout the night, touched, almost sensually bathed by the air beyond.

The thought made her flush uneasily, and remind herself that she hadn't been a lone female all that long, and that erotic imaginings were ridiculous.

She felt an odd sense of discomfort as well. Somewhere in the deep fog of sleep, she had felt as if she were home again, and Grant was there, staring at her. After the image, she had felt the strangest surge of fear, as if she should rise and lock the windows, but she didn't have the energy to do so.

Jet lag could do very strange things.

Ironically, after having arrived to find no one present for the first meeting of the group, she came in that afternoon to discover that she was the last to make it into the club.

"Hi! You must be Stephanie, our director!"

The first of her cast to greet her was a small, pretty woman with dark eyes, dark hair, who looked as if she could be a native—except that her English had no foreign accent. If anything, she had the slight twang of a Midwesterner.

The woman extended her hand, smiling, showing a mouthful of pearly whites. "I'm Lena Miro. Delighted to meet you."

"Lena, hi."

"This is Suzette Croix," Lena said, turning to the woman at her side. Suzette was Lena's antithesis—her eyes were a light green, almost a lime, and her hair was a soft blond.

"Hello," Suzette said. She smiled as well, but she seemed warier, giving Stephanie a grave surveillance.

"Suzette, hi."

Again she shook hands.

"Have you met the boys?" Suzette asked. "How silly of me, you just walked in. Slept late, huh? That first day after crossing the Atlantic is always a killer. Anyway, this is Drew"—she pointed out a very tall, slim fellow with red hair who was waiting to meet Stephanie—"and this is Doug Wharton." Doug was a little shorter than Drew, with brown hair, coffee-colored eyes, and a quick grin.

"We're really sorry about last night," Drew said, shaking her hand. "Who would have ever imagined that a broken hose would take 'til morning?"

"But the girls were stuck, too," Doug reminded them all.

"Yes," Suzette said, and shivered.

"Oh, it was really rather exciting!" Lena argued.

"Exciting! Ugh!" Suzette said, shaking her head as she

looked at Stephanie. "I hated it! They're still unearthing bones, and rather than just crate them up, they dust them off where they lie, they sift through the dirt . . . and the campsite was just a few feet away. After all those years . . . there's still hair and flesh and pieces of clothing and—trust me! It's just—ugh!"

"I found it very exciting," Lena argued.

"I think she found the *archeologists* exciting," Suzette said dryly.

"Hey, okay, so there was the one guy—"

"Oh, yeah!" Suzette said. "What a digger he was."

"You're into an archeologist?" Drew demanded. "Oh, come, please! The fellows who were in here from the dig the other night were downright . . . pathetic. So studious! Beady-eyed, scruffy."

"No, no, no, no!" Lena said, smiling at Stephanie. "Think Indiana Jones with this guy, except, not really. He's here through some kind of volunteer amateur program sponsored by *National Geographic*. Hey, in real life, he's an actor, or a director," Lena told them. "That's what the guide told me. He works someplace in the Midwest."

Stephanie felt a trickle of unease, then decided she was jumping to conclusions. Just because Grant Peterson had an obsession with ancient Egypt and spent most of his time watching the Discovery Channel, there was no reason to assume that he had taken time away from the Park Street Players to dig up ruins in Southern Italy. That would be too ironic.

"Gorgeous guy, that's for certain," Suzette murmured. She wrinkled her face. "Absolutely into the dig, though. Lena tried to flirt away, and he wasn't anything more than courteous."

"Remember his name?" Stephanie asked, trying to sound casual.

"No, because we didn't actually meet; he was on one side of the marked-off area, and we were on the other," Lena explained. "Then, at night . . . well, I guess he didn't come back to the campsite until it was really late."

"Until Lena gave up waiting for him," Suzette said dryly. "I have to admit . . . well, he was intriguing, no matter what his background or nationality. Abs like steel."

"Hey, you know what? We don't want to hear about this guy," Doug said. "We've seen plenty of beautiful Italian babes since we've been in the country, but they sure weren't around where we were stuck last night! Where we were, the whole town closed up, and the little pensione where we had to stay didn't even have television—or good magazines."

"Yeah, imagine that, Doug wanting to read," Drew said.

"I don't think he wanted to read," Lena said, smiling. "He's really fond of picture books."

"Eh! You spent the day staring at some guy's abs!" Doug ribbed her.

"Well, last night is over—the good and the bad of it—and we're together now," Stephanie said firmly. *Could this guy be Grant? That would be far too . . . bizarre. The American population was somewhere around three billion. Surely, lots of that number were into archeology and travel!*

And if it was Grant?

She was a professional. And she was running this show. And she hadn't seen a single archeologist yet—there was no reason she should!

She cleared her throat. "I'm glad you're all here. Except that, we're still missing two of our group?" She looked at all of them.

Arturo, who had been sitting idly at the back table, spoke up, "Clay Barton is on his way now. His plane from Rome to Naples was delayed."

"I see," Stephanie murmured. *Perhaps he should have started traveling earlier, since he'd been due yesterday.* "What about Gema Harris?"

At first, no one spoke.

Then, uneasily, Lena said, "I went by her place to get her on my way in. I thought she'd left already because there was no answer."

"Did you go in?" Doug asked.

"Of course I didn't go in!" Lena said. "I knocked and rang the little buzzer, and she didn't answer."

"Was her door locked?" Drew asked.

"I don't know. I didn't try it," Lena said.

"Might she have overslept?" Stephanie asked.

"I can go back," Lena said.

"No, we're still missing Clay, too, but the four of you are here. We'll get started," Stephanie said. "Arturo—would you mind sending someone to look for Gema?"

From the back of the café, he nodded and rose.

"She was talking about going to Rome," Drew murmured. Stephanie stared at him sharply and he shrugged. "She . . . well, you haven't met her yet. She's apparently the type who likes a little more action than we have around here. Nice girl, really. I think. But she's . . . I don't know. She's in a hurry. She made some comment the other day about the fact that it was unlikely that Hollywood was going to discover her here."

"So she would have just taken off without resigning?" Stephanie said.

Doug rubbed his chin. "I don't think so."

"Well, Arturo will see if he can find her," Stephanie said. "I was told that everyone had received our improv 'bible.' Is that correct?" Her question was answered by nods, and the four went about, picking up their notebooks where they'd been left on tables around the room. Suzette pointed out the coffeepot and cups, and Stephanie helped herself before the group gathered around one of the café tables. "Let's just make sure we're all going in the same direction. There are seven loose outlines, allowing us to change the script around every day with one extra, since we're going to be black on Monday nights. The café becomes the World Traveler's Club—Suzette, you're the maid—"

"Great. With her background, she's a French maid," Drew observed.

"No, we're going to go with some stereotypes and work with others. She's going to be the American maid," Stephanie said.

"I can actually speak French, though," Suzette said. "My dad's from Nice," she explained.

"There's a terrific bit for your character," Stephanie pointed out. "You can be the American maid who always tries to pretend that she's the French maid."

"Cool," Suzette agreed.

"But she's sexy and wears a short skirt, right?" Drew asked.

Stephanie smiled. "Well, we can play off that, too. She has a great skirt, but some really silly stockings. We'll all see the costumes soon. Drew—you're the want-to-be guy. You're president of the club, but most of your adventures are made up, and you can add to the outrageous lines of your stories at any time, okay?"

"I like it. Horn-rimmed glasses?"

"You bet. Coke-bottle lenses," Stephanie assured him.

"Lena, you're Drew's cohort in the area of creativity—the only reason you're back in Southern Italy is a family connection, but you like to pretend that you've been to the farthest reaches of the earth. You're the one down on everyone else's antics, dying for a little more sex in your own life."

"Wow! It's my real life story!" Lena said, and the others laughed. She might have been afraid that she was getting too much agreement and sympathy, because she quickly added, "Hey, my family is in the Milano area, and I'm not really down on fun, and my sex life has gone along just swimmingly, okay? And hey, be nice to me. I'm the only one in this crowd who does speak fluent Italian."

"I'll be as nice as you can imagine! And you can ask me for help anytime you feel that the sex life is a disaster," Doug offered.

"So I can feel that it's really hit rock bottom?" Lena teased.

"Ouch! I feel like . . . well, like my character," he said, grinning at Stephanie dryly.

"That's right. Poor Doug is to be known as Poindexter. A brilliant scholar, but a nerd in the worst degree. The others can't imagine that you even got into the club. They're jealous as well, though, because your exploits are all real. When Gema shows up, she's the vamp. She really has been everywhere, and what she misses is a real home. Her efforts for an actual love life have basically sucked, and the rest of you try to help her retain dignity. Literally, at times, pulling her away from the guys in the audience she uses for her little schticks."

She stopped speaking, looking up as Arturo returned to the back of the café. She arched a brow to him.

He shook his head.

"Well, so far, Gema is a no-show," she murmured.

"And Clay," Drew reminded her, frowning.

"He'll be here soon—we know that," Stephanie said. "Let's go ahead and read through the outlines, see how they sound, bounce ideas back and forth with one another."

The four were a good group; Stephanie acted as both still-missing Gema and just-not-present Clay, and she was more pleased as the minutes ticked by. Her cast appeared to be excellent natural comedians, quick to see how to milk any idea. She reminded them several times that they were to play with their audience, and, as they moved into the fifth scenario, they reminded her.

"So," Drew said when they had finished with the next to

the last scene, "Clay Barton gets to have all the real fun, huh?"

"Yes, and no," Stephanie agreed, idly drawing a line with her pencil and smiling as she answered him. "He's the swaggerer. He has been around, but he hasn't really got any money, and when his conquests don't work out, he tries to pretend that they have."

"So . . . he is supposed to be the good-looking one, huh?" Doug said with a sigh.

"Hopefully, a team like this works so well that after we get going, we'll switch roles around as well as scenarios," Stephanie told him. "No one gets stale, and anyone can fill in for anyone else. Normally, we'd have a few more cast members, but since we're just starting out with this, we're forming the company. Of course, it would help if we had the full group." Arturo had been sitting at the back of the café. She looked over, and didn't see him. Maybe he'd gone in search of Gema again.

As she stared toward the table, the outside door opened.

There was a man there. For a moment, he seemed to block out the sun. Despite herself, Stephanie felt a sense of unease streak down her spine. It was as if he were there, a presence that all but swept away daylight. Then, he might have been a shadow, a trick of the light.

She blinked, and he was walking through the aisle of tables to reach them.

He was, beyond a doubt, a striking individual. Tall—six-three, maybe—a shade shorter than Drew. His hair was very dark, and, as he drew closer, she saw that he had very unusual eyes—maybe brown, or hazel, but a strange shade of such colors, seeming both yellow and red. His features were strong and classical. He definitely had a continental look, smooth and sleek, and wore jeans and a polo shirt as if he were in a tux. He smiled as he reached the table, swinging a leather backpack around and setting it on the table, ready to reach in for his copy of the "bible" and notes. "I'm really sorry. Transportation takes some doing these days. I'm Clay Barton."

They all just stared at him.

His smiled deepened. "Clay Barton. I'm expected. I was bounced off a plane yesterday. I'm really sorry—I can see that you've been working."

Lena looked across the table at Stephanie. "Type-casting, or what?"

"I hope not," Clay said, grinning ever more deeply as he pulled up a chair. "My character is supposed to be something of a braggart and a jerk."

Stephanie reached out a hand to him at last. The touch of his fingers caused a jerk in her own. She tried to hide the feeling. "Stephanie Cahill, and hi, I'm your director. The rest of the cast . . . Drew Cunningham, our very tall redhead, Doug Wharton is there . . ."

Clay leaned forward, shaking hands around the table.

"Doug Wharton, not a redhead, and not quite so tall," Doug introduced himself with a grin.

"Suzette Croix," Suzette said, still staring.

"And this is Lena Miro," Stephanie finished out.

"Hi to all of you, and it's a pleasure, and once again, I'm sorry," Clay said.

"It's all right—we've been settling in, playing with ideas, and apparently, you had no choice," Stephanie said. "But we start on Friday night. We were working our last outline, so we'll go forward, and you can hop in when we work with the room and blocking once we've finished with the read-throughs."

"Great," he said, but then frowned. "Thought it was a cast of six."

"It is. We have a missing member," Doug explained.

"You are perfect!" Lena breathed, speaking at last.

"A perfect jerk?" he inquired, eyes sparkling. "I'll try not to be." He turned to Stephanie. "What do you mean, missing?"

"I mean, she hasn't shown up. I haven't met her, so I'm not sure whether to worry or not," Stephanie told him.

Doug snorted. "Worry about whether she's broken her contract or not. Seriously, while it's still early in the game, we ought to get Arturo to check out her place. See if she's gone—hook, line, and sinker."

Lena flashed a grimace at Stephanie. "Well, I don't like to say it, but . . . she wasn't impressed once she arrived."

"We can all take a walk over to meet her," Clay suggested.

"We'll finish the last outline," Stephanie said, looking quickly at her clipboard. Strange, as soon as he spoke, she'd felt oddly compelled to do whatever he said, no matter how simple. She was the director. She might have lost a cast member, but she wasn't losing control so quickly.

"This is good—we have Clay now, and I just have to fill in for Gema. Let's give it a go."

An hour later, they'd read through the outlines, and in just the afternoon, it seemed, the little group had bonded nicely, feeding one another with ad-libs and suggestions, and they were very good. For the first time since her arrival, Stephanie thought that the enterprise could really work.

Clay Barton had turned out to be wonderful. He could put a swagger into his voice, just as he could sound a little bit desperate, making explanations for boasts he'd made and been caught on. Stephanie was pleased to see that they made her laugh, and she knew the scenarios better than anyone else.

"Great! A great afternoon's work," she applauded them, closing her notebook at the end. Arturo, having taken his seat at the back of the café again, applauded.

"Bravo, bravo!" he called, rising and striding toward them.

"Thank you, Arturo. You met Clay when he came in?" Stephanie said.

"But of course!" Arturo said. He, too, looked at the newcomer with a bit of wonder. There was something very unusual about the man. Actually, with his looks and talent, Stephanie thought, it was amazing that he was here. The road to fame and fortune via Hollywood and the movies might be difficult, but this guy could probably have been raking in the bucks just doing underwear commercials.

"But no Gema?" Clay said.

Stephanie rose before he could make suggestions or commands. "Arturo, we're going to have to get a pass key and check her place," she said.

"*Sì, sì,*" Arturo said with a sigh. Then he looked worried. "You don't think she is hurt? That she slipped in her shower?"

"No, no, we're afraid she's just flown the coop," Doug said.

"*Scusi?* I'm sorry," Arturo said, arching a brow.

"He's afraid she's just walked out on us," Stephanie explained.

"Why would she?" Arturo asked, truly baffled. He apparently loved the town, the village, the surroundings.

"She's a different breed, Arturo, a different breed. Hey, maybe she's just sleeping off a hell of a hangover?" Doug offered.

"Well, I'll go check on her right now," Arturo said.

"I'll come with you," Stephanie told him.

"Hey, we'll all go," Clay said.

Stephanie looked at him.

"We're a team, right?" Doug said.

"If anything did happen . . ." Drew murmured.

"Let's go, then."

Arturo nodded. He led the way through the side door to

the café from the resort area, through the pleasant, airy, and spacious white marble lobby to the rear doors from the main building. There were a few people seated in the chairs in the center of the lobby, and they all looked up from their newspapers or conversations, watching as they walked through.

Out back, to the right of the area where Stephanie's cottage stood, there was a staggered row of such dwellings, but most of them smaller than Stephanie's, some of them single-story bungalows.

They went through the pine-tree-bordered paths and reached one of the two-storied buildings. Arturo knocked firmly, and hit the little buzzer.

They all waited.

Nothing.

"I think we need to open it and go in," Stephanie said.

"Yes . . . yes."

Arturo looked very unhappy.

He rummaged in his pockets for his passkeys, then opened the door. He stuck his head in and called out, "Gema! Gema, are you there?"

There was no answer.

Stephanie stepped past him. The place was similar to her own, just smaller.

She walked on into the living room.

"I'll look upstairs," Suzette murmured.

Stephanie wandered on into the little kitchenette area. She turned, aware that Clay Barton was standing in the middle of the living room or parlor area, his head slightly bowed. He stood so strangely, as if he were listening, or . . .

As if he saw himself as some kind of psychic. As if he were trying to *feel* or *envision* what might have taken place in the room.

He looked up, as if he had been aware she was watching him.

"What is it?" she asked.

"Pardon?" he said politely.

Stephanie opened her mouth to speak, but words never left her lips.

From upstairs, Suzette let out a bloodcurdling scream.

Chapter 3

"Eh! Americano!"

Grant Peterson looked up. He'd been painstakingly brushing away the dirt atop a centuries-old skeleton. The brush was almost as small as a kid's kindergarten watercolor brush. The task required tremendous patience. The area in which he worked had been roped off by the real archeologists, the fellows who knew what they were doing.

It was a woman's skeleton. Some of the scholars were convinced that they had found the remains of a legendary countess. But Carlo Ponti, head of the excavations at the site, so recently unearthed by a minor earthquake, was not convinced.

"So far, with the bits and pieces of fabric left . . . I don't think that these are the remains of such a woman," Carlo said. "I believe we will discover that we have found a peasant. I do think that these remains will prove that a legendary battle was fought, and that the stories told beyond the history books will be verified. The ground shifted, as it reportedly did centuries ago. To those poor people, it brought death. To us, it brings a treasure of knowledge."

Carlo walked toward him now, a jacket casually thrown over his shoulder. "*Americano*! Come on. We're calling it quits for the day. The road is nice and clear. We'll go into the town and have a real cooked meal and some drinks."

Grant stood, arching a brow, gesturing to the dirt that covered him.

"So, shower quickly. We'll be on our way in."

"It's all right. Go in without me," Grant said.

Carlo walked to the tape surrounding the ground where Grant worked. "Go—alone? With my German comrade Heinrich and the Swiss, Jacques? No, no, no. They are too serious. They know nothing but the earth and history. I want to hear music, and talk about movies. We'll go see the new club. I want to see the young ladies who will be working at the new club. The two who were stuck out here with the rocks in the road, eh?"

Grant shook his head. "You're a lascivious old fart, Carlo," he told the renowned archeologist. Carlo grinned. Actually, he was in his early fifties, and had a bearded, rustic kind of easy charm. He loved his work, but his every move was not dead serious, or geared in only one direction. He loved archeology because he loved history because he loved people, and what made them tick.

"*Sì*, let's go look at live women, eh? Besides, the forensic anthropologists arrive tomorrow, and they will likely not want much more dirt gone before they take their photos, yes? Take a shower, and let's go. Dusk is coming quick. And I've been eating from cans cooked over a fire and sleeping in a tent too long, even for me. *Andiamo!*"

Grant hesitated. He should really be staying out of the town. He didn't know for certain, but he was pretty sure that *la bella direttrice* of the new *teatro americano* was Stéphanie. He'd had no idea when he signed on here as an amateur volunteer that he and Steph might wind up in the same place, but when he had arrived and heard about the resort, the club, and the theatre, he had learned almost immediately that it was owned by an Italian-American named Victoria Reggia, and once he knew that, it was an educated assumption that Reggie would have brought Steph in on the project.

Steph, he was certain, had taken on the project to get out of Chicago—and away from him. He wasn't at all sure how he could prove that he had made his plans the day she had walked out—way ahead of her own. And if he tried to explain that he'd felt as if he'd been waiting all his life for this particular opportunity, she'd think he was in a stranger state than she had apparently considered him to be in when she left.

Maybe the new woman wasn't Steph.

Bull. Had to be, if Reggie owned the place.

But what the hell. Maybe she wouldn't be around. And he couldn't spend the next months refusing to go into town. Stephanie was going to have to believe whatever she chose.

"Grant?" Carlo said. "Are you all right?"

He wasn't. A fierce pain had suddenly snaked throughout his limbs, gripping them with tension. Everything that had happened with Steph had been torture, just as it was a constant agony now to wonder just what the hell was wrong with him, why he was here, and why he had all but thrown away the person who had meant more than anything in the world to him. A woman who was beautiful, sensual, evocative, intelligent, fun, and richly talented.

"Grant?"

"Yeah, sorry, daydreaming, I guess. About the bones, that's all," Grant said.

Carlo shook his head with patient tolerance. "Grant, *mio amico*—if you must daydream, make it about living women, eh? So—we go?"

"Sure. Give me a few minutes."

Daydream about living women . . .

Bizarre. There was something about the dig. He felt as if

he could unearth the bones, an entire section of history, a moment in time. Patience here had been difficult. He couldn't help that really strange feeling that if he really kept at it, searched and tore into the dirt, he'd have the answer he was so desperately seeking.

Problem was, he didn't even know the question.

"What, good God! What?" Stephanie cried, heading quickly for the stairs.

There seemed to be a pounding from all around as the lot of them joined Suzette where she stood, just inside the doorway of Gema's bedroom.

"It's a roach the size of Texas! I didn't know that they even got roaches in Italy!" Suzette said, horrified.

Her words were greeted by silence as those around her stared at one another, not sure whether to laugh, strangle Suzette, or simply be relieved.

"Where?" Arturo said with quiet dignity at last. "Naturally, we have a great deal of foliage, we are by the seaside. We are very, very clean . . . but upon occasion, an insect will make its way inside."

"Roaches are survivors. Older than dinosaurs, I believe," Clay said, a spark of amusement in his eyes. He was standing slightly in front of her. She could have sworn that he had been behind her as she came flying up the stairs.

"Suzette, you dip!" Lena let out suddenly. "You scared us all to death! My heart is still racing a million miles an hour. I thought that you'd . . . that you'd . . ."

"She thought you'd found Gema—splat on the floor," Drew said, grinning impishly.

"Drew, that's horrible!" Lena protested.

"Oh, come on!" Drew said. "It would be horrible if we had found Gema . . . hurt. Or worse," Drew said. "But she's not here. That much is evident."

Clay Barton went striding past them all to the closet. He swung the doors open.

They were all silent again as they stared in.

The closet was empty.

Suzette let out a long breath. "Well . . . there you have it. She's gone."

"But . . . but . . . she just walked out!" Arturo exclaimed, incredulous and outraged.

"Apparently," Drew said. "The bright lights of Rome and all, you know."

"I didn't know her," Stephanie said, looking at Arturo, and then the group. "Would she really have done such a thing?"

"I have to admit, I didn't think she would," Doug said. He shrugged. "She talked a lot. She is good-looking, and she certainly has balls, if you know what I mean. She's the type who intends to make it. But . . . well, we all knew where we were going when we took the job, so I really thought that all of her talk was just that . . . talk."

"I don't know. It doesn't really surprise me," Suzette said. "I mean, think about it, Lena. It's not that I dislike Gema, mind you—she can be really funny—but she was that . . . well, type. I mean, you wouldn't trust her, really, with anything terribly important. And if I had a boyfriend or husband, well, quite frankly, I wouldn't trust her in the room with him for five minutes! Lena, you know that I'm right. Okay, come on, really, think about it. When women have friends, they have good friends, people they trust. And then they have friends like Gema, who kind of move to their own tune. They can be friendly as hell, but you know that they don't really have the same ethics or feelings, or whatever and . . . oh, quit staring at me like that! I know that you all know what I mean. She thought she could better herself by leaving, so she left. For her, it wasn't a bad thing to do."

"But not to even mention it?" Stephanie asked.

Suzette shrugged.

"Well, I'd like to know that she's really all right," Stephanie said.

Arturo sniffed. "The closet is empty."

"Let's take a look around anyway, just make sure that we don't see anything funny, huh?" Stephanie said.

"Funny?" Drew said, arching a brow. "Like what?"

"Like blood on the floor," Lena said.

"My God, no!" Suzette cried.

"Suzette, we're not going to find blood on the floor," Stephanie said, but a strange unease filled her.

Suzette let out another little squeal.

"Suzette, really, we're just looking for a note or some-thing—" Stephanie began.

"No, no, it's the roach again. Moving! There, on the wall!"

Clay Barton strode across the room, picked up a tourist magazine from the dresser top, and whacked the roach.

"Ugh!" Suzette said.

"Hey, he just did the manly thing. The roach is dead," Doug told her impatiently.

"Dead as a doorknob!" Drew added cheerfully.

"Yes, it's still ugh!" Suzette said.

Clay shook his head and walked into the bathroom, came back out with toilet paper, and picked up the insect's re-mains.

They heard a flush as he sent the tissue and mini-carcass down the toilet. When he walked back out, he told Steph-anie, "I'll look around downstairs."

"Suzette, you and Lena look around in here," Stephanie told them.

"In the roach room! Hey, look, Clay was a manly man, all right, but there are still roach guts on the wall, even if he wiped it," Suzette said.

"We don't need to look at the wall," Lena told her. "Come

on, Suzette, let's just check out the drawers and the bath . . . it will only take a minute."

"Drew, Doug, please take a look around outside, and I'll head downstairs as well," Stephanie told them.

"Aye, aye!" Doug said, saluting. Drew followed his example. They both stared at her, standing at attention.

She forced a smile. That was what you got when you worked with improv players. "Cute, cute. Save it all for Friday night, huh?"

She turned, and nearly walked into Arturo, he had been standing so close behind her.

"What can I do?"

"Why don't you go to the lobby, see if you can find the maid who did this room today, and ask her if Gema left a message, or if she found anything," Stephanie suggested.

"Yes, yes . . . then we'll all meet in the lobby bar . . . it's just opposite the club. And the restaurant is behind—we can have a few drinks . . . have some dinner. You haven't had a dinner here yet. *Fantastico!*" he assured her.

"That will be great."

Arturo, pleased that he could help, started down the stairs. Stephanie glanced at Suzette and Lena. Suzette seemed to have gotten over her bug phobia, and was working on a dresser, going through it, drawer by drawer.

Stephanie went down the stairs, slowly.

She paused as she reached the bottom step.

Clay Barton was on his knees by the front door, studying the tile at the entry.

"What is it?" she said sharply.

He glanced up quickly, then rose, dusting his hands on his jeans. He had a rueful expression, and yet . . .

She could have sworn that before, he had been intense. As if he had seen something on the tile.

"Clay?" she said.

"Nothing."

"What?"

"I'm sorry. There was nothing," he said.

"What were you expecting?"

"Ah, well, you've got me playing detective, I guess," he said with a shrug.

"But you can see the floor easily enough—even from here. It's white tile," she pointed out.

"Yes, so it is. And like I said, there's nothing." He strode back toward the center of the living area. "No note—I've looked. Nothing broken, no sign of a struggle . . ."

"But the floor was fascinating?" she pressed.

"I guess I thought I saw a footprint, but hell, we've all walked over the entry area, so . . . and a footprint wouldn't mean anything, anyway. Hey, Arturo said something about drinks. I'm going on over to the bar."

He smiled, and exited.

She stared after him, and felt the strangest wave of fire and ice wash over her.

Then it was gone.

And she wondered if she was still suffering from jet lag . . .

Or if it was all part of the strangeness—that which made her feel wonderful, and that which made her feel uneasy— that had wrapped around her from the time she had first arrived.

As she stood at the base of the stairs, she heard the pounding of footsteps behind her. She took the last few steps to the landing and waited as Suzette and Lena joined her.

"Nothing, nothing at all," Lena said. "Every drawer is empty."

"She just left," Suzette said firmly.

"So it seems," Stephanie said.

"Wow, we're screwed then, huh?" Lena said. "Well, I suppose the outlines could all be redone. But hey, a vamp is usually necessary."

"We're not screwed," Suzette said, staring at Stephanie. "That's what you did in the States, right? Didn't you work with an improv group?"

"Yes, well, we'll see," Stephanie murmured. She was suddenly feeling the urgent need for a drink herself. "Let's just head on over to the bar for now. Arturo has suggested drinks before dinner."

"Great. What about the boys?" Lena asked.

"Doug and Drew? They'll find the bar," Suzette assured them.

Stephanie started across from the cottages to the rear doors to the main resort, followed by the other two. Behind her, they argued about Gema.

She had no idea what to think herself, but since the woman had apparently spoken to anyone who would listen about giving up her gig before she even started it, maybe it shouldn't be such a surprise.

Or a worry.

She walked across the lobby, slightly ahead of the other two, irritated at feeling the hint of a headache coming on. What the hell. A drink would kill or cure her.

She walked through the scattered tables where, it seemed, the locals had already found a place to relax and gather. A few people looked at her, some with curiosity, and some with smiles and acknowledgments. She smiled back, and headed around the curve of the bar.

And stopped short.

Arturo was there, waiting as he had suggested.

He wasn't alone.

There was a dignified, scholarly looking gentleman with gray hair and a beard, at his one side.

And at his other side . . .

Grant.

He looked up just as she stopped. His eyes, so deep a blue they were like the ocean at night, were wary. They offered both a rueful apology, and fuck-you-if-you-don't-like-it amusement.

"Ah, gentlemen!" Arturo said, noticing that the men's eyes had strayed, and their attention had wandered from the conversation. "You must meet Stephanie Cahill. Stephanie is here to direct our first venture into entertainment. Carlo Ponti, Miss Cahill—Stephanie, Dr. Carlo Ponti. And this! A fellow American, Stephanie, here to work the dig. Mr. Grant Peterson. Mr. Peterson, Miss Cahill!"

Carlo Ponti offered her a pleasant appreciation with a kiss on the hand and a sparkle in his eyes.

Grant didn't leave his chair.

"It's a small world, Arturo. Stephanie and I are old friends. Very good friends, as a matter of fact. Steph . . ."

Then he rose at last, coming toward her. He kissed her on both cheeks.

And they seemed to burn, as if she had been brushed by the most searing fire, a blaze that burned brighter than the sun.

"Well, hello!" Suzette said, inching her way between Stephanie and Grant. "Suzette Croix, hi. We saw you working last night—we were stuck after the rock slide—but you never made it back to the camp. I'm part of the comedy improv group."

"How do you do," Grant said politely. "This is Dr. Carlo Ponti."

"Hello, Suzette!" Carlo Ponti said, his voice full of the flattery that Italian men seemed so capable of giving, a very simple and pleasant appreciation that was usually lovely. "We almost met before. You were out at the dig."

"Yes, yes! And this is Lena Miro–who was with me," Suzette said quickly.

"*Il piacere è mio*," Lena murmured, which caused Carlo Ponti to ask about her Italian, and the two went into a conversation in the language, which left Carlo appearing very pleased.

"So! You two worked together!" Suzette said, taking Grant's arm and looking from one of them to the other.

"Grant owns the club in Chicago where I worked," Stephanie said. To her own ears, her words sounded stiff and forced. But she must have been speaking fairly normally, because Suzette didn't seem to notice a strained tone.

"Really! Imagine that! Did you know you would both be here? Well, actually, how could you not—"

"We didn't," Stephanie said sharply. Too sharply.

Grant's eyes were very cold. "We didn't. Stephanie had left the club when she accepted this offer, I believe. And I knew nothing about the club here when I signed up to volunteer at the dig."

"Wow! Small world, huh?"

"Way too small, isn't it?" Grant murmured.

"Hey!" Drew said, coming up behind Stephanie and placing an arm casually on her shoulders. "Hi," he said to Grant, aware that the women were grouped around him, and he was obviously someone they had met who was interesting. "Drew Cunningham."

"Grant Peterson."

Doug was behind Drew; introductions went around again, with both men meeting Carlo Ponti as well.

"We should get a big table, huh?" Drew said. "Arturo— you still buying?"

"Tonight, yes!" Arturo called back to him, grinning. "After tonight—no! Then the bar must begin to make money, not spend it."

"Let's push a couple of smaller tables together, huh?" Drew said. "We can all get acquainted. And Arturo, Carlo— thank the good Lord you're among us! This is Italy, and we're surrounded by Americans!"

"Americans are good friends to have," Arturo assured him.

"Yes, but when we go to dinner, you can actually read the menu."

"It's in English as well as Italian," Arturo reminded him.

"But it's more fun when it's in Italian and we have to figure it out," Drew assured him. "Come on, everyone have a seat—this is great!"

Apparently, everyone but Stephanie thought that it was just great. Suzette, apparently completely oblivious to the fact that there might have been anything other than a working relationship between Grant and Stephanie, had somewhat latched on to Grant, for which Stephanie realized she actually blessed her. Grant was drawn to the other side of the table. Doug was to her left, and a free chair wound up at her right.

"We need the extra chair?" Arturo asked.

"Clay is coming in right behind us," Doug said.

"That's right—Clay isn't here. Strange, I thought he was headed here before Suzette, Lena, and I started over," Stephanie said.

"Ran into him outside the cottage. He was giving it a good go-round," Drew explained.

"One of our cast has disappeared," Lena explained.

"Disappeared?" Carlo Ponti said, intrigued.

"Skedaddled, as we say in the West," Drew drawled.

"You're from Boston," Doug reminded him.

"She's gone, however you want to say it," Lena explained.

"Should you call the police?" Grant suggested.

"Well, I think the laws in Italy are pretty much the same as they are in the States," Drew said pragmatically. "She packed up and left. Apparently, this corner of Italy wasn't exciting enough for her."

"She'd been talking about taking off for Rome, and we're assuming that's what she did—since all her belongings are gone," Suzette said.

"Dr. Ponti, your profession is digging for clues, isn't it?" Doug asked.

"Ah, but I'm a detective of ancient artifacts," Ponti said. "I dig in the ground for objects and people who are there—and stay there. The past rarely moves around on one."

"There's Clay, coming now," Doug noted.

Stephanie turned to see that Clay was coming across the room to join them. He was staring intently at Carlo and Grant as he came to the chair by her side.

Arturo performed the introductions. Grant and Carlo stood to shake hands with Clay, then the three men sat down. Stephanie wasn't sure why, but it seemed that a new electricity had come to the table.

The men were wary of one another. She wondered why, or if it was just an instinctive alpha-type male thing going on between Grant and Clay. They spoke politely enough to one another, and yet there was something there, a strange, underlying hostility.

"Just curious," Grant said, "but if you all knew that the woman was unhappy here, and she mentioned leaving, why are you so worried?"

"We're not *so* worried," Stephanie said. "Just concerned."

"But you think you're going to find a clue to her disappearance by searching her empty room . . . or bungalow, wherever she was living?" Grant said.

Stephanie turned to Arturo. "Maybe we should call the police."

He sighed. "The 'police' are sitting on the other side of the café."

"Really?" Stephanie said, turning.

At a table in the opposite corner a handsome young Italian man with very dark hair and eyes was sitting with an older, slightly graying, broad-shouldered fellow.

"Come. I'll introduce you," Arturo said.

Stephanie stood, following Arturo.

The two men rose the minute they saw her coming with Arturo. They greeted one another warmly with a quick exchange in Italian, then Stephanie was introduced to Franco Mercurio the elder, and his son, Franco Mercurio the younger. The elder was called Merc, and the younger, Franco.

As they spoke, Stephanie felt the warm sensation of someone behind her; then a hand fell on her shoulder.

It was Clay Barton.

He had come to be supportive, she assumed. He introduced himself with ease, explained that one of their number had left quite abruptly, and that they would appreciate it if the officers would look into the situation.

They agreed immediately.

"If you wouldn't mind. We've trampled through the bungalow, I'm afraid," Stephanie said. "But we did discover that Gema's clothing was gone, as well as all her personal effects. We didn't really mean to disturb you right now, but . . ."

"*Signorina*, we will be happy to look into it immediately," Merc said, and at his side, his handsome young son and protégé nodded as well.

"The drinks will not go away," he said. "Arturo?"

"I'll come with you—I have the passkey," Arturo said.

The three walked back through the lobby.

"Feel better?" Clay said.

"Yes, thank you," she murmured, stepping slightly away from him to study him. His presence, she realized, made her feel good at that moment. He was strikingly—almost hypnotically—good-looking. Grant, she was certain, was watching them. She didn't particularly feel the need to create an atmosphere of jealousy; rather, she felt the need to protect herself from the feelings she had for Grant. When he had touched her earlier, she had wanted to forget everything. Even the fact that she'd almost questioned his sanity. And had, beyond a doubt, questioned the reality of his passion for her, when in his dream world, it was a name other than hers that came to his lips.

"They will do what is necessary," Clay said.

"Yes." His eyes were gold, or red. Or perhaps they changed color. Hazel eyes did that, of course.

She had never really seen such strange colors, though.

But when he looked at her the way he did, he created a feeling of well-being in her.

"Shall we return to the table?" he suggested.

"Ah, yes."

"You are all right, aren't you?"

"Of course!"

"It is surprising to run into someone you don't expect to see in a foreign country."

"Yes." She said the word casually, and yet, she had the feeling that he knew exactly what her relationship with Grant had been, and that he meant to be there, a total bastion of support for her.

"Ah, yes, surprising. Well . . . certainly, we can sit."

They returned to the table. He pulled out her chair for her. He didn't touch her as they sat, but he rested his hand and arm on the back rail of her chair.

"Everything taken care of?" Carlo Ponti asked.

"Yes, well, the Merc and Franco are looking at the bungalow now," Stephanie said. "Perhaps there's nothing for them to find, and it's most logical that Gema just went on to Rome, but at least the police are aware that she is not here."

"Good. We can move on, then!" Drew said cheerfully. "So—we've been discussing our illustrious, and not always so illustrious, careers. My last gig was a comedy club in Vegas—not a bad gig, really. It was fun, too. But I accepted this offer because it was a chance to spend some real time being paid in a foreign country—instead of having to stay. And to me, it's heaven, and I hope we wow our audiences.

The beach here is glorious. And the view of the mountains, *magnifico!*"

"I came because my background, as you all know, is Italian," Lena said. "And Drew, you're right. The scenery here is beyond beautiful."

"Thank you!" Carlo said.

"You're from here?" Suzette asked.

"Bari, originally—close enough!" Carlo said. "My offices are in Rome these days, but I will always love the country-side."

"So, Clay, you've been working comedy or improv as well? Straight theater? Film?" Grant asked.

He had leaned back in his chair. It was a macho pose, Stephanie thought. Not posed, but it was a way of sitting that spoke of confidence—and determination. He also seemed to be on the offensive. As if he were looking for something to be wrong with Clay Barton.

"I was working at a venue in Scotland," Clay said.

"Where, exactly?" Grant persisted.

"Outside Edinburgh," Clay told him.

"Did the place have a name?" Grant asked politely enough.

"The group is called 'Ye Olde Time Players,'" Clay said, keeping his voice just as level. Again, the electricity around the table seemed thick.

"I've heard of them!" Suzette said enthusiastically. "I was working in Paris last month, and some of the folks from England had been up to see your group. They said the shows were wonderful."

"They play of politics and Shakespeare," Clay explained. "And you?" he asked Grant.

"I own the Park Street Playhouse in Chicago," Grant said.

"How interesting. And yet you're here—not as an actor, but as an *archeologist*?"

"Amateur. An avid student of the past," Grant said. Again,

he spoke pleasantly. But Stephanie knew him. He'd found the question irritating. Maybe he knew how ridiculous his presence here seemed. "Stephanie used to work for me."

"I see. So now she has her own club and cast to direct," Clay mused. "And you . . . followed her here?"

"Pure coincidence," Grant said.

"Oh, I don't believe in pure coincidence!" Lena said. "Fate is just too strange, don't you think?" Lena was guileless with her words, and smile.

No one replied to her because Arturo bustled back to the table then. "Well, that is that. Merc and Franco have gone over the bungalow, and they are left with the same conclusion—our Gema has simply called it quits with us. So . . . it's nearly eight. Not so late, but you wish to start your rehearsals in the morning, so I understand. We can move into the dining room?"

"Yes, dinner sounds lovely," Stephanie said.

"We will excuse ourselves—" Carlo began.

"No, no! You two will join us tonight—I insist," Arturo said.

And so, they all trailed in to dinner together.

This time, Stephanie found herself between Grant and Clay Barton. She felt as if she sat between rival geysers, though surely, no one else had this perception, for the talk around the table was as casual and pleasant as could possibly be desired. Drew, Doug, Suzette, and Lena gave the archeologist and Grant a lively description of how the improv theater would run, and Carlo asked a number of questions and expressed his enthusiasm for the project and, naturally, asked about the work being done in English since they were in Italy.

"Reggie loves this area—the American lady who has bought the club. Like Lena, she is Italian-American," Arturo told him. "Because so little has really been done in many areas of

Calabria to draw on tourism dollars, Reggie is trying to pull visitors not just from the United States, but from around Europe. Whether deserving or not," he said dryly, "English has become the second language of many other nationalities."

"And we'll all be working on our Italian," Stephanie said. "Eventually, we intend to work in shows that draw on both languages. To get the club up and started, we're working with English—and the premise, of course, that our world travelers are working hard on their Italian."

"But sadly, it seems, you have run into a bit of a snag already, eh?" Carlo said. "Down a cast member, as it is."

"There's no problem there," Grant put in. He had leaned back to stare at Stephanie. "She's a wonderful director, of course. But Steph has quite a resumé. She's worked in touring groups, on Broadway, and, the last year, at the least, with a comedy improv group. She'll be able to step right in."

"That's what we assumed, of course," Lena said cheerfully.

"So, you will have your work cut out for you, Miss Cahill," Carlo said.

She shrugged. "I can fill in. It's just that we've started out so small. I would have preferred not to have to be on stage—there are too many technical aspects to be watched. I'd already intended to be my own stage manager, wardrobe mistress, and prop master."

"Each one of us can take on technical duty," Drew Cunningham reminded her, his tone serious and businesslike. She liked him, she thought, watching him from across the table. Both he and Doug were cutups, natural for their choice of profession. But she realized as well that they both had a deep core of determination. Like most actors and comedians, they knew their choice of work created a hard road to follow, and she was certain she was going to find them to be diligent in their ethics regarding discipline and principle.

"That's true, and it's what's going to happen, so it seems," Stephanie murmured.

Then, to her horror, Suzette chimed in. "And imagine! In this little corner of the world, you've accidentally run into your old boss, Stephanie. Surely, Grant, if we run into a problem here, the professional diggers will give you up for a night or two to help out here with your own speciality!"

Stephanie leaned forward, drawing a circle around the rim of her water glass, thinking quickly. "Grant is definitely a talented man. The Park Street Players win all kinds of awards, but hey, he's here to fulfill a dream—working with archeological experts. I wouldn't want to intrude on that."

"Seriously, just how much can you dig?" Lena asked. "There are other volunteers working, right? And many more professionals."

"But of course," Carlo said.

"If Stephanie wants or needs me, I'm sure I can be available," Grant said. He grinned then, suddenly, and it was a strange moment of normalcy in the midst of what felt like a very bizarre night to Stephanie.

"Steph is boss here. She likes being boss. And she's good. I don't like to step into a situation like that," Grant continued.

"But you've created and run your own company for years!" Lena said.

"My point. I like to be boss. So does Steph. And this is her baby."

"Are you saying that you don't think that you could listen to someone else's direction?" Clay Barton asked him politely.

"I don't know. It's been a long time since I haven't had total artistic control of such a project," Grant answered.

"Ah, well, it's hard in life. We all have to learn to listen—and take direction upon occasion," Clay said.

"Well, as to being the director of a theater group, I don't know," Carlo said, "but in the field, Grant is a wonderful worker." He laughed. "All that muscle! Many of my colleagues tend to be very scholarly—and not terribly athletic."

"I'm sure that Grant simply doesn't want to give up any time at the dig," Stephanie said, very aware of him sitting next to her, and watching her.

"But then again, we do have free time," Carlo said cheerfully.

"It would certainly be interesting to have Grant give us a hand," Suzette said.

"It's all really up to Steph," Grant said.

"Oh, well, we've gotten to spend the day with Stephanie," Suzette told him. "And she's wonderful, not hung up at all on being boss. She listened to every one of us. I know that she would always do what was best for the show, and Stephanie, I mean that as the most sincere compliment!"

A murmur of agreement went up around the table, and Stephanie forced a smile. With the size of their group, it wouldn't hurt at any time to have Grant's help, and he was capable of being the ultimate professional.

"Well, we'll see how things go," she said lightly. "Oh, my Lord, Arturo!" she added, grateful for the distraction of the food coming toward their table. They'd already been served a fantastic antipasto and huge salad; now, waiters were bearing huge plates of different pastas. "We'll all be playing very fat world travelers soon."

Food was passed around the table. Suzette asked Carlo and Grant more about the dig.

"It's fascinating!" Carlo assured her. "Well, if you have the patience to dig very carefully, dusting away layers of dirt with little brushes—and never, never rushing."

"Lena and I were there, remember?" Suzette said. "You two were busy and students showed us around, but we got a taste of what it takes."

"Hard work," Carlo agreed. "But to me . . . well, there is

a truly wonderful history to this area, much of it revolving around the Crusades. We were a stop on the way to the Holy Lands, and once many a lord or knight found his way here, he wanted to stay behind and live—and conquer. There has long been a story told in Italy about Norman conquerors—and a great battle between them that rocked the area. A nobleman named Conan de Burgh came beneath the flag of the king in Paris, and set his hand upon the land. As the story goes, he wound up being part of the land, respected and loved by the locals. He fell in love with a native Calabrian woman, but she was a known witch, wicked through and through! She was known to schoolchildren simply as Valeria," Carlo told them dramatically. "She seduced de Burgh, but then left him for a man more ferocious in the art of conquest, a kinsman of the French king named François de Venue, and so, in time, a great battle ensued. It was quite terrible; the witch controlled heinous monsters—they said that she created them by forcing the dead in the cemeteries to rise and become fighting demons. De Burgh went to battle against the two, but was so smitten that, in the end, he tried to prevent the local people from executing the witch, and at that moment, the earth began to tremble and quake, and nature herself decided that they must all die. The stories were half legend and half history, and now—since the earth shifted again for us!—we are able to prove the history part of what occurred. Naturally, since I was a child hearing all these stories, this dig is very special to me," Carlo finished.

"What a wonderful story! Witches and demons!" Lena said with a pleasant little shiver.

They were all startled then when a woman suddenly burst into the restaurant, crying out in Italian. For a moment, she stood in the center of the room, spinning around, obviously looking for someone. Stephanie thought that she was probably in her mid-forties, and that she had spent her years in hard work. Her hair was gray and drawn back in a bun, she wore no makeup, and was wearing a dress that fell nearly to her ankles; her features showed the aging of a life spent in the sun.

Then, she looked directly at Stephanie, and screamed.

Chapter 4

Stephanie leapt up, but by then, the woman had turned again.

"What is it?" Stephanie asked Arturo, alarmed.

"I am trying to understand," he said, rising.

The woman's eyes lit upon the two town policemen, Merc and Franco, who were dining at another table. She rushed to them, and in her excitement, fell to her knees at the elder man's feet. She tugged at his sleeve, though the man was already giving her his undivided attention.

Lena said, "She's talking about her daughter. Her daughter has disappeared."

"Why did she look at me, and scream?" Stephanie asked.

"Oh, I don't think she was really looking at you . . . or at us," Lena said. "She's just very distraught, you know. A bit hysterical."

Arturo started toward the table. Carlo Ponti excused himself as well, approaching the table behind Arturo.

The talk was very excited and mournful, and Arturo tried to speak with the woman, his voice soothing, as was that of the policeman. Merc rose, drawing the woman to her feet.

Uneasily, Stephanie glanced over at Grant.

He was staring at her, eyes grave. *Whatever the others thought, he knew, too, that the woman had stared directly at her.*

Or had she stared at him?

He offered her a shrug. She turned back to the action, and felt his hand on her shoulder, briefly. He meant to be reassuring, she knew. She stiffened, not wanting him to think that she was afraid, or that she had been unnerved in any way.

Lena was right. The woman was simply wild.

Stephanie heard Franco say, "*Il conto?*" to Arturo, which she knew to mean that he was asking for the check. Arturo waved a hand in the air, and the two policemen left with the distraught woman.

Arturo and Carlo returned to the table.

"What was that all about?" Drew asked.

"That was Lucretia Britto. Her daughter, Maria, has not come home," Arturo explained.

"How long has she been missing?" Grant asked.

Arturo shrugged ruefully. "Just a few hours. She didn't return for dinner. She works in the souvenir and furniture shop up the cliff."

"She's been missing just a few hours—and her mother is that upset?" Suzette said. "Perhaps she just met some friends for dinner—or, Lord! Just stopped to be alone a bit. Maybe she went for a walk on the beach—it's so beautiful at night."

"Ah, yes, just a few hours, we should not be too worried," Arturo said. "But . . . you must understand. Here, girls come home after work, even when they are twenty. Their mamas— and their papas!—keep a stern eye on them. Maria's father has been dead many years. Her brother is working in the United States at a theme park. So Lucretia and Maria are alone, and Maria is very good about telling her mother anything she wants to do. So . . . though it is just a few hours, Lucretia is very worried."

"Can we help?" Stephanie asked.

Arturo shook his head. "No—as you see, the police here are very different, too. They are going with Lucretia now. They'll go to the shop with Lucretia, and they will gather together many of the local people to look for her. I'm sure they'll find her."

Stephanie didn't think that he looked very sure.

She suddenly decided that the entire day had been long enough for her. "Arturo, the chef was wonderful, the food was delicious. I think I'm still feeling some of the effects of jet lag. If you'll all excuse me, I'm off to bed. Tomorrow, we've got to get an earlier start. Say, ten?" She looked around at her cast members.

There were nods of assent, and every man at the table rose.

"Steph, I'll walk you wherever you're going," Grant said.

"Hey, I'm fine, just out back and to the left," she said lightly.

"I can walk you," Clay said.

"I just gave her the same offer," Grant said.

In a minute, Stephanie feared, fists would be flying. At that particular moment, she didn't want either of them walking her anywhere.

"I'm fine, honestly. Sit down, both of you—have coffee, dessert, and after-dinner drinks," she said.

"Actually, I'd like a word with you," Grant told her.

She was aware then that everything said was being heard—and that at the table, eyes were going from one to the other of them as if they were at a tennis match.

"All right, fine. Thanks, Grant, and thank you, Clay." She gave Arturo a kiss on the top of the head and waved to the others.

There was an exit to the beach at the back of the restaurant, Arturo pointed out, and they headed that way. They were barely out the door before Grant said, "There's something about that guy I don't like."

"Which guy?"

"Clay Barton."

"I think there's something about you that *he* doesn't like," Stephanie said with a shrug.

"Because he knows that I don't fall for that polite exterior of his," Grant said.

Stephanie laughed. "Oh, Grant, really! He's an actor."

"He's not. I'm willing to bet that he isn't really an actor."

She stopped, and she wasn't amused, just serious as she looked at him in the moonlight. "Are you jealous?"

"No. Yes, probably, but that's not what it is. There's something strange about him, and I'm worried sick about you." He ran his fingers abstractedly through his hair, frowning, as if he didn't understand what he was saying himself. "Stephanie, whatever happened between us, I don't really know or understand. But you can believe in the fact that I care about you. Watch out for him."

She let out an impatient sigh. "Grant! I went my way, you went yours. Pure coincidence brought us to the same place. Unless you did follow me?"

"Don't be silly. This came through one of those societies I subscribe to," he told her, aggravated. "Did you follow me?" he asked.

"Now that's really ridiculous. Reggie owns the place."

"Where is Reggie?" he asked.

"Off getting customers. Grant, I'm fine. I can deal with Clay Barton, and any problem that may come up. Really."

"I should stick around," he murmured.

"You're not responsible for me!" she exclaimed.

He slipped an arm around her shoulder, drawing her from

the rear of the restaurant, as if he was afraid that their words would be overheard. As they moved her along, he was tense. "Stephanie, there's something very wrong here."

"What do you mean?"

"Your actress is missing. Another local girl is missing."

"We don't know anything about the local girl yet. And my actress probably took off for Rome. Rude and very unprofessional, but that's what appears to have happened," Stephanie told him.

"Yes, one would think," he murmured.

They came to her door.

"This is it," she said. "I'm back, safe and sound."

He took a step back from the doorway and looked skeptically at the cottage. "Anyone could break into this place way too easily."

"Grant, no one is going to break in here. Really," she told him.

"Stephanie," he said, and she was startled by the passion in the single whisper of her name. He reached out, as if compulsively, and touched her cheek with his fingertips. She was stunned by the emotions and sensations that such a little caress created within her. "You know—I pray you know, at least—that no matter what has gone on between us, your welfare means more to me than . . . life itself."

His fingertips awakened all the hungers she had repressed. She wanted nothing more than to step forward, and pretend that the bizarre estrangement had never come between them. They shifted, just slightly, and in split seconds she remembered only nights where she lay cocooned against his naked flesh, felt his arms around her. Times when she would awaken and turn, and see his eyes, and then a slow, lazy smile, and feel his hands or his lips, stroking somewhere erotically against the most erogenous areas of skin. Those times when she had wakened slowly, rather, and known the feathery brush of fingers against her spine, lips against her nape. Gentle security suddenly turned to erotic fantasy and more.

She stepped back.

Those times had ended. His arms had grown too fierce. He had whispered another woman's name.

"Grant, I'll be fine, really."

"I'm sorry I came here, I think, and sorrier that you did so." He held his distance, but his speech remained as passionate.

"Grant, I'll lock all the doors tonight. I swear it, all right?" He was, she believed in her heart, strangely sincere.

"I don't mind helping with this, you know," he said.

"You're here fulfilling your life's dream," she reminded him.

"I'm here," he said with a wave of his hand. "That's what's important. Because there is something going on, Stephanie. I know it."

"I told you. I will lock up tightly." He still didn't look happy. "Hey," she teased, "want me to run back to the restaurant and ask Arturo for a big bag of garlic? I can deck it around all the windows."

She was surprised when he didn't even crack a smile. "Hell, maybe that's not a bad idea," he murmured.

She sighed. "Grant, good night. Thank you for walking me here." She moved forward, meaning to stand on her toes, and give him a brief thank-you kiss on the cheek. Somehow, she moved too close. His arms wrapped around her. His knuckles were below her chin, and his lips were on hers, open-mouthed, forceful, tremulous, and passionate. His tongue moved against the walls of her mouth, plunged with sensual insinuation, and she felt the wild birth of a wicked, aching arousal. She wanted nothing more than to stay there, feel what he would do next, return the urgent quest with a hunger all her own.

She stepped back, ever so slightly afraid. He released her, yet his eyes remained dark and searching, with a strange anguish she found hard to bear.

"Good night," she told him quickly. "I'll lock up—I swear it."

She escaped quickly then, and stepped inside, locking the door.

Clay Barton watched Grant as he returned to the restaurant. Both Suzette and Lena had opted for bed earlier, while the men had remained, Carlo and Arturo with their cigars, Doug, Drew, and Clay sipping on brandies. Merc had returned, asking them if they would help with the search for the missing girl. They were just rising to do so, having been given the territory they were to travel.

"We're going to search the beach along the resort area, see if Maria is anywhere around," Clay told Grant.

"I said that we'd be delighted to help, of course," Carlo said.

"Sure. Does anyone really think that the girl might be lost on the beach?" Grant asked.

"No," Clay said flatly. His answer said much more. They were afraid that the girl might be dead, and that she had washed up on the beach.

"All right. Which way do I go?" Grant asked.

"You and I will walk south to where the rocks jut out, and then back," Clay told him. "Drew and Doug are walking all around the immediate resort area, and Arturo and Carlo will head north along the beach."

"Fine."

Grant eyed him suspiciously. Clay shrugged with a small smile.

"We meet back here, right?" Doug said.

"Yes, we come back here," Arturo said.

They exited together by the rear of the restaurant, then split to go their separate ways.

"So," Clay said to Grant as they walked, "you own a playhouse. You've a reputation for excellence in comedy, satire, and improv—and you're here at a dig site."

Grant flashed him a sharp and wary glance. "Yes."

"Really? I mean, sorry, but it does look as if you followed Stephanie here."

Grant stiffened. Clay observed him—physical features, stance, bearing. The guy was assured, and tall, broad-shouldered, and apparently composed of pure muscle. He was built like a rock, but seemed to have an easy coordination and agility.

"I've always had a fascination with archeology, the past, anthropology, you name it," Grant said. "I grew up in Chicago—one of my first memories is of the Egyptian exhibit at the Field Museum. This came up, and I came here."

"You didn't know about Reggie's place?" Clay asked casually.

Again, Grant shot him one of those looks that assured Clay that the fellow was barely controlling his temper. "I've seen Reggie three times. I knew she was Italian. That hardly meant that she was going to open a resort in Calabria and put a comedy club in her resort."

"Kind of strange, though, huh?" Clay said lightly.

Grant was assessing him as well, Clay knew.

"Strange. Yes. But then, a lot of things seem strange. Somehow, you just don't look like the usual comedian."

"No?" Clay said. He shrugged. "Well, hell, I always thought that actors and comedians came in all shapes and sizes."

Grant stopped suddenly. He'd veered very close to the water. Clay hadn't gone so far. The sand was deep, and the air was filled with the scent of the salt water. And something more.

The smell of death.

"There," Grant said.

Despite the darkness and the night, they could both see a clump of something ahead of them on the beach. They looked at one another for a split second, then headed toward it. They hunched down. The clump was covered in seaweed.

Grant let out a sound of relief. "Dolphin," he said.

"Poor thing," Clay murmured. "Looks like it beached itself."

"Maybe. I don't know a damned thing about dolphins," Grant said. He stood. He seemed inordinately relieved. "We'll have to tell Arturo. He won't have any tourists out on the beach for a week if they don't dispose of the carcass."

Clay nodded, and stood as well. "The cliffs are just there. There's nothing, no one, out here."

"I didn't think there would be, but what the hell," Grant said.

They started back. Again, Grant seemed drawn to the edge of the water. Clay kept to the sand, watching.

When they returned to the restaurant, the others were there, just as frustrated. They told Arturo about the dead dolphin, and he assured them that he'd have it taken care of by morning.

"Well, we should head back," Carlo Ponti told Grant.

Grant took a long, wary look at Clay. "Carlo, I'll be out first thing in the morning. I'm going to take a room here for the night . . . maybe for the week." He stared at Clay as he spoke, as if warning him.

Or threatening him?

Clay wasn't certain.

Grant kept looking at him. "I intend to be around here," he continued. "In case. Just in case Stephanie decides that she needs some help. You know, putting up the show."

Putting up the show. He didn't mean that at all. Nor did he mean "needs some help." What he meant was, "needs me."

That was fine, Clay determined, smiling deeply.

He was glad that Grant Peterson would be exactly where he could keep a close eye on him.

Just as, he was certain, Grant Peterson would be watching him.

She didn't owe Grant anything, Stephanie reminded herself. And still, that night, she locked the front door, and the back door, and when she went upstairs, she closed and locked the entry from the balcony as well.

Too bad. She had loved the breeze.

It was all silly, really—it had to be. Gema Harris had taken off for the bright lights of Rome, and the missing girl would be found soon as well. Maybe she had run away with a lover who would not be approved by her family. Such things were surely known to have happened before. By tomorrow, the mystery would be solved.

Still . . .

She wondered if it was more than Grant urging her to be careful that made her walk around the place with nervous determination. She felt edgy herself. She wasn't certain if she was really feeling anything unusual, or if the fact that there were missing persons in the area, and Grant's assertion that something was off, causing her to experience the unease.

She was really tired. Jet lag was a part of it. Her sleep having been beset by dreams was part of it as well.

Feeling certain that she had closed and locked every possible entrance, she showered and went to bed.

When she closed her eyes at first, they opened again immediately. She had locked the doors to the balcony, but hadn't closed the drapes.

The darkness outside seemed to hold shapes.

Stephanie rose, and closed the curtains, and went back to

bed. The events of the day kept going through her mind.
They would always end with one thought.

Grant was here.

And she would think about her cast again, and how pleased
she had been with the few intense hours she had spent working with Doug, Drew, Suzette, and Lena.

Then Clay Barton had arrived. In the night, her eyes
closed, attempting to sleep, she saw again the man's very unusual eyes. Cat eyes, lion eyes, dragon eyes. Like pinpoints
of red-gold light in the ebony of the shadows.

Tossing and turning, at last she slept.

But only a few minutes were restful.

Grant was here.

She dreamed that he was in the room. The drapes were
fluttering, and she thought that they couldn't be, because the
doors were closed. The breeze was drifting over her. She was
lying naked on the bed, and she could feel the air, as if it
were part of an erotic seduction. She tried to tell herself that
it was ridiculous, she had on a long T-shirt, she was swathed
in cotton, but still . . .

The air against her flesh was cool, and she was mesmer-
ized by the lightly billowing drapes; every inch of her skin
seemed to be touched by the breeze, damp and cool, teasing,
touching. And there was the man in the darkness, and by the
shape, she was certain that she knew him, knew him so well.

Grant was there.

Broad-shouldered, a lean muscle mass, hot and vital, and
moving with slow, sinewed ease, coming toward her. Sleek
and bronze, fluid and sensual, the pad of his step silent
across the room, his confidence complete, as if he knew the
air rushing over her held her spellbound, and she wouldn't
begin to protest . . . not at all, she would be waiting, anxious
for the liquid energy and spiraling heat that would come
with his touch.

Grant . . . or someone like Grant.

Hard-toned, agile, and the darkness hid the face, but there was a smile of amusement and assurance, and a knowledge . . .

He reached the foot of the bed. Crawled there, crouched, with that same animal beauty of movement and ease and sleek agility. Fingers slid along her calf, and the pure, searing ember of a kiss slid with liquid seduction along the flesh of her leg, teased beneath her kneecap. Her limbs were parted to allow for the force of the body coming against hers with slow, sure solicitation and she was powerless to move. There was darkness now where the drapes had appeared to billow. As if something had come behind him. Something winged and huge . . .

But she couldn't concentrate on it, couldn't remember to think, or even allow the rush of fear to touch her, because the sensation now streaming upward along her thigh was like a flow of lava, and she knew where it was coming, and she wanted it, and the hunger evoked was almost more than she could bear. She wanted to reach out and touch the man's hair, dig her fingers into it, feel the warmth and power of the body, and the life within the man, but she couldn't move, because the pulse between her legs had grown to a desperate fever pitch, and if the surge did not come completely to her soon . . .

The darkness rose like a great, sweeping cape. It would engulf them both. She didn't care. She wanted the man with a growing urgency that eclipsed all else. She writhed where she lay, still unable to make her limbs move. She tried to whisper his name, and remembered that they were not together, that there was something wrong, something so very wrong, no matter how cataclysmic their passion could be . . .

Closer, oh, God, yes . . . closer.

Then . . .

Someone else was there. At her side. Sitting, as if it were

perfectly natural for someone else to be present at the crux of such an erotically intimate moment.

No . . . you must be careful, you don't know who he is, the shadow is rising behind him, come to me, come with me, listen to me . . . it's here, in the past . . .

The man at her side was Clay Barton.

But then, the seduction between her legs became complete.

The shadow fell down, and she was screaming . . .

Stephanie awoke abruptly, catching the scream before it tore from her lips.

The glass doors were closed. The draperies were still. The room was empty. She was clad as she had been when she had gone to bed, in the soft, old, worn cotton T-gown. She was shaking, and bathed in sweat.

"Damn!" she breathed aloud, and she knew, of course, that she had been dreaming, and once again, the dream itself was simply embarrassing.

She flushed, jumped up, ran to the bathroom, flicked on the light, and doused her face with cold water. And then, in the light, the whole thing seemed to fade, and be ridiculous.

"Damn Grant for showing up here!" she said aloud. She walked back into the bedroom. The shadows there then seemed entirely natural.

Still, she turned on the bedroom light. And despite the fact that the dream was already fading, and it was ridiculous to think that she'd really felt anything at all or that anyone could have been in her cottage in any way, shape, or form, she went down the stairs and turned the lights on throughout the place.

By then, she was feeling really silly, but she wasn't quite ready to go back to bed. She made a cup of tea, and turned on the television. There was an all-night music channel in Italian, she discovered. Something like MTV or VH1. Curling into a chair, she watched the musicians on the screen.

When she fell asleep again, it was in the chair, with every light in the cottage on, and a rock rhythm permeating her mind.

He stood outside, taken by the darkness and the sea breeze, stock-still, as time ticked by, aware . . .

There.

With her.

He had to be with her.

The vigil had to continue, he knew. What might stand between them, he didn't know, only that he had to be there, to watch, to force himself into her consciousness, or subconsciousness. There was danger . . . deeper than any that might be imagined. There was a reason for everything. A reason for the torment . . .

And to watch.

Then, out of the shadows . . .

Light. A field of light. He fell back.

He gave himself a shake.

The vigil was over.

Breakfast was a buffet.

When Stephanie made it over to the restaurant in the morning, she headed immediately for the coffeepot, then noted just how beautifully and completely it was all arrayed. Every taste was catered to; there was even an assortment of foods that catered to any Japanese or Oriental clientele.

She selected a croissant, yogurt, and a fruit cup and headed for the large, round table where she had noted that Drew and Suzette were already sitting.

"Good morning," she said.

"*Buongiorno!*" Drew told her.

"Hey," Suzette said.

Stephanie slid into her chair. "Did they find the girl, Maria, do you know?"

Suzette shook her head. "I haven't seen Arturo yet this morning, but Giovanni was through here a few minutes ago." She smiled. "That is one good-looking young man. I think he wants in on the comedy club, but he says that he is too busy right now. Anyway, he said that they hadn't found the girl. Merc and Franco called into the next town—much bigger than this place—and they're sending a few men down to help."

"Maybe she eloped with an archeologist," Drew said.

Suzette shrugged. "Not the ones I've seen!" she said. "Except, of course, for Grant Peterson, and he's not really an archeologist. Stephanie! I still can't imagine that the guy you worked for at a comedy house is actually here—as an amateur digger."

Stephanie forced a smile. "I still can't quite believe it myself."

"He just left," Drew said.

"What do you mean?" Stephanie asked sharply.

"He was just in here, having breakfast. He's taken one of the cottages," Suzette said.

"You're kidding me!" Stephanie said, without thinking. A surge of anger filled her. It was bad enough that coincidence—as he swore—had brought them to the same place. He should have at least had the decency to keep sleeping out in his tent!

"No," Suzette said, and cast her head at an angle as she studied Stephanie. "Is that bad? He's devastating. The best-looking, most macho thing around here."

"Ouch!" Drew protested.

Suzette quickly put a hand on his shoulder. "I'm sorry! Drew, you, of course, are adorable!"

"I don't want to be adorable. I want to be macho!" he protested.

"Of course, then there's Clay Barton. He's a hottie, too," Suzette said.

"And I'm adorable!" Drew moaned.

"Adorable is good," Suzette assured him.

Drew rolled his eyes.

"Really, you know, it seems that Grant is really willing to help in any way. I mean, Lord knows, props . . . lighting. You can surely use him, Stephanie," Suzette said.

"Suzie, Suzie, Suzie!" Drew said, sitting back. "Women are supposed to be intuitive, and I think I've got it all over you on this one—of course, that may be since I'm the 'adorable' man that I am. There was something more than a working relationship that went on between our esteemed director and her ex-boss."

Suzette gasped. "Really?"

Stephanie shook her head, glaring at Drew. "Believe me, both Grant and I are totally professional."

"I would never doubt that," Drew said, but he was still smiling.

"I don't know how I didn't realize!" Suzette said. "I'm sorry . . . I wasn't honing in. I mean, he is just as sexy as all hell, but I'm not the type of woman . . . my hands are off now, I assure you."

"There's nothing between us now, really," Stephanie said.

"Maybe there's nothing between you, but there's something there," Drew said.

"There's not. We split up. We both thought that we were going places miles away from one another," Stephanie said.

"Bad breakup, huh?" Drew said.

"It's nothing like that. I care about him very much. As a human being, of course," Stephanie told him.

"As a human being!" Suzette nudged Drew, grinning.

Stephanie sighed. "Yes, I mean that he's a fine person,

we're still . . . friends, yes. I hope his life goes well, that he lives long and happily, and all that."

"Right," Suzette murmured.

"Hey, good morning all." With a coffee cup in one hand and a plate in the other, Lena stood behind one of the chairs. Drew jumped up and drew it out for her and she sat. "So—they never found that girl last night, huh?" she asked. "That's what the waitress told me, anyway."

"No, apparently not," Stephanie said.

Lena yawned. "Wow—weird, huh?" She shook her head. "Damn, I am tired. I must have been worried for her last night, because I hardly slept. Or when I slept . . . I can't remember them now, but man, I had some bizarre dreams."

"Probably because of that scream Maria's mom let out," Drew said. "And, of course, in a small place like this, you can't help but feel that traumas are more personal, huh?"

"Who's in trauma?"

They all spun around. Clay Barton had arrived. He was wearing sunglasses that enhanced the sophistication and classic perfection of his features.

"They never found the missing girl," Drew told him.

"That's bad," he said, joining them. Apparently, he wasn't a breakfast eater. He had brought only a cup of coffee to the table.

"Well, there's a voice of doom," Drew said. "I tend to think that she found the right guy and eloped. This could be romantic rather than tragic."

"She was supposed to be getting married to a local boy within a year," Clay said.

"Oh?" Stephanie said.

"I talked to Franco late last night," Clay said.

"Well, that's great. Just scare us all," Lena said with a shiver.

"Maybe we should be a little scared—scared enough to be careful," Clay said.

"That works for me," Suzette said with a shiver. "We stick together as much as possible, then."

"Since I'm your average 'adorable' guy," Drew teased her, "I can safely volunteer to hang around you girls and keep you safe."

Clay Barton didn't crack a smile. "Seriously, we have a cast member missing, and a village girl who has disappeared. Yes, we should lock our doors, and look out for one another."

"Well, if that's agreed, we should finish up and head over to the café," Stephanie said, glancing at her watch.

"We're missing Doug," Lena noted.

"Maybe he headed straight over to the café," Suzette suggested.

"Maybe," Stephanie said. "Anyway, I'm going over now. We need to get started. Finish your food, but then, let's get going."

Clay stood. "I'll go in with you. We stick together, right?"

Stephanie smiled. "Well, that's fine, but I'm only going through the bar and the lobby to the club area."

"And I'm not eating. I'll come with you."

"Great."

As she started through the tables, Stephanie had an acute moment of discomfort. A snatch of her dream seemed to come vividly to mind. *He had been there. In her dream. While Grant had been . . . doing very erotic things to her. If it had, indeed, been Grant.*

It had been a dream, for God's sake! she told herself impatiently.

And still . . .

He set a hand upon her shoulder as they walked. Doug or Drew might have done the same.

Doug and Drew did not look like this man, or have his . . .

Raw sense of competence, assurance, power . . .

Sensuality.

"You know, you were a bit of a voice of alarm back there," she told him.

"I just suggested that everyone be careful," he said. He smiled at her then, and squeezed her shoulder. "Hey, I'm sorry. I know we've got a show Friday night. It's going to be fine, I'm certain. You'll do great."

"Thanks." The sense of discomfort left her. She felt the most bizarre urge to rest against his shoulder.

They came into the club area. Doug was there, sitting on the edge of the stage, reading over his notes.

"Morning!" he called cheerfully.

Stephanie felt a keen sense of relief.

"Good morning," she told him.

"Hey, Doug! You mean you made it in here without coffee?" Suzette called out from behind Stephanie. She turned to see that the rest of her cast had assembled, coming right behind her and Clay Barton.

Doug laughed. "I came right in here, and that blessed young Giovanni fellow brought in a pot of coffee right away. Good fellow. Anyway, it's over there on the table, with cups and cream and sugar, so help yourselves, for those who are in dire need of more caffeine!"

Stephanie decided that she *was* in dire need. She got a cup of coffee, then said, "All right, guys, let's go through the first outline. Without scripts or notes."

"You're Gema's character?" Suzette asked.

"I guess so," Stephanie said. "Anyway . . . let's go. Lights . . . Lena, you enter from the back of the room."

The rehearsal began, and despite the fact that she had to be on stage, Stephanie was pleased. She did have an incredible ensemble group. She let the first run-through go without stopping; the second time around, she did her role with her notebook in hand. Drew called out to her after they had picked up the action when she had given him a stage direction, and she had to jump down from the stage to watch the piece of business he was asking about.

"Stephanie, my question is this," Drew said. "If you and Clay are stage right, and I'm coming in that way, won't I disrupt you while you're still in your intellectual argument about the guy in the audience you're going to be teasing?"

"Maybe, thanks, good point," she said. "Let me take a look."

"It is disruptive," came a voice from the back of the room. "Stephanie, maybe you want him to circle either around the audience, or enter stage left."

Looking to the rear of the café area, she saw Grant.

He was in jeans and a polo shirt, hair clean, damp, and somewhat slicked back. He hadn't been digging in the last hour or so, she was certain.

How long had he been there, watching them all in silence?

She was immediately tempted to ask him to please get the hell away.

But it would be a mistake.

"Are you here for a while?" she called out instead, hoping her voice wasn't as brittle as it sounded to her own ears.

"However long you need me," he said.

"Fine. Thanks. Then we'll run it again. And you can watch the blocking for me."

He came forward. Stephanie heard Lena whisper, "Damn, he arrived at a good time!" There was pleasure in her voice.

Damn, he arrived at a good time!

No! Damn, it was purely bizarre that he had arrived at all!

Stephanie took her place next to Clay Barton. Their characters were the two who considered themselves to be the hot ones—he, the international gigolo, at least in his own mind, and she, the flirt, the tease, tsked at by the other two women, who still tolerated her and tried to clean her up all the time. They ran the piece.

She didn't miss a beat, or an innuendo, and she was rewarded by the laughter of her fellow cast mates.

And still . . .

She had done it all by rote.

Because again, snatches of her dreams were far too vivid in her mind.

And having Grant there, watching her . . .

She suddenly thought of him as a giant black panther, a shadow, then a man, stalking her in the night . . .

Chapter 5

"He knows what he's doing, huh?" Clay Barton asked softly. He and Stephanie had just walked off stage, and Grant was courteously moving toward the rear of the café section, a casual motion that simply said he was turning direction back over to Stephanie.

"Yes. He's very good," Stephanie agreed. And he had been. She was going to call it quits. They hadn't taken a lunch break, and it was nearly six. No one had complained. They'd covered three of the outlines, and she already knew they were going to be fine. They established the course of action for the nights, and the cast had already come up with great ad-libs. They'd run over a few of the songs, and every member of the cast had, at least, a pleasant voice. Drew had an exceptional tenor.

Each night, Lena was giving a few sentences and lessons in Italian, as it was part of her character to be a bit of a braggart and know-it-all and flout her ability with the native tongue in front of her co-world travelers. Stephanie had been a little worried about how that would work out, but it had been perfect. Suzette spoke fluent French and tried to turn the tables on Lena, only to be informed that hey, this was Italy.

Every night, of course, would be different. Some nights would be better than others—it was always so when the audience was an integral part of the performance. Fortunately, it appeared that they were going to have a hit, and, according to Arturo, they were definitely going to have an audience.

"The situation is totally bizarre, but I guess I should just be grateful," Stephanie murmured to Clay. "Hey, guys!" she called, raising her voice and wending her way back close to the stage. "That was phenomenal, really. We've been together just a few days, and we seem to be doing great as an ensemble. Thank you all."

"Hey, cool!" Drew called out, still center stage. "Does that mean it's Miller time?"

"Peroni!" Lena teased back. "This is—"

"I know, I know!" Drew groaned, breaking in on her. "This is Italy."

"Are we breaking?" Suzette asked. "Since this is Italy, I'd give a lot for a glass of the truly delicious local red wine!"

"Yes, we're breaking," Stephanie said. "Once again, I want to thank you all."

"Suzette, does that mean you're willing to join me in the bar?" Drew asked.

"Only because we're an ensemble," Suzette said.

"I'm with you—nothing like keeping the cast close," Doug said. "And Lena . . . you're having a Peroni?"

"You bet," Lena assured him. "Clay, Grant . . . Stephanie?"

"Sure," Clay said.

"I'll be right along," Stephanie said. "I've scattered a few notes around. You can order me a Peroni, too, okay?"

"Peroni for me, too," Grant said. "I'll help Stephanie—I might have scattered a few of her pages."

The others hopped down from the stage. Suzette was the

last out, giving them a little wave. "Two Peronis—they'll be waiting."

"Thanks!" Stephanie called. When they were gone, she turned to stare at Grant. "I really do owe you a thank-you," she told him.

He shrugged. "I figure I can be around in the afternoons."

"I appreciate what you did," she said. "But you're really here for the dig. Carlo Ponti said that you're good, a help out there, too. You don't owe me, or this enterprise, anything."

"I can work at the dig in the mornings." He lifted his shoulders in a casual shrug once again. "As long as there are no rock slides, it's about thirty, forty minutes out and the same back in. I'd rather work there in the mornings—ten o'clock seems to be your choice of time around here, so I might as well get the early hours in out there."

"You took a cottage here?" she said.

"Yes."

"Because . . . because you decided I needed help?"

"Because the tent in the wilderness thing was getting old," he said impatiently. "I'm happier being around here, okay?"

She sighed. "Grant, there have been a few strange things happening here, but I'm not in any danger. I don't want you to feel responsible for looking after me."

"Like I said, I'm happier here. And don't worry—I'm not expecting anything from you, I'm not looking for payback of any kind."

She felt a flush cover her cheeks. "I didn't suggest that you were. You wouldn't. And that was hardly the crux of our problem."

"What exactly was it, would you say?" he asked her flatly.

"You," she whispered softly.

He lifted his hands. For a moment, it was as if he was going to deny that there had been anything different about him at all. But then he turned, starting toward the rear of the café. "Humor me, huh? I won't get in your way."

"You won't get in my way?" she called after him. "Hmm. What if I decided that I wanted to get into an affair with another man?" she queried.

He turned, hands on hips, staring at her.

"Clay Barton?"

"I didn't say that."

"Who else?" he queried. Then he said, "You should take your time. Take it slow, and take your time. Whatever."

"And what if someone else wanted to rush?" she asked.

"Let me suggest that they don't."

"And why is that?"

"I'd flatten him," Grant said simply. "Anything else? My Peroni is waiting."

"Please, go on. I wouldn't want your Peroni getting warm," she said.

He started out, but then paused. "Are you coming?"

"Yes."

She gathered her notes and stuffed them into her tote bag. She walked by him at a distance; he followed her, never close enough to touch.

They joined the others at the bar. The seats that had been left for them were not together. Stephanie was grateful.

She slid between Lena and Doug, who both greeted her. Clay, at Doug's left, had been speaking to him, and the men returned to the conversation. Lena moved in close to Stephanie. "Is everything all right?"

"It's great—why?"

Lena sighed, leaning back. "I'm envious, that's all."

Stephanie shook her head. "Really, there's nothing between us now. We're professional associates."

"He doesn't look at you like a professional associate," Lena said. "And that one!" She indicated Clay. "He's always watching you."

"I'm the director. You're all supposed to be watching me."

Lena laughed softly. "I do—and you're doing a great job.

And I admired you even more today when you were willing to hand over the reins and listen to other opinions. You don't have any of those insecure hang-ups where you're afraid to listen to others. I guess I'm just at that stage in my life where . . . I turned thirty-six this year. I've loved my profession—I haven't gotten rich, but I have managed to keep working. So I'm happy. But every once in a while . . . wow. I would just love to fall in love! Find the right guy, and fall in love. I think I'd trade anything for it, right now."

"Well, you never know. Mr. Right could be in the audience any night," Stephanie murmured. "But . . . well, you're beautiful, smart, and talented. A guy shouldn't be the focus of your life. Romance kind of happens when . . . when it happens."

"Easy for you to say. The two hunks in our company are always watching you!"

Stephanie groaned. "Lena, I don't think that Clay Barton is looking at me in any special way. And as to Grant . . . well, there was a past history."

"Yeah, yeah!" Lena said, waving a hand in the air. "Strange place, though, huh? I am Italian–Italian-American, all four grandparents from here—I've spent months of my life with family in the north, and I know the country well. But . . . this place is special. The beach, the colors of the water, the mountains behind . . . special, but strange. Jeez, the dreams I'm having!" She grinned suddenly. "Well, I guess they'll have to do for now. Until that guy shows up in the audience, huh?"

"He's waiting somewhere," Stephanie said. "Just remember, don't be in such a rush! You could be out with Mr. Wrong when Mr. Right finally comes along."

"I'll keep that in mind," Lena said.

"Arturo, my man!" Drew called suddenly. They all fell silent, turning to watch as Arturo strode through the bar.

He stopped at the table.

"Any word on the missing girl?" Grant asked.

"I'm afraid not. We have had so many search parties . . . officers in from other towns and villages. They've questioned the boyfriend, and he is at a loss, too. Poor boy, he cries almost as much as the girl's mother."

"We're so sorry," Stephanie said.

"They've really checked out the boyfriend's alibi and all?" Doug asked.

They must have all stared at him because he continued defensively with, "Well, in the United States, sadly enough, I know the police always start with the husband or boyfriend. There have been terrible cases in the United States where a man who supposedly loved a woman brutalized her. Of course, wives have killed husbands, too."

"They don't think it was the boy," Arturo said.

"Did he have an alibi?" Suzette asked.

"I think not. Actually, Maria never even showed up to work the day she disappeared. She left her house when her mother was still sleeping. So . . . she might have gone out anytime in the night, even. It might not have even been morning yet."

"Maybe she'll still turn up," Lena said hopefully.

"Maybe," Arturo agreed. He sounded sad. "Ah, well. You are having dinner in the restaurant here again?"

"Yes, I guess so," Stephanie said, looking around. It seemed as if they were agreed to spend the evening together again.

"Sure, why not?" Clay said.

"There are a few local places. And of course, part of starting this place was to pick up all of the local tourist trade, but . . . I'll see that the chef prepares a meal especially for you tonight," Arturo said. "I'll have that calamari you like so much brought to the table, Lena. And for you, Suzette, the shrimp pasta dish."

"Sounds lovely, thank you," Suzette told him, and Lena echoed her sentiment.

"Anything else?" Arturo asked.

"Everything here is great," Grant said.

Arturo smiled at last, pleased with the compliment.

"*Grazie*. I'm pleased you are all happy. The first real test of tourism begins this weekend. We've had guests here, of course, as you've seen, but local so far . . . some people down from Naples and even Rome. But what we really want is to bring in foreign money, of course!"

With a wave, he left them.

"Well, shall we all tromp on in and have dinner, then?" Doug suggested. "We skipped the whole lunch thing, remember?"

"And actually, that's a sin in Italy," Lena said.

"Let's go eat, then," Stephanie said.

They filed into the restaurant area. As Arturo promised, they were quickly served appetizers, the calamari, and an antipasto. For the area, they were dining fairly early, and the chef was able to come out himself, and bask in their pleasure. The conversation revolved around their work that day, and Stephanie was pleased with herself when she was able to tell them all casually that Grant had said that he'd work with them every afternoon.

"What about for the actual shows?" Suzette asked.

"Sure. I can stage manage for you once they open. We never dig in the dark," Grant said.

Stephanie dug in her bag and found her notes and schedules. "Tomorrow morning, the wardrobe mistress is supposed to bring around the costumes that were ordered. Lena, thank God we have you, because my Italian wouldn't be good enough if we were to encounter any problems. For now, we'll worry about having the right costume for our original roles. Next week, she'll come back and we'll be physically fitted for the other characters so that once we're under way, we can switch characters around so it will be fresh, and keep ourselves stretching."

"That's good—have our tailoring done when Grant isn't here, and work when he is," Lena approved. Stephanie thought that she sounded a little distracted. She had been looking across the room as she spoke.

Turning around slightly to see what had caught Lena's attention, Stephanie saw that the back door to the restaurant was swinging closed.

She shrugged. "Everything all right?" she asked Lena.

"Of course!"

The pasta bowl had been going around the table. She turned to pass it on to Clay Barton, at her left.

But Clay was watching Lena, and he seemed tense. His eyes, too, strayed to the rear door.

"Clay? Pasta?"

"Sure. Thanks," he said, recovering quickly.

And yet . . .

Strange. Very strange.

After a few minutes, Lena yawned suddenly. "Wow, guys, forgive me. That was so rude. It wasn't the company, honestly. You know, I'm going to have to forego dessert and coffee. Will you all excuse me? I'm heading for bed."

"Are you really that tired?" Clay asked her.

"Really." She flashed him a rueful smile. Clay didn't seem assured, but the men stood as Lena rose, bid them all good night, running around the table and kissing them, Italian style.

"Look what's coming. You're going to miss the tiramisu!" Doug warned her.

She grinned, and left.

After that, it seemed that the night broke up quickly. Suzette said she felt like exploring a few of the streets and local places. Doug and Drew volunteered to go with her, and Clay appeared to want to join the group as well.

"Stephanie?" Suzette asked.

She shook her head. "I'm feeling like Lena. Tired."

"Grant?" Suzette asked sweetly.

"I'll take a rain check."

"Hey, just because I'm opting out, you feel free to go," Stephanie said.

"I do feel free to go. It's just a long day for me, digging— and gophering," he said.

"Yeah, like you're a gopher!" Suzette said.

"Hey, I learned that early. In any form of live theater, you do whatever it takes. Steph, if you're heading to the cottage, I'll walk you over," he said.

Suzette flashed Stephanie a glance with a sly, secret smile, convinced that whatever had been going on between them still was.

"Hey, you guys, stick close with our little Franco-American hottie, huh?" Stephanie teased the others.

"We won't leave her for a second," Drew assured her, a little too solemnly.

"What if I find the love of my life?" Suzette demanded.

"Too bad. He'll have to wait," Doug said.

"What if you two find the loves of your lives?" Suzette asked.

"Wow. Hmm. We'll have to think about that one," Drew said, laughing. "Oh, not to worry. The chances of us both getting lucky in a small town like this are so far out of the spectrum! And Clay will be around, right?"

"I'll be around," Clay said. "Speaking of which, one of us should have walked Lena to her little place. I think I'll go check on her first."

"Steph and I will come with you," Grant said.

"We will?" Stephanie said, irritated just because he had answered for her.

He arched a brow at her, and she was further annoyed to realize that she had sounded sharp.

"Sorry, just thought I might volunteer on my own," she murmured.

"Maybe we should come, too," Drew said.

"No, you guys go on out and have a good time," Clay advised. "I think the three of us will be force enough."

The others started out the front and Stephanie, Clay, and Grant rose, heading out the back to the beach. The night was another balmy, beautiful sight.

"Full moon in less than a week," Clay noted.

They could hear the waves rushing in, and it seemed that a very gentle light, with just the touch of a red-gold glow, bathed the area.

"This stretch of Italy is simply gorgeous," Stephanie murmured. Their conversation seemed absurdly casual.

"That one is Lena's, just there—I think," Grant said.

"How do you know?" Stephanie asked him.

He arched a brow at her and again pointed. "Because that one is mine, over there. When I checked in, Giovanni showed me the place, and pointed out the cottages where I could find all of you."

"Ah," she murmured, feeling a little rebuffed. She hadn't been accusing him of anything. Had she?

Clay walked ahead of them, heading for Lena's door. He knocked on it firmly. They waited, and nothing happened.

"There's a buzzer," Grant pointed out.

Clay punched the little doorbell.

This time, they heard footsteps on the stairs.

Then, Lena opened the door.

It appeared that she had hastily thrown a terry robe over a far more revealing night garment in some kind of turquoise silk and gauze. Her hair was definitely mussed, and she appeared flushed and nervous.

She stared at the three of them. "Yes?"

"We were just checking to see that you got back okay," Grant said.

She sighed. "I'm fine. Just fine. As you can see."

"Right," Clay murmured. Stephanie noted that he was looking at her little cottage strangely, as if he were trying to *sense* whether everything was really all right or not.

"I'm okay, honest!" Lena said. "I'm tired. I was actually in bed."

"So, you're not inviting us in, huh?" Clay said lightly.

"No, no, no—you may definitely not come in! I'm going back to bed. I'm sorry—how rude. Thank you all for checking on me. But please, go away. Hey, my director is here. And I intend to do good work for her in the morning, so . . ."

"We're out of here, then," Grant said. "Good night."

"Good night. And really. Thank you all for caring," Lena said.

They turned and started to walk away. Clay Barton paused on the path, looking back.

"What is it? What's wrong?" Grant demanded.

"She swore she was fine," Clay murmured.

"And it definitely looked as if we dragged her out of bed," Stephanie commented.

"Right," Clay said. "Well." He looked from Grant to Stephanie and offered a wry grimace. "I guess I'm on my way out, then. See you all tomorrow."

He turned and left them. They watched him until he disappeared back into the resort, then turned toward Stephanie's cottage.

At the door, Stephanie inserted her key, then turned back to Grant. "Well, I'm here. Safe and sound. Thanks."

He nodded. "Mind if I come in and see it?"

She hesitated. "Look, Grant, we're managing to do fairly well on a professional level. And it's not as if I don't have feelings for you—you know that I do. But—"

"Steph, I didn't ask to sleep with you. I just want to make sure . . . that the place is safe. Oh, come on, Stephanie, really. Tell me that you haven't . . . *felt* strange things here."

"Wow, that's fanciful," she murmured. "Not at all like you. Or maybe completely like you, that's just it—I don't really know you at all anymore."

"You've always known me."

"Right," she murmured. "So well that in the middle of a highly intimate and even climactic moment, you called out another woman's name."

He waved a hand in the air. "Yes, so you said."

"And you don't believe me?"

"I'm not saying that you're lying. I just don't know why—I have never met anyone named Valeria."

"I don't think you were even really there," Stephanie said, searching his eyes.

"If it was such a cataclysmic moment, I had to have been there."

Physically, yes. Leading her to believe that he was the very air she breathed. In the sense that he could touch and tease and meld, and she could feel as if they were one . . .

Except, in a very strange way, part of him hadn't been with her!

"That's just it. Oh, never mind. There's something strange going on *inside* of you, Grant."

"There's something strange going on *here*," he insisted. He took her by the shoulders. "Stephanie, I swear I knew nothing about Reggie having a place here when I signed up as a volunteer on the dig. And you didn't know I was coming here when you accepted Reggie's offer. Don't you think it's strange to begin with?"

Oddly, before she answered, she thought how she would always be in love with his hands. They had such length, his fingers tapered. They were tanned, and his palms and fingertips were slightly rough because he'd dig into construction work on a set just as quickly as he'd step out on stage himself, when need be. They were incredible hands when they moved against flesh; they could caress like a bare breeze, and hold someone with enough power and strength so that it seemed that nothing in the world could interfere . . .

Maybe something not really of this world?

It was just the words he was saying. Creating fantasy in her own heart.

"Grant, there are such things as wild coincidences that do happen," she said. But his eyes were filled with tension, and she felt it in his fingertips as well. He really wasn't trying to sleep with her, she thought dryly, and wondered if she should feel insulted.

Especially after her dreams . . .

"Come in. Walk around if you want. There's nothing unusual in the cottage, I assure you. It's a pretty place, brand new, delightfully designed."

She walked in and turned back. "Come in."

He did so. He wandered around the downstairs, then glanced at her, arching a brow as he looked at the steps up to her bedroom area. "May I?"

"Go ahead."

She waited on the ground floor. A few minutes later he came back down. "The balcony is glorious, the breeze is great. I locked the windows out to the balcony."

"I thought that I locked them."

"Maybe the maid opened them," Grant said.

"Probably. I mean, normally, a person would love to sleep with the ocean breeze and the stars shining just beyond," Stephanie said dryly.

"Keep them locked."

"I told you—I do lock them," she said. She shook her head. "Grant—"

"Stephanie, believe me, there's something going on."

She felt a trickling of unease, as if she knew that he was right, but also knew that she was refusing to accept it.

"Grant, maybe that poor girl was kidnapped or killed. But if so . . . surely the police will find the man who did it."

"Just swear to me that you will keep yourself locked in at night, all right?" he asked her. "I'm going to leave—I'm not doing this to force you into anything. But if you need me . . . well, I showed you where my cottage is, right? And there's a phone, and my cell works here—it's a Chicago number, but it works here."

"Mine is European, too," she murmured. "Grant, if I'm afraid in any way, I'll call you, I swear."

"Right," he murmured. He didn't sound satisfied.

"Grant, what more can I really say right now?" she asked, a little desperately. It would be so easy to let him stay. To let all her fantastically sexual dreams find release in the real thing. Except that she had been in love with him. She'd wanted a life, forever and ever, children, a house . . .

But there was something seriously, seriously wrong.

Even if she was still in love with him.

And even if she suddenly wanted, more than anything, for him to just grab her, run with her up to the bedroom, and make all the dreams real . . .

No.

"I'm just afraid that . . ."

"That what?" She swallowed hard and forced herself to speak normally.

"I'm afraid you may not have time to be afraid," he said softly.

"Grant, that's it. Good night. Thank you for the concern, and good night."

He nodded.

Tall, broad-shouldered, built like steel, he turned and left her, just as she had asked.

And she wondered if she wasn't the biggest fool in the entire world.

* * *

"Yes, oh, God, yes!"

Lena was ever so slightly embarrassed, and yet in the flush of such physical excitement that she barely gave her words a passing thought. *So what if they'd been used in every schlocky porn film since the beginning of moviemaking!*

"Lord, yes, please!"

Good heavens, the man was an animal!

She'd never been so titillated, and in her life, she'd never been tempted before to fall so quickly into the arms of a near-stranger. And so boldly. No real talk, no pretense of a sudden, dying devotion or affection, just *sex*.

A look at one another, a knowing . . . clothing strewn in a matter of seconds. Just an initial kiss as the whole getting-to-know-you-foreplay thing, and then sex—raw, base, first on the table, then on the floor. He was rough, but it didn't matter, because the slide of his teeth and force of his mouth against her were the most erotic things she'd felt in all her life. She'd knelt, she'd stood, she'd parted her legs in a way she'd never even imagined before. He played at her thighs, between them, coerced her into curling her fingers around him, returning every wet intimacy . . .

And then . . .

He was like a jackrabbit. Like the wind.

It might not be the romantic love affair she had thought she wanted, but . . .

"Yes, yes, do it, do it."

He did.

She thought she was going to die. She was wet as a leaky faucet. Drenched inside and out, shaking, flying, climbing . . . climaxing like a madwoman.

And he just laughed.

"There's more, baby, so much more!" he whispered.

No. There couldn't be. She couldn't take it. She felt drained and exhausted, sucked dry. A weary smile played at her lips.

"Wow."

He was going to stay with her, she thought. If just for a while.

Yet suddenly, abruptly, he jumped up. As if he had heard something, or someone.

Almost as if . . . someone was coming. Well, they had done so before. But that had just been when she'd been waiting, and, well, of course he'd known—and waited himself. So clever.

Everyone would know that she was fine. For the life of her, she wouldn't open the door now.

"What's the matter?" she whispered. She couldn't really speak.

He didn't reply. She realized vaguely that he wasn't even there anymore, but it didn't matter. She couldn't move. Couldn't have done it again. She closed her eyes, feeling the overpowering desire to sleep, to rest . . .

No, no . . . she couldn't move now.

But all she wanted in the whole wide world was for him to come again.

Her eyes . . .

She couldn't keep them open.

They closed. And she felt consciousness . . . fading away.

Night progressed.

Grant despaired of sleeping. Really sleeping. He'd dozed off several times, only to awaken as if he'd heard a cannon fired, nearly jumping out of bed. And there would be nothing. No reason for him to have awakened at all.

He walked out to the balcony area of his cottage, but the way it was positioned, he could see the ocean, the waves, the beach, the horizon, no more. The view was absurdly peaceful, the sound of the waves, lulling.

Restlessly, he returned to his bedroom, dressed, and exited his cottage via the front door. All the little bungalows seemed still and quiet. Naturally. It was four a.m. Even the barhoppers would be tucked in, sleeping now.

He started out along the beach, recalling the smell of death that had assailed him when he'd taken the same walk with Clay Barton. Arturo had seen to it that the carcass of the dead mammal had been taken away.

There was no smell of death tonight.

He paused on the beach, feeling the breeze wrap around him, watching in the pale light as foam flecked against the sand. How very, very normal. Lovely. From where he stood, he stared back at the scattered assembly of beach houses, cottages, or bungalows. Night-lights glowed on the little paths surrounding them. At most front doors, small lanterns burned as well.

There was nothing . . .

There . . . two down from his own. That was where Giovanni had told him Clay Barton was staying. It was dark, except for a pale illumination that spread from the balcony area. A night-light? Or was the very strange Mr. Barton up and restless as well?

Curious man. He seemed intent on sticking with Stephanie as well, and yet . . .

As cool, attractive, and suave as the man might be, it didn't seem that he was actually coming on to any of the women. Even as he followed Stephanie—watched her ceaselessly— he didn't make any moves that weren't respectable.

Maybe he was gay.

Uh-uh. That was something he was certain he would know. No—in fact, there was something about the guy that seemed to tick off every alpha-male fiber of Grant's being, and he knew that he edged closer to Stephanie every time the guy was around, and that he gritted his teeth during some of their playful scenes together, aware that it was acting. It had best be acting. *Was* acting.

He could have sworn that the man was no actor. Why? He was fine on stage, had a damned good memory for lines, moved easily enough . . .

There was no reason to suspect him.

Yes, there was. Instinct.

Instinct that said what?

He didn't know.

Grant glanced at his watch. Four-forty-five. At least it was getting closer to morning. This was strange as hell, too—he didn't mind being away at the first light. He'd be damned if he'd leave the area of the resort after dark—or before the light.

As he stood there, then, looking back at the field of cottages, he froze suddenly. There seemed to be an odd, sweeping shadow circling over them. There couldn't be. Not beneath the partial moon, with the few stars scattering the night sky. Not with the little lights that shone out from here and there.

But there was. A shadow like . . .

Wings. Immense wings.

Fear clutched his throat. Tension soared through him. He blinked.

The shadows was there . . . high. And then it seemed to settle.

He forced movement into his body, terror gripping him that the shadow had fallen around Stephanie's place. Sand flew up around his feet as he ran, heedless then of sight or sound or anything, he was so anxious to get to Stephanie's.

He arrived by the back and flew up the stairs to the balcony, hopping the little guardrail.

Racing to the glass doors with his hand raised, he noted that her curtain was fully closed. She had gone to bed with a fair amount of light shedding around from the bathroom, and from the hallway and staircase.

He could see her.

She was sleeping. Curled up, with her dark hair spilled

over the pillow, hands prayer-fashion, beautiful face toward the glass. She was sleeping peacefully.

He stood there, hand raised, not moving—like an asshole.

Yet it seemed that the strange fear that had gripped his throat had wended its way into his heart and soul. He knew again that no matter what it was that was going on . . .

He loved her. Deeply, passionately. And just watching her, he felt a heat rise in his body, muscles constrict, body contort . . .

He swore at himself, turned, wondered if he should just go and walk into the frigging ocean water and douse himself.

But back on the beach, he paused, looking around again.

There had been a shadow.

And it had oddly settled somewhere.

Where?

Chapter 6

Their costume designer was a small woman with a delightful, big smile. Stephanie didn't understand how the woman had managed to make so many things so right, but she had. She'd been worried since the woman had arrived early, and Lena had arrived late. But she knew a few words of English, and Stephanie's growing knowledge of Italian had done well enough as Drew, Doug, and Suzette went through their fittings. Her own was off, but then, the costume had originally been planned for Gema. And there were a few problems with Clay Barton's—the trousers were too short, and the arms weren't long enough.

Leeza D'Onofrio, the costumer, tsked at herself, looked at her notes, and looked at Clay, and shook her head. Stephanie didn't need to be a language expert to know that Leeza was baffled, but still, apparently, she had expected some problems.

She was startled when Clay went into a conversation with the woman—in Italian. Leeza smiled, and remeasured, and apparently seemed charmed, and ready to redo the costume in plenty of time.

"She wants you to know that she'll be back with both costumes by tomorrow afternoon—she's very happy to be working with us, and can do almost anything we want," Clay told Stephanie.

"Great," she murmured, staring at him. "I didn't know you spoke Italian. And please don't tell me that you took a Berlitz program two weeks before coming here."

He shook his head. "Just something I picked up during my lifetime," he told her.

"But it doesn't even sound as if you have an accent," Stephanie told him.

"I like languages," he said.

"You speak others?"

"A few."

"Like?"

"French."

"Ah. And?"

"I'm pretty good with Spanish."

"Well, great," Stephanie murmured. It *was* great. She wondered why the information made her feel uneasy. Especially when it was just then that Lena walked in, looking pale and ill.

"I'm so sorry!" Lena told Stephanie. "I just couldn't wake up this morning. I was awake, but then fell back to sleep. I must have eaten something . . . except that I'm not sick to my stomach."

Stephanie, concerned, felt Lena's forehead. She wasn't hot. In fact, she seemed to be too cold.

"Maybe you should take the afternoon off," Stephanie advised her.

"There's more to run through," Lena said ruefully.

"Yes, but . . . I think we've already proven that we're a great ensemble. It's going to be hard if you can't stand up on Friday night. Have your fitting, then take your outline scripts and go back to bed. You can study there. Maybe you're getting a flu."

"I guess it must be something like that," Lena said. "I am so sorry!"

"You don't need to apologize—just get well," Stephanie told her.

It was very strange. If Lena had been with the group partying the night before, Stephanie might have understood it better.

She felt good herself that morning. But she'd taken a sleeping aid the night before and been mercifully undisturbed by dreams.

Clay came up as the two women talked. He frowned, looking at Lena with real concern. He, too, touched her forehead. He didn't appeared to be relieved in the least that she didn't have a fever.

"Let me walk you back to your place," he told her.

She let out a little sigh. "Actually, that would be great. I feel so weak!"

The two of them left, Clay saying they should go through the restaurant and get her something to eat so she could bolster her strength. Lena demurred, but then agreed.

Disturbed, and not at all sure why, Stephanie called to Doug.

"Yeah?"

"Do me a favor. Clay is walking Lena back to her room, but will you go, too? She really doesn't seem to be well at all. Just make sure that everything is all right."

"Whatever you say," Doug said. "Hey, now there's a change for you. Suzette is the one who should be down this morning."

"Oh? We were at the local café, an old place that opened . . . well, centuries ago, I guess. And we had a lot of local wine. But here we are—Drew, Suzette, and myself—hale and hearty."

"I thought Clay Barton was joining you as well," Stephanie said.

Doug lifted his shoulders and let them fall. "Yeah, we thought he was coming, too. He never showed up. Anyway, I'll go after them, just make sure they're both all right."

"Thanks."

Stephanie watched him go. She glanced at her watch. It was barely eleven; Grant wouldn't be there until one. She'd been fitted; Lena's costume had been left behind, Clay's was already set for alterations as well. They'd worked hard for long hours yesterday, and the rehearsals would go much smoother once Grant showed up.

"Hey, boss lady!" Drew called to her. "I think our costumer is leaving. So what's up next?"

"The beach," Stephanie said.

"What?" Suzette demanded, coming toward her.

"The beach. We'll break today. I don't think any of us made it in to breakfast. It's eleven now—we'll meet here again at one. Until then . . . get some lunch, get some sun, or run around the local shops."

"Really?" Suzette said.

Drew nudged her with an elbow. "Hey, yeah, really! I'm hitting the streets. You can come with me if you want. We can wait for Drew and Clay. Two hours of daylight. We need to move fast. Then we can grab food that we can carry—"

"You know, there actually is no McDonald's here," Suzette said.

"Okay, okay, we sit down, we eat, we run. We dash back to our places, jump into suits, and lie on the sand. Stephanie, are you with us?"

She shook her head. "I'm grabbing bread, cheese, meat, a few bottles of water, and heading straight for the sand."

"Bread and wine and thee. Maybe we should do the same?" he suggested to Suzette.

"I don't care what we do, but make up your mind. Our minutes are a-wasting!" Suzette said, grinning at Stephanie.

Stephanie started toward the rear of the café.

"Hey, your bungalow is that way!" Drew told her.

"I'm just going to check with Arturo, see if he can't get the local doctor to look in on Lena. Then I'll be out there, okay?"

"Sound decision," Drew said gravely. "We'll just grab Doug and Clay, and be with you in the wink of an eye!"

What hadn't seemed at all painstaking or tedious to Grant before now seemed like utmost misery.

He didn't want to give up his work on the dig because of a far-fetched belief that something strange was going on. Something he didn't understand, couldn't figure out, and might be a total fabrication of his imagination. While he dusted bones—with a smaller brush than ever before, now that the forensic anthropologists had arrived—he tried to decide just what it was that disturbed him so deeply. He tried to tell himself that he was in a mid-life crisis, but if so, it was a sad thing, since he was only thirty-three. But it wasn't, and he knew it, and what bothered him more than anything was that he was pretty sure his own bizarre behavior had begun right about the time that the site here had originally been discovered.

All right—maybe, somewhere, he had read about all the activity in the region in the centuries in which the Crusades had taken place. Maybe he'd even heard the legends about the place, and so, in his subconscious, with his love of the ancient, he had come up with some correlation that was so deeply imbedded in his mind that he couldn't tell reality from fantasy.

Man, that was a load of bull!

He paused in his work. He was alone at his particular site, but right around the bend of the cliff, he could hear Carlo Ponti droning on along with some of the new people who had arrived; they were disinterring one of the skeletons, and the work there was being performed by the experts, and only the experts.

Today, he was working on his hands and knees on the very fine task of preparing the next fellow to be lifted and taken to the museum in Naples. This fellow had patches of naturally mummified skin remaining, and many fragments of clothing. Though he certainly hadn't been dressed in the full armor of a knight, he'd owned some kind of metal-and-wood shield, and though in pieces, there were lots of fragments to be delicately worked around. Yet, as he knelt on the ground, taking extreme care as he had been taught, his eyes wandered, and he frowned.

Just beneath the yellow stretch of plastic cord that designated the work area, there appeared to be a mound of dirt. Grant didn't remember the earth rising in that strange fashion before.

He sat back and stared at it.

A cold sensation swept his neck.

He dropped his work brush and came to his feet. Striding over to the area, he knelt down again.

The cold continued.

He began to dig, with his hands alone.

There was something there.

There was *someone there.*

Dirt, foliage, and tiny pebbles flew.

He stopped, his breath caught in his throat. The dirt filled his lungs, and he started to cough. He had come upon another body.

Only, this one wasn't centuries old.

The scent of death struck him, and he choked again, then fought down a swift rise of nausea.

Indeed, it was the smell of death.

And he'd not discovered a beached dolphin.

He sank back on his legs, exhausted, overwhelmed by a sense of sadness and despair. Then, after a moment, he managed to rise.

Sweaty, covered in dirt, he walked around to where Carlo Ponti worked.

"You found something else!" Carlo exclaimed.

"I'm afraid so."

"Afraid?"

"Yes, afraid. I think I've found the missing girl. Maria Britto."

Arturo assured Stephanie that he would get a doctor for Lena. "There is a local man, of course. Doctor Antinella. I will make sure that he sees Lena this afternoon. How odd, though! None of our staff or guests has shown the least sign of a flu."

"Well, she definitely has something," Stephanie assured him. "Anyway, I'm heading to the sand for a while."

"The sand?"

"The beach. We're going to take a little break."

"Lovely, lovely!" Arturo applauded.

"Think we could take some bread and cheese out there, something like that?" Stephanie asked.

"But of course!" Arturo assured her happily. "I will have it sent."

Stephanie thanked him and returned to her own cottage.

This morning, it looked bright and beautiful. It was amazing what one good night's sleep could do. Usually, she hated taking sleep aids of any kind. They usually left her tired in the morning, or groggy. Apparently, she had simply needed the deep sleep, because she didn't feel groggy at all. Just pleased that the world seemed so . . . normal.

She changed into a bathing suit, grabbed her towel, lotion, and a book. When she went out back, there were a few sunbathers stretched out on towels or resort lawn chairs, and a woman with two young children was watching them as they frolicked in the surf.

She stretched out her own towel, but the water was inviting. She wondered if it would be warm, and decided to find out. Hurrying to the shore, she felt the water trickle over her feet and was delighted.

She plunged in, swimming out, thinking that the salt water was absolutely wonderful. It felt especially delicious, since even at the best of times, the lake water in Illinois was chilly. She floated for several minutes, swam again, enjoying the feel of using her muscles, then headed back into shore.

She paused, a bit out, and saw that the others had arrived. Suzette was fetching in a risqué bikini, Doug and Drew were in shorts, and Clay was there, but he was wearing jeans and a short-sleeved, tailored shirt. He didn't look like he was going swimming.

She swam to the shallow, and stood in water that was about two feet deep and started walking out.

She had just stepped from the water when she heard screaming. Turning quickly to the sound, she was horrified to see one of the two chubby-cheeked children who had been playing in the shallows was too far out, and struggling in stronger waves. She started to run to the water, plunged in, and headed out.

It had seemed a calm day with easy waves, but the water could always be deceptive. The child was being quickly washed southward and away from shore. The woman who had been with him was still screaming.

Stephanie swam as hard and as fast as she could. Though it couldn't have been long, it seemed like forever. Finally, her fingers contacted a little leg. She caught the child across the chest in a lifesaving hold and made for the shore.

As she neared it, hands reached out. Doug had come into the shallows and was reaching for the child. Though he was small, Stephanie quickly gave up her little burden. She was panting.

She rested a moment, then came somewhat awkwardly to her feet and walked against the water to reach the sand.

The boy was down on a towel. Doug had come to her assistance, but it was Clay manipulating the boy to clear his lungs and throat, and giving him mouth-to-mouth. Just as she reached his side, the little boy rocketed out a geyser of water and began to cough and sputter. The woman stepped in then, sweeping him up, patting him on the back. She was crying and laughing at the same time, speaking in rapid Italian. She kept trying to hug and kiss Clay and Doug while holding the child. Stephanie watched, feeling a little underappreciated, but yet, delighted that the little one seemed fine, and had suffered no serious consequences. The little boy started to cry, clinging to his mother. Doug kept saying in English that everything was fine, and that he'd done nothing, and Clay was saying something to her in Italian.

She saw Stephanie then and rushed over to her, hugging, smashing the child between them, and thanking her effusively again. Stephanie felt ashamed.

The noise had alerted Arturo. He came out with extra towels, and, after a great deal of excitement, he, the woman, and both children left the beach area.

"Well, *there's* some excitement for you!" Suzette said, standing near their towels. "Maybe that means we're just supposed to work through the days, no matter what."

"Ah—or it meant that we were supposed to be right where we were! Hey, good for you, Steph! You are the woman of the moment."

She shrugged. "I was closest."

"And good thing you were. Clay can't swim."

Amused, Stephanie looked at him with surprise. "You—can't swim?"

"I loathe the water," he admitted.

"Imagine—Mr. Macho, Muscles, and facial-features-to-grace-a-Grecian-coin, can't swim!" Drew said, finding it somewhat amusing—and, apparently, pleasing.

She laughed as well, looking at Clay. "Everyone has different talents. But, hey, good place to be working then—right on the beach!"

"I don't mind looking at the water," Clay said. "Well, congratulations—you did do great."

"Doug helped, and hey, you did the CPR."

"Well, you know, what the heck, we are an ensemble," Clay said with a shrug.

"Arturo brought us out a special sparkling wine. I accepted it graciously, but was going to save it for later, since we have the afternoon ahead of us," Suzette said. "The food came out before your glorious rescue—don't go getting the idea that Arturo paused to extol the wine in the middle of a trauma! Anyway, after that, I say we pop the cork on the stuff!"

"Sure," Stephanie agreed. "How loaded can we all get on one bottle? We can have a pot of coffee brought in to our rehearsals." She noticed that Clay had a wet towel on his arm. "Hey!" she told him. "Let me take that—you're dressed, and you'll wind up soaked."

"It's all right. I'm already soaked," he said.

She reached for the towel impatiently. "I'll take it!"

Apparently, he hadn't expected her to grab at the towel. She took it easily.

Her eyes widened.

His arm looked horrible. As if he had just been badly burned. She gasped aloud. "Your arm! What on earth—"

"What? I didn't see anything wrong with him," Suzette said.

"Look! You've got blisters—" Stephanie said.

"It's nothing!" Clay snapped out the words, then gritted his teeth. "Honestly . . . a reaction to the sun and salt. It's all right. It will be fine tomorrow."

"You need to see a doctor!" Stephanie protested.

"I'm telling you, it's just a reaction. Honestly, please don't worry. Listen, I'm not hanging around to picnic anyway. Don't worry about me. I'll put some lotion on it—and I'll change to a long-sleeved shirt. It will be fine, really. Hey, good picnic, guys. I'll see you at one!"

With a wave, he left them, long strides taking him quickly away, toward his bungalow.

"Wow, poor guy!" Drew said.

"Yeah, but. . . ." Doug began

"But what?" Stephanie demanded.

Doug grinned. "I don't know. He's too perfect. So there's his flaw. Get him baked in the sun, and he looks like salsa! I gotta kind of enjoy that."

Drew sighed. "Irish with freckles—I look like that when I'm not careful, so don't go making fun of skin that comes out like mincemeat, huh?"

"Sorry!" Doug said. But he smiled again. "I, on the other hand," he said, making his voice very deep, "bronze nicely, and come out of the sun looking just like an Adonis!"

They all laughed, but Stephanie did so uneasily.

Clay Barton didn't just look like he'd suffered sunburn, or even a reaction like a rash. He looked as if he'd charbroiled—and just on the arm.

The arm where he'd had saltwater.

The police came.

They took picture after picture.

Everyone spoke excitedly—some of the men came close to shedding tears. Maria had been a beautiful young girl.

No more.

"The animals must have gotten to her," Carlo said, shaking his head sadly.

Grant thought that was a very curious conjecture.

Had the animals chewed her up—and then reburied her?

She'd been ripped to shreds—yes, that much was obvious. But still, how was it that she had been buried in a mound of dirt?

He was certain that the police had to be asking the same questions.

A number of cars had come, all of them carrying different policemen from different local areas. Word would be put out across all of Calabria, Sicily, and the rest of Italy, and even over to Greece that the police should be on the lookout for a psychotic killer. There had been something of a fierce argument between the lawmen, and Carlo told Grant it was because certain of the officers wanted the body taken as far away as Naples for an autopsy, but the local authorities were adamantly against the idea—her mother was going to be hysterical enough. She was traditional and Catholic, and the body needed to remain in the area.

Grant was sure that the higher state authorities would prevail.

They didn't. Maria's body would remain here.

At first glance, the local coroner—who was an M.D. and a respected medical man—could only tell them that he would assume from the temperature of the body and other signs, it appeared that she had been dead before her mother had even reported her missing or even before she would have been at the job where her mother had certainly thought she had been all day.

And after that . . . ?

And as to the condition of the body . . . ?

There had been so many cars arriving that Grant hadn't

even noticed the last arrival. He was sitting on a log with a bottle of water, just feeling the misery of their find, when the person he least expected—and least wanted to see—found a place beside him on the log.

"What the hell are you doing out here?" he asked Clay Barton.

"We had a break. I figured if I drove out, and traffic was good, I'd have about fifteen minutes to take a look at the place before driving back," Clay replied. He gazed toward where they were just taking the girl's remains from the earth. "So they found her."

"Chewed to smithereens," Grant said dully.

"Did you see the body?" Clay asked him tensely.

"See it? I fucking found it."

"How . . . did she die?"

"Are you kidding? I don't think that an entire forensic team could tell you that. She's chewed . . . in pieces. I don't know what the hell kind of an animal got hold of her—a wild dog, they're thinking—but we're talking . . . limbs barely still attached."

"Did you see . . . her neck. Her throat?" Clay persisted.

Grant turned to stare at him. "Yes, as a matter of fact, I did. It was crusted with dried blood—like the rest of her. *Chewed. Gnawed.* What the hell? Are you into practicing some strange form of really demented necrophilia?"

The man was angered by the question, strange eyes flashing a warning sign. Fine. Bring it on. Grant was dying to throw a punch at his jaw. More than that. He was dying to tear into him, beat him to a pulp.

He took a breath, trying to control his temper. Amazingly, he realized that the other man was trying to do the same thing.

"I've heard of other such deaths," Clay said.

"Maybe you should talk to the police. The place is crawling with them. Carlo can be your interpreter."

Clay Barton cast him another glance, which seemed to carry contempt. "No need," he said simply.

To Grant's amazement, the other man walked over to the area where they were bagging the dead girl. He began to speak in Italian, rapidly, and it seemed that his accent was perfect. For some reason, the man's easy use of the language rubbed savagely against the raw edges of his temper.

He was further astounded when the cops and forensics people replied to him, stepped back and away, and allowed him to view the body.

They gave him time, offered him a pair of gloves. It seemed the most natural thing in the world that a stranger— an actor, for God's sake—had asked to see the corpse. And inspect it.

Then Maria Britto was zipped up, and there was shouting, and she was taken to a morgue car, and at last it began to drive away.

Clay walked back to him. "Are you going to the rehearsal?"

"Oh, you bet," Grant assured him

Grant shook off the lethargy that had gripped him and headed for his own rental car. There was no way in hell he wasn't going to be there—ahead of Clay—for the rehearsal.

Word reached Stephanie regarding the horrible discovery of Maria Britto as soon as she entered the club through the backstage doors.

Drew was there, and he looked ashen. "They found the girl," he told her.

"The young Italian girl?"

"Maria Britto."

She knew, of course, from the way that he looked that they hadn't found the girl alive.

"Where?"

"At the dig."

"She didn't fall . . . or have an accident?"

"I don't think they know the actual cause of death, but no, it wasn't accidental. You don't die accidentally, and then bury yourself."

"Who found her?"

"Grant," Drew said. "They say he's shaken, but . . . I guess he should be here any minute."

"How do you know all this?" Stephanie asked suspiciously.

The cop, Merc, called Arturo, and I just saw Arturo."

"Ah."

"Depressing, huh?" Drew said.

"Scary!" Suzette announced, coming in through the back, and evidently hearing their words, or simply certain of what they had to be talking about.

"Horrible!" Doug said, coming in behind Suzette.

"Yeah, kind of makes the concept of rehearsing a comedy show rather rude," Stephanie murmured.

"Ah, Steph . . . it's a small town, but none of us ever met this girl," Drew reminded her. "And we're under contract. And I imagine it's going to be bad enough for the place, once word of the girl's death gets out. They need tourists. We're supposed to help draw in American money."

"Right," Stephanie murmured. "Except that I just went by to see Lena, and she looks a little better, but the doctor went to see her and he suggested she seriously needed some bed rest, that her pulse was barely beating."

"Man, that's bizarre!" Drew said, shaking his head. "She was fine last night."

"She might have gotten a strange insect bite, or something like that?" Suzette asked.

"According to the doctor," Stephanie said, "she needs red meat, and lots of rest."

"We're in some serious trouble, then," Suzette said. "We're supposed to put on a show this Friday night."

"We could cancel," Drew said gloomily.

Stephanie was quiet for a minute. "We'll ask Arturo. I have a number for Reggie, too . . . but this is his home. I think that this has to be Arturo's call."

As she spoke, the rear door to the café area of the club opened and Grant came in. He looked extremely grim.

"Hey!" Drew said to him quietly. "You okay, man?"

"Yeah," Grant said. "It's a sad business, though. Really horrible."

"So . . . how . . ." Drew began awkwardly.

"Who do they . . . suspect?" Suzette asked.

Grant shook his head, walking straight for the coffeepot. He was streaked with mud and looked like hell, hair a mess, shirt ripped. "I don't think they have a suspect. I'm sure they'll talk to the boyfriend again, but . . . I don't think he's much of a suspect. Actually, according to Carlo, there hasn't been anything like this here . . . ever. This area never even got caught up in any of the Mafia wars, so . . . the last history of horrible violence here goes back centuries."

Clay came in the same way that Grant had.

Drew watched him come in, studying him curiously for a minute.

"You went out to the dig?" he asked.

"Yes. It wasn't what I was expecting," Clay said.

Grant stiffened, but held his silence. "Stephanie, why don't you get started. I'm going to go and take a shower."

"We were just wondering if we should be rehearsing," she murmured.

He looked her in the eye. "Do you know how many murders there are in Chicago in a year?" he asked her.

"A lot, but . . . that's Chicago. This place is so small!"

"Whether the show goes on Friday night or not, we'll wait

and see. But as far as the rehearsal goes . . . yeah. We should do it." He had drained the coffee in a swallow. He set the cup down by the pot. "I'll be right back." He started out through the back, but then paused. "Where's Lena?"

"Sick," Stephanie told him.

"Sick?" Grant said suspiciously

"Really sick. The doctor said she had to have bed rest."

"Down another cast member?" Grant said, and seemed deeply disturbed.

"Yeah, and Steph's already taking Gema's part, so . . . she can't do both. Well, being Steph, she probably can, but it really all works around a cast of six." Drew grimaced. "If one of us guys were down, you could fill in, Grant, and we could all be doing props, lighting, and stage management. But . . . what do we do about Lena?"

"She's just ill for a few days—she doesn't need to be replaced," Stephanie said sharply.

"Actually . . . I may have a solution for you," Clay said.

They all turned and stared at him.

"A friend of mine is in town. She's a writer, so she's doing kind of a lazy trip through Italy, and came here to wish me a 'break a leg' for opening night. She's done some theater work, and she isn't looking to steal anyone's job—she has her own. I'm sure she'd be willing to step in until we see how Lena's doing."

"You just happen to have a friend, huh?" Grant said softly.

"What's that supposed to mean?" Stephanie demanded.

Grant looked away and shrugged, but he was still tense as piano wire. Stephanie ignored him and mulled the matter.

Lena had looked really sick. And she had apologized over and over again. The doctor had hoped some good meals and vitamins might make a change, but he had also suggested she might wind up having to go to the hospital for a blood transfusion.

"Clay, call your friend. If she really doesn't mind a job that could end any second, we'd be grateful if she wants to fill in. That is . . . well, we have created a bit of an ensemble. She'd kind of have to audition."

"She wouldn't mind, and she'll be fine. Honestly. Wait until you see her."

"Is that all right with you, Grant?" Stephanie demanded, eyeing him sharply.

He lifted his shoulders again. "Hey, babe, it's your show."

He turned and walked out.

When Grant was gone, Stephanie turned to Clay. "I'm sorry, Clay. He was rather rude."

"He was the one who found the body," Clay said. "He has a right to be off right now."

"He found the body?"

"Yep. It was right next to the ancient remains he had been excavating," Clay said.

"Wow, no wonder he seems in bad shape," Suzette murmured. "Oh, God!" she exclaimed, and shivered suddenly.

"What?" Stephanie demanded.

"Well . . . they found Maria Britto," Suzette murmured.

"Yes?" Stephanie said.

"Dead," Suzette whispered.

"Yes, it's terrible, and of course, it does mean that . . . well, since she didn't bury herself, it does mean that there is a killer out there. We know it. We know to be careful. We're going to be all right, Suzette," Stephanie said, determined to be reassuring.

"That's not it," Suzette murmured, staring at her.

"Then *what*?" Stephanie demanded.

"I know what she's getting at," Clay said, striding closer

to them, hands on his hips. His eyes lit on Stephanie, their strange red-gold color bright.

"She's afraid that we just might find Gema as well, that she didn't run off to Rome, that . . . that she's dead and buried somewhere, just the same."

Chapter 7

Grant showered for a long time, letting the hot water work into his muscles. He couldn't seem to leave the deep, cleansing effect of the water, but once he was out, he dressed quickly, anxious to see Lena Miro himself, then get back to the rehearsal.

As he approached her cottage, he wondered if he should walk on by, and leave her to rest. Knocking on the door would get her out of bed, and not help her any. But just as he approached, he saw the young Italian houseboy, Giovanni, leaving with a tray.

"*Buongiorno*, Signor Peterson!" the man said cheerfully.

"*Buongiorno*, Giovanni," Grant returned. "Is Miss Miro sleeping?"

"No, no. Arturo insisted that I bring her lots of food, and red wine." He shrugged. "We believe here that red wine can cure anything."

Grant smiled. "How is she doing?"

"Better, I think. A few days of rest, and . . . she'll be fine!" he said cheerfully. "The door is open now, just go on in. When you leave, just press the little button behind you, and she will be locked in again. She is upstairs, resting in bed. Just call out so you don't scare her, eh?"

"Thanks. *Grazie*."

Grant entered. The stairs to Lena's loft area were right at the door. "Lena, are you awake?" he called.

"Yes! Grant? Come up, please!"

"On my way," he said, and hurried up the stairs.

Lena was watching the BBC on the one English language station that they received.

She was very pale, her color seeming all the more ashen because she was typically so beautifully tan or olive-toned by nature. Her eyes, however, were very bright, and she seemed pleased and somewhat revitalized to see Grant.

"Hey, kid," he said, drawing the chair from the dressing table over to her bed. "How are you doing?"

"Not so bad—as long as I stay down," she said, smiling wanly. "I'm just so sorry!"

"When you're sick, you can't be sorry," Grant said.

"Yeah, but . . . there's a show in two nights."

"Clay says he has some friend in the area who can fill in for you."

"Great. I'll be out of a job."

Grant shook his head. "No, no, nothing like that. The girl is a writer, but with some theater experience, and she'll just fill in while you're feeling so badly. But hey, you know, seriously, I know Stephanie pretty well. She'd never take your job for something like this, and if you're not feeling better in a day or two . . . I think you need to head to a spot with specialists and maybe a hospital."

"Oh, no—I don't want to leave here," Lena protested.

She sat up. She was wearing a nightgown that didn't seem to have too much substance to it. The gown wasn't actually see-through, but it was made of a light pink silk that clung to her form. She was a well-built woman, with large, round breasts; their size seemed apparent in the gown, her nipples clearly etched beneath it.

An odd choice for lying in a bed, being ill, he thought.

"Lena, if you're sick . . ."

"I'm going to get better. In fact," she offered what he first thought was simply a friendly smile, "with you in the room, I feel better already. Stronger."

She reached out and touched his cheek. There was a definite suggestion to the stroke of her fingers against his flesh.

He caught her hand, squeezing it warmly as a friend. "Lena, everyone wants you here—you're sweet, charming, and talented, but if a specialist can get to the bottom of this . . ."

"Oh, I just slept badly, that's all," she told him, eyes very wide. "This is where I can get better. I've never known anything like being in a place like this before." She laughed. There was a throaty sound to it. "And I'm Italian! The north is beautiful. Milan is a happening place. Florence is . . . well, it's art and leather. Venice is romantic. But there's nothing like this. I never want to leave. Ever."

"Wow, you do like it here," Grant murmured.

She edged closer to him, and as she did so, one shoulder of the gown slipped, exposing the roundness of her breast.

"Like it? I love it!" She gripped his hand, drawing it to her chest. She stared at him with a curious, seductive smile. "Feel my heart, Grant. It's beating for this place."

He had little choice, without ripping his hand away.

"A place doesn't mean that much, Lena, not when your health is involved."

"Oh, but it does. And you know . . . you smell divine."

"Good soap," he said lightly.

"You know, you really are something. So . . . masculine . . . you can tease about soap, but there's something else to you, you know, down deep. So sensual. You're kind of like a volcano, you know . . . I can just imagine you . . . erupting."

"I'm glad you've got a good heartbeat going, Lena," he murmured, trying to extract his hand from her breasts.

She clung tightly, with a startling strength.

She moved her head even closer to his, whispering against his ear. "Feel more than the heartbeat. . . you're giving me strength."

She moved his fingers, splaying them over her breast, moving against him, the tip of her tongue suddenly playing against his ear.

And for a minute, he found himself caught in a strange form of mesmerization. Tempted to seize her, lose himself in her lips, bury himself in the expanse of her breasts. She had his hand, and he didn't stop her as she drew it along the length of her body, down between her legs.

He jerked back abruptly, shaking his head, taking her hand firmly and placing it back against her breasts. Her eyes met his again. She wasn't offended; she seemed pleased that she had taken him as far as she had. She wore a secret, cat-like smile.

"I'd never tell," she told him.

"Tell who?" he asked, exasperated with himself.

"Stephanie, of course—you're in love with her, right? Oh, yes, yes, you two are split up, but . . . *this* is different, and you know that it is. I want you . . . you want me. There's a rise in your pants, Mr. Peterson, I can tell. So . . . make love to me. Let me make love to you. You want it, I know that you do. I can make you feel . . . you can't imagine how I can make you feel. And I'll never tell. It will be our little secret."

She came upon a sudden, swift strength, her smile deepening, back straightened, arms powerful as she reached out and grabbed him, aiming right at his crotch, and getting a good grip on his penis despite the denim of his jeans.

It didn't seem like Lena talking at all. Not that he'd gotten to know her all that well, but this just wasn't her.

And yet her fingers, gripping, caressing, stroking . . .

He caught her hands, aware himself of what she had managed to do, but placing them back on the bed once again. Oddly enough, though, it was her eyes that seemed to have a more potent grip on him.

He rose, putting some distance between them.

"Lena, get better," he told her, managing to make his voice firm. "I've got to get over to the rehearsal."

She eased herself back down against the sheets, doing so with an undulation in her hips, stretching her fingers out over the fabric, still smiling at him. She ran her fingers over her breasts then, and down, pressing them against her belly, then cupping them at the base of her Venus mound. "I'm so much better with you just in the room," she purred.

"Feel better," he said.

She laughed. "I can make myself feel better," she said, "but I'd feel much, much better if you were to do it for me." With that, she slowly arched her hips, and pulled the nightgown up, and pressed her fingers against her own bare hips. She was going to start masturbating there and then.

He didn't say anything else to her but turned and left, aware that he was feeling the almost urgent desire to drop down at her side, and . . .

Do whatever she wanted. He gritted his teeth, hurrying out, and down the stairs. He heard the sound of her taunting, pleased laughter in his wake. Too husky, too deep . . .

"You'll come back for me, Grant. You know you want it!" she called in his wake.

He reached the landing. There was a sheen of sweat on his forehead, and he felt a pounding that remained, a vicious drumbeat in his penis.

Outside her cottage, a cool breeze struck his face, and he was deflated as instantly as he had been aroused.

Lena had to go. Someone needed to insist that she see a

specialist in a bigger city. There was something wrong here, really wrong.

Stephanie.

With hurried footsteps, he headed for the rehearsal.

Clay Barton's friend was a girl named Liz.

She was very attractive and friendly, happy to meet the rest of the group, and quick to assure Stephanie that she didn't really want a job, but that she was pleased to fill in for whatever time was needed. "The comedy is based on their characters and their relationships, right?"

"Yes. Actually, Lena's character is the one with an Italian background. She had a few Italian asides to the audience. We'll just rework it as we go along."

"Um . . . actually, I speak Italian," Liz told Stephanie.

Stephanie wondered why she wasn't surprised. "Great," she said.

"Tomorrow night is the opening, right?" Liz asked.

"Yes. There's a lot for you to go through . . . but we'll just work with the first outline. That's what we'll use Friday night, and you can look over the second, which we'll use Saturday night, and since the tour group is only here for those two days, we'll probably go black on Sunday as well as Monday, in respect for what happened here, in the community," Stephanie told her. She had been talking to Arturo, and since they were having the tour group come in, there seemed no way out of the two shows, but as the tour group was leaving Sunday afternoon, there seemed little reason to be open for a community that would be in mourning.

"That's fine," Liz said, giving Stephanie a soft and beautiful smile.

Drew, smitten by the newcomer, was seated on the stage near them. "We are an ensemble group, so don't you worry about anything!" he told her. "Anything you miss, we can pick up for you. There's so much ad-libbing in the show to begin with . . . you really can't have a problem. We won't let you have a problem."

"Thanks, that sounds great, then," Liz said.

"You know, it's really super that you were here," Suzette said. "What a coincidence."

"Amazing, really," Grant said, reappearing from the stage-end entry to the club.

"Grant, Liz, Liz, Grant," Stephanie said. He had a look of thunder on his face, and she expected this to go as badly as possible.

As he'd said, though—this was her show. She did have the right just to tell Grant to get the hell out.

Luckily, as well as being extremely attractive and sweet, Liz seemed to have a real enthusiasm for improv theater, or a tremendous sense of diplomacy.

"Grant Peterson, this is a pleasure. I had told Clay I was eager to meet you. I was at your club a few times when I was in the Chicago area. It was tremendous. I do travel books—I mentioned your place in one. I'll have to get you a copy," Liz told Grant. Stephanie studied the woman, curious. Either she was a far greater actress than they might have dared hope, or what she was telling Grant was true.

"Thank you," Grant said, taking her hand. "I'd love to see a copy.

"We haven't much time, not if we're sliding Liz into the show," he added.

"You're right." Stephanie slid off the stage. "Liz, just keep that little book with notes and the outline on you. I'm assuming you'll need it. Grant?"

"Places, everyone," Grant directed.

And so they began.

Liz wasn't Lena, but for a newcomer, a writer, filling in and working with the others for the first time, she was extraordinary. Of course, the outlines and concept of the show allowed for an awful lot of leeway.

Still . . .

It was amazing that Clay had known Liz, that Liz had been able to come, and that it was all working out so well.

The first run-through was, naturally, a little slow. Stephanie decided to stick to acting, and she let Grant call stops, and give Liz her bits of stage direction and suggestions as to what to do with her lines. Liz listened to him carefully and incorporated everything he said into her lines and actions. Strangely, for that first run-through, no one else made any comments, but then again, they weren't really needed. Grant was good on stage himself, but directing and management were his specialties.

When she stepped off stage, Stephanie was glad to see that Grant looked at her with a simple shrug. It was his way of admitting that Liz was going to work out just fine.

"Everyone has put in a lot of hard work, and that was excellent," he said, complimenting the cast. "Since we're having a show tomorrow night, I'd like to do it once more. That way, tomorrow, we do a really quick run-through . . . in costume—right, Steph?"

"Yes, the pieces we needed altered will be here by tonight," she told him.

He nodded. "Then we can spend the rest of the day working on the second outline for Saturday night, and if we can make it tight . . . everyone can take Saturday off until show time, and come into it fresh." He stared at Stephanie. "Does that work for you?"

"Absolutely," she agreed.

"Fine, then . . . places, everyone."

They completed a second run-through. It was going to be fine.

Early that evening when they finished, no one suggested drinks. It seemed that everyone was anxious just to return to their private space.

"We could meet for dinner—anyone who wanted to show up, that is—around eight-thirty?" Drew suggested.

"Sure," Stephanie murmured.

Then she gave them all a wave, and hurried out the back.

Dr. Barello, the local coroner, was still feeling somewhat irritated that there had been so much as a suggestion that he couldn't handle an autopsy on poor, sweet, young Maria. Leave it to big-city people to have such an aura of superiority!

But he had the law on his side. Maria was staying right here, and he would have Dr. Antinella assist him.

There wasn't a big hospital in the town, but their small facility was up-to-date. State funding had done a lot for them—along with the fact that they didn't have a terrible overhead, that no one in this region was out to cheat anyone, or to make a great deal of money off the misfortune of others.

Barello admitted to himself that there was not often a cause for an autopsy in the town—people usually died of old age. But the service had been performed before, and would be again. He had known Maria since she was a baby, and he would be tender with her, as would Antinella. She was one of their own.

Nor would the autopsy wait. He didn't care if he and Antinella worked all night.

At six, as arranged, he met Dr. Antinella in the basement morgue area of the small hospital. The police were there as well, since the police photographer was doubling as the morgue photographer. Pictures were taken of the remains with scraps of clothing still on the body. Then Dr. Barello ordered everyone out except for the photographer, and pictures were taken of the bloodied remains after the remaining clothing had been tenderly removed.

No assistant was called to bathe the body; Dr. Antinella, the girl's physician since her birth, performed that task as well, with equal respect and tenderness.

Scrubbed and masked, the doctors arranged the autopsy tools on a table by the gurney, then set about searching the flesh for signs of death as well as clues. It was while they were thus engaged that the door opened and closed.

Barello looked up angrily. "We're not to be disturbed!" he announced, and frowned. What the hell was the man doing there, in the autopsy room? What was he? Among the morbidly curious? Disgraceful.

"Get out!" he said, outraged. How on earth had the man gotten in to begin with? Though small, the hospital employed security guards, four of them, one man for each shift and an extra to allow for days off and holidays. Knowing what was going on, the young student on the night shift had been seated at the desk at the morgue door.

Antinella looked up as well, outraged. Maria did not deserve any disrespect now.

"There will be no cutting," the man said.

"What?" Barello said.

"No cutting. Sew her back together," the man said, walking on into the room.

"Yes, we'll carefully sew her back together," Antinella said, and looked at Barello. And Barello nodded.

An hour and a half later, he found that he was sitting at the desk himself, filling out the death certificate and the autopsy report.

He had no memory of the arrival of the man, not even a subconscious suspicion that anyone had interrupted his work with Antinella.

All that filled his mind was the thought that they had made Maria look beautiful again. Somehow, all the right things had been done. They had taken scrapings from her nails. There were vials filled with all the samples the police would expect; it had all been done correctly, professionally, and by the book. No big-city law or medical man could find fault with their procedures in the least.

Cause of death—an encounter with a wild animal, apparently a wolf, despite the fact there were few in the area, and there hadn't been a documented case of such an attack in . . . well, in eight or nine hundred years, at least.

The poor girl.

Barello knew Maria's fiancé, just as he knew Maria. The boy hadn't murdered her. She had been killed by an animal or animals.

But how was it that she had been discovered, buried deep in the earth, and at the excavation site?

Barello shook his head. That was a matter for the police. Perhaps one of the townsfolk had found her . . . and despite the agony of her mother knowing that the girl was missing, the person thought it would be better to hide the body, and let the mother believe that the girl had run away, seeking a life in a larger place, with greater promise.

Antinella came out of the morgue.

"She is . . . finished for the evening?"

"Yes, resting upon the gurney, sheeted . . . in the cold," he said sadly. "Tomorrow, we'll bring her to the funeral home . . . they will embalm her, and she will rest in peace."

"Yes. The poor girl. Imagine! Wolves attacking, now!"

"Yes, wolves attacking. The police will have to put out warnings for anyone traveling out to the cliffs."

"Poor, poor girl!" Barello said.

"Poor, poor girl," Antinella agreed.

He stood on the beach. From there, he had an excellent view of Lena Miro's door.

He waited, biding his time. He had always found it fasci-
nating to stare at the water. If only . . . well, there was no "if
only." And still, he enjoyed the view, and the feel of the air.

And then . . .

He saw the maid.

She saw him.

He moved along the path, not even hurrying. The woman
just stared at him, like a doe caught in the headlights. She
moved aside, allowing him entry, holding the door open for
him.

He smiled, and thanked her.

It didn't matter. She would never remember that he had
been there.

He entered the cottage, and quietly closed the door be-
hind him.

And started up the stairs.

It was nearly nine when they met for dinner.

By the time Stephanie came into the restaurant, the others
had gathered, Liz Henderson among them. Arturo was at the
table, and he was very sad, telling them that there was some
news that was a relief, and still sad—and dangerous.

The doctors had just finished with the body of Maria
Britto.

"I have to say, I was very, very worried myself!" Arturo
was telling them. "The way she was found . . . but there is
not a murderer loose among us. Dr. Barello—the coroner—
is certain that she was killed by wild animals. And there!
There is where people must worry, and be very, very careful!"

Grant, already seated, stared at Arturo as if the man had
gone insane.

"Animals buried the girl?" he said incredulously.

"Well, no, no, of course not!" Arturo said. He shook his

head, sighing sadly. "The police will investigate. Right now, they believe that someone found the girl in a horribly ravaged condition and thought that the kindest thing would be to cover her up."

"Without reporting that she was discovered?" Grant said.

"She was in sad shape."

"I know," Grant said flatly, "but that makes no sense. I'm pretty sure that psychologists and psychiatrists around the world believe that closure in the event of the disappearance of a loved one is far kinder than letting a parent, child, spouse, or any loved one spend the rest of their life wondering what happened!"

"Yes, that's reasonable," Arturo said. "But . . ." He shrugged. "As I said, the police will search and investigate until they have the answers. In the meantime, and this is most important for you, Grant—be careful! Maria must have gone near the dig site, because there are no wolves in town, I can assure you!"

"I'm sorry, it still makes no sense," Grant said. "A normal person, coming upon that body, would have been horrified. Their first instinct would have been to get the police, get help! And how do you just happen upon a body at a dig? There are people around—even at night, the campsite isn't that far from the excavation areas."

"Yes, but . . . well, maybe someone was just thinking about the girl's mother—and thought she'd be too horrible to find," Drew suggested.

Grant shook his head. "Sorry—to me, it just doesn't jell."

"Yes, but again, there's really not anything *we* can do about it," Suzette said. "Except that, Grant, Arturo is right— you have to be very careful out there."

"Right," Grant murmured.

He still wasn't buying it—any of it, Stephanie thought.

"You still think we should go with the show tomorrow night?" Stephanie asked Arturo.

"I think we have to go with the show tomorrow night," Arturo told her. "We have people coming in—they arrive in Naples tomorrow morning, and they'll be here by early afternoon." He brightened slightly. "I will send you some nice red wine—local, naturally. It makes everything better."

He left them.

"It just still seems rather in bad taste," Stephanie murmured.

"Stephanie, the local people are trying very hard to make a success out of this place. They won't be here, of course, but we're planning the show for Americans, and they will come and spend money. It's important for the community," Suzette reminded her.

"I guess," Stephanie murmured.

"Hey, Liz, you're doing great, by the way," Doug said.

"Amazingly so," Drew agreed enthusiastically.

"I told you she'd be fine," Clay said quietly.

"Well, thank you, all of you," Liz said. A waiter brought the wine. There was no pouring of it into one glass to be tasted—this was Arturo's suggestion. It was going to be great. Glasses were passed all around.

"Wait," Grant said, looking across the table. "To Liz—for being in the right place at the right time. It's a little like a miracle."

He sounded genuine. He was not. He was suspicious of Liz, and of Clay. Stephanie determined to ignore him. He was the strange one these days.

"To Liz! With thanks," she said.

Liz Henderson graciously accepted their toast, and told Stephanie then that the dressmaker had brought her costume to her room, and that it was fine. They all agreed that they were ready.

"Hey, has anyone checked in on Lena lately?" Suzette asked.

"I was over there earlier," Grant said.

"How was she?"

He hesitated strangely. "More energetic than I expected." He shook his head. "She needs to see a doctor elsewhere."

"The man here is supposed to be very good," Clay said. "He studied in Paris, Rome, and the States, before deciding that he wanted to be his hometown physician."

"Yes, but . . . I don't know. We'll have to see, I guess," Grant murmured.

Their conversation turned to the show. Grant gave Stephanie his suggestion for lighting, and told her that he'd be managing that and the music cues from the booth, so they'd have to be careful to see that their own props were placed correctly. Everyone agreed that they'd have no difficulty being responsible for their own pieces.

"Anyway, if we lose something, it will still fit into the improv," Drew said.

"True. The best thing about these shows is that it's possible to make anything work, as long as you remain in character," Grant said.

Arturo sent dessert to the table, and the waiter, bringing espressos, assured them all that it was decaf. Stephanie noted that they were the last ones dining. She glanced at her watch. It was midnight.

She yawned, excused herself, stretched, and rose. "I hadn't realized it was so late."

"Wait up—everyone gets walked to their cottage, right?" Grant said.

"Everyone? How can we all walk one another?" Drew asked.

"I'll get Stephanie back, Clay can see to Liz, and Drew and Doug can see to Suzette," Grant suggested.

"Good," Drew said, grinning. "And then, Doug, you can walk me back. I'm not big on wolves myself."

"We're not going to run into a wolf on the beach," Doug said, grimacing.

"There are different kinds of wolves, you know," Suzette reminded him.

"True, but apparently, none of you thinks of either of us as the other type," Drew said. "Sadly! So . . . come on, Suzette, let's get you tucked in."

"Hey, what about Lena? Shouldn't we check on her?"

"I'll go see her," Stephanie volunteered.

"What if she's sleeping?" Grant asked, a little sharply.

"I have a key to her room," Suzette said. "She has one to mine, too. We thought it was a good idea when we checked in—we're both pretty capable of misplacing them, and that way, we wouldn't find ourselves locked out." She dug in her purse and handed the key to Stephanie. "You can give it back to me sometime tomorrow, okay?"

"Yep. Good night, then," Stephanie said.

They all started out the back together. Grant was silent as they headed for Lena's. "What's wrong with you?" Stephanie asked him.

"Lena was very, very strange before," he said. "I'll wait downstairs for you, if you don't mind."

Stephanie frowned, looking at him. "You don't want to see her for yourself?"

"As I said, she was very, very strange."

"How?"

Grant stopped walking, waiting until he was certain the others were out of earshot. "She tried to . . . come on to me."

"What?"

"Believe me, I don't mean this as any kind of an ego trip. She tried to . . . come on to me," he explained again.

"Grant, she likes you—she was just flirting. She's sick, remember?" Stephanie said.

"Stephanie, she grabbed me!"

"You're sure?" Stephanie asked, staring at him, and very surprised by the situation. Lena just wasn't the type. She might flirt and laugh, but . . .

"Yes, I'm sure." He took the key from Stephanie's fingers and opened the door. "You go on up. I'll be right here."

Grant was behaving odder and odder. Still, Stephanie didn't want to argue with him any more that night. She wondered briefly if he would say such a thing in the hopes of making her jealous, but she just didn't think so. And still . . . *Lena* doing such a thing? Even if Stephanie had assured her that she and Grant were no longer a couple, Lena wasn't the type to be . . . lascivious.

Stephanie hurried up the stairs. The hall and bathroom lights were on; the bedroom itself was dark. The windows were closed.

She walked over to the bed. Placing a hand on Lena's forehead, she was relieved to feel that it seemed a more normal temperature.

"Stephanie?" Lena asked. She sounded like a little girl.

"Yes, it's me. I'm just seeing how you're doing."

"Better . . . just weak. Hey, the sliding glass doors are closed. There's no air in here," Lena said fretfully.

"I'm not sure you need air tonight. The temperature in here is just right, Lena."

Stephanie's eyes were growing more accustomed to the dim light. Lena looked restless. Her fingers were curled around a medallion or cross she was wearing around her neck.

"Maybe you're right," Lena murmured. "But you know . . . the doctor left me some sleeping pills right on the dresser. Would you give me one? I had one earlier . . . sleep seems to help a lot."

"Sure, hang on."

Stephanie went for the vial, thinking it was strange—sleeping pills were helping Lena. They had definitely helped her. And maybe having the place shut up was good, too. The dreams didn't seem to be as bad with the sliding doors closed.

Could *dreams* have made Lena ill, she wondered.

She brought Lena a pill. She had a bottle of water at her bedside, and used it to take the pill. Settling back, she smiled at Stephanie. "Thanks."

Stephanie looked at the cross Lena was wearing. She hadn't seen it on her before.

"That's a pretty piece," she said.

Lena touched it, troubled. "This . . . yes, thanks. I think I bought it here. I must be losing it somewhat, because I don't remember putting it on. It's strange, though. It's irritating around my neck. Want to help me get it off?"

"Sure."

Stephanie sat at her side, and Lena twisted around. For several minutes, Stephanie struggled with the clasp. "This is ridiculous, but . . . it's a strange hook. I can't quite get it."

"Never mind, then. I'll live with it until the morning," Lena said. "Hey . . . you know, just in the last few hours, I really have started to feel better."

"That's great!" Stephanie told her.

"Hey, how is the new girl?"

"She's working out fine, so you shouldn't worry."

"Now I *am* worried! She's not so fine that you'd rather have her permanently?" Lena said.

"No—you're still the better comedian. But she's fine."

"Thank God!" Lena breathed. "Still, I'm so sorry to miss the opening."

"Well, better to miss the opening than be really ill."

"Right."

"I'll see you in the morning, then," Stephanie said.

"Thanks. Thanks a lot! You're the busiest one, and the only one to come by and see me!" Lena told her.

Stephanie had been halfway out of the room. She paused, looking back. "What?"

"You're the only one who has come!"

"Grant said he was up earlier."

"If he was, I didn't see him," Lena told her.

"But . . ."

Lena shrugged. "Maybe I was asleep."

"Maybe," Stephanie said. "Well, good night."

"Good night!"

Stephanie hurried down the stairs. Grant was waiting. His expression was guarded. "How was she?"

"Doing much better."

"Well, good. I'm glad to hear that."

Stephanie studied him as they went out. He turned and checked that the door was relocked.

"She says she never saw you today," Stephanie told him.

He whirled around and looked at her. She didn't think he was acting.

And yet . . . it was Grant.

"I told you the truth," he said flatly.

"Okay, so . . . maybe she was a little delirious?" Stephanie suggested.

"She was a little something," he muttered.

They crossed the distance to her cottage. Stephanie opened her door. Even as she did so, she was aware of him behind her. And she was startled by the sudden, almost desperate urge she had to ask him in. She felt . . .

Stimulated . . . as if she'd been engaged in heavy petting for the last hour. As if she had to grab hold of him, rip into his clothing . . .

"Good night!" she gasped out quickly.

She didn't let him hover, or even respond. She got into her cottage, closed and locked the door, and leaned against it, stunned at herself, and alarmed.

"Stephanie! Make sure—"

"Yes, yes, I'll lock up. I'll lock everything," she assured him. She didn't wait then, but ran up the stairs to the bedroom, making certain that her footsteps were heavy, audible just outside where Grant stood.

She walked straight to the shower, shedding her clothing. She turned on the water, and let it slush over her in cold rivulets.

In just seconds, she thought she'd been crazy. She turned the water to warm. After a few minutes, she stepped out, dried, brushed her teeth, and crawled into one of her long, cotton T nightgowns.

She hesitated, left the bathroom and stairway lights on, turned off the bedroom overhead, and crawled in.

The room was too silent.

She turned on the television, and lay down again.

After a while, the lulling sound of the BBC reporter's smooth voice wrapped around her, making the world seem normal, and she began to drift to sleep.

She bolted up.

There, at the foot of her bed, was Grant.

Bronzed, naked, erect. It looked as if he had been greased, as if for some kind of bodybuilding competition. Every shadow and nuance of his muscles seemed to glimmer and excite. Though he was still, he seemed filled with electricity and vibrance. She felt her breath catch in her throat, and it started to happen again. She ached. Agonized. Sexually, sensually . . . and felt that if she didn't reach out and touch him . . .

Stephanie . . . I'm waiting. You can see . . . come . . . come on . . . come to me . . .

Yes. She was an idiot. He wanted her, and she had thrown him away. And nothing else in the world mattered now except getting to him, touching him, having him inside of her, having him . . .

No.

Another voice. Someone else in her room again. Someone calling her back. She turned . . . silly, there was nothing behind her except for the wall.

She turned back to where Grant had stood, hair falling in

his eyes, body as sleek, muscle-bound, and aroused as a hungry Adonis . . .

Except that . . . he wasn't there. There just seemed to be a . . . shadow. A huge, eclipsing shadow where he had stood.

A shadow like wings.

A sharp sound exploded nearby. She jumped up with a scream, and realized that the sound had woken her and that she had been dreaming.

Just dreaming again.

But the sound had been real. It was coming from the glass doors.

A slam exploded against them again. Terrified, Stephanie let her hand fly to her throat. She barely swallowed back a hysterical scream.

She forced herself to rip open the draperies.

Chapter 8

"So . . . everyone is tucked in?" Liz asked, closing the drapes as she turned and saw that Clay had come into the room.

"All tucked in."

"And Lena? Did you see to her?"

"Oh, yes."

Smiling, Liz strolled over to where he stood. She touched his face, and then reached for the top button of his shirt, and methodically, to undo it, and then the others. She slid her hands against his bare chest, then stood on her toes, whispering against his ear.

"Stephanie is very . . . I do mean *very* beautiful. Those blue eyes, and that dark, dark, nearly ebony hair. And the way she's built . . . I don't need to be jealous, do I?"

"You?" He smiled, struggling out of the shirt, letting it fall to the floor. "Never!" He slid his hands beneath the silky shoulders of her see-through nightgown, causing it to fall to the floor. He crushed her against him, feeling the pressure of her breasts against his flesh.

She reached for his belt buckle, undid it. Slowly, listening to the rasping sound of it, pulled down the zipper. Palms against his hips and lowering, she pressed down the jeans.

"Never!" he repeated, pressing his lips against her throat.

The thrill of desire swept through her. She cradled his buttocks, and felt the pressure of his sex hard against her.

She hesitated, just briefly. "The cross?" she whispered.

"Taken care of," he murmured against her flesh.

"You're sure?"

"It will all break soon enough."

"But tonight . . . ?" she asked.

"Tonight . . . tonight, now, we . . . rest."

"Rest wasn't what I had in mind."

"Let me rephrase . . . tonight, there's just you. And I. It's been too long," he told her.

They parted, just briefly. Long enough for him to shed shoes, socks, and the jeans.

"My love!" she whispered, flying against him.

His touch was as desperate, as savage as her own. And in the darkness of the night, they fell upon one another.

"Grant!"

Stephanie was stunned. He stood outside her window—no, he was almost attached to it, like a silly little stuffed creature, suction-cupped to a car window.

Except that he wasn't little. He was towering. And his eyes were a blue that blazed with a terrible intensity.

"Let me in!" he demanded.

She wasn't sure why, but she obeyed, snapping the lock, sliding the windows open. He entered, fingers tearing through his hair as he brushed past her, looked wildly through the room, entered the bath, and ran down the stairs.

"Grant, what the hell is the matter with you?" she cried after him.

"Lock those windows again!" he called back up.

A few minutes later, he returned. He looked baffled, but not at all apologetic.

"Grant, what are you doing?" Stephanie demanded.

"I saw it come here."

"You saw *what* come here?" She crossed her arms over her chest.

"A . . . shadow."

He was still frowning and looking around the room. Despite herself, his words created a chill in her.

A shadow. She could only dimly remember now, but there had been a shadow . . .

In the room. There, at the foot of the bed. Where he had been. Except that he hadn't really been there.

"Let me get this straight. You saw a shadow. At night, in the moonlight. Imagine. And so you raced up my back steps, pounded on the glass as if you needed to wake the dead, and burst in here—to catch the shadow?" she said.

"There was . . . someone," he said.

"Grant, what are you doing?" she whispered, a little desperately. "There's no one in here—as you've seen."

"No," he agreed, looking at her. He still seemed so troubled that she couldn't just scream and order him out. "There's no *one* in here."

"Okay . . . is the shadow in here?"

"Stephanie, I haven't lost my mind."

"Right. But the next thing I know, you'll be telling me to wear a cross and buy a gun and fill it with silver bullets, or the like," she said dryly.

He didn't laugh, or crack so much as a rueful grin.

"Maybe that wouldn't be such a bad idea," he told her.

"Oh, Grant, please. I'd be understanding if it were just—finding that girl must have been horrible for you. But you started this very strange behavior in Chicago. That's why we split up, remember?"

"Stephanie, please. I keep telling you that there is something very wrong here."

She walked across the room, coming to him. "You saw a shadow. Maybe someone was walking to get to their own place, and walked by mine to get to it. Grant, I'm alone here, and there's nothing wrong."

She set a hand on his chest, looking up into his eyes, trying to get him to pay deep and serious attention to her.

He met her gaze, then shook his head, distracted. He seemed to be listening to something in the night. There was nothing to hear.

He looked back at her again. She saw the vein thundering at his throat. He was as electric and keyed as he had been in her dream. Vital. Heat seemed to emanate from him. She stepped back slightly.

"Grant, you've got to go."

He shook his head.

"Stephanie, I have to stay."

"Grant! We split up because we really needed to. It's not because I hate you—you know I don't. It's not that we weren't good together—we were. But *we're* what's wrong. Please, Grant, you don't know how hard it was for me . . . I came here to make it on my own, to get myself together. Then you were here! You can't stay."

He shook his head impatiently. "Stephanie." He gripped both her hands, holding them between his. "I don't mean here, right here. I don't mean to crawl in with you to sleep. I don't mean to coerce or trick you back into bed. I just need to stay here. At your doorway. Make sure all the doors are locked, and then just throw me a pillow."

She backed away from him.

"You're crazy."

"But I'm not leaving. Scream or call the cops if you feel you really have to. I am not leaving." He released her, walked by her, and grabbed a pillow off the bed. She watched as he assured himself that the sliding doors had been relocked.

"This is getting ridiculous. Beyond what I owe you in respect to the past, or out of friendship," she said, walking to her bedside phone. "I am calling the cops," she told him.

She damned the fact that he knew she wouldn't. With the pillow he had taken from the bed, he walked to the doorway, and just outside. Plumping the pillow behind him, he leaned against the wall.

She set the phone down and walked to where he stood. "Grant, I am really, really worried about you."

"Go to sleep, Steph," he said wearily. He sounded drained. There was no emotion in his voice.

"Grant! You're going to stay all night, leaned against a wall?"

"Yes."

"Aren't you supposed to be at the dig tomorrow?"

"Yes."

"And then there's the last rehearsal, and a show tomorrow night."

"Yes."

"But you're going to stay up against a wall all night?"

"I'll doze off, I'm certain. But at least, I'll be here."

She threw up her hands, exasperated. "Fine. Stay there, then. I'm going back to bed." So, determined, she walked back to the bed, and crawled into it, drawing the covers to her chin. She listened, and waited.

Grant didn't move.

And she realized that he really intended to spend the night sitting up against the wall.

She lay in bed, listening again. The voice of the BBC journalists went on and on.

Shadows . . .

Dreams that were so vivid they seemed real.

Yes, maybe she should buy a cross.

Time passed. Grant didn't come near her, but neither did she rest. How could she? He was with her. It wasn't a dream, a sexual fantasy caused by their sudden parting, and her self-enforced deprivation.

She was certain that he was worried. But . . . he was *crazy* worried. In Chicago, he had been distracted.

He had called out another woman's name.

That still hurt. Maybe it was the real crux of the matter. Then, tonight, he had said that Lena had come on to him. Lena said she hadn't even seen him.

She'd be an idiot to get up and go to him. He was with her, he was quiet, he was on guard against whatever danger threatened in his own mind. Leave it lie, leave it lie . . .

But thirty minutes later, she was still wide awake.

She rose, and walked to the hall.

His eyes were closed, his head against the pillow pressed to the wall. His handsome features were so stressed and riddled with tension that she felt her heart flip.

"Grant." She whispered his name.

His eyes flew open and he jerked bolt upright.

"I'm sorry!" she murmured, coming down to sit cross-legged before him.

He exhaled with relief.

"Do you want some tea . . . a drink, or something?" she asked softly.

"Just go to sleep, Stephanie," he said.

She rose. "I think I'll have a Tia Maria with milk. That could help."

He groaned. "All right. I'll have a Tia Maria with you."

She went on down the steps. He followed. In the kitchen, she found glasses, milk, and the Tia Maria stuffed into one of the cabinets.

"I'll take it neat," he told her.

She nodded, and added milk only to her glass of liqueur.

She handed him his glass.

"Grant, I admit that what has happened has been really terrible. You spend your days working on bones. Then, today, you found the dead girl. But you have to understand. Something very sad happened—it doesn't mean that we're all in danger. The girl was attacked by animals."

The look he gave her was filled with disbelief. "You cannot tell me that you believe that!" he exclaimed.

"Grant! Doctors did an autopsy," she argued.

"They're lying," he said simply.

"Why would they lie?"

"A cover-up—I don't know."

"You said yourself that the body was . . . ravaged."

"She wasn't killed by an animal," he said flatly. "Not by a wolf, not as we know wolves," he muttered.

"All right—maybe the boyfriend did it. The fiancé. And the community is covering up. That still wouldn't put any of us into a high-risk zone."

"Stephanie, if you tell me you haven't felt anything strange since you've been here, I will call you an out-and-out liar."

She hesitated. "We're in a foreign country. We all had some jet lag. The night sky is different, the language on the streets is different . . . everything is different."

Again, he gave her that look. "You know what I'm talking about."

"Oh, Grant," she murmured.

"Stephanie, I'm not asking anything of you," he reminded her.

She sighed. "Fine. Be crazy. I'm going back to bed."

She rinsed her glass and set it in the sink and started back upstairs. She heard him follow, heard him take up his position again.

And then she couldn't stand it again. She kept seeing flashes of the image she had seen in her dream. It had once seemed so wrong to be together when it seemed that it wasn't what she really wanted, or the way she craved to be needed and loved as well. Tonight . . .

He was here.

He was Grant.

And if it was only for the night . . .

She walked out to the hallway. He was awake this time, and he looked up at her, a brow rising sardonically.

"Stephanie, you're supposed to feel safe and secure with me out here, and therefore, you should be able to sleep."

She didn't answer. She offered him her hand. He took it, eyes narrowing somewhat warily. He rose, towering over her.

"I can't sleep with you out here," she said.

"I'm not leaving."

"I know."

Their eyes met.

A slow, rueful smile touched his lips. "Stephanie, if you think I can lie on one side of the bed and keep my distance, I'm not sure I can make that kind of a promise."

She angled her head to study him, and slowly smiled as well. "I think I might actually be rather insulted if you could make such a promise."

She felt his thumb fall against her cheekbone, the pad of it callused, but almost excruciatingly gentle. Then she caught his hand.

"I'm not saying that anything has changed," she told him roughly.

His hand fell. "Well, then, I'll try not to be too tender."

She let that be as it would, not replying, turning back to the bedroom. Yet, at the foot of the bed she stopped, dead still for a minute.

He had stood here, in all his naked glory, flesh flawed here and there with scars obtained from various exploits. He had stood in a purely carnal state . . .

Like an animal.

Only in a dream.

And yet . . .

Remaining where she was, back to him, she caught the hem of her cotton T gown and pulled it over her head, tossing it aside. She would have caught at the elastic of her panties to discard them in the same manner, but he was already behind her.

It was stunning, the speed with which he had managed to disrobe.

But she felt his naked flesh. Felt his chest, flush against her back, felt the hot, moist whisper of his breath against her shoulders and neck and he lifted her hair, and placed his lips there, the texture of his lips running slowly from her earlobe to her collarbone. His fingers feathered down her spine. He was on his knees then. His fingers found the elastic hers had not, and the last flimsy garment was lowered down the length of her legs. She stepped free of them, and felt the searing seduction of his lips against the base of her spine, the small of her back. He turned her to face him, and buried himself against her, fingers stroking the inside of the length of her thighs, kisses delving deeply between them.

She caught her breath, immobilized in a sea of sensation. She felt as if her blood had been instantly set afire, that her limbs were electric, and yet . . . losing strength. It was as if great waves from the ocean were washing over her, flooding her with an urgent, desperate, dying need. She gripped his shoulders, her fingers tore into his hair . . .

Then he was standing, pushing her back. She fell against the bed, and saw him.

And he was there, as he had been in her dream, muscles heated and glistening in the pale light that seeped into them. Legs like sculpted columns, shoulders like metallic beams, his stance and added breath of excitement in a sea of sensual desire that gripped her in an all-encompassing hold. He crawled down atop her, and she reached for him. His scent was familiar, his arms were a bastion, and despite the fact that nothing mattered but the satiation of the hunger riddling her senses, she was aware as well that there was something far, far more . . .

He came to her . . . into her. She felt the force of his body like a shock, and yet she couldn't get enough. He moved, and she felt herself arching against him like a madwoman herself. He gripped her shoulders, fell lower, caught her buttocks, pressed them ever closer. His rhythm became fast, almost frantic . . . the speed, staggering . . . the rise, almost unbelievable . . . and yet so real. The feel of his flesh, the masculine scent of him, the sound of him breathing, the steady, then rising, pounding of his heart, soft, louder, engulfing. She cried out, body constricting into a taut knot, as the climax she had so desperately writhed and arched to achieve came racing explosively through her, and for long moments that seemed like an eternity, she couldn't have moved if she tried . . . she just allowed it to bathe her, the sweet aftermath . . . jolt after jolt . . . pulse and pulse . . . slower . . . slower . . . until her muscles eased. She felt the dampness then between them, the sheets, the night. And all that occurred to her at first was the sweetest gratitude. *It hadn't been a dream. It had been real, all real. And he was here with her, and outside, she could hear the ocean breeze as it rustled by . . .*

He didn't try to speak. Neither did she. She felt his arm around her, holding her.

Later in the night, she felt his touch again. And she was eager to turn to him. More eager, still, to press her lips against the vibrance of his flesh . . . to seduce in turn. And again, to feel that wonder of sensation, like the wind, like thunder, sweeping through her . . .

Real. Every anguished or ecstatic moment real. Grant, real, at her side . . .

Once again, neither tried for words.

When she awoke, he had showered. A bath towel wrapped

around his waist, coffee cup in his hand, he was staring out the back glass doors.

It was morning.

With that light dispelling any illusions or fears of the night gone by, she wasn't sure what she wanted to say to him, where she wanted to go from here. She feigned sleep.

She heard him dress.

She heard him leave.

And she heard him check that he had duly locked her door after he had gone.

She lay still for a while, reflecting on the night. Then she rose and showered. It promised to be a long day.

So far, she realized, every day here had been long. Very long.

At ten o'clock, the body of Maria Britto arrived at the funeral home.

Danielo Vedero, the town's mortician, knew the girl, just as the police and doctors had known her. He intended to do his very best with her, despite the fact that he was deeply worried about the work.

He had heard how she had been chewed up. And then . . . after an autopsy. Well, she would have her wake in the following two days.

On Monday, she would be interred in the graveyard. It was very, very said. Merc and Franco, with whom Danielo had shared espresso early last evening, said that Maria's mother had done nothing but cry since the girl had disappeared. She had known, somehow, they said, that her daughter was dead. Intuition.

But for Maria, and for her mother, Danielo would see to it that she looked as if she was sleeping, and completely at peace.

He told his receptionist to hold all calls; he would be busy for hours.

He closed himself into his embalming room. His assistant had lain the girl out for him.

Coming to the body, he frowned. There was no autopsy scar on her chest. In fact . . . had they been wrong? She didn't look as if she had been chewed by animals! She was amazing. Her skin had color. In fact, she might have been just sleeping as she lay there, before he even touched her, began the embalming process, much less her hair and makeup.

He came close to her. It was so wrong, this child, dead. Laid out on her back, she showed none of the signs of the ravaging that she had endured. In fact . . . she was gorgeous, as only such a young woman could be. Her waist was slender, her limbs long and shapely. Her breasts were high and proud, full, despite the way she lay upon her back. Peering more closely at her chest and abdomen, he thought he could see the faint lines of scars.

Scars. Not fresh wounds. Not gaping holes created by the teeth of beasts.

Troubled, he leaned closer, and ran his finger along one of the pale lines that stretched from her breast to her abdomen.

"Danielo! You lascivious old dog!"

He jumped back, a scream rising in his throat.

Maria's eyes were open, and on him. He blinked, wondering if he'd not had enough sleep, or if all the overwhelming sadness hadn't caused a malfunction in his brain.

She sat up. His corpse sat up. And smiled. But it wasn't Maria's usual smile. It was easy and twisted. "What, are you horny, old man? Poor thing—that withered, screaming harpy of a wife you've got must not be putting out, eh, Danielo?"

She laughed as he stood there, stupefied.

He gave his head a shake, thinking he would wake up.

She crooked a finger at him. "Come here, Danielo. Come, come to me . . . I'll fulfill your deepest, darkest, *filthiest* desires, old man."

Then, he really wanted to scream. His knees were buckling. His heart was pounding as if it would burst out of his chest. He was terrified.

But no sound would come to his lips.

"Come, come . . ."

He didn't feel her reach for him, but she must have done so. He was in front of her, and she was laughing again. She took his hand and brought it to her breast. Once again, cruel laughter rang from her lips. "Dear, dear, you mustn't die on me, Danielo, come on, I need you. Here, here . . . come closer, closer . . . there."

She was going to whisper something in his ear. He felt her tongue flickering out, touching his flesh. Then . . .

There was a sharp pain.

And the noise . . .

A slurping sound. It went on and on and on. . . .

And as he stood there, he realized it was delicious. And in the first time in recent memory, he felt . . .

Good. *Sì, sì, sì* . . . so good.

His body began to shake.

The sound continued . . .

Slowly, slowly . . . he sank to the ground.

Carlo greeted Grant at his rental car. "I tried to call you," he told him. "Arturo said that you had already gone when I reached the resort, and your cell phone went straight to your answering machine. I'm afraid the satellites are not very good here."

"Why were you trying to reach me?" Grant asked him.

"There's no work today. The police have cordoned off the area. There are crime scene specialists here."

Grant nodded. At last, something made sense to him.

"They're hoping to discover who buried the girl?" he asked Carlo.

Carlo nodded gravely. "It is strange, isn't it? Why bury the girl, when so many were looking for her so desperately."

"Have they questioned the fiancé?"

"Yes, but he seems to be innocent, from what they have told me. Maybe there was someone—a lover she shouldn't have been seeing—who saw the attack. And since he might have felt that it was his fault . . . well, he buried Maria so that he wouldn't be blamed. If so, hopefully they will discover the truth soon enough."

"You really believe that animals did it?" Grant asked Carlo.

Carlo seemed surprised. "Well, you come from a very big city. Maybe you think that our men aren't as learned as those you know. But I can swear to you, both Barello and Antinella are superb physicians, and know what they're doing."

"I'm sorry—I didn't mean to imply that they weren't," Grant told him. He wondered if he was telling the truth. Because he simply didn't believe the autopsy report. "It's just . . ."

"It's just terrible, and that's that!" Carlo said, shaking his head. "Anyway, I'm so sorry you had to drive out."

"It's all right. I'll just head back. The first show is tonight. The tour group should be flocking in as we speak," Grant said.

"Check with Arturo in the morning!" Carlo told him. "I'll let him know if they've opened the dig back up to us!"

"I'll do that. Thanks!" Grant called.

He turned the car around on the little road and started back. Looking in his rearview mirror, he was momentarily blinded. It seemed that a swatch of black had settled over the sky.

He pulled the car to a halt, stopped, got out, and looked back at the dig. An eerie sensation he couldn't fathom gripped him.

The dig.

It all had to do with the dig, he thought.

He got back into the car, very anxious to return to the resort.

Danielo rose, feeling the back of his head. As he came to his feet, stars appeared before his eyes, and he thought he was going to black out again.

How strange!

He'd never had such an occurrence before in his life.

What had happened?

All he remembered was walking into the embalming room and then . . .

He blinked, trying to regain his vision. Then a sigh left him.

Well, whatever he had done—struck his head? Inhaled too much fluid?—at least, it had happened when he had finished.

Amazing—he couldn't remember a minute of it. And yet, what an outstanding job he had done!

There was Maria. Oh, she was so beautiful! Her hair curled around her shoulders, onto her breasts. Her mother had given them a beautiful blue dress for her burial. And her makeup! He had done an outstanding job.

She was truly so lovely. He had succeeded well.

She did look as if she slept. As if any moment . . .

She might awake.

Chapter 9

The rehearsal went so well, Stephanie was amazed.

A lot of it had to do with the simplicity of their plan. Arturo had been sent ahead of time to acquire the set and props Stephanie had requested, and by the time she arrived on Friday, everything was set. Giovanni had taken care of it all, Arturo told her. She made a mental note to thank him, since she had seen very little of him since her first arrival. It was almost a pity that it seemed they kept losing their women players—had a man gotten ill, she mused, she would have been tempted to give him his time on stage.

Grant had come back early. Stephanie had actually been nervous about seeing him, but he gave no indication that there had been anything between them other than the usual, and they had made an easy segue into the day's work after he explained to her that there was to be no digging that day. He told her briefly that the area was still cordoned off.

For the show, it was all the better.

Lena was actually looking better as well. She was still weak, but much better. She made it out of bed to come and sit in the rear of the café with Arturo, and though she was naturally a bit suspicious of Liz at first, their newest player won Lena over as well, asking for her advice on character, and listening with an intense respect that seemed to please Lena.

They were due to welcome their first crowd at eight. They finished by five, and decided it would be a good time to have dinner. They were all exhilarated, on a high from the success of their work. The place was filled with tourists—most of them American military men and members of their families, but some were Germans who had civilian jobs at the base. In the restaurant, they were talking, laughing, eating, and drinking in very good humor.

There was a lot of laughter, and Stephanie realized that it was actually too easy to forget that a young girl had just died a savage death, and that the town was in mourning.

Arturo rushed by their table, just a little flustered for once. Stephanie called him, he stopped, and rushed back. "Did Reggie come with these guys?" she asked him.

"Reggie . . . no. I don't think so, anyway. I haven't seen her," he said. "Tonight, you'll excuse me, please? It is our first evening with this kind of crowd," he said.

"Certainly, do what you need to do!" Stephanie told him. He smiled, and went on.

"Why wouldn't Reggie come in with this group?" Grant murmured.

"Maybe she is here—maybe he just hasn't seen her yet," Clay suggested.

"And where would she be, then?" Suzette asked.

"Could I have more of that Florentine steak?" Lena asked. "My God, suddenly, I'm just ravenous. And the meat . . . I wish it were just a bit more rare."

"Lena! It's mooing all over the plate as it is!" Drew told her, passing her the meat. Lena smiled. Stephanie was glad to see that she was so much better.

"I'll bet Reggie just got tied up booking more trips," Doug suggested.

"It's strange, though. You'd think she'd want to see her opening night," Suzette said. She looked around. "I haven't actually met her, you know."

"None of us has," Drew said. "I never even sent in a resume—she pulled mine off the computer. I received the offer by e-mail, and then my contract by Federal Express."

"That's how she hired all of us," Suzette said. "I think. Well, except for Steph, right?"

"She's some kind of a distant relation," Stephanie told Suzette. "But actually, even I agreed to this over the phone. I figured she'd show up sooner or later."

Lena giggled. "Well, the rest of us won't know her if we see her."

"Oh, you can't miss Reggie," Grant told them. "She has a certain way about her . . . she walks as if she's royalty."

Stephanie frowned. "What did you mean by that?"

"I meant what I said—and nothing bad. Reggie is tall, slim, has coloring a lot like Stephanie's, and she's traveled the world and has a certain elegance about her. She has a certain way," Grant repeated, staring at Stephanie, and almost daring her to contradict him. He hadn't said anything bad, not really. She just hadn't liked the way he'd said it.

Stephanie pushed back her chair. "Let's take our coffee backstage and get into costume."

"If you ask me," Suzette said, rising, "this show should be great. Look how happy these people are! And they're drinking, so all the jokes about booze should go well."

"Yeah, thank God they're not driving," Drew muttered.

"Thank God," Liz agreed.

As they exited, Arturo came breezing through again. He caught Stephanie's arm, and said, "Can you take a minute, please? I'd like you to meet Captain Mallory."

She had no idea who Captain Mallory was, but she quickly found out. Even as Arturo stopped her, the young man with the buzz haircut was standing by the next table.

"Captain Mallory, this is our young director for the club—director, producer, actress, I should say—Miss Stephanie Cahill," Arturo said, introducing her with a certain pride. "Stephanie, Captain Thomas Mallory."

"How do you do?" He offered her a handshake and a smile. "I'm afraid I'm in charge of this expedition, so if there's any difficulty with folks getting rowdy, I'm the one you complain to."

Stephanie smiled. "I'm sure we'll be fine, but it's a pleasure to meet you. I hope you'll enjoy our show."

"I know we will."

"Well, then, excuse me. You know, you all are the audience for our opening night."

"We may all go down in history," he said wryly.

She smiled, starting to leave, but then she hesitated. "Captain Mallory, did Reggie come with you all?"

"Reggie?"

"Victoria Reggia—the real producer of the whole enterprise."

"Oh, I'm sorry—Vickie."

Reggie was suddenly going by *Vickie*?

"Right, Vickie. Did she come with your group?"

"No, no, she was moving on. To The Hague, I believe."

"Ah, well, thank you, and I'll see you in there."

He gave her a wave. As she walked away, she heard his friends at the table teasing him, commenting that it was too bad that he seemed to have such an "in."

Hurrying backstage, she found that the others were already in costume. Lena was helping Liz with her makeup.

"Do you think you ought to be back in bed?" Stephanie asked her.

Lena shrugged. "I seem to be okay. Since last night . . . I

honestly think I'm gaining strength every minute. I'll stay with Grant in the booth, sitting, and I know I'll be all right."

"Okay, but . . . you get right back into bed if you start feeling worse."

"Yes, ma'am!" Lena promised.

There were two large dressing areas, one for the men, another for the women. Stephanie quickly changed into her costume, a crimson getup with a side slit and a feathered hat. In costume and makeup, she joined the others in the eaves stage left.

Since Grant was in the booth, managing the lights and sound, he'd set up a mike system that warned them of their cues.

"Five minutes." His voice came softly out of the wire.

"Well, guys, have fun. That's always the best direction," Stephanie said.

"Break a leg, everyone," Suzette said cheerfully. The group quickly went through the motions of offering one another hugs and kisses.

Clay Barton offered her no more than anyone else. And yet . . .

His touch seemed more magnetic. There it was, she mused, that strange power about him that seemed to make him more . . .

More. Just more. Intriguing, strange, and, oddly, he seemed to offer a sense of leashed power.

"Sixty seconds." The house lights dimmed, the stage lights came up. They were all aware that drinks would be served throughout by the restaurant staff, and that they couldn't allow themselves to be distracted—unless they did so on purpose because they were playing with the audience.

"Curtain," came Grant's voice.

Suzette went out on stage with her feather duster.

Her costume alone was a hit. And she played to the applause and the catcalls, then began to explain that she was the maid for the World Traveler's Club, but really, she was much more; she'd probably been far more places than any of the members, but then she'd hit Monte Carlo, and since she was broke . . .

She was great. The servicemen offered her money and she brought her fingers to her lips and suggested that they leave an extra tip for the waitstaff, who worked very hard. Even that brought applause.

Drew was next on stage, admonishing Suzette for the dust, and when she claimed there was none, he blew on top of a stack of books and enough dust started flying to bring about more laughter. The two did a song, played with the audience, and next out to join them were Liz and Doug. Liz was wonderful, throwing out phrases in Italian and German, being silly as she played with the audience. Doug pretended to have been just about everywhere, but had all his facts very obviously wrong.

Clay made his entrance, playing with every female he passed, managing to do so with such a caricature of a playboy that even the men whose wives or girlfriends he stopped to ridiculously seduce were laughing right along with the women. Stephanie gave him a few moments in the spotlight, then made her own entrance, admonishing him, but then stopping to muss someone's hair, sit on a lap, or simply stare at a man. She pretended to be so caught up in one of the servicemen that Clay had to come to get her. They did their number, the group came out to argue about who really knew the world the most, and Doug did his best with a "what did it matter" speech—they were in Italy, on the water, in the sun, and wherever else any of them had been, the club was the finest place in the world.

The show ran an hour and a half. Much of it was bantering with the audience, asking questions about who was married, who was dating, where they all came from originally. The group was wonderful, eager to get in on the action.

When Stephanie pretended to teach Doug to bump and grind, their hapless audience "volunteer" put on a spectacular show himself, and they were all impressed, and the ad-libs flew because the guy could really dance.

It was near the end of the show when Stephanie was in the background as Doug and Liz did a question-and-answer session about marriage when she looked toward the rear of the café. She missed a beat, frowning. It was dark in the back, but she could have sworn, if only for a second, that she saw Reggie. But as she looked that way, the woman turned. She seemed to see someone, or something, that frightened her.

Because she bolted from the doorway, as if she were hurrying out before she could be seen.

It was Reggie . . . it had been, hadn't it?

"Well?" Clay was staring at her. She remembered where they were in the play.

"*You* can make a group sing louder than I can." She swung her little purse around and assessed the audience. "Oh, honey, I don't think so." She skipped down into the audience, picking on a young lieutenant. "Don't you think my half of the audience could sing much, much louder?"

"I'd be a soprano for you!" the man told her solemnly, causing a rise of laughter.

Soon, they were taking their last bows. Their audience was on its feet, clapping and laughing as they exited the theater. Waiters from the restaurant saw to it that the group filed out—not rushed, but moving along.

Back in the eaves stage left, Stephanie found herself lifted and whirled around. Drew was delighted. Once again, they were on a high of excitement.

"It was fabulous! Who ever would have believed it!" Suzette exclaimed.

By then, Grant and Lena reached them. Again, hugs and kisses went around the group. Arturo burst in on them, and joined in the hugging and kissing. He had brought several bottles of champagne, and they were quickly popped.

"What an opening night! Wait until Reggie hears!" he said.

"You know, I could have sworn that I saw Reggie tonight, in the back of the house," Stephanie said, accepting a glass of champagne. "Did you see her—or the woman who looked just like her, Arturo?"

Arturo stared at her blankly. "Reggie, no. A woman who looked like her . . . no, I don't think I saw anyone like her."

"Grant, did you see who I'm talking about?" Stephanie asked.

He shook his head. "Sorry, my attention was on the stage."

Stephanie shrugged. "Well, anyway, there's someone here who looks an awful lot like Reggie. Maybe I'll see her again tomorrow."

"Strange," Grant said.

"What?" Stephanie asked him.

"Reggie is so unique, that's all," he said.

He was right. And still . . . she had to have seen someone who resembled Reggie to some extent. She felt a slight irritation. Reggie *should* have been here for tonight. The cast had really performed magnificently.

Laughter, champagne, and happy comments about each other's ad-libs and audience members continued for a while. Everyone was thrilled. But at last, they realized that they'd stayed backstage very late, and that there was a lot of work to do in the morning.

"Lena," Liz asked, "think you'll be taking your role back soon?"

"I hope so. But probably not tomorrow. And you were wonderful."

"Thanks," Liz said. "Well, we're going black on Sunday and Monday, so probably by Tuesday, you'll be ready."

"I hope," Lena said. She stared at Liz, then gave her a hug. "Thank you. You were a godsend!"

"Let's just be thankful you're doing so much better. I've had fun," Liz said.

They started out the backstage doors to the beach.

"Hey!" Grant said, suddenly somber. "Let's not forget the stick-together rule here."

"Right!" Drew said. "Okay, Grant, I take it you're escorting Stephanie. Clay, you'll walk Liz to her place. I'll get Lena back safe and sound, and Doug, that leaves you with Suzette."

"Sorry," Doug grimaced at Suzette.

"Hey, you're like a knight in shining armor, okay? Good night, all." She caught Doug's tie, and started walking him.

"Good night, everyone," Stephanie said. She walked ahead of Grant. At her door, she paused.

"You know I won't go away," he said softly.

She opened the door, and let him follow behind her. She walked into the kitchen, trying to be casual. "You know, I'm not sure that I thanked you for all you've put in."

"It was nothing, ma'am."

"But seriously, you came here because of your fascination with archeology—the old, the ancient, and the Crusaders and knights."

He didn't answer her right away. "I think I'm here because I had to be here."

She felt a slight chill. "I don't know what you mean."

"I can't explain. And it doesn't really matter." There was something more that he could have said, but she knew Grant; he had decided he'd said enough.

"Grant, I'm still very worried about you," she murmured.

"And there you go, backing away again. In a thousand years, Stephanie, I would never hurt you," he told her.

She sighed. "You've talked about something strange

going on here. But Maria was killed by animals—that's what doctors, men of medical science, had to say. And Gema . . . well, the wolves would have had to have packed up for her. So there has been a very tragic occurrence, but nothing so terribly strange, Grant."

"Um. Right. Well, I'm not leaving, so where do you want me sleeping?"

She realized that she might be acting as strangely as he was, pulling him close one minute, pushing him away the next.

There was still something about the way he was acting . . . his thought processes, even, that was very, very scary.

But that minute, in the seclusion of her little kitchen, it didn't matter. He was there. She was there. And when she was with him . . .

Same as always. She felt that she breathed him in, that she drowned within him.

She poured a glass of water and drank it quickly.

"Steph, where am I sleeping?"

"Wherever you want," she told him, setting the glass down. She started up the steps to the bedroom, and a slight smile of anticipation teased at her lips.

As she walked, she began shedding clothing, leaving her shoes on the first step, casting her shirt off to lie on the fourth step, then her skirt on the seventh, her bra on the ninth.

At the loft landing, she skimmed out of her jeans and thong. She turned back, and saw that he was mounting the steps in the same fashion, loafers on the second step, shirt on the fifth, jeans on the eighth.

She met his eyes, and the night became electric. She let out a little cry as he reached her, swept her up, and caught her lips with fierce passion as his stride brought them both crashing down in the bed.

Night . . .

There were no dreams.
Only the reality of him.

When she heard the knock, Suzette assumed that Doug had come back to say something; she had barely gotten in her cottage when she heard the sound.

She opened the door.

"Suzette."

She heard her name. It was like the sweetest caress, a sound that touched and evoked and hypnotized. She heard the sound, a pleasant breeze that wrapped around her, soft as the brush of a flower petal. And then she saw the man.

She was dimly aware that he had no right to be there, certainly not at that time.

Then she heard the whisper of her name again.

"May I come in?" he asked.

"But . . . of course," she whispered.

And it seemed that the night wrapped around her.

Carlo Ponti met Grant in the restaurant at the breakfast buffet. He was frustrated, and yet excited.

"We've been asked to hold back again," he explained to Grant, "but there was a piece of metal armor that Heinrich had found before all this happened, and we sent it off to the museum to be studied. I just got a call back this morning, and the markings definitely indicate the house of de Burgh. And if that is the case, I believe we will shortly discover the remains of Conan de Burgh himself."

"That's wonderful," Grant said.

"Yes, we will be able to piece together a bit of history, prove what occurred here. And, of course, every time we are able to do something like this, we make the area more historical, and more exciting. I've been talking with the Discovery Channel, and they are interested. It's all more than we might have hoped. Except, of course, there is the sadness of Maria."

"Yes," Grant mused.

"If the stories passed down through the ages are accurate, we should find other bodies as well. The great clash of the Norman lords that occurred, right here!"

"We've already found a number of bodies," Grant reminded.

"Yes, yes . . . we know that the earthquake that broke up the cliff definitely happened. Exact dates are a bit sketchy. Those we have found already belonged to the local people. This little piece of metal is a tremendous find. Somewhere in the rubble, Conan de Burgh was buried, along with Valeria, and François. Others, yes, those who wanted her executed."

"Wait, wait, who?" Grant said.

"Valeria—the women with whom de Burgh fell in love. She must have been truly something. Wicked to no end, since she apparently forced her own people to war—we're assuming that the 'demons' or 'devil dogs' of legend were her own forces. She rode with François, and they were the ones who ravaged the countryside. Conan de Burgh won the last battle, but was then killed himself by the earthquake. He might have survived, had he not been trying to save Valeria's life."

Valeria.

That was the name.

Stephanie had claimed that he'd cried it in his sleep, cried it when he was awake.

When he was with her.

Coincidence?

He sipped his coffee, trying to keep a grip on the frightening sense of destiny, of the feeling that he'd had to come here—and that something was very wrong here. It was so hard to accept that he, who had so often scoffed at anything out of the ordinary, could have this strange sense of destiny. Stephanie had put it all into simple perspective last night. Gema had packed up and left. Maria had been attacked by wild animals. There was nothing so bizarre in any of it. So they all had dreams. They were in a foreign country. They slept to the sound of the waves and the sea breeze rustling through local palms.

"Grant?"

"Yes, yes, sorry."

"Are you still with me?"

"Of course."

"Come out tomorrow. The crime scene people have said that they will be out of the way by then. It's so very, very exciting!"

"Yes, of course. Sunday. We're going to be black, out of respect for the community," he murmured.

"I must go. I want to be there. I don't intend to get in the way of the detectives, but I must also guard my own interests. *A domani!*"

"Tomorrow," Grant said.

When he rose, he felt unsteady. He gave himself a mental shake. The last two nights . . . back with Steph. Incredible nights. He loved her so deeply. He believed she loved him. But now she was uneasy about him as well.

And why not? He wondered sometimes if he wasn't going crazy himself!

"I'm really beginning to feel so, so much better!" Lena said. She was lying on the sand, dark sunglasses shielding her eyes. "Well, maybe not great. And man, that sun is bothering my eyes today! But I think by Monday . . . well, we may not need Liz anymore. She has been great, though, huh?"

"Don't get rid of Liz so quickly," Suzette murmured.

On a towel next to Suzette, Stephanie frowned. "Are you feeling ill now?"

Suzette shook her head. "No, not really. Just tired today. I had the strangest dreams last night."

"Nightmares?" Lena asked sympathetically.

Suzette shook her head. She was wearing dark glasses as well, but it was apparent that she was flushing.

"No . . . not nightmares," she murmured.

She glanced at Stephanie, then at Lena. "I dreamt that I was with someone. And it was . . . I was . . . wild. Absolutely indecent. And yet . . . I was thrilled. It's rather embarrassing. Made me wonder what . . . well, maybe it's just sad."

Lena was silent. "You know, they say that we dream about being naked in a crowd, or find that we're giving a speech in the nude, because we're insecure."

"You've had dreams like that here?" Suzette asked her.

Lena shook her head. "I think . . . then I got sick, and then I started getting better, and you know . . . now this is really weird." She looked at them both and giggled. "I think I might have grown up too Catholic. We have all that guilt thing going, you know. But . . . I honestly think I feel better since I started wearing my cross."

"Oh, Lena! Faith is great and all that, but do you really think that wearing a cross could make you feel better?" Suzette said. Then she shrugged, answering herself. "Hey, they say that half of what you feel is in your mind, and people do travel the world to go to shrines, so who am I to comment? Besides, it's a beautiful cross."

"It is, isn't it?" Lena mused. She grinned at Suzette. "I even had a dream about someone trying to get me to take it off—can you imagine?"

"How have your dreams been, Steph?" Suzette asked.

Lena answered for her. "I don't think Steph has been

To start your membership, simply complete and return the Free Book Certificate. You'll receive your Introductory Shipment of 3 FREE Zebra Contemporary Romances, you only pay $1.99 for shipping and handling. Then, each month you will receive the 3 newest Zebra Contemporary Romances. Each shipment will be yours to examine FREE for 10 days. If you decide to keep the books, you'll pay the preferred subscriber price (a savings of up to 20% off the cover price), plus shipping and handling. If you want us to stop sending books, just say the word… it's that simple.

FREE BOOK CERTIFICATE

Yes! Please send me 3 FREE Zebra Contemporary romance novels. I only pay $1.99 for shipping and handling. I understand that each month thereafter I will be able to preview 3 brand-new Contemporary Romances FREE for 10 days. Then, if I should decide to keep them, I will pay the money-saving preferred subscriber's price (that's a savings of up to 20% off the retail price), plus shipping and handling. I understand I am under no obligation to purchase any books, as explained on this card.

Name_____

Address_____ Apt.____

City_____ State_____ Zip_____

Telephone (____)_____

Signature_____
(If under 18, parent or guardian must sign)

Offer limited to one per household and not to current subscribers. Terms, offer and prices subject to change. Orders subject to acceptance by Zebra Contemporary Book Club. Offer Valid in the U.S. only.

Thank You!

CN054A

Zebra Contemporary Romance Book Club
Zebra Home Subscription Service, Inc.
P.O. Box 5214
Clifton , NJ 07015-5214

dreaming lately. I think she's been dealing with the real thing."

"You and Grant are back?" Suzette said, and she sounded pleased.

"We're not actually back. We have a lot of . . . issues."

"I'd find a way around those issues!" Lena advised her. "He's so capable, and authoritative, and he's in the theater, and even if he weren't built like brick and sexy as all hell, in our line of work, sometimes you just have to go for hetero-sexual."

"Well, that's true," Suzette mused. "Seems to me, though, that too often, the kind of guy you'd like to be with, even marry, comes and goes too quickly. I actually love the the-ater because of my gay friends. They stay your friends."

"That's true," Lena mused. "But they don't do much for your sex life. Then again, since we seem to be so self-sufficient with dreams . . ."

Suzette started to laugh. "Look at Stephanie! I think the real thing has to be much better than a dream. And yet . . ." Her voice trailed as she flushed again.

"Yet what?" Stephanie asked her.

"It was so real!"

"There were some awfully good-looking servicemen around last night," Lena said.

"I know!" Suzette moaned. "And we were just on such a high . . . tonight, we have to stick around in the bar and flirt with a few!"

They ate early again. That night, the restaurant was filled, and now people knew and recognized them, so they came to the table in a constant flow, telling them how much they had enjoyed the show, and how they were looking forward to the evening.

Grant left the table before the others to check the set, and Stephanie followed soon after, feeling somewhat guilty. Since she'd wound up as part of the cast, and he'd been there, she'd left him to attend to the details that were really her responsibility.

But he didn't seem to mind. He didn't even want to hear her thank him that night. He seemed oddly distracted. She decided for the time to leave him alone.

The show went up. The second night was even more fun, with their audience aware that they'd be participating.

Yet, in the middle of it, Stephanie was startled when she was in the eaves with Suzette and she whispered to her, "You're not going to believe who I saw out there tonight!"

"Who?" Stephanie whispered back.

"Gema!"

"Gema—back here?"

"Look, she's in the rear, near the door to the resort lobby."

"I never met her," Stephanie reminded Suzette.

"I'll bet she's sorry she walked off!" Suzette said. "And please, Stephanie, if she comes begging, do not give her her job back. She left us high and dry."

"Try to show her to me when we're back out there," Stephanie said.

Suzette nodded. But when they had a chance to speak again, Suzette said, "I didn't see her again. Well, I'll just bet that she'll come around. This show is going to wind up in newspapers across the globe, if we keep doing this well. She doesn't deserve to be any part of our success!"

That night, when the show ended, the cast determined to mill with the men and women who had come, and who had headed back into the bar to enjoy the remnants of their last evening. Stephanie mulled that it might not be a bad thing for her to do as well.

But when she told Grant what she was thinking, he had other plans.

"You go ahead. I . . . I have to do something else."

"What?" she asked him.

"There's a wake for Maria tonight. The viewing goes on to eleven. Since I'm the one who found the body . . . well, I feel I should pay my respects," he told her.

Stephanie felt slightly ashamed. The shows had been so magnificently received that she had pushed the local tragedy out of her mind.

"I'm coming with you," she told him.

"You don't have to," he said.

"I want to. Just let me get out of this makeup."

"All right," he said. "But we have to hurry. The funeral home is just up the street, but it's also getting really late."

She scrubbed her face and didn't bother with reapplying street makeup. Grant ran back with her to her cottage to find something appropriate to wear. She chose a simple black dress. In the States she might not have been so concerned about color or tradition, but here, where old values were so important, she wanted to be in proper attire.

As they walked the distance, uphill, she glanced at her watch, hoping she hadn't made them so late that the wake would be over, but they still had a few minutes.

When they arrived, she felt the massive difference of emotions between being at the resort, and coming here, where the real heart of the community lay.

The funeral home was crowded. She saw a lot of the local people she had noticed in the café sipping espresso, having dinner, or just coming in to be social. Both of the police officers were there.

And Maria's mother.

She was on her knees before the coffin.

To Stephanie's amazement, the coffin was open. And to her greater amazement, the girl looked beautiful. Absolutely stunning. There were no marks on her flesh. Her face was reposed; it almost looked as if a gentle smile teased her lips.

"They must have the world's best morticians here," Grant murmured lightly.

As they stood back respectfully, Maria's mother began to cry. She touched her daughter's face, and a keening wail came from her lips.

The policeman, Merc, went to her, drawing her away from the coffin.

"Let's say a little prayer," Grant murmured.

They walked forward together and went to their knees on the little pew in front of the girl. They bowed their heads, closed their eyes.

Stephanie knew she should be asking God to welcome the soul of the deceased. She opened her eyes. A gasp formed in her throat.

Maria was looking at her.

Stephanie blinked.

The girl was as she had been, eyes closed. They were sewn closed, of course. She was dead, embalmed.

Grant nudged her. He hadn't seen what Stephanie had seen. Or imagined, she told herself ruefully. It had to have been a trick of her mind because Maria looked so very beautiful, and not at all dead.

They rose, walking to the side of the coffin. Grant nodded to people in acknowledgement, and she thought they must be scientists or other volunteers from the dig.

Carlo Ponti was there. He walked over and shook Grant's hand, and kissed Stephanie on the cheek. "It was good of you to come," he said.

They didn't get a chance to reply.

Maria's mother let out a terrible wail, a cry of anguish that brought agony to every heart there.

But then, she broke free from Merc and went running to the coffin. Her purse fell as she drew something from it.

It was a huge knife.

Before anyone could stop her, she pulled her daughter's hair, drawing her head up.

And she proceeded to saw away at Maria's neck, madly attempting to sever the head from the shoulders.

Chapter 10

Stephanie had never seen anything more horrible in her life.

Lucretia Britto didn't just slice at her daughter's throat; she hacked at it viciously.

Neither had Stephanie ever imagined what it took to remove a head from a body. The fevered energy and effort the woman displayed was insane. And at first, everyone there was apparently so shocked that they didn't move. There they were in the funeral home, soft, soothing music playing, and everyone just staring as the woman worked with maniacal verve to cut off her daughter's head.

At last, three men raced to the coffin.

By then, sweat had popped out all over Lucretia's face, and the oddest thing was that she was covered in blood. Stephanie didn't know a great deal about embalming, but she had always believed that the blood was removed from the veins and fluid put in.

What spouted from Maria Britto was definitely blood. That, or the town used the most macabre crimson embalming fluid known to man.

Everyone had been silent, staring, stupefied; then it seemed that everyone in the place was talking. Lucretia, dripping red, was hysterical, screaming as the men drew her away. The priest rushed up to the coffin, praying, tossing holy water upon the now nearly decapitated deceased, and the men in attendance all seemed to be fighting with one another.

The priest called out sharply; he walked to the two men trying to restrain Lucretia, and spoke very gently. She slumped suddenly into the arms of those who held her. Then, she began to sob softly.

Stephanie felt that she was at a total loss. She felt terribly awkward as well, as if she had intervened in something extremely personal, another person's terrible grief. She knew sorrow for the girl, and a tremendous sympathy for the woman maddened by her pain, yet there was nothing she could do.

Apparently, Grant was feeling the same.

He touched her arm gently. They didn't need to speak. They turned, and as the chaos continued around them, they slipped down the aisle to exit the viewing room. At the back of the room, they saw Carlo, watching, listening, shaking his head.

"Most unusual," he muttered.

"We feel we're in the way, like intruders," Grant said to him.

Carlo nodded. "Yes, even I feel this way. When a mother loses a daughter . . . she is beside herself, superstitious, and there is anger between the doctors, the mortician, and the police—she was not embalmed properly, which is against the law, and yet, their concern was for Lucretia, the living, and no one imagined that she might do such a bizarre thing . . . yet how unusual."

Stephanie wondered to just what Carlo referred since the entire scene had been, and still was, unusual to say the least.

"The blood *spurted*," he said. "No heart to pump it, and it spurted. This entire situation just becomes more and more tragic." He gave them a sad smile. "It was very good of you to come. Please think of us as people who love too deeply, not as lunatics."

"Carlo! Please, we've seen the anguish," Grant said softly. "Good night."

"*Sì, sì. Buonasera,*" Carlo murmured. "Tomorrow, then, Grant."

"Yes, of course."

Carlo smiled at Stephanie. "Miss Cahill, you should come out with Grant. Despite all this, there is a deep historical significance to the area."

"I'd like to come out and see the site," Stephanie said.

He nodded.

The voices near the coffin were rising shrilly once again.

"Excuse me, perhaps I can help with a calm voice of reason. Though I believe Dr. Antinella is going to help Lucretia most . . . I see that he is preparing a sedative for the woman."

"Yes, yes, please go," Grant murmured.

He took Stephanie's hand, and they walked out.

His grip was strong, supportive. "You're still shaking," he told Stephanie, once they were out into the night air. "Are you all right?"

"I don't know. I'm still dumbfounded," she admitted.

"I could tell some of what was going on, even before Carlo explained," he murmured.

Stephanie gazed at him. He shrugged. "I'm beginning to understand a great deal of Italian. And then, of course, there is the obvious. I think that the doctor, the coroner, and the mortician determined that they wouldn't slice Maria up any worse than . . . than she was. Apparently, they knew from certain signs on the body that death had been caused by animals, and so . . . why cause Lucretia more grief when they felt they could prepare her properly for her burial? There's a deep tradition here, you know. Laws about the disposal of the dead belong to larger, more tightly packed societies. They don't worry about the water being tainted, or some of the other problems that ensued in other places from burials in which the bodies weren't properly prepared or retained. So . . . anyway, the police are furious about that. And Lucretia . . . she's insisting to everyone that her daughter was the victim of demons, or some otherworldly creature, and that the only way she will lie at peace is if her head is severed."

Stephanie shivered. "She did look . . . alive," she murmured. A memory of the trick of light that had caused the girl's eyes to appear open filled her mind. Uncanny. Weird. Terrifying.

The night was balmy, but the air suddenly seemed cold. There was a mild breeze, but it seemed to be whistling. She realized that she was afraid. Very afraid. And she should have felt some sense of security with Grant at her side, and yet . . .

It too often seemed that he was part of the bizarre events occurring and the frightening dreams and suspicions that teased at her reason and logic!

Yet he held her hand, firmly. His size alone seemed imposing in the night.

"She was dead," Grant said. He exhaled on a sigh. "Believe me. I'm the one who found her. She was dead. What I can't believe is how whole they made her appear. When I first found her, her limbs . . . her throat . . . well, they'll bury her, and she'll be at peace."

"I wonder if I'll ever erase that picture from my mind's eye," Stephanie said.

He released her hand, slipping his arm around her. She was still shaking, she realized.

"Let's get back to your cottage," he murmured.

She noted that he was watching the night sky. It could be as strange as everything else around them, with a touch of the moon and stars one minute, and a darkness that was disturbingly complete the next. As if a huge swath of black cloth was tossed up to cover the heavens.

Like a shadow in the darkness. An ebony beyond black.

She quickened her footsteps, matching the natural long stride he had previously slowed for her sake.

When they reached the cottage, she still felt as if she was in shock. Cold, numb, and scared on a level she didn't even understand.

"Is this place stocked with brandy?" Grant asked.

"Yes."

"Good. Let's drink the bottle."

Stephanie realized that Grant was shaken, too.

Every human being, male or female, macho or squeamish, who had witnessed the scene in the funeral home had to have been shaken.

"A bottle of brandy sounds very good," she said.

Drew had definitely had a few drinks. No, he corrected himself, making his way to his cottage—he'd definitely had *more* than a few drinks. But what a great night. The show going so well, and then the time in the bar with servicemen complimenting them all, servicewomen flirting with him, and the wives, sisters—*whatevers!*—of others telling him what a fine natural comedian he was, and that it was the best little excursion they'd had in all the time they'd been stationed abroad, traveling whenever they could.

He was probably going to have one hell of a headache in the morning. People had been buying him drinks—all kinds of drinks. Through the course of the evening he'd had beer, wine, shots, and mixed drinks.

Big mistake, but . . .

Aspirin. Aspirin now . . . and maybe he should chew on

some bread. Someone had told him once that bread soaked up alcohol, and that aspirin before going to bed definitely helped defeat the morning hangover.

What the hell. Whether any of it was true or not, he might as well try.

In his kitchen, he popped the aspirin, and found that he was thirsty, so he drank two glasses of water. Did that help dilute the alcohol—or did it just make it slosh around more?

He really had no clue.

The sharp knocking at his door made him jump.

Who the hell . . . ?

He walked back to the door. He may not have been in great shape, but he had just seen to it that Suzette had gotten back to her place safely. She wouldn't have left and come back for any reason—would she?

Well, there had been a few women in the bar to whom he had just happened to casually mention his cabin number . . .

Great. He might just get lucky. And if he did, he'd probably pass out before he was able to pass in to anything!

Looking through the peephole, he was astonished to see Gema standing on his doorstep.

He threw open the door.

"You!" He wasn't drunk enough not to feel a rise of anger. "What are you doing here now, Gema? The show went up without you—as you certainly must have seen. And it went up well."

She arched a brow and just smiled. "Don't get in a huff, Drew. The show was wonderful. I just came to tell you. And don't worry—I'm not trying to get my job back, I'm just passing through for the night. Aren't you going to invite me in?"

"No! You screwed us all, and we came out all right in spite of it!"

He slammed the door in her face.

Should he have done that? He didn't know. He wasn't

going to have to wait for the morning; his head was pounding already.

"Drew, come on, please . . . I just need to talk to you for a few minutes. I'll make it worth your while!" she teased.

He turned, leaning against the door.

He toyed with the idea of opening it. She'd treated him like dog poop before. Neither he nor Doug had seemed to be the least interesting as human beings to her at all.

And still . . .

Gema was stacked. Had she paid for the boobs? If so, she'd gotten her money's worth.

"Drew . . . ?" Her voice was coercive.

Yes, tempting.

But he was sliding against the door. His knees were just giving.

"You ass! I'll fuck you like you've never been fucked before!" she said.

Too late.

His keister hit the floor, and his head fell forward toward his knees. He was passing out.

Too bad.

It would have been nice to see just what she had intended. It wasn't like he got an offer like that every day of his life.

That was his last thought . . . then the swimming in his brain went still.

And dark.

They did consume most of the brandy.

They had done so sitting on the sofa downstairs. And they hadn't talked a lot. They'd mention something about the show, and then something about the wake. And then Stephanie would shiver again, and they'd fall silent. Then they'd mention something about the show . . .

And something about the wake.

And drink more brandy.

Stephanie had gone from sitting beside him to resting her head on his shoulder. And now, she was lying on his lap, and as he gently moved his fingers over her forehead, smoothing dark strands of her hair from it, he saw that she had fallen asleep. Thank God. He needed sleep, too. He needed time to try to forget.

He waited, just watching her, as she breathed in and out. For a moment, the love he felt for her was so fierce that he shivered, and shivered with a fear that made no sense.

It was this place.

No, it had started before they had come to this place. They hadn't even come together. And yet . . .

He had been drawn here.

And despite Reggie, maybe Stephanie had been drawn as well.

Whatever was happening had torn them apart.

He gritted his teeth. He had to make whatever was happening put them back together again.

She shuddered slightly in her sleep, then a sigh escaped her and she settled against his lap again. He waited a few minutes, then rose carefully, balancing her weight. He brought her upstairs to the bedroom and slipped her shoes off, leaving her in her clothes. Settling her head on her pillow, he drew the covers to her shoulders, then slid off his own shoes and crawled in next to her.

Once again, he just watched as she breathed.

And the sense that he had to protect her, above all else, against all odds, swept over him.

And with it, suddenly, an anger.

Whatever the hell it was, he damned sure was going to beat it.

He lay awake a long time, and realized that he was waiting for the light. That night, he intended to wait out the darkness.

At one point, he rose restlessly, walked to the sliding glass windows, and looked out at the night. The heavens seemed shaded again, as if the moon and stars were blocked by a giant, sweeping cloak that enwrapped the area.

He gripped the balcony railing. He could hear the breeze. It seemed that there were whispers in it. Voices that called to him.

He closed his eyes, on the one hand telling himself that he was being absurd, and on the other hand . . . listening. He sat on the balcony, leaned against the glass, feeling the air, smelling the salt from the water.

Again, his eyes closed. As if it were a physical presence as solid as the arms of a woman, the air seemed to enwrap him . . .

Doug was already lying down when he heard the rapping sound. Groggy, he listened for several minutes before he realized that the tapping was coming from the sliding glass doors just feet away from his bed.

He buried his head back into his pillow, exhausted. It had been one hell of a night, and the mingling with others after the show had been a definite boon to his ego. They might be working a new, small club in Southern Italy, but for a stage performer, there was little so sweet as being received with such tremendous enthusiasm.

The tapping continued.

"Go away," he muttered aloud. He hadn't gotten quite as carried away with alcohol as the others, but . . . was the tapping real, or was it in his mind?

It was real.

He struggled out of bed, anxious to stop the noise. Padding softly in his Calvin Kleins, he reached the doors and drew back the draperies.

He was astounded to see Gema Harris standing there.

But then, maybe he shouldn't have been quite so surprised. Suzette had sworn that she had seem Gema; she had kept trying to find her among the people thronging the bar after the show.

She had her nerve, coming back. He intended to tell her so. Knowing Gema, though, she'd have some ridiculous story about being spirited away for just a few days by Steven Spielberg, or something of the like. Yeah, right, Gema.

He found the lock and opened the door, sliding the glass back wide. The ocean air hit him, and for a minute, it was sobering. He stared at Gema, ready to yell, to tell her that he was sleeping, that she wasn't wanted.

The words froze in his mouth. His boxers were spacious, and the material was suddenly standing like a tent.

Gema looked incredible. She was blessed with a real hourglass figure—paid for or not, he had no idea—but in the last week, certain of her assets seemed to have grown. And she didn't have a hard look to her at all. Her eyes were bright, her smile was amazingly sweet.

"You're not getting your job back, you know," he heard himself say.

"I know. I just really wanted to apologize." Her eyes swept him up and down. Surely, she was aware of the physical reaction she had caused.

"You're knocking at my door in the middle of the night to apologize to me? Stephanie is the one you walked out on, you know. You were here earlier—Suzette saw you. While people were actually still awake would have been a nice time to apologize or explain, or whatever."

"Doug, you were always the most decent to me, you understood me best," she said, and for the life of him, she actually seemed distraught. "Let me in, please. Let me just talk for a minute?"

He sighed. Gema would be pleased, of course, knowing

that she had the charm and ability to manipulate him. But, hey, what the hell?

"Sure. You want a drink?"

"A drink? You're offering?" she said, and giggled slightly. "Oh, Doug, that would be lovely."

"We can go down to the kitchen. Let me just grab a robe."

He started to head for his closet. He felt her fingers on his bare back. If his Calvin Kleins had been in trouble before, they were instantly strained to the breaking point by that one touch.

"Doug . . . you don't need a robe."

Astounded, he turned to her. She had never shown the least sexual interest in him before—he wasn't rich enough, or muscle-bound enough.

She was wearing a knit, halter-type dress. With no underwear, he quickly discovered.

She was sliding out of it, the very act a tease of the highest variety, her every little nuance of movement sensual enough to wake a dead man.

"Gema?" His voice sounded funny. High and cracking.

He backed away at first. She didn't care a hoot about him. She was going to use him to get back in Stephanie's good graces, somehow.

She was naked, breasts huge as pendulums, hair falling around her shoulders, lips moist, pouting slightly.

She wants something, he reminded himself.

But then . . .

Who the hell cared?

He did manage to ask her, "Gema, what do you want?"

"You," she whispered. The simple word was delightfully lascivious.

Then she moved against him. She came to her toes, tongue teasing his lips as she pressed against him. His insides seemed to explode.

Screw it. She could have whatever she wanted.

He felt her tongue moving against his earlobe, felt her body press firmly to his. He seemed to be fitting to her just like a glove.

He grabbed at the waistband of his boxers, nearly stumbling in his haste to be rid of them. She started to press him toward the bed. His arms wrapped around her. He wanted her down.

Lord, but she was a strong one!

He was twisted around, forced down. She straddled him and started kissing him again in a frenzy.

"Gema . . . if you want it, you'd better go for it now!" he said hoarsely.

Then . . . in the midst of her erotic play, he felt the sharpness of pain.

Like the tapping, at first, he didn't know where it had come from. He realized that she'd been nibbling against his neck . . .

Fire flashed through him . . .

Then ice.

And distantly, he heard a sound. A smacking, suckling sound.

"Gema, what . . . ?"

"You did offer me a drink," she whispered.

His mind began to fade. He heard her . . . drinking, suckling, all in a frenzy, and it didn't matter. He was distant, cold, numb, and still aware of a feeling of the deepest, most amazing sexual gratification . . .

Slurp.

Lord, Lord, yes . . .

"That's it!"

The sound of a new voice in his bedroom should have been alarming, but Doug didn't really hear it.

He didn't even know when Gema was wrenched from her place atop him.

"No!" Gema cried to the newcomer. "No . . . I need . . . I need . . ."

"You'll never survive!" she was told harshly.

The man who had slipped in through the glass windows behind her angrily threw her clothing toward her. "You didn't listen to a thing I've said. I don't want any more dead yet—what the hell is the matter with you?"

"I don't need you!" Gema cried, starting forward.

He struck her, backhanding her across the face with a force that was staggering. Gema went flying back against the closet door. The noise was like thunder.

Doug, however, didn't notice or move. His eyes were open, and he was just staring into the night.

The man walked over to where Gema had landed, on the floor, having slipped down the wall to fall to her knees. He caught her by her hair, forcing her to look up at him. "You do have to listen to me. The lord giveth, and the lord taketh. And I am your lord. Get up, and get out. You've had enough. I don't want this one dead—yet."

"You kill!" she cried.

"I am the lord. I do what I want," he said.

He tugged harder on her hair, forcing her to her feet.

She became petulant. "Please, I need—"

"You get what I say. Now, out!"

She looked at Doug one last time. His member was flaccid then. His boxers were still wrapped around his feet.

His head was slightly twisted to the side. She could see the irritation at his neck, but there wasn't a drop of blood wasted. Something inside her burned. He wasn't used up. There was more, more, and . . .

"Out!"

She was shoved outside. She actually began to laugh, wondering just what he would remember when he woke up and found himself in that ridiculous position.

* * *

Grant and Stephanie decided to drive out to the dig for the afternoon.

They both had slept late.

Stephanie awoke to find that Grant was lying quietly at her side, watching her. He looked worn, and she wanted to reach out, caress his face, and somehow soothe the torment that seemed to be racking him.

She wondered if he looked so because he couldn't forget what they had witnessed the night before.

Or if it went deeper.

Despite the fact that they'd been as intimate as ever—if not more so—she still felt the urge to hold back something of herself. She didn't understand him, and as she had been when they had argued so fiercely and she had left him, she was afraid for herself. She loved him far too much. Needed him. And she couldn't allow that, not when the love she felt was filled with so much confusion and fear.

"A penny for your thoughts," Grant murmured.

"I'm not sure I've formed any yet this morning," she told him. She realized that they were both still fully clad, other than the fact that they were shoeless. "How about *your* thoughts?" Stephanie asked. He was going to talk about last night, she was certain.

But he didn't. He touched her cheek with his thumb. "I was thinking that you were the most beautiful creature in the world," he told her gently. And his gaze was very serious and somber. "Actually, I was thinking that you are the world, everything good in it, light and laughter and sanity and caring . . . you know that I love you, Stephanie."

She shook her head, withdrawing slightly. "Grant—"

"Don't go panicking on me. I won't say it again," he told her, rising. "I'll settle for you letting me hang around. I'm going to hit the shower."

He left her.

Did he really love her so deeply?

It couldn't be with a greater force than what she felt for him.

But then . . .

What was so wrong?

She rose, suddenly eager to make some kind of amends. As she stepped from the foot of the bed to the carpet, she frowned.

He had left a little trail of sand on his walk to the bathroom. Where the hell had that come from, she wondered.

The beach, she told herself.

He must have picked it up when they walked back to her cottage after attending the wake. But he'd had his shoes on then, and they had stuck to the paths.

She shrugged. Didn't matter. The maids around here were incredible, vacuuming every day, keeping the cottages just beautiful.

She walked to the bathroom, then hesitated. He had the door closed. She could hear the shower running.

Let it be, she told herself.

But she couldn't.

She tapped lightly, then entered. She could see his form through the lightly fogged glass enclosure of the shower. Tall, sleek, tightly muscled. A terrible urge to come close to him ripped through her.

She shed her clothing quickly and opened the door just as he was sudsing his chest.

He arched a brow, looked her up and down.

"Let me do that for you."

"Only if I get to wash your chest, too," he said.

"I intend to wash lots of places on you," she informed him.

"Well, then it's only fair that you be as clean," he returned.

"I wouldn't want to be anything less," she assured him. She stepped in, closing the door behind herself. The space was tight. It didn't matter. The water was hot, and the pressure was even better. The soap was slick, and she took it out of his hands.

It was good, running it down his flesh.

It was better when he took it, all playful sparks gone from his eyes, his intent vividly clear as he used it on her . . . soap, hands, fingers . . . all manipulating.

She felt the ferocity of the water. The sound in her ears seemed to drown out all else, except for the beat of her pulse, and the rhythm of desire rising in her. She closed her eyes, and let sensation take over. In a matter of minutes, it was madness.

The shower worked for a few minutes . . .

Then they burst out of it.

Bed, carpet . . . everything was soaked. And it didn't matter in the least. There was nothing like being alive in his arms . . . nothing like dying a little there . . . nothing like the raw heat, the feel of flesh, the urgency, striving, flying, falling . . .

Or the tenderness that followed. But that was what seemed to scare her then. She was afraid that she was in love with someone who was becoming a bit of a madman.

Leaving him quickly when he would have held her longer, she ran back to the shower. She was quick, and she dressed immediately, running out then without looking at him, saying that she'd fix coffee.

As she did so, she was shaking, and she didn't know why. How could she love him so much, and be so afraid, deep in the pit of her soul?

They made it into the restaurant in good time—the tour group had just departed. The Sunday brunch was a really magnificent display.

There were a number of townspeople back in the restaurant; they seemed to prefer the resort when the tourists were present.

To Stephanie, it seemed that everyone was whispering. She felt, as well, that people looked at her and Grant, and whispered some more. They were speaking in Italian, and doing so rapidly, so it didn't really matter that they whispered. Still, she knew that they were talking about the wake the night before.

Arturo stopped by their table and joined them, telling them he was sorry they had witnessed the horror the night before.

"It's Lucretia we feel so badly for," Stephanie told him. "The poor woman is simply demented with grief."

"Yes, of course," Arturo murmured.

"What will happen now?" Grant asked.

"She will be properly embalmed, and the funeral will take place tomorrow," he said.

"Will there be repercussions against the doctor and the coroner?" Grant asked.

Arturo shook his head. "Not here," he said softly.

"That's interesting," Grant murmured. "I mean . . . isn't saying that something was done when it wasn't . . . illegal?"

Arturo shrugged. "Oh, the state authorities could try to make something of it, but . . . there would be such an outcry here that everyone intends just to let it all slip by. There were discussions and meetings last night, but . . . everyone is back in harmony. There was no wrong intended." Arturo hesitated. "We are still a little superstitious here, you know? Some people are certain that if Lucretia was compelled to sever her daughter's head, there might be good cause."

"Good cause!" Stephanie exclaimed, shocked.

"As I said, we're superstitious here."

"Severing a dead child's head is taking superstition to extremes, don't you think?" Stephanie said.

Arturo shrugged. "Yes. It's also an insane act of someone in terrible pain. So . . . the priest said that no one must be made to suffer more for what happened, so . . . Maria will be buried, and life will go on." He rose. "Excuse me. There is still a lot to be done today."

Just as Arturo left the table, Clay Barton arrived with Liz, and the two took chairs at their customary table.

"Good morning," Liz said. She looked at Stephanie. "Are you all right?"

"Of course," Stephanie said, frowning.

"We heard you'd been at the funeral parlor last night," Clay said.

At Stephanie's side, Grant had already stiffened. He did so the minute Clay Barton came near him, she knew. She didn't understand it. Clay was responsible, good at his work, and always polite. She couldn't believe that Grant was suddenly suffering a bout of low self-esteem, so she didn't think that he would dislike the man simply because he was so good-looking and macho-esque.

"We were there. It was sad. And it's over," Grant said.

"Yes, the girl will be buried on Monday," Clay said. "And whatever pain her mother might have been feeling, in her own mind, at least, her daughter will be at peace."

Grant stared at him.

"We were there, too, last night. Before you, I imagine. We had actually intended to go back just to ask if there was anything we could do," Liz said. "But then . . . we heard about what happened."

"I ran into one of the cops on the beach this morning," Clay explained.

"Yes, and of course, you speak Italian, so you probably understood much more than we possibly could," Stephanie said.

Grant looked at her sharply.

"What happened when you ran into the cop this morning?" Grant asked Clay. His voice had an edge.

"Nothing. He told me that everything was fine now, and calm. Apparently, the townspeople are going to get together and buy an airline ticket for Lucretia—and send her to America to be with her sons," Clay said.

"That's a wonderful idea," Stephanie said. "Here . . . she would be forced to remember her daughter every single day."

"Well," Liz said, "we've decided that we'd take the day and go out and see the dig."

"Really? Aren't you two exhausted? We heard that the partying went on very late here," Grant said. "And Clay—you were out there the other day."

"I came out—but that was when you found Maria. It wasn't a good time at all to see what has been uncovered," Clay reminded him.

"That's right. You were there," Grant said.

He wasn't quite rude, but close.

"Well, I'm anxious to get out there," Liz said, trying to put a light note into the conversation.

"You're not exhausted? You didn't have a late night?" Grant was more courteous when he spoke to Liz. He might dislike Clay, but there was no reason at all not to like Liz.

"There was some partying, yes. We weren't part of it. And Grant, everyone walked someone to their cottage, just as they were supposed to do!" Liz said. "So, what are you two up to?"

"We're going to the dig, too," Stephanie said.

"We can go together," Liz said, as if pleasantly surprised that they'd planned the same day.

"Great," Stephanie said.

"Well, we were going to head out right after brunch," Grant said. He didn't want to be accompanied by the pair, Stephanie realized.

Too bad. She was pleased to have the company.

"That will work fine for us," Clay assured her.

"Great. I'm going to get more eggs first," Stephanie said. "Grant, if the waiter comes by, could you ask for more coffee, please."

It was while she was standing at the omelette station that she saw Clay at the next table, helping himself to bacon. She frowned, thinking there was something wrong, but not sure what it was.

Then she knew.

He was in a sleeveless shirt. She saw his arms. Both arms. Neither showed the least bit of irritation. They just looked tanned, sleek, and well-muscled.

That was amazing. Just the other day, when they'd dragged the boy from the surf, he had looked as if he'd suffered third-degree burns!

And now . . .

There was nothing. Nothing at all. It appeared as if he had never suffered the least injury to his flesh.

Chapter 11

Clay Barton turned, aware she was staring at him.

She flushed. "Sorry. I can't believe the way your arm healed!" she told him.

"Oh, that!" he said. "I told you—it was just an irritation. Rises, and goes back down. That's all."

"That's all! Medical science would surely pay you a bundle. I've never seen anyone heal like that."

"That's because what you saw looked a whole lot worse than it was," he assured her. He pointed behind the table where the chef was working.

"What I saw was bad! And actually, I was not a particularly good director, come to think of it. I should have asked how you were doing, but I honestly forgot. You've been wearing longsleeved shirts."

"Stephanie, I told you that I'd be fine. I am. Hey, your omelette is ready."

"Oh! Thanks!" She turned back, and thanked the man who had cooked her omelette. But even as she accepted it, she marveled that it seemed impossible that he could have healed so completely in such a short period of time.

As they walked back to the table, she saw that Grant was watching her with dark, pensive eyes. He had been watching the conversation. She had no intention of telling him what it had been about. It would only add to his hostility against Clay.

As they sat, Liz smiled at Stephanie. "I was just telling Grant how anxious I've been to get out to the dig. And I haven't had a chance to go. Now, it will really be a lot nicer—Grant will be almost like having an expert guide."

"I'm not an expert at all," Grant protested.

"He has a keen interest in archeology and ancient cultures," Stephanie said. She shrugged. "Carlo said you were quite an asset," she reminded.

"Anyone who sat there for hours dusting bones with a paint brush would be considered an asset," Grant said. "But Carlo will be there," he told Liz, "and he is an expert."

Suzette came in then, sitting down with just a cup of coffee. She looked exhausted.

"Hey," she said.

"Good morning," Stephanie said.

Suzette groaned and leaned her head on the table. "No, it's not a good morning," she assured them.

"Too much partying, hum?" Liz said sympathetically.

Suzette shrugged. "I didn't realize it, but I guess so. Thank God that it's a day off!"

"We're going out to the dig," Stephanie told her. "Do you want to come?"

Suzette grimaced ruefully. "I want to drown in this coffee right now. I'm going to try food, and see if that improves anything. Then I'm going to spend the day on the beach. I'll get Lena back out with me, hopefully. I tried knocking on both Doug's door and Drew's. Neither one of them stumbled down to answer. And they're not in here, so . . . besides, I've been to the dig. The only thing I saw there of real interest was Grant, and turns out the two of you are . . . old friends. *C'est la vie*! Anyway, I'm too dragged out this morning to get in a car and drive anywhere." She shook her head and her eyes widened. "I wouldn't even want to go shopping today!"

Clay touched her forehead, causing Suzette to turn and gaze at him strangely. "You don't think you've caught a bit of Lena's flu, do you?"

"I've no idea. But I think a day of doing nothing but lying in the sun is going to help. Have a good time, though."

"We were just going to leave," Stephanie said. "Want us to wait until you've had breakfast?"

"No, no, I'm fine here. Besides, the boys will appear eventually. Go, have a great day. Damn, I really didn't know I drank so much!"

"Dreams keeping you awake?" Clay asked.

It was such a casual question. But so right on the mark, Stephanie saw, as Suzette lowered her head and flushed.

"Too much of a good thing. Sorry, Steph, but boy, you have a cast full of kids! We were like a college group last night, celebrating graduation or something. Please, all of you, get going. My coffee cup and I are going to bond."

"Want some toast or something?" Grant asked her.

"You know, that would be great," Suzette said.

He left the table and brought her back a plate of toast. She smiled her thanks, then said, "Go, please! You're making me feel guilty."

"We'll be back by dark," Clay said.

Stephanie wasn't sure why, but his words sounded ominous. She rose along with the others and they exited by the front.

"Shall I drive?" Clay suggested.

"We'll take mine," Grant said.

Yep, he even feels he has to drive! Stephanie thought.

But he continued with, "I've driven out there almost every day. I can probably get us out there the fastest."

That made sense. *She still had the feeling that Grant wasn't about to let Clay have control in any way.*

"Great," Clay said.

Grant had rented a Jeep. They piled into it, and started out of town.

Suzette had been on the beach for nearly an hour by the time Drew showed up.

She knew that someone was standing over her, because she was suddenly shaded from the sun. Opening her eyes and moving her sunglasses down her nose, she saw Drew.

"So, look what the cat dragged in—or out, as the case may be," she said.

He grunted, threw down a towel, and took a seat next to her. "Damn, I feel like hell—mouth like a trash can," he said.

"It was too much, huh?" Suzette said.

"Well, it was worth it, though, huh? What a night. I felt on top of the world."

"So did I. I think I passed out, though. The minute I walked in the cottage."

"Yeah . . . I woke up on the floor," Drew admitted. He was quiet a few minutes. "Had a crazy dream, though."

"Oh?" Suzette said, her interest seriously piqued.

"Yeah . . ."

"Oh, come on, Drew! Tell me about it."

"Well, I *think* it was a dream. Or a fantasy brought on by an alcoholic stupor."

"Drew, really, you can tell me," Suzette said. "Oh, come on, please. If you can't tell me . . . we've gotten to be good friends, haven't we?"

He shrugged. "All right. I dreamed that Gema was here, that she came to my door, and wanted to have hot, wild sex with me."

"With you!" Suzette exclaimed.

"Hey," he said, hurt. "I thought we agreed the other day that I was cute. Adorable."

"Drew, you *are* adorable," Suzette assured him quickly. "It's just that . . . you're talking about Gema. And she didn't like anything about any of us. Neither Lena nor I was worldly or sophisticated, and she could understand how *we* were willing to play a two-bit town. And she made it rather clear that she didn't think that either you or Doug was . . . was . . . sexy enough for her. Sorry—that's not a personal opinion, it's just the way Gema was with us."

"Yeah, it was a bizarre dream, huh?"

"Did you have sex with her—in the dream?" Suzette asked.

Drew grinned. "No, I was so cool, you would have loved it. I told her where to get off."

"You know . . ." Suzette began.

"What?"

"It's just funny. Really strange."

"What's funny?"

They both looked up. Doug had come out. He, too, was wearing sunglasses. He had on a long-sleeved shirt. It wasn't buttoned, but he was holding it closed.

He looked the worst of the three of them, Suzette decided.

Drew let out a long sigh. "Suzette is putting me in a sane frame of mind."

"Oh? How?" Doug sat down at the end of Drew's towel.

"She's reminding me that Gema just about thought I was a red-headed eunuch."

"Gema?" Doug said.

Drew let out a dry laugh. "I had a liquor-enhanced fantasy dream that Gema came to my door and nearly ripped her clothes off, just trying to get in. But I told her . . . well, I think I basically told her she was a bitch and we didn't want to see her. I didn't let her get past my front door. Weird, huh?"

Doug flushed. Odd—he looked red, because he had looked so pale. "Weird—you bet, weird."

"Thanks—so you think she'd as soon sleep with a spitting camel as me, too, huh?"

Doug shook his head. "I had the same dream—only I did let her in the front door."

"What?" Suzette exploded.

"Well, she didn't come to the front door," Doug explained.

"She fell down from heaven?" Drew said sarcastically.

But Doug didn't smile or laugh. "She came to my back doors . . . you know, the loft glass doors." His color deepened. "The next thing I knew . . ." He glanced at Suzette, then shrugged again. "She was in my boxers."

"Wow," Drew murmured. "I wonder which was the bigger fantasy—me kicking her out, or you actually getting it on with her!"

"It wasn't a good dream," Doug murmured. "It was weird, and I woke up feeling . . . weird. Headache. Like I hadn't slept at all, and I was . . ."

"You were what?" Suzette demanded, nearly pouncing on him.

"Nothing. Forget I said that," Doug said quickly.

"I will *not* forget!"

"Suzette, I'm not about to say—"

"Listen," she said, "and maybe this will make you feel better. I've been having these really, really weird sexual fantasy things going on here, too. I dream about this guy . . . and in the dream, I know him, know I shouldn't be fooling around with him, but he looks at me, and does things to me and . . . they're like the most erotic things ever. When I wake up, it's like it happened, but I can't remember who I was meeting . . . or who came to the door, or just appeared, or whatever. I keep thinking the guy is Italian, but maybe he's not. So . . . dammit, Doug, what?"

"I woke up with my boxers knotted around my ankles," he said.

Drew burst out laughing.

"Hey!" Doug protested in a growing fury. "Like you really would have thrown Gema out—no matter what a bitch she might be—if she'd gotten that close to you. A piece of ass is a piece of ass, right?"

"Doug!" Suzette said primly.

"Sorry, we're talking about Gema. Who *is* a bitch. And would sleep with the right guy to get ahead. She might have invented the damn casting couch," Doug said. "I said it from the beginning. The whole thing was . . . weird!"

"Um, well, it gets weirder," Suzette said. They both stared at her. "I could have sworn that Gema was here last night."

"What?" Drew said hoarsely.

"I didn't talk to her or anything, and I could have been wrong. I was on stage, looking toward the rear of the café. I thought I saw her, standing at the doorway between the café door and the little hallway into the lobby of the resort. I told Stephanie, but she never met Gema, so even if she'd still been there, Stephanie couldn't have said, hell, yes, that's Gema."

Drew looked at Doug. "Do you think she could have really been here?"

Doug shook his head. "No . . . when I woke up, it was all too vague. It was a dream. It had to have been!"

"How the hell did we both have the same dream?" Drew demanded.

"Well, we didn't. You threw her out, I had sex," Doug reminded him.

"But what if she *was* here?" Suzette mused.

"Then Doug definitely had a better night with her than I did," Drew said. "Hell, and I was laughing at you, Doug."

Doug stared out at the water, not smiling. He shuddered, almost imperceptibly. "No . . . there was something . . . not right about it."

"What the hell do you think all this means?" Suzette asked. "You both dreaming about Gema—and she couldn't have been here. We didn't see her after the show. Arturo didn't see her—he would have mentioned it. But you both dream about sex with her—"

"Hot, wet, steamy, luscious sex," Doug corrected lightly.

"Okay, okay, don't get carried away," Suzette said. "While I have these fantasies about a passionate Adonis who . . . I don't know how he gets there, either, but he's in my room. Anyway, a good doctor would probably have a heyday with us. What do you think it means?"

Doug and Drew looked at one another, and suddenly grinned.

"What?" Suzette demanded.

"Shall I?" Drew asked Doug.

"Yep, you go ahead."

Drew stared at Suzette. "It means we're sex-starved. We're wonderful, healthy adults with raging sex drives, and they're sadly going to waste. It means, Suzette, that you need to invite us over—both of us. One at a time—we don't need to get kinky or anything."

She stared at him, and realized he was teasing her. She managed a smile. Then she got the cap off her water bottle and squirted him with it.

"Hey!"

"Weird. You two are weird, all right! In your dreams!" she said.

But then, they all stared at one another.

It was all in their dreams.

* * *

"The earthquake, of course, was documented," Carlo said, walking with Stephanie, Grant, Clay, and Liz around the expanse of the site. "The names of the Norman lords are documented, along with the battles they fought, and so on and so on. This was like a jumping-off place for the Holy Lands, so it was natural that tremendous forces came through here. As a matter of fact, to this day, you'll find that there are a number of French surnames here along with the Italian. A few English, a few Spanish . . . but then, of course, most of the English nobility was actually Norman, or French, so those rather combine. We know that there was a Norman lord named Conan de Burgh. We know he had conquered vast lands, and that the people hailed him as something of a hero—apparently, the conquering lord was better than the one they'd been born to serve. We know as well, it's documented, that François de Venue—a half cousin, or illegitimate brother or cousin—of the king of France came here as well. There was tremendous friction between them. De Burgh had finished with his battles and wanted to settle down to a life of prosperity. Nominally, he still served his king in France. De Venue apparently thought that de Burgh owed him homage. This we know through historical documentation. That they were both killed when the earthquake struck is assumed because their names disappear from the historic logs. The legends that abound are sheer romance, and yet, this dig may well prove that there was a lot of fact to the tales. An earthquake buried them all, and an earthquake is bringing them all back to light."

"Fascinating!" Liz said.

"I agree. We've been stopped for the last few days, but as you can see—" He pointed. There were a number of different areas roped off low to the ground with differently colored ties, all indicating something to the archeologists, Stephanie was certain. People were working away in their little plots and areas. Some had apparatuses that looked like giant sifters—the type of equipment someone might have if they were panning for gold out West.

Some had small hoes or tiny, trowel-like shovels. And some had brushes. Small brushes.

"As you can see," Carlo Ponti continued, "we are back to work."

Despite his poorly masked antipathy for Clay, Grant changed at the site. Clay asked questions. Grant did love this work. He answered when he could.

Clay looked up at the cliffs that rose above the site.

"The final battle took place just above, then?" he queried.

"There, up above. The fighting was here, and all around," Carlo told him. "Sometimes, it's hard to piece together exactly what happened, because the earth has shifted several times. The fighting was here. Conan de Burgh had a fortress just east and south of where the club is now—he would have ridden from there. François de Venue was inland. These cliffs are riddled with caves, so it's likely he kept arms, perhaps hid spies, and used some of the labyrinth within for various purposes. The orders from the king of France were for the men to divide the area. Most historians believe that de Venue never intended to obey such an order. He meant to dominate Conan de Burgh and seize control of the entire area. Since they clashed here, it's likely that was the case. Since de Burgh did put down the attack before dying himself, the status of the people here was maintained. The cliffs have been used for every war and insurrection since, naturally."

"So, have you gotten into the cliffs yet?" Clay asked.

"No, we have found such a rich field here, where the armies fought, we have worked hard to find all we can before the earth decides to shift again," Carlo said. "Eventually, we will get into the caves. But for now . . . it's slow work. Very tedious. Grant can tell you. And as for me, I am most anxious to find the body of Conan de Burgh, and we believe we are close. Naturally, we are also searching for the remains of de Venue—and his Valeria." He grimaced. "So far, we've found nothing to suggest the remains of 'demon' dogs—or even hunting dogs. But we imagine that de Venue must have had a pack of some kind of very vicious hounds that ran with his army. There were no automatic rifles then, so . . . imagine the damage that dogs, trained to kill, might have done."

"Imagine," Clay murmured.

"Well," Carlo said, "please, there is a lot to see here, really, even beyond the actual ground, where, you will note, it is slow work. Grant is well aware of this. The scenery here is quite beautiful. Wander as you wish—areas where the integrity of the find are being preserved are clearly marked, but if you walk along the heights and look down, you can imagine the forces coming together. Be careful if you climb around any of the cliffs—the many earthquakes here leave areas that are not secure. But, please, enjoy. The campsite is there . . . chat with the workers, have water or coffee if you like. I'm afraid there is no refreshment stand as yet."

They thanked him.

"Grant, may I have a moment? I wanted to ask you a few questions about your work the other day," Carlo said.

"Certainly," Grant told him. Then he glanced at Stephanie. "Maybe later—"

"Don't be ridiculous!" Stephanie said. "I'm fine, I love it here. I feel encapsulated by beauty and history. The afternoon is gorgeous."

"He won't be long," Carlo assured her.

"Don't worry, we'll be fine," Stephanie told him.

"Stephanie," Grant began.

"I'll be here, right here."

"We'll just wander around, exploring," Liz said.

"Stephanie . . . you can wander with Liz and Clay," Grant told her. She had the feeling that he didn't actually want her to do that.

"I'm fine—just go!"

Grant nodded, and left with Carlo, the two heading for the campsite where a number of tents had been set up.

"I think I'd love to see the area from that little plateau, just up the hill," Clay said.

"You two go ahead," Stephanie told him. "I'll wait."

"You sure? You probably shouldn't be alone in this area," Liz said. "The ground could be unsteady."

"I don't think it's just going to open up and suck me in," Stephanie said. "I'll just wait for Grant, honestly. You two go ahead."

Clay pointed to the rise about a hundred feet from them. It appeared that there was a trail that wove through the trees and foliage to a small plateau overlooking the immediate area. "We're going that way. If you need us, just give a call."

"I'll be fine," Stephanie assured them.

She watched as they started for the trail, and found herself wondering just what the relationship was between the two. They were obviously close, but—in front of others, at least, they were never demonstrative or intimate in any way.

There was a log near the area where cords and little numbered cards indicated little work areas. She sat and stared at them, and wondered what the numbers indicated.

It was beautiful here. The entire landscape of this part of Italy was stunning. Far below them now, the water shimmered in the dying sun with a beautiful array of colors. In the distance, she could see the rise of cities and towns on different cliffs; they were very old, for the most part, the majority having been built right into the mountainous terrain through the centuries in which European knights were making their way south to fight the Crusades. The medieval enchantment was picture-postcard perfect, and she reflected that the area should become a great destination for visitors, especially art students and those who simply loved the authenticity of the glorious places that did remain.

The afternoon was waning; she hadn't realized they had spent so much time with Carlo. Maybe it had taken them longer to get out here than she had thought, too.

She sank down to the ground in front of the log, leaning against it. The sky was lovely. She lay her head back against the log, felt the air sweeping around her. Her eyes closed. She couldn't believe it, but it was really so gorgeous and lulling . . . she was tempted to doze off while she waited. Even the log seemed to be making the most wonderful pillow.

The air . . .

The air here was so good. She'd felt it that first night she had come. As if there was something magic in the very breeze.

Magic . . .

Mesmerizing.

With her eyes closed, she felt the sweetest sense of lightness, as if the very ground offered a sense of warmth and security.

It was just the breeze. And her own weariness.

And there was no reason not to nod off . . .

They had come to the plateau.

Liz stood some distance back, watching.

Clay stood at the edge of the remaining ground, and Liz suddenly found herself imagining the scene that legend had passed down—a beautiful woman, on her knees, her executioner ready, her lover fighting to reach her . . .

And then fate, or nature, stepping in. The earth rumbling, and the ground disintegrating beneath them. Casting them all to their deaths.

Or had they all died?

Clay was tense, eyes closed, teeth grating. Tension gripped the length of him.

"Here . . . God, yes, the center is here . . . there is so much that I feel . . . and can't quite touch!" he said in frustration.

"There is a difference here," she murmured.

He turned and looked at her, eyes vividly red-gold at that moment.

"It's Stephanie," he said.

"But we don't know enough!" she protested.

"It's her. And I've waited too long," he said.

"No . . . it's too soon," Liz protested.

"No. The time has come."

Stephanie awoke with a start.

Looking toward the hill and plateau, she saw no sign of Clay and Liz.

She glanced toward the area of the encampment, but saw no sign of Grant, either. She stretched, wondering if she shouldn't just head toward the tents and find him.

She realized then that she wasn't really growing restless. She liked being where she was. There was a very gentle breeze that day. The streaks of color in the sky as the sun began to settle in the west were magnificent. The nap had been deliciously refreshing.

She surveyed her surroundings again.

The ground around her had been well trampled, and she noted the spot where Maria Britto's body had been found.

By Grant.

Near it, there were other areas where bodies had been discovered. Some had been taken away. Some remained, shielded by tarps and the plastic cords that designated a find. Most of the bodies found had been reduced to bone, but some had yielded scraps of clothing, remnants of weapons, and, something that had deeply excited Carlo—an almost perfect pair of leather shoes circa the late eleventh century.

Bodies . . . bones . . .

It was growing dark.

She had an absurd vision of the bones suddenly rising from the graves, coming together, and staring at her from empty eye sockets.

She stood suddenly, having unnerved herself.

Still, she managed to laugh as she did so. Her vision hadn't really been all that terrifying; rather like a remake of Ray Harryhausen special effects; she saw Jason and the Argonauts battling the bones as they pursued their way through Greek myth.

And still . . .

She decided that it was time to find Grant.

She started along the path, then paused, certain that she'd heard her name being called.

"Stephanie!"

"Grant?" It was his voice, wasn't it?

But there was no reply.

"Stephanie!"

The voice was slightly different.

She turned around. "Liz? Clay? Are you two around here somewhere?"

Stephanie . . . Steph . . . Stephanie. Where are you?

Puzzled, she stood her ground for several minutes. She looked toward the encampment, and then toward the trail where Liz and Clay had gone. Once again, she was certain that it was Grant's voice.

"Just head to the encampment," she told herself aloud, irritated.

But she felt the overwhelming desire to go the other way. Maybe one of them was in trouble.

Stephanie!

The last sounded like a weak and desperate cry of pain.

Was someone hurt, or was she imagining it?

There was still just a bit of light remaining.

She wasn't frightened. There were actually many people in the vicinity—the camp was not far away at all.

Tempted, she started toward the trail.

"There is always a balancing act between the needs of the living, the present, and the discovery and preservation of history," Carlo said. He was deeply pleased, showing Grant a muddied piece of metal that meant nothing to him. "Much work was destroyed as well as delayed when the police were here, but . . . then there was this!"

Grant wanted to be as impressed and pleased as Carlo apparently wanted him to be. He nodded, looking at Carlo, waiting.

"This is a boot buckle!" Carlo told him.

"That's great."

"Not just any boot buckle."

"No, of course not. It's a medieval boot buckle, right?"

Carlo nodded, tenderly holding the piece. "Look . . . here. That is the coat of arms of the king of France, and there, beneath, the arms of François de Venue! Believe it or not, the police unearthed this gem for me in their search for clues to the circumstances of Maria's death and burial."

"It's a fine discovery," Grant said.

"It is your work area," Carlo murmured. "I realize that events here have been disturbing, to say the least, and, of course, now you are involved with the theater. But hopefully, you will continue to work with us, and it's important that you realize just how dear every little discovery is. This means that François de Venue was definitely fighting right in this very area, and if he was killed, his remains must be very near."

"He was killed in the battle, wasn't he?" Grant asked.

"That is the assumption, yes. He, Valeria, and Conan de Burgh were all reported to have died that day. They disappear from history, that much is certain, and de Burgh was hailed as a hero by the locals, who apparently went on to live for years in peace and prosperity. So far, we have found little proof of the fact that these men indeed came to great blows right here. And we have found many bones. But, ah! If we could just find the remains of the key players, then, what triumph!"

Carlo's eyes glowed.

"Well, you've just begun. I'm sure you'll find what you're seeking."

"Um, yes, well, you're right. We've only just begun. The excavations here could go on for years, and, of course, I know you haven't that kind of time, but your work is deeply appreciated. I know as well, of course, where your true vocation lies."

Something about the way Carlo spoke was disturbing, but Grant wasn't sure why. He should have understood the man's passion. He knew what it was to have a feeling for a line of work that was a dedication and desire, far more than just a job.

"I do intend to spend my time working here as well," Grant said.

Carlo nodded then, apparently pleased. "Well, I have kept you from your friends far too long. You'll forgive me for not including them—you have been a part of this, they have not. And we are scholars here, of course, determined to give our finds to the world. Every now and then, however, we have moments of selfishness and pride!"

"Of course. And thank you. I am honored to be working here," Grant assured him. "If you'll excuse me, though . . . I've been away some time now."

"Certainly!"

With a smile and a wave, Grant started back down the

trail to where he had left Stephanie. When he reached the site, he wasn't alarmed at first when he didn't see her.

"Steph?" he called her name, but there was no answer.

He looked around, and the first unease filled him. It was growing dark.

He could see the trail up the little cliff that led to the precipice and decided she must have gone that way—though it occurred to him there were many places she might be. But he had to start somewhere.

He started up the trail. It was steep in a few places, but not dangerously so.

"Stephanie!" He called her name, waited, and heard nothing.

He quickened his pace, and was panting when he reached the top.

Stepping out, he saw that there was a spectacular view of the region. Great castles and walled cities could be seen from here, and at this distance, the ruin wasn't visible as it would be up close. From here, he might have entered a different world.

Then, as he stood there, he experienced the oddest sensation.

He'd been here before.

He'd climbed the trail . . .

He'd felt a terrible sense of urgency, and he'd come here, and . . .

The wind picked up. It whispered first, then whistled. It wasn't that strong, he tried to tell himself, and yet . . .

It even seemed to be screaming.

"Stephanie!" He shouted her name in growing panic.

The light was beginning to fade in earnest.

He needed to hurry, to find her. And yet . . .

For a minute, he couldn't force himself to move. The sense of *déjà-vu* was more than he could stand. *Ass, you've been working in the area!* he reminded himself.

And yet . . .

It took the most ridiculous effort to fight the urge to stay, to turn away and start down again. Fear suddenly fueled anger.

Where the hell had she gone?

Stephanie realized that she should have been growing a bit uneasy.

She thought she had taken the trail upward—but at some point, her trek had taken her down again. She had left the area where trees and foliage surrounded the path. The terrain was growing rockier. The cliff had become rugged stone, rising almost straight to the sky.

"Liz? Clay?" she called.

Against the rock, it seemed that the wind was stronger.

She swore softly, turned around, walked what she thought was the way she had come, and encountered only more rock and cliff.

"Grant!" she shouted, and waited.

The last sun slipped out of the sky, and she was surrounded by darkness. Too bad she wasn't home, she told herself. Her key chain had an alarm, and a flashlight.

But she wasn't home. She was in the hills in Italy, and like an idiot, she had wandered off alone.

There was a moon out, providing a touch of light, but . . .

What if she just kept wandering, endlessly? What if she couldn't find her way back? She didn't know the area to begin with, and now, in the dark . . .

She wasn't going to panic, she assured herself. She wouldn't starve, and she wouldn't even die of dehydration. Even if she had to just stop and sit here, eventually, someone would come for her. Grant would never just leave her.

And even if he did, Clay and Liz were here.

That thought shamed her; Grant would never leave her.

Grant was very strange these days.

Carlo Ponti even knew that she was here! And if Grant was so strange, dangerously strange, her intuition would have warned her by now. She was still sleeping with him!

But that might be because . . .

There was something about him. She couldn't resist him . . . there was a raw sensuality there, sometimes, it was as if she couldn't refuse, as if he awakened something in her almost like a blood lust. She was desperate . . .

She was desperate all right! Where the hell was she?

"**Don't** panic!" she said aloud. Then she decided one way **not to panic** was to avoid talking to herself.

She would be fine, she assured herself.

All she had to do was sit and wait.

Wait . . .

Right.

Had Maria Britto come here? Had she been waiting for a lover **when** the . . . animals, the wild dogs, whatever . . . had come upon her?

"Oh, God!"

She was talking to herself aloud again.

"That's because I am going to panic!" she said.

Maria Britto . . . Lord! First, attacked by savage animals. *Chewed*, Grant had said.

And then . . .

Her own mother had attacked her coffin to sever her head.

"Sweet Jesu, don't think about that!" she commanded herself. *If you do, in just a few minutes, you'll be tearing your hair out and jumping off a cliff like a madwoman!*

Then, she saw a light. It was ahead, somewhere in the rock.

A light in the rocks?

Maybe they were there, searching for her.

Searching for her in the rocks?

Why not? Trails, darkness, light, voices . . . all were de-

ceptive out here! It had to be help, people coming for her, looking for her.

The thought was steadying.

And then, once again, she thought she heard her name. A whisper, a call on the wind. They would be looking for her, of course. Maybe they had gotten ahead of her—or maybe they were behind her, she was so turned around.

Head for the light. What else was there to do?

It was the logical thing to do.

And yet . . .

Even as she walked, using logic, she thought it strange again. It was almost as if she was compelled to come this way.

He waited. Yes! This was it, the moment . . .

Stretching out, he could feel her, coming to him.

The aches, the hungers, the bitterness, the loathing, the waiting, the hatred . . . oh, yes, the hatred, simmering, waiting . . .

The time had come.

They would all be made to pay.

Even that knowledge made his sense of power increase and soar; his day had brought greater strength, but now . . . he felt invincible.

Immortal.

Closer . . .

Closer still.

She was coming.

And he would have what he wanted, the fulfillment that no other subject of hunger and lust had provided; he would have vengeance, and the taste of it was already so sweet upon his lips.

This way . . .

Yes. She was coming.

* * *

Great. If it hadn't already been dark and windy, there was a fog rising. Stephanie swore again at her own stupidity.

The way the wind rose, she was certain that there wasn't going to be just fog; pretty soon, she wouldn't have to worry so much about that because it was going to rain.

She stood still. It was growing very chilly. It might be beautiful and balmy down by the beach, but here, once the wind picked up, it was more than cold. It was nippy. She felt as if little trickles of ice water were suddenly slipping down the length of her spine.

She couldn't see in front of her.

And still, ahead . . . seeming to come from the very rocks, was that light. They were close, she was certain.

They had to be looking for her! Surely, certainly. They would know by now that she was lost. It had been a long time, though just how long, she didn't know.

The wind blew with a mighty howl.

A bolt of lightning suddenly slashed across the sky. For a moment, she could see.

Clearly.

And she stopped dead, thinking that she had lost her mind.

Grant was ahead of her, far ahead on the trail, and it seemed that he was framed by the rock.

He was naked.

Impossibly tall, shoulders gleaming and bronzed, nuance and shadow of sleek muscle sculpture so apparent, everything about him . . .

Animalistic.

Raw.

Carnal . . .

In the dark, in the mist, he was coming toward her. His eyes smouldered with a sensuality like nothing she had ever seen before. What they did to her . . . her limbs were molten, as if he had somehow transmitted that sense of heat to her.

Nothing in the world seemed so important as reaching him.

A voice warned her there was something wrong with the vision.

But there was something so powerful about it as well. Light and fire seemed to radiate from him, sweeping across the space between them. Limb and muscles, flesh and bone, face and stance, were all so overwhelmingly compelling that she could do nothing but walk forward, yearning to reach him . . .

To touch him.

To be touched.

It was as if her very blood boiled, and the beat of his hunger pounded within her own mind.

"Yes, I'm coming!" she cried.

She wasn't crazy at all. This was what she was supposed to be doing—it was the most natural thing in the world.

And heedless of the rock, the terrain, the darkness, and the fog, she began to move forward, bidden by the light.

She didn't think at all.

She was called.

And so she came.

Chapter 12

It had gotten dark.

Doug had come in from the beach an hour earlier; it had been good, being out there with Drew and Suzette. Lena had appeared for a while as well, but she had been scratching her neck, and she hadn't seemed really comfortable.

"I am feeling better," she'd assured them. But the sun had bothered her, so she had gone in.

The sun had bothered him that day, too. But he had felt safe with the others.

Odd, he hadn't realized that he hadn't felt safe alone.

Finally, though, he'd felt that he needed a shower, so he had rinsed off a long, long time, towel-dried, and flopped down on his bed, feeling a total lack of energy.

He had appreciated the BBC, but felt then as if there was really nothing to watch on television.

The news just never seemed to get any better.

They were due to meet for dinner, but not for another hour or so. He was clean, he was presentable. He was ready.

Doug flicked the channels. There was an Italian game

show on with lovely, scantily clad girls. He watched it for a few minutes, then switched the channel.

He wished that he had more energy. He just didn't. Maybe a nap wouldn't be a bad thing.

His lashes fell, then rose, then fell, then rose.

He jerked, flicked the channel changer again.

He came back to the Italian game show. Now, the girls were topless. They were playing some kind of strip poker. Men in tuxedos were egging them on.

He realized that his eyes were glued to the television.

Somebody apparently made some kind of a bet. A giant card was played, and one girl lost. She let out a little cry and everyone laughed, and so she walked out on the stage in high heels and a teeny-weeny thong. Turning her backside to the camera, she made an art form of removing the thong.

He saw that another woman was walking toward her. At first, he saw only the back of the other woman. She, too, was in heels and a thong. She walked right up against the back-side of the blonde and began stroking her. The blonde turned and the two began to caress one another.

"One hell of a game show!" he muttered out loud.

Then the woman with the blonde turned, and Doug jerked up, staring at the television.

It was Gema.

And suddenly, she was talking to him from the television screen.

"Hi, Doug. Come on in . . . you know you like it. You know you want it."

His jaw dropped. So Gema had . . .

Well, achieved some kind of stardom. Even if it was on an Italian porn game show.

Should they really be showing this stuff? Kids could be watching.

"Doug! Pay attention," Gema called with a pout.

He did. And she and her partner began doing things . . .

Gema, her hands still all over the other woman, turned to him. "You let me in once, Dougie. Come on . . . give me a nice, sweet, wet welcome!"

He was dreaming again, he realized. He needed to wake up.

Why wake up?

It was the most action he'd had in ages.

"Hey, baby, let the dreams begin!" he told Gema.

Suddenly, she was there with him. Just as she had been on the television. Breasts . . . purely global. And that outfit . . . stiletto heels, tiny lace thong . . .

"Doug . . . I am just so hungry for you!"

"Come and eat me up then," he responded.

"Oh, I intend to," she whispered.

Once again, she was stalking him. *Bring it on.* He lay with his hands laced behind his head, a grin of pure, unadulterated pleasure splitting his features from ear to ear.

She came to him, paused near his feet, then lifted one long leg onto the bed, giving him a magnificent view.

A second long leg came up. She stood over him.

Then she dropped down, agile as a contortionist, spread-eagle over his hips.

Pure glory raced through him. She shook her hair teasingly over him as she lowered her face to his chest, kissing and nipping at the flesh. She inched against him, undulating like a pole dancer. Her lips found his while her hands zoned in, low on his body, gloving him, leading him deep into the heat of her body.

Her lips . . . slid. Her hips moved.

He felt like an eighteen-year-old on a roller-coaster ride. She moved like a riveter, and it worked—Lord, yes, it worked—it was flying faster than an SST, and he was exploding like a teenybopper and he felt the magic work through his muscles, he felt it . . .

A prick . . .

Not even pain.

Then he heard it.

A slurping sound. Slow and sensual as all else, and . . .

"You're delicious, Doug," she whispered, "and tonight, we've got all night. There's no one here to stop me."

She giggled.

"I can eat and eat and eat and eat and eat until . . . you die!"

"Stephanie!"

"Steph!"

"Stop!"

Stephanie jerked, as if she had just awakened. Something . . .

A noise.

Voices.

She wasn't sure who was shouting, or why.

She didn't even know what she had been doing, but it suddenly seemed as if there was a cacophony of voices coming at her, calling her name.

She blinked furiously, and she was terrified, because she didn't know what she was doing, or where she was going.

And she suddenly found herself on an outcropping surrounding a cliff. There was barely room for her feet. A frigging goat might have had a problem getting where she was.

"Stephanie, careful! Stay where you are."

Grant's voice. She blinked, oddly thinking that it was Grant who had gotten her here. She felt a surge of anger against him.

"Stephanie . . . stay still. He's coming!" Another voice, female . . . it was Liz.

There was no rain, and no lightning, but the ground fog had risen. Through it, to her right, she could see Grant hugging the cliff side, making his way to her.

She swallowed and turned. Clay Barton was coming from the other direction. She tried to look behind her.

There was a sheer drop.

Fingers touched her. They were cold as ice. She had a vision again, bones rising from the ground, touching her with an icy blast. She nearly screamed.

"Steph, it's me—don't jerk away!"

Grant had reached her. He sounded angry, but as if he were trying to control the emotion in his voice. "Take my hand—walk with me."

She balked.

"Steph!"

She swallowed hard, recent memory cascading down upon her. This couldn't be Grant's fault. She hadn't been with him. All right, so she had been looking for him, but . . .

How the hell had she gotten here?

"I'm on your other side, Stephanie." It was Clay.

"Careful! All of you!" Liz called from down below.

"Slowly . . . the ground isn't solid," Grant warned. They were inching his way. Bit by bit. And he was right. She could feel the earth crumbling and giving way as they moved.

Her right foot slipped. She started to slide down. A scream escaped her.

Both men caught her by the arms, drawing her back up. Grant staggered backward against the cliff, crushing her to him, pressing her forward, ahead of him, then. He turned to give Clay a hand—there was no footing remaining where she had stood. With Grant's hand, Clay made a leap over the gap.

His body crushed against hers as he passed her, putting her between the two of them again. She closed her eyes, still trembling from the close call.

"It's widening . . . we're almost back on a trail again," Grant said.

She nodded. He was right. In another minute, they were

on a trail. Two minutes after that, they were on a broad plateau that slopped gently downward, back toward the area of the dig.

That was when Grant let loose.

Swinging her around before him with barely controlled rage tightening his every muscle, he very nearly barked out his words. "What the hell were you doing?"

She didn't know herself. She was shaking and afraid, and therefore, defensive. And once again, it was slipping into the corner of her mind that it was somehow all his fault.

"You *ass*! I was looking for you!"

"Against a sheer drop? What the hell did you think—that I'd become part of the rock?"

"Hey, you two," Clay said, coming behind Stephanie.

"You, dammit, get the fuck out of it!" Grant all but roared.

"Grant!" Stephanie exploded, stunned.

Liz had run up to meet them by then. She was obviously upset. "Please, all of you, stop! Let's not say things we don't mean . . . and, Lord! Let's not get violent, huh? Please?"

"Violent?" Stephanie should have kept silent, but she was still stunned by Grant's display of wrath, and his absolute rudeness and hostility toward Clay, who had risked his life for her as well!

"Actually, Liz, I wouldn't blame Clay if he slammed my very old acquaintance Mr. Peterson from here to China!" she said, staring at Grant.

"No one is decking anyone," Liz said, a prayer that it would be so in her tone. "Grant, please! You're scared because Stephanie could have been killed. You don't understand . . . it was like pea soup out here for a few minutes . . . we were all kind of wandering around like idiots. Please, all of you! Stop, think, cool down. I am begging you!"

She was right, and Stephanie knew it, and she didn't want Grant slugging Clay, or Clay slugging Grant.

She lifted a hand. "I'm sorry. Truly sorry. I feel like an idiot. I don't know how I got where I was, except . . . Liz is right. There was just . . . a fog. A mist. Something, I don't know. But I'm sorry. Really, really sorry, Grant. And both of you—you did save my life. Or, at the very least, you saved me from a broken neck and crushed bones. So I thank you both. Liz, can we get back to the car now, please?"

"Yes, yes, let's get back to the car." She slipped an arm around Stephanie's shoulders and shot a glance over her head at Clay. She sounded aggravated herself as she added, "We should never, *never* have stayed here after dark."

Neither Grant nor Clay said anything as they followed Liz and Stephanie back, so she assumed that, for the moment, neither one of them was going to cream the other.

They all reached Grant's rental car in stony silence and reclaimed the seats they'd taken for the ride in. No one spoke. Grant revved the car, and they began the drive back.

Stephanie looked out the window and shivered.

What the hell had she been doing?

Lena and Suzette were seated at the table when Drew arrived. He was a little bit late, but they had waited for him and Doug. Both women had ordered a glass of wine, but didn't seem to mind that they'd waited to order dinner.

"Hey, for a redhead, you're getting a nice tan," Lena approved.

He grimaced, taking a chair and waving to their waiter, motioning for a beer. The fellow grinned and nodded.

"Thanks. You are a kind woman, Lena, to call this rosy hue a tan. But I thank you. Maybe if I nurse it along, I can look good and buff by the time we finish our run." He frowned. "Did Doug say he was coming?"

"Oh, yes, he intends to join us," Suzette assured him.

The waiter brought Drew's beer. He drank it slowly, idly

chatting with the girls about little improvements they could make in the shows, now that they'd gotten their feet wet and had a better idea of how it would all go. "We'll have to check these ideas out with Stephanie, though," he said.

Lena waved a hand in the air. "Of course! But she loves it when people come up with ideas. I think that's why she's so good—she isn't afraid to let others have artistic opinions."

Drew shrugged. "Yeah, she's cool. She can even give up control to be able to get in a smoother flow with the rest of us as an ensemble. So . . . hey, what do you all think the story is between Liz and Clay?"

"They're sleeping together. Definitely," Suzette said sagely.

Lena arched a brow. "Hmm. I don't know. He has an interest in Stephanie."

"Well, we all have an interest in her," Suzette argued. "She's the boss."

"No, no, no, the way he watches her . . . he has an *interest* in her," Lena said.

"Ah, but there's Grant!" Suzette said.

"Um," Lena agreed.

"Did you have to make that sound as if the man were a rare filet?" Drew said, wincing.

"Sorry. There's something about him," Lena said, grinning.

"Yeah, yeah, and Clay, too, and I'm adorable. I don't know why I get into these conversations," Drew said. Then he frowned. "Doug really should have been here by now. And he didn't look so good today. I'm going to run over to his cottage, okay?"

"You're right—that sounds like a really good idea."

Drew went to Doug's and pounded on the front door. There was no answer, so he hesitated, then went around back and climbed the stairs to his friend's balcony.

The doors were open. The draperies were blowing in the breeze.

"Doug?" Drew called carefully.

There was no answer. He fought a mild struggle with the billowing drapes, and entered.

The television was on. Loud.

And there was Doug. He was collapsed beside the bed.

"Sweet Lord!" Drew cried out, reaching down quickly to feel for a pulse. His friend was cold, as cold as ice. For a moment Drew recoiled, terrified that Doug was dead. He forced himself to reach out again. At his throat, he found a pulse.

Staggering to his feet, he hurried to the phone.

It might be a small town, but the emergency response was swift. Within minutes, he heard the sound of sirens.

Arturo came to translate for him as the men asked him questions. He couldn't tell them much, just that Doug had complained of feeling weak, that he hadn't looked great that afternoon, and that he'd found him on the floor.

The girls rushed up in a panic, and Drew tried to calm them. In the end, they all—including Arturo—drove to the hospital behind the ambulance bearing Doug.

They drove for at least ten minutes in tense and painful silence before Grant spoke at last. His steely gaze caught Stephanie's in the rearview mirror. "I apologize," he said rigidly.

He didn't actually ask for forgiveness, so she didn't offer it.

"All right."

"You were in a really dangerous place!" he reminded her.

"They need more light out there. All those workers . . . they could wander at night, too," Liz said. "It's just . . . a dangerous place. Once it gets dark."

"It's an archeological dig!" Clay said. "Not an Italian theme park."

They all fell silent again.

The drive back was interminable.

And then, at last, they saw the resort ahead of them, and Grant found his parking place to the far left of the entry.

"Ah, a shower, a drink, and dinner!" Liz said. "Everything will look better then. Grant, thanks for driving. It was a fantastic place to see, and thanks to you, of course, we were given really special treatment by Carlo Ponti."

"Carlo is a nice guy. He would have given you special treatment anyway, I'm certain, but I'm glad you enjoyed seeing the excavations," Grant told her.

Clay was already out of the car. When Stephanie exited, she saw that he was standing rigidly. He certainly didn't have a forked tongue he injected into the air or anything of the like, and yet Stephanie had the notion that he was *feeling* it.

"There's something wrong," he murmured.

Grant slammed the driver's side door. "There's definitely something wrong," he muttered.

Clay ignored him, striding into the resort. He walked straight up to the receptionist's desk and began speaking to the clerk on duty in rapid Italian. The clerk spoke back excitedly. Stephanie caught Doug's name, and the word *mal* or bad, but the rest of it, she could only surmise.

"The hospital!" Grant, slightly behind her, said.

Clay turned at the same time, nodding at Grant.

Whatever hostility was still simmering between the two men, they capped it for the moment. The four of them returned to the car, and started off once again.

"What happened?" Stephanie demanded, looking back at Clay.

Clay now seemed to be as tense as Grant. "He collapsed."

"Where?"

"In his room. Alone. He was supposed to have met the others. Drew went to find him, and he'd collapsed."

"It sounds like what Lena had . . . except worse," Stephanie murmured.

"Yes, that's how it sounds," Clay said flatly.

They reached the small hospital. The one good thing about such a small town was that they had no problem parking. And when they burst into the waiting room, they immediately saw Lena, Suzette, Drew, and Arturo.

"How is he?" Stephanie asked anxiously.

"Dr. Antinella says that we got to him in the nick of time," Drew assured her. He was holding his arm at an angle, and there was a bandage on it. He saw her staring at it and quickly added, "I'm not hurt. Their blood bank is low, and they're pretty desperate. No time for the usual tests, and I'm O positive. Any of the rest of you O positive?"

"I'm AB," Stephanie said with a wince.

"I'm O positive," Grant said.

As he spoke, a harried-looking Dr. Antinella came out of the white doors that led to the ER.

"Here, here!" Drew said, indicating Grant. Antinella spoke English fluently. "O positive—you're certain?" he said to Grant.

"Yes."

"No diseases?"

"None."

"Please, come in quickly, then."

Grant disappeared with the doctor. Stephanie sat down, or rather collapsed, next to Suzette, who was shaky.

"It's all right. They'll take care of him," Stephanie said, setting her hand on Suzette's.

Suzette shook her head. "You—you should have seen him, Stephanie. He was white. Not just ashen, but *white*."

"They'll take care of him. He'll be fine."

Both Suzette and Lena stared at her. Drew coughed. "Stephanie, Lena was sick first. Suzette began to feel the same symptoms. And now . . . Doug almost died. They're scared. Hell! I'm scared. What the hell is this?"

She didn't get to answer. Clay spun around, heading for the exit.

"Where are you going?" Suzette called after him.

"My blood is worthless to Doug," he said briefly. "I think I can be of more help back at the resort."

He left, distracted, not allowing them to say more.

"He speaks Italian," Liz said, as if that explained his behavior. "I'll go with him. Maybe we can find out if there's been a . . . sickness like this before."

She followed Clay out.

There was silence in the waiting room. At last, Suzette said, "Antinella said there was no way he could take blood from Lena . . . then he said that I couldn't give, either. Arturo gave . . . and one of the nurses, and both of the young fellows who came as the emergency unit."

"He wasn't even . . . cut. Or hurt," Drew said dully.

Stephanie stood and started pacing. Doug had to be all right.

"Strange, isn't it?" Doug murmured suddenly. "It seems almost to have something to do with . . . dreams."

"Dreams?" Stephanie said, startled.

"Well, you were having some bizarre fantasies, right, Lena? When you got so sick?"

Lena flushed. "Well, I don't see how it relates."

"Neither do I, but it seems to," Drew said.

"What are you talking about?" Stephanie asked.

"Gema."

"What?"

"Gema—and, well, Lena's fantasy lover."

"I had a dream, too—then I woke up feeling as if I had no energy. I was really afraid that it was because . . . because I was . . . well, you know, tossing and turning all night, by my lonesome," Suzette murmured, not looking at them.

Drew came to Stephanie, taking her hands. "I know this makes no sense, but both Doug and I had dreams about Gema the night before. I dreamt that she showed up at my place, and I threw her out. Doug dreamed that she had hot sex with him."

Stephanie just stared at him.

"Remember, Steph, I told you that I thought I saw Gema in the audience," Suzette reminded her.

"But . . . I don't get it. How could dreams make someone ill?" Stephanie asked, shaking her head.

She'd had her own share of dreams and fantasies. But still . . .

"Maybe . . . maybe Gema is here. You think you saw her, Suzette. And both of you and Doug supposedly dreamed about her. Maybe she . . . maybe she's ill. Wandering. And carrying some kind of terrible flu with her," Stephanie said.

"Yeah, maybe," Doug said dryly.

"And why not?" Stephanie asked.

"How would that explain Lena getting so ill first—before anyone saw or imagined Gema's having returned?"

Stephanie had no logical explanation.

Grant came out through the emergency room doors, a bandage around his arm. Antinella followed him, speaking in Italian. Grant seemed to understand him, because he shook his head, giving the doctor a rueful grimace. "I don't need to lie down—I'm fine. I swear, I'm fine." He looked around. "Where are Clay and Liz? They could use another pint for Doug."

"They left," Suzette said.

"He has bad blood, or the wrong blood," Lena added.

Grant shook his head with disgust, looking annoyed again.

"He's welcome to a bunch of mine, but it won't do him any good," Stephanie said, hearing the rise in her voice.

Drew sighed. "They went back to the resort. He seemed to think he could find out something more about Doug's illness. By talking to people, I guess."

Grant let out a sound of irritation. "I'm going back—I think I'm going to try and find out a few things on my own as well."

He headed out the door. Stephanie suddenly chased after him. She caught him out in the parking lot, grabbed his arm, spinning him back around to face her.

She thought that she didn't know him. His features were taut, ferocious. She stepped back, feeling the wave of his heat and anger wash over her. She gritted her teeth, amazed that she still felt the urge to simply touch him. He was infuriating her, but he had never seemed more attractive or compelling.

"Grant, you've got to stop this," she told him.

"Stop what?"

"You're going after Clay."

"You're wrong. I'm not going after Clay."

"Well, you've got something against him that's ridiculous," she said. "And you're going to cause a terrible schism in everything, as if we're not having enough trouble with this disease, whatever this thing might be—"

"The disease is Clay."

"Grant!"

"Somehow, it is. I'm telling you."

She forced herself to step back, to shake her head. "Grant, I swear to you, I'm beginning to believe that *you're* the disease."

He was still, staring back at her. Shoulders broad and square, blue eyes nearly ebony and narrowed with tension.

"Think what you like," he said, and turned again.

"Grant!"

He paused, his back to her for several seconds. Then he spun again.

"What, Stephanie?"

"Stay in your own cottage tonight."

"I can't leave you alone."

"Oh, yes, you can. Because I'm afraid to have you with me."

He stared at her and seconds passed like heartbeats. He muttered something.

She thought it might well have been the word *bitch*.

Then he took the few steps back to her and gripped her arms. She saw the muscles twitch in his throat, the beat of his pulse against a vein. "I will never leave you alone. Never. Lock me out. You'll never be alone."

But he released her then, as if she were somehow tainted, turned and strode for his car. As she watched him go, she was shaking. Her knees were weak. She was hot, and chilled, and she was angry . . .

And she was glad.

She could force herself to behave sanely.

But she didn't feel that way at all.

She was afraid . . .

But she wanted him more than ever. She wanted him so much that . . .

Fear be damned.

She squared her shoulders, furious with herself. She'd meant it. She was locking herself into her cottage that night. Somehow, Grant was simply going to have to get a grip on his anger and emotions.

She loved him. But it was far too easy to see herself . . . a moth drawn to the flame. The way she felt was too deep, too fevered. Too desperate. As if . . . as if her emotions were even deeper than the time they'd been together, of the flesh, not of the flesh . . .

She groaned aloud, clenching her hands into fists at her side.

Then, as she stood there, it seemed that a deep, sweeping cloud came over the moon. And standing alone in the darkness outside the hospital, she felt vulnerable, as she never had before.

Stephanie . . . come!

It was the darkness, the strange shadows. She clamped her hands over her ears. She was letting her imagination play terrible tricks on her.

Stephanie . . .

She thought she heard throaty laughter.

It was only the sound of the wind, whispering through the trees.

She turned and ran back to the hospital.

Back to the blazing light that she knew, beyond a doubt, to be real.

Because she knew, deep in her heart, that she was being called.

Called . . .

Into the darkness.

Chapter 13

He knew instantly, before he returned, that something had gone wrong, something that didn't fit the plan.

And he knew what.

He found her in his private quarters.

And it was what he'd expected.

She was like a well-fed cat, stretched out on the little love-seat, the look of absolute pleasure and satiation in her eyes. He tried to remember that she was young, that the hunger could be an overwhelming desire, but that did little to ease his temper. She was as disposable as any other; she had been useful, but she had turned that usefulness now into a situation that could destroy his careful plans.

She smiled when she saw him, and he knew she was feeling her strength and power.

"So . . . you disobeyed me," he said.

She rose, still sleek as a cat, perhaps more sinuous than ever, so aware of herself, of her new being. "Yes, I disobeyed you," she said, and she came to him, playfully teasing at his hair, sending a finger to draw a line down his cheek. "I," she *informed him, "am the same as you. And I have wants and desires as well. And the power to take what I will."*

He shook his head, calm despite the rage burning inside.

"No, no, little one, you don't understand. I have a certain protection. One that you are lacking. You will be caught."

"Caught? What would it matter? Why . . . if a big, bad wolf came after me, I would just eat him all up."

Again, he shook his head. He placed his hands on her shoulders and looked into her eyes. "There are still things beneath heaven and earth that you don't understand. Different beings, different strengths, those who live and let others live, and those who think to rule the universe for those they consider to be evil and out of control. But that doesn't really matter now. You disobeyed me."

"I am my own power," she insisted.

"I told you, I am the lord."

"I want to be my own master."

"I am the lord, and the lord giveth, and the lord taketh away."

She never knew what was happening. It was almost a pity. She should have learned some humility.

His hands moved dexterously from her shoulders to cradle her head.

Then he snapped, and twisted.

There was an odd and horrible popping sound.

Her body fell into a pile at his feet.

Time to feed the demon dogs.

Doug had been taken to a room. He slept, and seemed to do so peacefully. Machines monitored his vital signs, and an IV brought vital fluids into his body.

Arturo had gone back to the resort, but Liz had returned to the hospital, saying that she wanted to take a turn sitting at Doug's side.

Stephanie was curious that she spent so much time speaking with the doctor in Italian, but whatever she was saying, Antinella seemed to agree with her. They looked grave when they spoke.

Stephanie decided that she didn't want Liz in with Doug alone. Then she began to wonder why it seemed that she didn't trust anyone anymore. Even the doctor seemed suspicious, and that was because he was talking to Liz. Liz was suspicious because she had come to them through Clay; Clay was suspicious because Grant made her so nervous about the man, but then, there was Grant, and he was suspicious because . . . there were a million reasons. She wasn't even sure what they all were.

For the first hour they were allowed in, she and Suzette sat with Doug. He had color, Stephanie was glad to see, and Drew, coming in with Lena and Liz to spell them, seemed to be greatly relieved.

She asked Drew to follow her as she left the room.

When he was in the hallway with her, she hesitated, then told him, "Whatever happens, let's keep two people with him at all times."

He frowned. "All right," he said slowly. He kept staring at her. "You're worried about someone in particular, aren't you?"

"No . . . yes. Drew, I'm just not secure with Liz being alone with him."

He seemed really surprised. "She's one of the nicest people I've ever met," he told her.

"I know. I think so, too."

"But?"

"Drew, I'm beginning to get the feeling that none of us should be alone."

"Maybe I spooked you with that talk about dreams. I had to sound crazy, right?"

"I wish you had sounded entirely crazy," she told him.

"Maybe it is crazy. Just please don't let Doug be alone . . . especially with Liz."

"You got it, kid."

"Did you find a place to eat while we were in with Doug?" she asked him.

He nodded. "A little café right around the corner. I'm pretty sure the woman said they were open until eleven. Luckily, this is Italy, and having dinner late is natural."

"Great. Okay, Suzette and I will get some dinner, and be back."

"Are we staying here all night?" he asked her.

"You think *you* sound crazy?" she asked him. "I just think that we need to be around a while, okay? Maybe until dawn, and then we can go back and get some sleep ourselves."

Drew agreed. Stephanie went back for Suzette, and the two headed out, looking for the café. They found the place, and when they went in and sat down, the woman who was apparently cook, waitress, and owner came over. She didn't speak English, but Stephanie had learned enough to get by in a restaurant. The woman was pleasant, and took their order.

They both had a glass of wine as they waited for their food. "Do you think that . . . that Gema might be like . . . I don't know—skulking around somewhere? Perhaps really ill, and passing it on?" Suzette asked.

"I don't know. Sometimes I think we're all losing it."

"It's a miracle that Doug is alive. You should have seen him when we first got here," Suzette said.

Stephanie nodded, somewhat distracted. There was an elderly Italian man sitting with a group at the rear of the café. The five men had apparently long since finished eating, but as was often the custom here, they were sitting and talking with their cigars and brandy, drawing the evening out.

The one elderly gentleman was staring at her intently. It

was the kind of serious study that made her feel uncomfortable.

The waitress came, delivering their salads.

She said something to them that Stephanie didn't understand, but it was friendly. She finished with a cheerful, "*Mangia!*"

They thanked her.

As they ate, Stephanie told Suzette, "There's an older man back there, staring at me."

Suzette grinned. "He probably thinks you're hot stuff."

"I don't think it's that," Stephanie assured her.

"Hey, Italian men are appreciative of women. It's nice. You have to be nineteen and perfect not to feel a little flattered when a man compliments you." She paused, taking a quick glance back. "Even if he is old enough to be Methuselah."

"I really don't think he's appreciating me," Stephanie murmured.

Suzette sighed. "Oh, well, let him look. It's a free country. Okay, it's not the United States, but it's a free country. Can't stop the old boy from looking. Strange, isn't it? I just love it here so very much! I mean, I'll always be an American, but I was so delighted to realize that we were really a success here, that we could have had a very long and prosperous run! What a base! I want to go to Sicily, and so many of the wonderful little spots around here. And hey, a few days in France, Greece . . . anywhere in Europe would be easy from here. Okay, well, not so easy, since we have to get into Naples, but still . . . I had really dreamed that I could put in a couple of years here, and now . . . pray God, that this is just some flu bug! I feel better today, but I knew how Doug felt, because the other morning when I woke up . . . it was terrible. It was like being . . . drained. Can a flu make you have strange dreams? I imagine. I mean, a fever can make you delirious."

Stephanie was barely paying attention. The old man was not looking at her with appreciation. His stare was hard and cold.

"Yes, a fever can make you delirious," she murmured.

The waitress returned with their pasta dishes. Again, she was sweet, urging them to eat up.

"Stephanie?"

"Yes, Suzette?"

"You're not listening to me."

"I am, really."

"Get over the old guy in the back."

"Sorry. And listen, we are a tremendous success. We will continue to be so."

"We can't be a success if we're all in the hospital, sick, or—as in Doug's case—at death's door!" Suzette said. "The pasta is delicious!"

"Yes, it is," Stephanie murmured. And it was. Still, it was hard to enjoy her food, she was so aware of the man, just staring at her.

She forced herself to look at Suzette. "We will get to the bottom of what's going on. Lena has been getting better on her own, you said that you feel better already, and Dr. Antinella has taken good care of Doug." She hesitated a minute. "You know what, though? I think it might be a good idea if you moved in with Lena, or if Lena moved in with you."

"Why?"

"Because if you guys are getting fevers in the night, tossing or turning with dreams, you can wake one another up, get aspirin for one another . . . just be there for one another."

"Maybe that's a good idea," Suzette murmured slowly. "We became really good friends quickly here, but . . . we both enjoyed our own space. The little cottages are so special, you know? But you're probably right. And it will only be for a bit . . . I'll talk to her tonight. What about you? Oh, silly me, never mind. I forgot. There's Grant."

Yes, there was Grant.

"Here comes our fish . . . wow, smell it! This place is like the find of the century. And you know what? I don't even think we're going to wind up really fat. I read a column on AOL News that said the Italians don't put all the bad stuff into pasta, the way we do in America."

"Probably not," Stephanie murmured.

The group of men was rising. She felt a tremendous relief. But the man who had been staring at her didn't walk out along with his friends.

He finally came toward their table.

Stephanie set her fork down.

He rested a hand on the table, facing her, and speaking so quickly she couldn't catch so much as a word he was saying in his deep, urgent voice.

He was angry.

At one point, he raised his fist, then lowered it.

She shook her head. "*Per favore! Non capisco!*" she told him, trying to make him comprehend that she didn't understand a word.

But he didn't stop speaking. At the end, he suddenly pulled something from his pocket. At that point, she jumped. He was so adamant that she thought he was about to pull a pistol.

It wasn't a pistol. It was a beautiful little piece of jewelry. A small silver cross.

Suzette, stunned, just sat with her mouth open.

The old man pressed the cross into Stephanie's hands.

She tried to tell him no, that she couldn't take it. He became even more excited.

At that point, a young man came out of the kitchen. He bore a resemblance to the woman who had served them, and

Stephanie assumed that he had to be her son. He spoke soothing words to the old man, then smiled ruefully at Stephanie. "Thank you for your . . . patience. Adalio Davanti is old, yes, and he fears that you have brought bad things down upon us, with the theater. Please, don't take offense. He wants you to have this. To wear it. To make the town safe for all of us."

Stephanie stared at the young man. "I—I—this is a beautiful piece. It is obviously worth something. I can't take it from him."

The young man grinned. "He's a jeweler. It's what he does. The cross is not so expensive for him, and he really wants you to have it, to wear it. Please do. It's all right, really. My mother is about to get really angry with him, and he's actually a good man. My mother likes the customers that come into the new resort. Please, you will make both my mother and an old man very happy."

Stephanie stared at the old fellow. He was still watching her so intently, so urgently.

She forced a smile. "*Mille grazie*. Thank you, thank you so very much." She took the cross and put it on, clenching her teeth when he came to life and helped her with the catch.

She let her hair fall back into place and smiled again. "Thank you."

He found some English and told her, "You—you wear. Not off. *Capisce?*"

"*Sì, grazie*," she said solemnly.

At last, he seemed satisfied. He turned and left the restaurant. The young man sighed. "The fish is good, yes?"

"Excellent," Suzette assured him.

They smiled at one another.

They were smiles of appreciation. The young man lingered, watching Suzette. At last he returned to the kitchen.

Suzette burst out laughing.

"What on earth was funny about all that?" Stephanie demanded.

"Sorry. Most people just get a pinch on the behind. You wind up with a gorgeous piece of jewelry! Steph, did you really look at that? The handwork on the silver is just beautiful."

"Um, beautiful," she murmured. "Let's hurry up and get back to the hospital. We can spell the others so they can get a late coffee or drink, maybe. Then they can come back . . . and I guess we can head back and get some sleep then. It will be nearly late enough—or early enough," she murmured.

Grant didn't see Clay Barton or Liz anywhere when he returned to the resort.

There were people still in the restaurant, but they were mostly locals, and the head waiter told them that they had people down from Northern Italy and even France, but only a few.

It was a quiet night. It was Sunday, and in Southern Italy, Sunday still meant a day of rest for most people. Besides, tomorrow was Maria Britto's funeral, and many of the local populace would be attending it.

Grant walked into the club café, but the theater was, of course, closed for the night, and it was empty. He walked around anyway, where so much activity happened, feeling the strangeness of such a place when it was dark, actors and audience gone.

He walked out on the beach, but still found no sign of Clay and Liz. He realized that he didn't know if Liz was in a cottage or if she had a room in the actual resort building, but he did know where Clay's cottage was. Not sure of just what he was going to say to the man, he still walked to his door and banged on it, then rang the bell.

There was no answer.

He didn't have a key to Stephanie's cottage since he only

entered it with her and hadn't thought to suggest that she give him one.

She probably would have refused.

Still, a few words in the Italian language that was coming more and more naturally to him as the days passed helped to secure him a second key to the cottage from the young man working the front desk.

He went into Stephanie's room, not certain at first what he was doing there.

Then, he knew.

Trying not to disturb her belongings, he searched through them until he found the resumés that she had on the cast. He was fairly certain that Reggie had done the hiring, and sent the resumés on to Stephanie so she would know who she was working with. It didn't seem plausible that she would have had enough time to advertise the positions and then sift through the applicants before coming over here.

He found them in a canvas shoulder bag she brought to rehearsals. Sitting on the edge of her bed, he scanned them with a practiced eye.

Suzette . . . she'd spent some time studying with a school of mime in Paris, and she'd worked various clubs in both Europe and America. Lena . . . her letter of introduction made note of her Italian background. Drew's letter began with the fact that he knew absolutely no Italian, but would be delighted to learn. Doug's was similar . . . Gema's was extensive and somewhat boastful. And then . . . there was Clay Barton's. It was a very normal resumé. Educated at Tulane . . . worked in a number of New Orleans clubs . . . a stint in New York, and a few gigs in London.

There was no mention of his knowledge of Italian.

He scanned the resumé again, replaced it in Stephanie's bag, and headed out, anxious to reach his own cottage.

As he neared his doorway, he stopped.

There was something lying there, right on the mat before the front door.

He came in a little closer, then stood dead still.

It was the lower half of an arm. A human arm. The flesh was mottled and gray . . . the fingers were contorted. They seemed to be reaching out.

For him. The hand pointed toward his door.

The flesh on the arm was withered . . . as if the human being to whom it had once belonged had been dead for a fair amount of time. And yet . . . yet there was flesh to it.

For a moment, he was still, frozen with the shock. Then he thought that someone had wanted him to find the arm, and to feel this horror.

Was it a warning? Or a taunt?

He came closer, bending down, and determined that it had belonged to a woman—and that it was not so old that it might have come from the excavations or the dig.

He was not about to touch it and leave any imprint on it.

He turned around sharply and headed back to the resort, hoping that Merc or Franco would be sitting in the restaurant, and if they weren't, he'd have the young man at the registration desk call the police.

He felt ill.

He was suddenly certain that he had found the missing Gema Harris.

Part of her, at least.

Stephanie had almost dozed in a chair when Drew burst into Doug's room, obviously in a high state of agitation.

He glanced at Doug where he lay on the bed, and then at Suzette, who was sleeping in the plush, convertible chairbed on the far side of the room. He motioned to Stephanie to follow him out.

Curious, she did so.

In the dimly lit hospital hallway, he cleared his throat.

"You know that stuff I told you about dreams?"

"About Gema?"

"Yeah, yeah. And we were talking about how Suzette had thought that she'd seen her, and maybe she was coming around, and she had some flu, and we were all getting it from her?"

"Yes?"

"Well, I was wrong. Dead wrong. No pun intended," he said, and laughed dryly.

"Drew, you're not making any sense."

"Sorry, sorry." He hesitated, inhaling deeply. "I don't think Suzette saw Gema, and I sure as hell don't think she was ever standing at my door. Nor could she have had any wild nights with Doug."

"Why not?"

He inhaled again.

"Grant just called the hospital. There was an arm in his doorway."

"You're really not making sense! An arm?"

"An arm—just an arm. A human arm. The police came and picked it up, and there were no real identifying features on it, but . . . they think it might be Gema's."

Ice became an eddy in the pit of Stephanie's stomach. She shook her head in denial. "They found a human arm in front of Grant's door?"

"Yes. Grant found it."

Grant. Again.

Her heart skipped a beat. "Maybe someone is playing a cruel joke on him. Maybe it came from the dig."

Doug shook his head emphatically.

"No. It's not an *old* arm. Not that kind of old. There was . . . there was flesh. But apparently, the flesh . . . well, I don't know anything about forensics, but the person has been dead a while. *A week at least!"*

A dull pain hit her. She hadn't met Gema. The woman hadn't been a favorite in this group. But that didn't matter. There was another woman dead.

"Maybe . . . it's not Gema's arm," she said hopefully.

"Well, from what Grant said, so far the coroner hasn't had much to say. But it appears to have belonged to a young woman, somewhere between twenty and thirty."

"Still," Stephanie said desperately, "maybe it's not Gema's arm."

"Tomorrow they'll try fingerprints, but if Gema didn't have them on file anywhere, they may not know. I'll get down to the morgue with the coroner and . . . and look, and see if there's something that I can identify, but . . . we may never know for certain. Unless . . ."

"Unless what?"

"Well, unless the rest of the body appears," Drew said miserably.

The police and the coroner had come and gone. They had been as puzzled and shocked as Grant himself.

Arturo, too, had come, wringing his hands, tremendously distressed. He was now gone as well.

Grant had patiently answered questions posed to him by the police on his own, and through Arturo.

He also assured the local officers that he wasn't planning on leaving the area. He had gotten a little information from them, and he called the hospital to talk to Drew, anxious that he know about the discovery before they all returned—perhaps heedlessly, believing that there wasn't any danger in the area other than forest "animals." He told Drew both the assumptions being made—that the arm, yes, could have easily belonged to Gema—and the fact that they couldn't be certain, not yet.

Hours had passed since he had first returned. With all the commotion that the arrival of the police had brought, he still hadn't seen Clay Barton, though Drew had informed him that Liz had gone back to the hospital.

Stephanie was still there as well. They were all sticking together, taking turns stretching and walking around the lobby, and sitting quietly in Doug's room.

Hanging up from Drew, Grant paused.

With the arm bagged and taken away, the police finished with their questioning for the evening, and, his call made to insure that the others knew about the discovery and were still together, he was free to return to his own cottage.

He did so.

Hurrying to the bedroom, he connected to the Internet. And he began to look up names, actors, actresses, and resumés.

When Stephanie went in for her last stint with Doug, she was glad to see that he was breathing normally.

Lena was excited. They had almost lost him. He had flat-lined for a few seconds while she and Suzette had been gone, and there had been all kinds of feverish activity in the hospital. They had brought Doug back.

And minutes later, he had opened his eyes. He had talked to them all.

It had been like a miracle—he had even asked for dinner.

Stephanie glanced at the peacefully sleeping Doug. She smiled, then looked anxiously back at Drew.

"Did he remember what happened? Anything at all?" she asked.

"Nope, nothing," Drew said.

According to Doug, he'd just come in from the beach, showered, and lain down on his bed for a nap.

That was it. All that he could recall. He'd had dreams . . . seemed he was always having dreams, but nothing he could remember.

Apparently, they had decided not to tell him about the arm left on Drew's doorstep. Stephanie decided that they'd been right. He had just managed to squeak by . . . he had nearly died. There was no reason to tell him things that would be deeply upsetting.

He remained in a restful sleep while Stephanie sat vigil, sitting by his side on the bed while Suzette curled into the chair again. He was wearing a standard white hospital gown. Looking down at him, Stephanie frowned.

He was wearing a medallion around his neck as well. She frowned, certain that she hadn't seen it on him earlier.

She reached out to touch it.

It was a silver cross. Bigger, heavier, but similar to the one she was now wearing.

As she fingered the cross, she realized there was a peculiar odor in the air as well.

It was a hospital. Hospitals always smelled a little funky.

No . . . it wasn't that kind of odor.

"Garlic," Suzette said suddenly, causing her to jump.

She looked at Suzette, who shrugged.

"I think it's me," she said apologetically. "I ate more than you did. A lot, I guess."

Stephanie smiled. "I don't remember Doug having this cross."

Suzette rose, walking across the room to her and reaching down to touch and study the piece as well. "Looks a lot like yours."

"But, did he have it before?"

"I don't think so."

"Well, I haven't seen the crazy old man in the hospital, so he didn't bring it."

"Maybe we just never noticed Doug wearing it before," Suzette suggested. "Who knows? Maybe he shopped at the old man's place one day."

"Maybe. Odd, though. I think someone just put it on him."

"Who?"

"I don't know."

"Well, I guess something like that should be a choice," Suzette said. "Should we . . . take it off of him?"

"I don't think so," Stephanie murmured. She shrugged. "I'm wearing mine. And . . . I think Doug is Christian."

"He could be an atheist, for all I know. The discussion never came up between us. But I don't think that he's Jewish, Buddhist, Hindu, or Moslem, so . . . I guess it's all right to leave it. No, we should definitely leave it. It may actually be his, and we just don't know it."

"I think you're right . . . besides, he might have gotten it from someone who just wants to be nice and probably thinks it's a very good thing," Stephanie murmured.

Suzette nodded. "They're gorgeous. I'd like one. Maybe I'll find the old guy's place and buy one tomorrow myself." She shivered fiercely. "May not help, but can't hurt. Stephanie, do you think that the arm Grant found . . . that it did belong to Gema?"

"I have no idea," Stephanie said honestly.

"So scary!" Suzette said.

Stephanie reached back and unhooked her cross, offering it to Suzette. "Here, take this."

"I can't!"

"Why not?"

"The old fellow gave it to you."

"I know, but you take this one. I'll go and buy one from

him tomorrow. I'll take someone with me—someone who really speaks Italian. I want to know what he was trying to say to me."

"I think he was just talking crazy."

"*He* was talking crazy!" Stephanie exclaimed. "Right. A girl is found buried—but they decide she was killed by animals. Then her mother lops her head off when she's lying in her coffin. We all dream—weird things. Then Grant finds a human arm on his porch. And the old fellow is talking crazy? Hmm. I think I want to know what he was saying."

Suzette nodded miserably. She strode across the room, then glanced at her watch. "It's five. Think it will be okay if we go soon?"

"Yes," Stephanie said.

"It's okay if you go right now," Drew said from the doorway. "I'm going to hang out a while longer. Arturo just sent Giovanni with a car from the resort to pick you girls up. Go back and get some sleep. I'll stay until after he wakes up for real, has some breakfast, and talks me into believing it's okay if I leave."

"I should stay," Stephanie murmured.

"No. You look like hell. If you all go, I'll sleep in the chair. I'll be fine. Then, when I'm totally crashed tomorrow, you guys can take over."

Doug tossed on the bed and flopped over, restlessly clawing at his neck.

"What's he doing now?" Drew wondered worriedly.

"Think he's . . . allergic to metal?" Suzette suggested.

Drew frowned, looking at the cross. "Is this his?"

"We don't know—I don't remember seeing it on him, either," Stephanie said.

"Maybe one of the nurses is praying for him . . . and thought he needed it," Suzette said. "You know how some people feel about actors—especially comedians.

Maybe she—or he—thought he needed all the help he could get."

"Yeah, but look," Doug murmured. "It looks like it's irritating his skin! We'd better get it off."

"Maybe," Stephanie murmured.

And maybe Doug did indeed have an allergy. Once Drew had turned Doug over and Stephanie had gotten the clasp undone, he seemed to be fine, falling back into a restless sleep. The irritation on his throat seemed to disappear almost immediately.

"There, feel better?" Drew asked Stephanie. "Get going—Giovanni is here."

At last, Stephanie agreed. She felt guilty leaving, but the others convinced her.

Outside, Giovanni was waiting for them with the resort van. He was sympathetic and charming. Despite the way he spoke, with the right words and duly respectful of the gravity of Doug's condition and the events of the day, he looked at them all—with appreciation. He was an attractive and charming young man, trying to lift their spirits as they returned.

"Lena agreed, she's bunking in with me," Suzette, in the middle seat, told Stephanie, who was up front.

"That's good," Stephanie said.

"Stephanie, Liz will be . . . alone?" Suzette said.

Lena elbowed her in the ribs.

"Oh, yeah, right . . . Clay?" she said, looking at Liz.

"We're very close, of course, but don't worry about me. I'm fine—really. Especially right now. I think I'm going to hang in the lobby until they open the restaurant for breakfast."

"And you . . . well, I guess you're fine, too," Lena said, looking at Stephanie.

"I'm fine," she assured them, looking ahead.

Fine.

Yes, she'd be fine. Alone!

Grant was surely in his own place. And surely exhausted by now as well. In the hours that they'd been at the hospital, he had probably spent most of his time with the police!

Giovanni pulled in front of the resort. Stephanie was the last out, thanking him for having come at such a late hour.

"My pleasure," he assured her. "But . . . Mr. Peterson . . . he went back to his place."

"Yes?" she said.

He flushed handsomely, dark lashes sweeping his cheeks as he looked down. She realized that Giovanni—like most of the resort—was surely aware of where Grant had been sleeping.

"I thought you might want to know where he was."

"Thank you, Giovanni. And good night."

She started toward the main entrance. Suzette was waiting for her; Liz and Lena were just ahead. "Was the sensuous-eyed young Italian trying to make you feel the need for male companionship through the night?" Suzette asked.

Stephanie had to laugh. "I get the impression he'd like to spread love around the world. But he's always respectful. Hey, you all still be careful, okay?" she said. Then she gave them a wave, hurrying out, anxious. She felt nothing but absolute exhaustion. And she wanted desperately to be alone.

She nearly ran out back, grateful that it was so close to morning—to dawn, to the bright light of the sun. And yet, when she hurried from the rear doors of the resort down the trail to her own place, she realized it was still very dark.

Fumbling in her purse, she found her room key.

As she neared her door, she found herself thinking about Grant

What had he felt when he approached his own door—and saw a human arm there?

Or had he put it there?

Chills ripped into her, and she ran the last few steps to her door, opening it quickly. She loathed herself for having such vicious thoughts—surely, he was having his problems, but to suspect such things about a man she . . .

Loved.

That was just it! Oh, Lord, women could be such fools, letting an all-consuming passion, a hunger for the intimacy of such a sex life, interfere with logic and sense. She couldn't do that. She couldn't tell herself that just because she needed him beside her, because he made the earth and the heavens rise and explode like fireworks, that there couldn't be something wrong with him.

Very wrong.

Shaking her head, she pushed open the door. As she did so, she had a sense of a shadow, huge, bat-like, sweeping the night behind her.

She stepped in and slammed her door, and turned on every light in the place.

She ran up the stairs, turned on more lights, and washed her face. She stepped into the shower and let the water run, then froze.

A shadow seemed to have swept through her room.

She turned off the water and stood dead still.

Listening.

She waited. Nothing.

At last, as quietly as she could, she opened the glass door and groped for her towel, looking out to the bedroom.

Nothing.

She wrapped the towel around her, and tentatively stepped into the bedroom. The lights were on, as she had left them. The glass doors were locked; the draperies were still.

She exhaled, and knew she had to run downstairs—if she didn't, she'd never sleep.

Clutching her towel, she started down the stairs. Step by step.

The lights were blazing. As she had left them.

She stepped more quickly, hurrying down to the first-floor landing. She checked the hall closet, then the kitchen, and the doors that led to the beach. Everything was locked, as she had left it. And she wasn't turning the lights off. She'd have to worry about conservation at some later date.

At the foot of the stairs, she made one long, last assessment of her ground-floor area.

Lights were on, doors were locked, place was empty.

She started back up the stairs, reached the landing, and headed to her bedroom area. There, she paused, dead still, terror gripping her heart.

The draperies were breezing in, like great, puffy white ghosts, billowing.

The back door was open.

There seemed to be . . . a shadow. A shadow emerging, growing, from the corner of the room.

A shadow . . .

Quickly gone.

For suddenly, the whole of the little cottage was plunged into darkness.

Chapter 14

Liz had waited until Suzette and Lena left the lobby, walking out arm in arm to Suzette's cottage.

She had no intention of waiting around until breakfast.

Her room was on the second floor of the main resort, facing the cottages. She hurried to it. Opening the door, she looked in. "Clay?"

There was no answer. Nor had he left her a message of any kind.

She strode across to the window. From her vantage point, she could see the area of the beach on both the left and the right, and the entries to most of the cottages.

She could see Stephanie's place, ablaze with light.

She could see Lena and Suzette, just reaching the latter's cottage. Lena was standing at the door, looking around, apparently urging Suzette to join her. Her arms were wrapped around her chest.

Lena was digging in her purse for her room key.

She surveyed the beach area the best she could.

It remained quiet.

Then, she saw it.

A sweeping black shadow, descending.

Then, Stephanie Cahill's place plunged into darkness.

Her heart slammed.

The time had come.

Turning away from the window, she raced out of her room, heedless of the door flying closed behind her.

She was desperate to make it out of the resort, and over to the cottage in time.

Stephanie stood in the total darkness, blinking and frozen, staring into the corner where she had seen the shadow.

There was a commotion at the glass doors, someone coming through, entangling in the billowing drapes.

She wore nothing but a towel, and carried no weapon, but instinct warned her of the most acute and terrible danger.

She needed something, anything!

Then, suddenly, there was more noise at the sliding glass doors and the draperies weren't just billowing, they were exploding into her room. As they did so, the complete and sudden black was eased.

Outside, the dawn was coming at last.

And now, in the pale light, she saw that her draperies had been cleanly pulled from the curtain rod. It appeared that they had turned into a massive ball on her floor.

Staring in that direction, she caught some movement with her peripheral vision. But it was nothing, just the shadow fading.

She heard grunts then, and the sound of a well-delivered punch.

Her sense of terror faded, to be replaced by one of fury. She recognized the sounds coming from the knot of her ruined draperies.

"Dammit, what the hell are you two doing?"

Walking over to the ball of entangled humanity on her floor, she tore at the drapes, then yelled at Clay Barton and tugged at Grant's hair.

"What the hell are the two of you doing?" she demanded, struggling to maintain her dignity despite the towel.

Tousled, heaving, eyes lethal as they surveyed one another, both Clay and Grant rose, circling like boxers.

Stephanie still held several strands of Grant's hair in her hand. He hadn't even noticed losing them.

"Stop it! What's going on?" she demanded.

"He was headed here," Grant accused Clay. "And God knows what he intended."

"Hell, no! I was after you!" Clay fired back.

"Liar!" Grant shouted, ready to lunge again.

"Wait!" Stephanie caught hold of his arm. He shook her off without notice, eyes lethally narrowed on Clay, every muscle in his body clenched and taut. Clay stood his ground, surveying Grant in return with a cool contempt.

"No!" Stephanie roared, coming between the two. "This is insane. This is my room. You've ruined my drapes, you jerks. What the hell is it between you two? Stop it, now!"

"I saw the shadow," Clay said, staring at Grant.

"Yeah, I saw the damned shadow—you!" Grant accused him in return.

So far, neither one of them had made a jab at the other with her between them. But not a bit of the flaming anger or boiling testosterone seemed to diminish.

"Grant, I really, desperately, want you to calm down and talk to me," Stephanie said.

"Talk, all right! I'll talk. Guess what?—I just searched the Internet. There was a Clay Barton—a fellow with this man's name and resumé, and even his looks. Seems one thing was different about him, though. He had AIDS—and he died a year ago!"

"Oh, you checked the Internet, did you?" Clay demanded in return.

At that moment, Stephanie whirled around as someone else came flying through the glass sliding doors. Liz.

She flew in, catching hold of the frame, staring at them all first, and trying to assess the situation.

"Lucien!" she cried out, racing toward him.

"Lucien!" Grant exploded. "I told you the guy was an impostor. And a murderer, I think."

"No!" Liz protested. She had slipped an arm around the man she had called Lucien and stared at the both of them, and then at him. "Dammit, you've got to tell them the truth!"

"Yeah, I'd sure as hell like the truth!" Grant said, crossing his arms over his chest.

"Wait a minute! I'm the director of the show," Stephanie protested. "If someone has been lying to me—"

"Stephanie, this doesn't have a damned thing to do with the show, does it?" Grant demanded, staring at the two of them. "Does it—Liz? Or is that your name? It isn't, is it?"

"Jade," she said.

Stephanie, totally puzzled, stared blankly for a moment. She pointed at the man she had known as Clay. "All right, your name is Lucien. And you're Jade. And, of course, you know one another very well, I take it."

"We're married," Jade explained.

"Great. He's married. Trying to pick up other women."

"You ass! The hell I did!" Lucien responded.

"Will you two stop!" Liz exploded.

"Let's see, your real name is Lucien, you're married to this other fraud who is really named Jade, and you've been following my woman like a tick on a dog; so just what the hell is your story?"

"You ass!" Lucien repeated, standing with muscles as taut as Grant's.

"I'm not your 'woman,' like a serf, or a piece of property!" Stephanie exclaimed to Grant.

He turned to her then, frustrated, drawing ragged hair away from his eyes. His expression clearly denoted that she was arguing semantics in the middle of chaos. "It refers to the person I love!" he said, indignant and distracted. "And is meant in no way possessive or . . . Sweet Jesus! This is not the point. What is going on?"

"You've got to tell them the truth!" Jade said to Lucien. "You should have told them the truth from the beginning."

"Oh, indeed. I should have just said, hey, I'm a vampire, and something is going on here that's not right. Did I say 'vampire'? Sorry, don't panic—I'm a good one these days?" he said skeptically to Liz—or Jade.

"Vampire!" Grant exploded. "Get real, and do it fast."

"Or what?" Lucien said icily.

"Lucien!"

Lucien looked at his wife. "He's dying to take another really good jab at me. I should let him go for it."

"Feel free to strike first," Grant said with cold courtesy.

"Dammit! Both of you, stop!" Stephanie said, desperately trying to get control. She realized she'd reacted with sheer emotion to a few things said here tonight herself, but it was all beginning to border on the truly insane.

"You two have to listen!" Jade pleaded. Tense silence followed her words. "He . . . really is a vampire," she said, then she held up a hand, as if she could prevent people from talking by doing so. "I came close . . . so I know what's happening here. In the real world, you can be tainted, and not turned, and survive. Only if help is immediate, as it was for Doug tonight. Once someone dies from a bite . . . then it's over. And the only way to end it is fire, the ocean . . . sea water, or a stake through the heart and decapitation."

After her words, the silence remained. A pin could have been heard dropping.

Then Grant spoke at last. "We've got to get the police."

He turned to exit through the open glass doors. "Stephanie, you can't stay here with him," he called back.

"I'm in a towel!" she reminded him.

But Grant didn't go anywhere. She hadn't seen Lucien move, and she was certain that Grant hadn't, either.

But he was in front of Grant, blocking his way. "The police here will be involved," Lucien said, his temper seeming to have abated. He sounded tired, and little more.

"There's sun coming up out here, buddy. Sure you want to be in the light?" Grant asked. "I mean, you're a vampire."

Lucien let out a sound of irritation. "Sunlight robs vampires of some of their strength. It won't make them turn into ash or disappear," he said.

"Look, I'm not sure if you're lethal, or merely demented," Grant said firmly. "But one way or the other, we're going to the police."

"Will you two just listen?" Jade pleaded again. She strode to the two men, coming between them and placing a hand on Grant's chest, forcing him to look down at her. "I'm begging you—listen."

Grant's jaw was twisted but he looked over Jade's head, staring at Lucien. "Did you kill Maria Britto—or Gema Harris?"

"Before God, I didn't," Lucien said.

Grant frowned, staring skeptically at Jade again. "Did he say, 'before God'?"

"He's made his peace with his Maker," she said simply.

Grant stared a minute, then shook his head. "I'm sorry, this is just preposterous."

"Is it?" Jade demanded, staring at him again. "Admit it. You know that there is something really wrong here. You've been plagued by strange dreams. Your friends have experienced illnesses that can't be explained. A village girl was killed—and her own mother was willing to be judged insane in order to remove her head from her body." Grant was silent, staring at her. "When you're out at the dig, you find that you have a stranger feeling than ever. You two . . . you two split up because you were behaving so strangely—am I wrong?"

Grant darted a glance at Stephanie, then looked back at Jade. "He's a vampire?" he said, indicating Lucien with a thrust of his jaw.

"Actually, a vampire king," Jade murmured.

"Oh. The king," Grant said.

"There's a very long history that you can't begin to know or understand," Jade said.

"You're a vampire," Grant said to Lucien. "Prove it."

"Want me to snap your neck?" Lucien asked. "Or just bite it?"

Grant looked as if he were about to lunge at him. "Lucien!" Jade pleaded. She glared at her husband, then turned back to Grant. "There was a time when, naturally, his kind just did what they had to in order to survive. The world grew, the technological age came, and . . . anyway, a terrible dissension arose among those who wanted to survive with and protect humanity and those who wanted to live by the old rules. So now . . . the point is, he's here to protect you. Well, not just you, or even Stephanie, but to put down a really terrible evil that is alive in the world again."

"Okay . . . wait a minute, I think this is getting way too bizarre," Stephanie said, adding quickly, before Jade could protest, "but if you will all please go downstairs for a minute and let me get dressed, we can try—and I do mean try hard—to talk about it rationally."

All three of them stared at her.

"Please?" she said.

Jade turned and walked to the door and looked back at the men. "Lucien, Grant?"

Grant stepped by Lucien, following Jade. Lucien did the same.

When they were gone, Stephanie just stood there. *They were insane!* she tried to tell herself. But everything here lately was insane.

Maybe it had been so since she had arrived.

She flew into motion then, hurrying into the closet, scrambling into a pair of jeans and knit shirt, finding her shoes, putting them on. She hurried down the stairs.

Jade had begun to make coffee.

To Stephanie's amazement, Grant and Clay were suddenly speaking intensely to one another, but not with hostility. Grant seemed to be very seriously listening to what Lucien had to say.

Jade flashed Stephanie a smile. It was the smile most women would give one another if their husbands had nearly come to blows over the outcome of a football game, or some other silly thing, and it had been prevented.

Lucien and Grant were seated at the dining table. Stephanie realized that they were talking about the dig.

"I believe that the earthquake caused either François de Venue or Valeria to be released," Lucien said. "They must have been entombed when the quake struck centuries ago, but the recent shift caused them to be freed. As I said—one, or the other, or both. I felt it when it happened—and it was right after that, when I was reading *Variety*, that I saw the advertisements for comedians/improv actors who were willing to work indefinitely in Italy."

"Reggie put the ads out," Stephanie said, piping up. "And Reggie . . . well, she was around way before the last earthquake."

Lucien drummed on the table, mulling her words.

"Wait a minute," Grant said to Lucien. "You said that you felt it when it happened. What did you feel?"

"I have an extra . . . sense, I guess you'd say. I can usually feel it when there's a real rise of evil. I can usually pick out another vampire from miles away. But with this . . . I only felt the . . . rise. And a threat. A real threat."

"So what does that mean?" Grant asked cautiously.

"It means," Jade said, bringing the coffeepot and a handful of cups to the table, "that there's more involved than just a vampire."

"Just a vampire," Stephanie repeated. She accepted coffee from Jade and sat at the end of the table, shaking her head. "I'm sorry, but . . ."

Lucien turned back to Grant. "Valeria had some kind of a fantastic power. They called her a witch—nothing to do with wiccans, today or yesterday, I assure you. But a witch, as in the fact that she came from a long line of women with unearthly powers. What happened then was that François de Venue became a vampire—whether it was in Paris, fighting the Crusades, conquering native populations elsewhere, I'm not certain. The point is—he had a certain power of his own. It must have been pretty strong, because—according to history, at least—she very nearly married Conan de Burgh. Instead, she rode with François de Venue. The legends have it that she could raise the wind, bring fog and rain, and create an army of devil dogs."

"What are devil dogs?" Stephanie heard herself ask. She gave herself a shake. She was listening to this.

She shouldn't.

But the two seemed to be speaking as if this were all so par for the course!

And despite herself . . .

She couldn't forget the way Grant had been.

She couldn't forget her own dreams.

And mostly . . .

She couldn't forget how she had felt, finding herself on a precipice, not at all sure how or why she had gotten there.

She had been stirring sugar into her coffee. She realized that her hands were shaking. She set down her cup.

"Devil dogs, or demon dogs," Jade mused, looking at Lucien.

He looked at her and Grant. She realized that Lucien's eyes were really red and gold. She had always noted his eyes. Always noted a way about him, the smooth, easy, animal agility with which he moved. She had always recognized something different about him.

She checked herself—she was believing all of this.

And yet . . . with everything else . . .

Why not?

She found herself staring at Grant, who was looking back at her. She realized that, after his initial disdain, he was listening.

Maybe he was too willing to believe. He had a hardened look about his jaw. As if . . .

Almost as if he were feeling vindicated, and more powerful, now that he might have a direction in which to go. A sense of warmth snaked along her spine. Whatever she had said or done, no matter how confused things had been, she realized, he'd always been willing to fight for her. No matter how she'd rejected him, he'd come back.

She forced her eyes back to Lucien and Jade.

"Do you know what they were talking about—devil dogs?" she asked.

Jade deferred to Lucien. He shook his head. "Not werewolves," he murmured.

"Werewolves," Grant said flatly. "They exist?"

"Yes," Lucien said. "As a matter of fact—before you make a joke—one of my best friends and closest associates is a werewolf."

Stephanie glanced at Grant. He looked back.

Okay, maybe this is all insane, his look seemed to say.

"I believe that the demon dogs are something that the witch—or sorceress—Valeria is able to raise. But where she gets them, or what they are, exactly, I don't know," Lucien said. "Jade has been studying all the old texts she can get her hands on to find out more about them, but . . ."

Grant shook his head suddenly. "Okay, let's say that François de Venue was released from whatever tomb or prison the earth had held him in. He killed Maria Britto, and Gema. Let's say he even played with Lena, and probably Suzette. If he's a vampire, with all this power—and certainly, Maria's body was torn to shreds—why hasn't he just gone crazy? Why didn't he kill Lena outright? Or Suzette? And if the police came after him, assumably, he could make quick work of the police."

"I'm not sure he's to that point yet," Jade said.

"If he's been buried for centuries, he needed to slake his hunger first, regain his strength," Lucien said. "I'm willing to bet that, eventually, they'll find out that some missing persons were killed around here. Bodies will turn up. In the old days, there were rules—a vampire had to destroy his, or her, kills, and only create three new beings of his kind per century."

Again, Stephanie and Grant exchanged glances.

This time, Lucien sighed impatiently. "All right, I know that this is a lot for the two of you to take in. And that, of course, is why I didn't just come to you from the very beginning and try to say all this—you would have been completely determined to have me locked up."

"If you're really a vampire," Grant said, "couldn't you have just hypnotized us into some kind of submission? Or is that just myth, too?"

"No. I could have done all manner of things," Lucien said evenly. "I didn't."

Stephanie gasped suddenly. *This couldn't be real. The man couldn't be a vampire.*

And yet . . .

"Your arm!" she exclaimed to Lucien. "It was blistered horribly, but . . ."

"I have incredible powers of recuperation," he told her.

"So that was just from the seawater that was splashed on you when we dragged the little boy out of the water?" she said.

"Actually, everyone managed to get quite a bit of it on me," he said dryly. He looked at Grant. "You know my weakness. I hope you don't share it."

"We're still talking," Grant said.

"All right, so this vampire needs to gain strength," Stephanie said.

"I think there's more to it than that," Lucien told her.

"Like what?" Grant asked.

"He has a plan," Lucien said.

Stephanie shook her head. "Like what?"

"I don't know that yet. If he were just working with the growing powers of one of my own kind, I would know," Lucien said, and his frustration was very real. "But Valeria . . . whatever her sorcery, it's different, and very powerful. Because of her, he is somehow able to shield himself—just as she shields herself. If she has been awakened as well—which seems to be evident—she is very dangerous. Historically, reviews on her are mixed. Some people believe that François had a hold over her, and that she only used her power for evil—to kill and ravage—because François could hurt her—somehow. Then there are others who believed that she was simply evil incarnate herself. The truth, we don't know."

"What *do* you know?" Grant asked.

Lucien glanced at Jade, then sat back, drumming his fingers on the table again. He looked at Grant. "I know that you're involved."

"I'm not a vampire dug up out of the ground!" Grant protested strongly. "You can check on my background, all the way back to nursery school!"

"I never suggested that you were François. But I know it—and you know it. You're involved. Admit it. You felt you had to come here. And you really didn't know that Stephanie would be here."

Grant was silent, staring at him.

"Steph—you came because of the job. But if you look deep inside, you'll know that every word we're saying is true. You were being summoned. You can't deny it. And if you deny it to me, you still can't lie to yourself. When we found you on the cliff, you had no idea what you were doing, where you were going—or why. Right?"

She, too, just stared at him in silence.

"What do we do?" she asked carefully after a minute.

"First, I need some help. I can't keep slipping in and out of places, trying to get crosses around people's necks," Lucien said. "And dammit—where's yours?" he asked Stephanie.

She started. "You made that old man give me a cross?"

He shook his head. "He knows," he said softly. "A lot of these people know. They are actually smarter here than in many a place, because they haven't been so attuned to machinery, technology, and modern culture that they've forgotten there can be more than meets the eye."

"So . . . the people here just know . . . that there are vampires among them?" Stephanie said.

Grant inhaled suddenly and looked at Lucien. "This person, or creature—François. He did kill Gema—but he didn't destroy her immediately. She died, and became a vampire. And he let her go after Drew and Doug, and somehow, she failed with Drew, but she got to Doug . . . and he would have died, except that Drew found him and they got enough blood into him fast enough. But the arm on my doorstep—it was Gema's arm. Right?"

"Yes, I believe so," Lucien agreed.

"Why did he turn her into a vampire . . . and then destroy her?" Stephanie asked. "Wouldn't he need . . . helpers, assistants, fellow bloodsuckers? Sorry, Lucien," she murmured. But he didn't seem offended.

Insanity—she was worried about insulting a man who claimed to be a vampire.

"I think she went further than she was supposed to go with Doug. Whoever our fellow is, he didn't want things happening this fast. Gema disobeyed him. He destroyed her." Lucien grimaced. "Why do you think Maria Britto looked so alive at her wake?"

"Obviously," Stephanie said, arching a brow, "because she wasn't really dead. She was a vampire, with remarkable powers of recovery?"

"Exactly," Lucien said. "But if her mother hadn't destroyed her," he added grimly, "I'd have been there, watching her."

"Watching her? Not destroying her yourself?"

"In Maria's case . . . I would have gone to her."

"I don't believe I'm going to say this, but . . ." Stephanie said, looking at Lucien again. "Because she might have been a *good vampire*?"

"Something like that," Lucien said.

"Now I'm lost. When I found Maria, she was in . . . tatters. The police were there, and the coroner and the doctor, and her death was definitely not natural. Why didn't the doctor and coroner do the autopsy and embalm her correctly in the first place?" Grant asked.

"Because vampires have the power to hypnotize," Jade said softly.

"All right, so either Maria or this François got to both those men. Right?"

"That's what I believe," Lucien said.

Grant lifted his hands, staring at Lucien. "Why—why have

you been so mistrustful of me? I'm not sure myself who tackled who on Stephanie's balcony tonight—and I know I was damned suspicious of you. But why were you after me?" Grant demanded, staring at Lucien.

"Because you are involved somehow. I wasn't sure . . . on which side," Lucien told him. "Besides, I wasn't really after you—I was just watching you. You were the one always willing to pick a fight."

"Because you seemed to be following Stephanie. How could I have known you didn't intend any harm to her?" Grant demanded.

"I told you, Lucien—if you'd just come to them in the beginning," Jade murmured.

Lucien smiled, shaking his head. "They aren't really buying all of this tonight, Jade. But they've both felt enough of a disturbance that they have to listen with their minds open— a crack, at least."

"I still don't understand. You have all these powers. You're a king of your kind. Wait a minute—you're wearing a cross!" Grant said suddenly.

"There's an important point you need to learn," Lucien said, looking at them both. "Yes, I can wear a cross. I can walk into a church—I was born at a time when the Church was everything—and I can still feel a deep peace. Now. Because in the battle, there is black and white and shades between. But there is good and evil, the salvation of life, and the brutal destruction of it. I fight for life, and against the kind of evil that feeds on blood and pain. Such a creature as François? He could not wear a cross—or a Star of David, for that matter. He would cringe before a really holy man of any religion that respected the one Creator. There are tricks to dupe, disable, and slaughter priests and holy men, of course. But true believers have their weapons as well. François would not be able to enter consecrated ground. Holy water would hurt—badly. But you'd need a lot to really kill such a creature. I believe that during the daylight hours, François is still weak. That doesn't mean that he isn't about. It just means he can't cause the harm by day that he can at night. During the light today, what you two need to do is make the rest of this crew understand that no one should be invited in, crosses are far more important apparel than underwear, and no one should be alone."

"That's great for our crew, but this is a town, a village . . ." Grant reminded him. "There are many people at risk."

"You did notice, I'm certain, that there was no huge outcry when it was discovered that Maria Britto was not given an autopsy, or embalmed," Lucien said. He stared hard at Stephanie. "The person in question here is Victoria Reggia."

She shook her head firmly. "Reggie did not just pop out of the ground! She was there for me when my parents died, and that was nearly eleven years ago."

Lucien shrugged. "Still . . . the opening here—of the club—rather coincided with the growth of the dig. The earthquake that led to the discovery of the remains happened just about two months ago."

"You're not making any sense—the resort itself was surely started way before that!" Stephanie told him.

"The resort was built nearly a year ago by a group of American businessmen. They sold it to Victoria Reggia—just about two months ago."

"Are you suggesting that Reggie is an evil sorceress?" Stephanie demanded, growing angry. "Again, I tell you it makes no sense—I've known Reggie for more than a decade."

"Yes, yes, I understand that," Lucien said.

"You think she's a reincarnation of an evil sorceress?" Stephanie said, grating her teeth, unable to keep a disdainful note from her voice.

"No," Lucien said.

Stephanie threw up her hands. "Then just what are you getting at?"

"I'm trying very hard to determine just why . . . why it seems that you are so pivotal in all this," Lucien said quietly.

"Me!" Stephanie protested.

"And you, of course, Grant. But you already know that there's a connection for you here."

"Interesting. My name is Peterson," Grant said dryly.

"And I'm a Cahill!" Stephanie said.

Lucien smiled. "A lot of centuries have gone by since François de Venue, Valeria, and Conan de Burgh were caught up in an earthquake. Stephanie, you're related to Reggie somehow, right?"

She waved a hand in the air. "Vaguely. She's my mother's cousin, or something like that. Maybe a second cousin. I don't even know. She was there for me. She's a good friend."

"Interesting, though. She set all this up, she brought you over, hired everyone—including me—but hasn't come around to see her work," Lucien noted.

"She was in Germany, meeting with groups at military bases, getting them to come over here. The townspeople are very happy about it. They need the tourism dollars," Stephanie informed him.

"Yes, they need the tourism dollars," Lucien agreed. He was staring at Stephanie. "You've seen her, haven't you?"

"No!" Stephanie said.

"Yes, you have."

She flushed. Grant stared at her. He knew her so well, and he hadn't known she was lying. In a way, at least.

"I really haven't seen her. I just thought I saw her at the back of the café," Stephanie said.

"I see," Lucien murmured.

"It wasn't Reggie!" Stephanie said. "I asked . . . she wasn't with the group. And Arturo didn't see her. Did *you* see her."

"I wouldn't have known if I had," Lucien said. "I've never met her."

"Well, she's gorgeous," Stephanie told him, still feeling defensive.

"She looks a lot like Steph—or Steph looks like her. She has a mane of really dark hair, and blue, almost violet, eyes."

"Ah," Lucien said, as if that meant something.

"Honestly, she wasn't here. If she had been, she would have made a point to get to me. I know that," Stephanie said.

"Perhaps you're right," Lucien said. He turned to Grant. "Peterson. Names ending with 'son' are usually Scandinavian."

"Or American," Grant reminded him.

"Actually, with all the Viking activity, such names may be European as well, in many places. The great Norman lords had Scandinavian ancestry."

"My family has been in the States for years," Grant said. "What on earth are you getting at?"

"Nothing, really. Just thinking out loud," Lucien said.

"Well, it's going to be much easier to get to the bottom of everything now that things are out in the open," Jade said. She smiled. "Except that, looking at the two of you, I can see that you're not at all convinced that we're sane."

Grant was silent, then smiled. "The scary thing is that I'm not at all convinced that you are *insane.*"

"But," Jade continued, "you're both exhausted, and this is too much for you to accept in one sitting. That's entirely understandable."

"There is a connection, though—for both of you," Lucien said with certainty. "We have to discover exactly what it is. And sooner than later."

Jade glanced at Lucien. "It may be daytime, but no one has had any sleep. We need to try to get a few hours in. That was just decaf, by the way," she told them, indicating the coffee. "Thinking that you're filled with caffeine can keep you awake, really. The mind can do incredible things."

"Yes, it can, can't it?" Grant said. "After all, we're actually sitting here, talking to you, as if you could really be a vampire. As if such creatures could really exist."

"He doesn't take much on faith, does he?" Lucien mused to Jade.

"He did ask for proof," Jade said.

As she spoke, Lucien disappeared from the chair where he had been sitting. Grant leaped to his feet, wary, coming to stand protectively behind Stephanie in a split second and single stride.

There was no puff of smoke, nothing. The man simply disappeared.

He had been there, and then he wasn't.

"You wanted proof," Jade reminded Grant quietly.

Grant spun around suddenly. Lucien was standing behind him.

Grant had to be rattled, but he didn't show it. "You could just be a really excellent magician," he said.

"But I'm not, and you know it," Lucien said. "Don't you?"

Grant didn't reply.

Lucien shrugged. "We're going to get out of here now. It would be best if we remained Clay and Liz, as far as the others are concerned. I would prefer that the truth about me be on a need-to-know basis."

Jade smiled awkwardly. "Try to get some sleep. Things may speed up around here, now that it seems something has gone a little outside the line for our François."

"Speed up?" Stephanie murmured.

"He wants something. That something may be . . ."

"May be what?" Grant demanded.

Lucien met his gaze.

"Stephanie," he said simply.

Lena heard the rapping on the door and ran to it.

Her heart was thundering. She was so afraid that one of

the others had come back to bring them new word about Doug.

A bad word.

He couldn't have had a relapse . . .

He could have.

Without thinking, she threw the door open.

She stood stock-still for a minute, deeply confused.

She felt the eyes.

Felt them on her, and then . . .

She opened the door farther. It was what was wanted.

She was dimly aware of Suzette running back down the stairs, anxious to find out what the tapping had been.

"Lena?"

Suzette froze on the bottom stair.

He was already inside. And he looked at her, and smiled.

"Two for the price of one," he said lightly.

Suzette's mouth was working. But she remained where she stood, transfixed. Somewhere inside, though, she was trying to fight. He frowned. Walking toward her, he felt a sudden repulsion.

Then he knew why. He saw the silver piece around her neck, and swallowed. A shiver went through him. He shook off the discomfort angrily and backed away.

"First things first!" he said. "Lena, go take that . . . that *thing* off Suzette's neck!"

Obediently, Lena turned to her friend. Suzette managed to lift a hand, as if she could stop Lena. But then, she hadn't that much strength.

He was pleased with himself; he'd already visited both girls, and he'd toyed with the idea of only playing with one. And here they were, together. How lovely, and how convenient. And how very much fun.

Lena got the cross, ripping it from Suzette's neck. She cast it down on the living room floor.

He grabbed a pillow from the couch and threw it on top of the offensive piece.

"And now!" he said.

"The two of you . . . ah, well!"

They were huddled at the bottom of the stairs together, both wide-eyed, staring at him, awaiting his next order. The one, petite, dark, and gorgeous with her inky eyes; the other, a little snow princess, blond with blue eyes.

Oh, yes. This could be the greatest entertainment he had yet afforded himself. Better, even, he mused, than the prize he awaited.

But the real prize was power. And he craved that more than any other sensory pleasure he could take at will.

But for the moment . . .

He walked to the pair, ran a finger down Suzette's peaches-and-cream arm, then stroked the rise of Lena's breast.

"Suzette, you will undo those buttons from Lena . . ." he began.

Then, something struck him, and he glanced at his watch, and cursed.

It wasn't going to be quite as much fun as he had intended.

"Make it quick!" he barked at Lena.

He needed to hurry. And still . . .

It was indeed entertaining. He savored the taste of the blonde while the brunette stroked and soothed her.

And he all but drained the brunette while he watched what the blonde was doing between her thighs.

The ecstasy was almost his undoing. Still, it all seemed to please him with a volatile, sensory delight greater than an explosion from Etna.

He had to stop himself. He didn't want them dead.

Yet.

As he gently settled the girls on the ground, sated, nearly bloated, he felt a moment's chill.

The other was near!

He gritted his teeth and fought the fear.

He was cloaked in a way that masked him. He was safe. And when he was done . . .

He would have all the power he had ever craved. And a world, a huge world, with a massive population, in which to play.

And conquer.

Chapter 15

Grant sat at the table long after Lucien and Jade had gone, staring at his coffee cup. Stephanie did the same.

Then she rose. She smiled at him weakly. "I've got to get some sleep. And I've got to go up and do something about that curtain."

She left him sitting at the table. They hadn't exchanged a word with one another about the entire bizarre occurrence that night or the even more absurd conversation they had just had with Lucien and Jade—or Clay and Liz.

They were liars. They had to be liars. Fakers, magicians, liars.

But they weren't.

Stephanie was right. They were both so tired that they were bleary-eyed. There had been far too much happening in a day for either of them to understand or accept.

Or deny.

Grant rose.

He had seen Stephanie lock the front door. He checked it anyway. He checked the downstairs back door as well.

Daytime, he mocked himself. They were probably safe anyway.

He climbed the stairs to the loft, his footsteps heavy. When he reached the bedroom area, Stephanie was busy trying to balance the broken rod on the sliding glass doors and stuff the billowing white drapes back over it. He caught her in the act, pulling her against him. For a minute, he just held her there. Ridiculous thoughts filled him. *At least the suave bastard was married!*

Yep, he was a vampire, but hell, a married one. Surely, that made it all better.

And yet . . .

He felt again the fierce desire that he had felt for Stephanie from the moment he had met her, a love so intense it was frightening. *And he didn't need to be afraid of Clay Barton . . .*

Hell, no! Just some ancient, evil corpse brought back to life because of an earthquake. An evil being who, for some reason, wanted Stephanie.

He nuzzled his face against her nape, feeling her hair tease his skin. And he told her almost urgently, "I would die for you. I would die without you!"

She might have turned around and told him that he had best get a life—they weren't really together. She had let him stay because he was so insistent. She had made love with him because they were both healthy and vital and their chemistry was a combustible match.

But she didn't. She turned into his arms, and let him hold her. For a moment, she was vulnerable, grateful just to feel secure in the circle of his arms. He lifted her chin. So much of their lovemaking had been desperate and wild. He kissed her very gently, slowly, savoring the feel of his lips against her, the taste of her mouth, the depth and texture of it. She stirred. He instantly felt a quickening in himself. So much for a tender moment.

She drew away.

"The drapes," she reminded him.

"Um, we would be just about on television, huh?" he said.

"Well, kind of. And if you look below . . . Giovanni is delivering someone's luggage, the maids are moving about . . . and one of the cooks is outside, smoking," she said dryly.

He laughed, stepping forward with the bent rod, and lifting it. It wouldn't fit. He lowered it before himself and straightened it, then set it back on the hooks. Not perfect, but it was going to stay. Stephanie was behind him with the drapes. He took them from her, reaching up to see that they were attached to enough places to provide them complete privacy.

He turned back to her.

Her clothes were strewn. She was already in the bed. The room was cast in shadow again, while outside, the sun blazed.

He came to her.

She wasn't in a tender mood. She rose to meet him, her hands upon his clothing, her whisper hot in the shadows. "Tonight . . . God, I want to crawl into your skin, I need to be with you, a part of you, so badly!"

She was on her knees against him. He caught her jaw tenderly, firmly, and found her lips again. She returned the kiss with a wanton abandon, still tugging anxiously on his clothing. Their mouths remained meshed while they both struggled with buttons, zippers, and then the denim of his jeans. When they came together, flesh against flesh, it was as if they seared to one another. Her hands were everywhere on him. He gripped her tightly, melding her to him, but she tossed her head back, sending kisses flying in a sea of desperation against his chest and shoulders. She shoved him back. He allowed it. She rubbed her body down the length of his, the friction of her flesh against his an erotic sensation long before she made it far more intimate—teeth, lips, and tongue playing wickedly on his flesh, against his thighs, his abdomen, his sex. Acute arousal seared into him, and he halfway rose, lifting her, bringing her down against him, letting her ride the heat, the rhythm of his choice until the urge to increase the tempo soared in him like a wildfire of need, and caught her tightly, rolling against the sheets with her, taking her position on top. The world rocked and thundered; he felt his climax come upon him as explosively as fireworks. His very essence seemed to flow into her. *She had said that she'd wanted to crawl into his skin. He felt as if they did, somewhere, all but become one . . .*

Her body shuddered and quaked in his arms, and at last, still embraced, she went still. Her fingers played in his hair and he eased himself to her side, scooping her against him.

Then . . .

He heard the noise. Downstairs.

She tensed in his arms. But he'd heard it, too. Someone at the downstairs door, someone trying to get in.

He leapt out of the bed, assuring himself that the glass doors were locked; then, heedless of his state of total undress, he flew down the stairs. A crack of brilliant daylight was flooding in.

The top bolt was on; the door could only part an inch.

"*Buongiorno!*" a cheerful voice called.

He collapsed against the wall. The maid! It was daytime, morning.

"*Buongiorno,*" he returned, and all his Italian fled from his mind. "We're still, uh, sleeping!" he told her.

"*Mi dispiace! A più tardi!*" the maid assured him.

The door closed over the crack. He hit the bottom lock again.

Stephanie, raven's wing hair cascading in a wild tangle over her shoulders, was standing at the top of the stairs.

"The maid," he told her, but she already knew.

They both burst into laughter. He tore up the stairs, and

swept her back up into his arms. They both continued to laugh as they crashed down on the bed.

Not too terribly much later, they actually fell asleep.

"Drew?"

Drew had dozed in the chair. The sound of his name brought him instantly and fully awake. He felt a startled sense of panic, but he was awake.

"Doug?" he said anxiously.

"Yeah, man."

Doug was sitting up in the bed. He didn't look pale, haggard—hell, he didn't even look sick!

"Hey . . . you look great."

"Yeah? I feel . . . weird."

"You should. We nearly lost you last night," Drew told him.

Doug grimaced, and stretched his muscles. "Really weird. And hungry."

"I'll get you something."

Doug made a face. "No . . . I'm in the hospital, right? I don't want any hospital food."

"All right. I'll go out and get you something and bring it back."

"A steak. Really rare."

"Hey! Don't get too picky on me, buddy. I've got to see what I can find somewhere near here—the café is really good, though," Drew assured him.

Doug made a face. There was an IV dripping into his arm. He looked at it with distaste. "I gotta get out of here!" he said.

"You've got to sit tight, and deal with it," Drew said firmly. "Wait until Dr. Antinella sees you. I have a feeling he may want you to stay a few more days. In fact, I think I'll get one of the nurses to check with him—just make sure he doesn't want you on a special diet or anything."

"I'm feeling great," Doug said. He grinned. "Honestly."

"And you still don't remember anything?" Drew asked him curiously.

Doug shook his head. "Just . . . coming in from the beach." He hesitated, then stared at Drew beseechingly. "I really need something that's like real, live food. You all must have been through hell last night, and I really appreciate it, but . . . man, I'm hungry."

"All right, sit tight. I'm on it," Doug told him.

Out in the hallway, he ran into one of the nurses. He smiled awkwardly, knowing that he wouldn't begin to know how to ask her if it was okay for him to bring in outside food for Doug. Maybe she spoke English. He tried. "My friend . . . *mio amico* . . . ah . . . *desidero mangiare. Posso . . . io . . .*"

"What does he desire?" the nurse asked, smiling. She was an attractive woman in her late twenties or early thirties who apparently knew English just fine.

"He's very hungry, but he wants a steak. Is it all right if I go out and find him one?"

"Come," she said.

He followed her to the nurses' station, and she leafed through the charts.

"He is on no special diet. There are no instructions. Dr. Antinella will be around to see him very soon. He has been good through the night, and this morning, yes?"

"You've checked in on him?"

"But of course," she assured him. "You have been sleeping," she said, a small smile curving her lips. "A good friend you are, though. Trying to stay awake."

"Yeah, well . . ." He flushed. Damn, but he hated it when he flushed. He turned really red. "I'll be back. I'm going to try and find my buddy a steak."

"*Ciao!*" she said cheerfully.

"*Ciao.*" He waved awkwardly. Damn, but she was cute.

A tremendous feeling of well-being swept through him. Doug was better already. The world was good.

No, it wasn't, he remembered.

There had been a human arm left in front of Grant's cottage last night. And he was supposed to find his way to the mortuary and see . . . see if he could identify it as Gema's.

His stomach churned.

Good thing he was getting the steak for Doug, and not himself.

Antoinette smiled and hummed as she worked, her notepad in her hand. She had received a promotion to her recent position just a few weeks ago, and she was still very proud and pleased. She wasn't just head nurse for her shift now, but supervisor of her area.

That meant, of course, that she now had greater responsibility, and that she was required to know the extent of their supplies at all times, know when they were low, what must be ordered. Naturally, she was responsible as well to make sure that none of her fellow employees slipped out at night with any drugs.

There were many that could just give one a great high for an evening. Drugs that saved life could also be exceptionally entertaining in the recreational area.

She took her responsibilities very seriously, but not fretfully. This was a small place. It was tightly run. The employees took pride in it, and when a bad egg came along now and then, well . . . he or she didn't usually last very long.

When she first heard the sound at the door, she didn't even look up.

"Yes? I'm busy, as you can see."

She felt the touch on her shoulder first. Her first instinct was irritation. Who in the world! Did someone think that she, of all women, would be interested in an intimate little *tête-à-tête* in the supply room? And if not, did they think they could get her to let them slip out with supplies that belonged to the hospital?

Indignant, she spun around.

She inhaled, ready to be firm, angry, and definitely indignant.

Antoinette!

She heard the caress of her name, heard it as if it had been spoken inside of her, as if it were a stroke against her naked flesh.

She stared ahead into . . . fire.

"Yes?" she said, and it was a rasp.

She was aware of the smile. Of the euphoria that swept over her.

She heard the commands, and she obeyed.

Every last one . . .

When she woke up, she was on the floor. She looked at herself in horror and embarrassment, scrambled to her feet. Stunned and confused, with no memory of the last twenty minutes, she hastily made repairs to herself.

And then, she saw the supply room.

And she began to scream for help, still tucking her hair back into her cap.

Sleep was good. Delicious. Stephanie was aware of the warmth of Grant's body, and somehow, even sleeping, aware as well that beyond the darkness of the room, it was daylight.

Rest was wonderful.

And then . . .

She began to stir, aware that at her side, Grant was tossing. His flesh seemed on fire.

Grunts, sounds—words?—she couldn't understand suddenly began to tumble from his lips. His muscles tensed, lengthened, tensed again. His fingers wound tightly into fists, and he pounded the bed at his side.

She just stared at him at first.

Then she jumped out of the bed, stunned at the violence in the thrashing of his body. He shouted, and again, the sounds seemed like words, but she couldn't understand anything he said.

Suddenly and abruptly, he went still.

Then he sat up, jackknifed to a sitting position. His eyes were open, and he was staring ahead in fury and anger. He shouted out again, threatening someone. Vaguely, she was aware that she recognized the language.

She even thought she understood the words.

"Grant!" she called softly. He was dreaming; he had to be dreaming. She didn't know whether to shake him or maintain her gentle approach. And she was afraid to get too close to him; his volatility could send her flying if she didn't wake him fully and instantly.

He screamed something out again, something she couldn't discern, then leapt out of the bed. Stark naked, he strode for the doors, and fought with the billowing drapes. Ripping them open, he slammed against the glass.

"Grant!"

Back to her, buttocks and thigh muscles bronze and taut, he was pressed against the glass.

"Grant!"

She leapt up, suddenly heedless of physical danger, desperate to get him away from the glass before a young mother with a child or children looked up from the beach and decided to have him arrested for indecent exposure.

"Grant!"

Stephanie threw her arms around him, dragging him back. For a minute, it was terrifying. He was a powerhouse of heat and energy. With all her strength, she tried to draw him in. She fell back on the bed beneath him. His weight was smothering. She shoved him off her, dug her way out from beneath him, and, gasping, made it to her feet.

"Grant!"

He lay flat on the bed, silent and still, eyes closed.

To her absolute amazement, he rolled into a more comfortable position, just as if he had been easily, restfully sleeping all along.

Puzzled and frightened, she bit her lower lip, then realized that she was standing naked in front of an uncovered picture window. Groaning, she went for the drapes. As she tried to stuff them back around the rod, the whole thing fell down on her again.

"Steph, what on earth are you doing?" she heard Grant ask.

Turning, she saw him, hair tousled, yawning, eyes only half open against the light, staring at her as if she were the one losing her mind. But then, his gaze became troubled. He rose, untangling her from the wrecked curtains once again, returning them to the rod. He drew her to him, and stood still, just holding her for several long moments.

She determined not to prompt him, to give him time on his own.

"I remember . . ." he murmured.

"I remember . . . and then I lose it." Shaking his head, he stepped away, heading for the bathroom. She heard the shower, and let him be, straightening the bedding. He came out in one of the resort's terry robes, and told her, "I'll put on more coffee."

Her turn in the shower. She ran in, glancing at the clock. They'd had about five hours sleep. It was going to have to be enough.

When she emerged, showered, hair clean and damp, some makeup to minimize the effects of sleeplessness and wear and tear, she hurried down the stairs. The coffee was made. He wasn't downstairs, but he hadn't left. She ran back up the stairs, and found him standing out on the balcony, looking toward the west where the sea met land, and the mountains could be seen, climbing almost to the sky.

"I dreamed I was there," he told her, aware that she had come, that she was watching him.

"You—have been there," she reminded him.

He shook his head, and strangely, looked at his hands.

"No . . . I heard the screams, the clang of steel . . . I was watching a battle through the eyes of someone there. I felt the rush of a horse beneath, the weight of chain mail and armor . . . I . . ." He turned and stared at her. "I saw the demon dogs."

She was silent for a minute, then said, "Maybe it was a very natural dream. We were up for hours and hours, listening to things so fantastic, that even now, with just a few hours sleep, seem to be impossible. But the events all those centuries ago were what we were talking about, right before we went to sleep. Your dream was . . . normal, I think."

"It was in vivid color. I *could* smell the blood, feel the steel. I was looking through a visor . . . and it limited the field of vision. I was fighting, and somehow . . . I was learning as I went along. Learning how to fight. Not how to fight men—I seemed to know that. I could feel the ache in my muscles as I swung a sword. But the dogs . . . they had to lose their heads, or they wouldn't stay down."

She came and put a hand on his arm. "It was a dream, Grant. I was next to you. It was worse, though, than any that you had before, back home, in the States," she said. She stepped around, standing in front of him, seeking his eyes. "You were with me, all along. It was a dream. I was next to you. I have to make a real, concerted effort to wake you up from now on."

He shook his head slowly. "I hate it. I'm—I'm afraid of

it. But don't wake me up. You can't wake me up because . . .
I have to get to the end of it."

A real sense of fear suddenly filled her. "I—I don't think
you should get to the end of it."

"I have to."

"Listen, a good psychologist or psychiatrist would find us
fascinating subjects—and explain away a great deal, I'm
certain. But I've heard things about dreams, and, of course, I
don't know if they're true or not, but . . . I don't want you
dreaming about this. Everyone died in those hills and tors
that day. I don't want you to dream . . . that you die," she told
him.

He smiled suddenly, and cupped the back of her head tenderly with his hand. "I know this sounds ridiculous, but it's
almost like going back. Like being there. And I might be
able to see the truth of what went on."

"Dreams are what we make of them!" she whispered.

He pulled her close. "Are you forgetting the wee hours of
the day?" he asked huskily. Then he pulled away again. "We
have a friend who's a vampire, remember? And, hey, his best
friend is a werewolf."

"I haven't forgotten. It's just that now . . . after sleeping . . .
the total absurdity of it all is coming home, and I don't know
what I believe." She hesitated. "What do you believe?"

"I believe you're in danger. Maybe I'm in danger, too, but
. . . Stephanie, if this horrid creature exists, and they're right,
for some reason, he wants you."

"Grant, I promise you, I have no feeling at all about ever
being in this area before. I love it here—well, I did love it,
before people started . . . dying. Grant, I haven't been sick a
day. The others have been sick. Gema was the one taken."

"You need to call Reggie. You have a number for her,
don't you?" Grant demanded.

"I have a cell number, of course. But she never answers.

You've known me long enough to know how Reggie is," she reminded him.

"Call her. Tell her it's important that she call you back."

"Why?"

"Don't you at least want to know where she is?" he asked.

"Reggie is not the reincarnation or whatever of an evil witch!" Stephanie insisted.

"I repeat—don't you at least want to know where she is, and what she's doing? Try her cell. If we don't reach her, we'll talk to Arturo," Grant insisted. He kissed her forehead. "I'm going to get dressed. In my old clothes so I can go over to my place and get clean ones. Then . . . I think we should go check on Doug right away, what do you say?"

She nodded. "All right. I'll try to reach Reggie."

Reggie didn't answer when Stephanie dialed her cell number, but in a few minutes she called back.

"Darling, I know I've been just terrible about communication," Reggie told her, "but then you had this number, so I assumed that if you were having any problems, you'd call me. But I talked to Arturo. Such dreadful things are going on!"

"Yes," Stephanie said, feeling a little guilty. Grant had gone to his place to get clean clothing; if he'd been there, she'd be giving him a filthy look right now that said *I told you so*. But then, actually, Lucien had been the one convinced that there was something out of the ordinary with Reggie. "Did you know Maria Britto? And I don't know when you talked to Arturo last, but it seems that a body part left in front of Grant's doorway belonged to Gema Harris."

"I never met Maria, or even Gema," Reggie said. "Of course, I feel horrible. Just horrible. I hired Gema, so her death is certainly my fault."

"No, Reggie. It's the fault of the heinous person who did it to her," Stephanie said.

"She wouldn't have been here if I hadn't hired her, so . . . it is my fault. I'm in Belgium. I was getting together another tour group . . . there was supposed to be a group coming in from the U.K. on Tuesday, but I've managed to get them rescheduled. If they prove today that a piece of Gema's body has been discovered, why, of course, I intend to offer your actors severance pay, and give them the option to go home. Unless, of course, they can find this psychotic killer. When I first heard about Maria, they said she'd been killed by wild animals! Well, it's apparently an animal, all right. And I heard that Lena had gotten ill, but was better, and that Suzette had a bad day—and that Doug nearly died!"

"Doug is doing much better," Stephanie said. "Reggie . . . you didn't come in with the group from Germany the other night, did you?"

"Why on earth are you asking that?" Reggie asked.

"I could have sworn that I saw you."

"I told you, dear, I'm in Belgium."

"Yes . . . I know."

"What is Grant doing there? I thought you were so anxious to come to Italy to spend some time away from him!"

"He didn't know I was here. He came to be part of that dig."

"Ah, yes, the dig." Reggie sounded aggravated.

"Reggie, if they bring up some real historical treasures and set up some kind of a park, mapping a medieval battlefield, it will be spectacular for the region."

"I suppose. It's just that scientists are so dry. And cheap! Honestly, I know that we're talking Europe, and that service is included in a bill, but most people leave a few euros on the table! And they come in muddy! Never mind, Stephanie— with what I've heard, I want you to be careful. In fact, you should go home."

"I—I can't go home," Stephanie said, faltering.

"Why not?"

Why not, indeed? She should just pick up and leave. Leave the resort, the terrible things happening, and stories about witches and vampires that were impossible to believe.

Leave a place where people became strangely ill, one after another. Where girls supposedly killed by animals, but obviously buried by humans.

Here, body parts were discovered on doorsteps.

I can't leave, not now.

Her cast still remained, and still had hopes that the crimes could be solved, that the show—far more entertaining than they had dared hope—could have a long run.

That wasn't it. She couldn't leave because . . .

There were answers to be found here somewhere. And she didn't want to run away from Grant.

"I wouldn't leave while the others are still here, and I'm not sure they want to give it all up so quickly, Reggie. The town can't just give up—they have to solve what's going on here. We'll stick together. We'll be fine. When are you coming back?"

She could faintly hear Reggie's sigh over the distance. "Well, I've rescheduled a few groups, and I have to finish here, but I will be there as soon as I can get there." She was silent for a minute, but Stephanie was certain she was about to say something else. When she did, she sounded indignant. "Arturo has told me that there's a wild tale about a medieval witch, and the townspeople have whispered that things have started to go badly there because of me! I'm doing my best to help bring money into the area, and that's the thanks I get! If there's something going wrong, they need to look at the people who are digging up the past. This psycho is probably part of the scientific community that has come in!"

Stephanie hesitated, then knew there was no way she could possibly begin to explain that there was so much more going on than she had imagined! She could just envision herself trying to tell Reggie over the miles that one of the cast members was a fake, and that he claimed to be a vampire, a *good* vampire, aware of a terrible evil in the area, and searching for it himself. And that he was having trouble because his usual powers were blocked because there *was* a witch involved as well as a vampire.

She would sound as if she had gone certifiably insane herself.

"I hope you get here soon, Reggie," she said.

"As soon as I can, Steph. Poor dear! Who would have imagined that I would have done this to you!"

"You haven't done anything to me, Reggie," Stephanie assured her. "It's beautiful here, the show was great. What you intended was wonderful—and can still be. I'll let the cast know that we're going to be on hiatus until we get word from you."

"All right, dear. Naturally, they're welcome to stay—but they're also free to leave. They must do as they think best. And I will see you as soon as I can," Reggie said.

"Great. Take care of yourself," Stephanie said.

"You, too, dear. You, too. And Stephanie!"

"Yes."

"Thank you."

"For what?"

"I heard that the shows were brilliant, that the audience nearly rolled on the floor with laughter."

"Thanks. We hope to bring it all back. 'Bye, then."

"*Ciao.*"

When Drew returned to the hospital, he was startled to see the police car in front. When he entered, half the staff in the reception area was talking excitedly, angrily, and gesturing wildly to emphasize their words over those of others.

He stared blankly at the chaos for a minute. The older policeman, Merc, lifted a hand and said something firmly, and everyone fell silent.

The pretty nurse he had met earlier was standing on the fringes of the group. He made his way around to her and whispered, "What's happened?"

"Our blood was stolen."

"What?"

She sighed deeply. "I went to our supply room. I am a supervisor, and . . . there are drugs, and of course, our blood supply, which are always monitored. I do . . . what is the word? Inventory. When I got there, all our blood had been stolen! Dr. Antinella is very angry. He thinks it might have been a very mean prank, and he wants our police chief to round up all the teenagers in town and get a confession." She turned to Drew, her large, dark eyes somber. "It's really very serious. You know how low our supplies are—you gave type O for your friend last night. Now we have no A, B, or AB. It's all gone."

"That's terrible!"

"Yes."

"But . . . someone came in, got into the room where you kept the blood, stole it all, and got out—without being seen?" Drew said, somewhat incredulous.

"I'm afraid that's what happened," the nurse told him.

Merc was speaking sternly, and if nothing else, he managed to get the rest of them to stay silent. Dr. Antinella spoke quietly and calmly in response to something that Merc said, and if anything, he looked very weary and disgusted.

"Our chief is saying," the nurse explained to Drew, "that he will speak with everyone working here, one by one. And he wants the room closed off. He is calling the crime scene specialists from the next big town to come back. They were already here, you know, for quite some time, working the area where poor Maria Britto had been buried up in the hills."

"I know," Drew murmured. "Well, I hope they'll find some fingerprints, a shoe print . . . something that will help them. But, aren't supplies like that locked up?"

"That's why everyone is so upset. Yes, of course, they were locked up. Dr. Antinella has a key, the superintendent has a key, and the head nurse has a key. They all swear that their keys were in their possession at all times. But the room was not broken into. So . . . someone had to have used a key." Despite the gravity of her words, she smiled suddenly. "My name is Antoinette, by the way."

"Antoinette," Drew said. "That's a beautiful name."

She flashed him another smile, listening again, because Merc was talking. "He will use the superintendent's office and speak with everyone there. None of us is to leave the hospital." She sighed. "And to happen today!"

"Why today in particular?" Drew asked.

"Why, they are burying Maria Britto today. It is such a sad occasion. And word is all over town that an arm was found last night, at the resort, on a man's doorstep. Everyone thinks it belongs to the missing actress. Now, this . . . everyone is edgy, and excited. And afraid," she added softly. She turned back to him. "Well, it is a pleasure to know you. I'll be called soon enough. You must excuse me. I need to see to my patients. And that food is getting cold," she finished, indicating the bag Drew carried.

He had come back so proud of getting the steak and spaghetti. The concept of "to go" was not really recognized here.

Now, the food was indeed getting cold, and his sense of things going right was definitely flying out the window. Strange, he'd finally met a friend. A lovely Italian woman. And everything around him was going right to hell.

Worry filled him deeply as well. He was anxious to get back to Doug.

"Antoinette, despite everything, it's a pleasure to know

you, too," he said. "It's all right if I go through, right? I brought my friend a steak."

"Yes, yes, get the food to your friend. You're in the hospital now—they may not let you leave for a while yet," she told him.

"That's no problem. I have all day."

She gave him a little wave, and walked back toward the group. Franco, standing by his father's side, saw Drew, and nodded an acknowledgment. Drew nodded in turn, and lifted the bag of food in explanation, though he wasn't sure why. Franco nodded again.

Drew hurried through the reception area and down the hallway. As he walked, he patted his pocket, trying to make sure he still had his cell phone.

He had to call the others about this bizarre new development.

With one hand, he pulled out the cell as he headed along quickly, then entered Doug's room.

He started to dial Stephanie's phone number; it was the one he had actually memorized.

His fingers suddenly froze on the dial plate.

The bag of "to go" food fell from his hand and crashed on the floor as he stared into Doug's room.

Chapter 16

"She's very upset," Stephanie told Grant, referring to Reggie. "Think about it. She's off combing Europe for customers to get an area going. Then she calls back and hears everything that's happening, and, apparently, since a lot of this did seem to coincide, even Arturo tells her that there's talk about her being a sorceress. And as I said, all that is ridiculous—Reggie was not just 'dug up.' She's been in my life, at least, for a very long time."

"Where did she say she was?" Grant asked.

"Belgium."

"Steph, don't get angry with me. I'm not the one who suggested that she was a witch," Grant reminded her. They were seated at her dining room table.

There didn't seem to be enough coffee in the world that morning.

Not even espresso.

"We need to get over to the hospital," Grant said.

"Should we see if Lucien and Jade are awake?" Stephanie asked him. "Although, it is just about one o'clock." She hesitated. "Would he be . . . sleeping? Resting? Doing whatever vampires usually do in the afternoon?"

He stared back at her, his lips hinting at a rueful smile. "I don't know. I never knew a vampire before." He gave his head a slight shake. "There was something about him . . . *is* something about him . . . but can any of this be true?"

Stephanie took his hands. "Grant, there's something out of the ordinary that's true here, and we both know it."

"It's the most insane thing in the world—and it really scares me—but I do believe this guy. Either he's what he says he is, or he's the most sincere lunatic in the world. Come on, let's go and see how Doug is doing. We'll stop by Lucien's cottage and find out if he does sleep most of the day, and if not, if they're coming to the hospital with us."

They walked the short distance to the cottage that had been assigned to Clay Barton. Jade opened the door. She had apparently been up for some time.

"Good morning—afternoon," she told them. "Come on in."

"Is he—sleeping?" Stephanie asked.

"He's been gone for hours," Jade told them. "Something happened. I'm not sure what. He did one of those things where he kind of bolted awake . . . got really restless, and then went out. When he can explain what woke him so violently, he will. Anyway, we've all got to make sure we keep moving along here. I've been searching the Internet for information about the Norman presence here during the medieval ages, and trying to find out if there aren't any old texts somewhere that might help us. There's a library in town. I'm hoping to find a reference to a book that I might then locate."

"Ah," Grant murmured.

"We're dealing with an unknown, you see," Jade explained.

"Doesn't Lucien have to . . . I don't know, rest by day, at least? Does he have to return to his—er—coffin?"

"We travel with native dirt," she said. "And as for sleeping . . . he sleeps next to me," she said softly.

Stephanie cleared her throat and said, "Grant had a really terrible nightmare last night."

Grant flashed her a look, as if she were airing dirty laundry before a comparative stranger.

"Grant! Maybe Liz—Jade—can help, or even learn something from you," Stephanie pleaded.

Jade was looking at him with serious interest. "Do you remember the dream?"

"At first . . . at first, I could still smell the blood when I awoke. But it . . . it's fading now. What I remember is that I was riding, I was in full armor, and . . . it was terrible. There was a horrible slaughter. People, animals . . . the dead everywhere. And I knew . . ."

"You knew what?"

He shook his head. "I just knew that the situation was desperate. And that . . ."

"Grant! This could be important!" Jade said. "That what?"

"That heads had to be removed. That was the only way to kill—François. And it was also the only way to kill the devil dogs. And Valeria." He waved a hand in the air. "It might have all been a trick of the mind. You know, there's the dig, and the conversation we had . . . and the schism in my mind as I try to determine whether or not vampires can exist, and, if they do, if there's such a thing as a good vampire."

Jade smiled. "It's a lot, isn't it? But your dream might have been more important than you know."

"I've had it before," he said. "But each time, it's more vivid."

"That may be really important," she told him. A silence came between them.

"We're heading for the hospital, to see about Doug," Stephanie told her.

"Good idea. Make sure he's still wearing that cross."

"What?" Stephanie said.

"We got a cross on him last night. Make sure he's still wearing it."

"We—we took it off him. It seemed that the metal was bothering his throat," Stephanie told her.

"I'd better come with you," she said.

Drew rushed in.

A fierce struggle was ensuing—an elderly man with a huge knife was busy attacking Doug.

Doug was doing his best to defend himself, rolling, sliding, and then leaping as the man savagely struck at him.

"Hey!" Drew cried. "Get off of him!"

He charged the man.

The old man turned on him. Drew backed away, catching Doug's eye across the bed. The old man was crazy—and he was lethal.

"What the hell?" Drew said to Doug.

"The old geezer just came in and attacked me!" Doug shouted back.

The man began to speak to Drew in rapid Italian, his words earnest.

Drew shook his head, trying to indicate that he didn't understand. The man waved the knife. It appeared to be a butcher's knife. One slash from that, and . . .

"Now, sir, I can't let you chop up my friend," Drew said, keeping his voice low and even. That's how you were supposed to talk to the crazed, right? They needed to get the knife away from the fellow.

Where was the hospital staff? If the cops were here, and they were looking into a blood theft, why the hell weren't they coming now? Surely, someone was hearing this commotion.

But then, maybe not. People were awaiting their turn to talk. They were all distracted.

All right, he had to handle it himself. He took a step toward the fellow. "Now, buddy, listen, I need you to give me the knife."

The man took a step toward him then, the knife swinging.

"No! Dear God, what the hell . . . no, no, no! I don't have a weapon, see?" Drew said.

Doug was trying to get around the bed and make for the door, the exit. The Italian man might have been as old as God himself, but he was sharp as a tack. He lunged toward the foot of the bed, sending Drew back to the far corner of the room.

Drew looked wildly around himself. "Someone, help!" he shouted as loudly as he could. There was nothing.

He grabbed a bedpan, putting it in front of himself as a poor excuse for a shield.

He was quickly sorry that he did so. The old man bunched his slender muscles and started across the room with wild intent in his eyes.

"No!" Doug shrieked, coming forward.

The old man stopped and spun quickly, heading for Doug once again. He was nearly upon him when suddenly a figure burst into the room, making a flying tackle for the old fellow. He heard a shriek; the body that had flown in, catching the fellow's feet, bringing him down hard on the hospital bed, was Grant Peterson. Stephanie had let out the scream, and she and Liz were now standing in the doorway.

The old man twisted around, still fighting, slashing. Grant jumped back just in time, then lashed out with his leg. His foot connected with the old man's wrist, and at last, the knife went flying from his hand, slammed against the wall, and fell to the floor.

Doug made a dive for it.

"Whew!" Doug let out, doubling over, gripping his knees.

The old man just lay on the bed then. His head was twisted to the side. His eyes stared vacantly, glazed, across the room.

"Hey!" Grant said softly, approaching him. "Are you all right, is your wrist . . . can you move it?"

Liz hurried into the room, coming to the fellow's other side. She began to speak in Italian to him.

He didn't respond.

At last, the nurse, Antoinette, came to the door as well.

"What is going on here?" she demanded indignantly. "What have you done to him?" she cried, seeing the old man on the bed.

"Done to *him*!" Drew said indignantly. "He tried to kill Doug. Then he tried to kill me, and my friend Grant got here just in the nick of time to stop him!"

Antoinette stared at all of them. She walked in, pushing both Liz and Grant aside. She began to speak to the old man, smoothing back his white hair.

Suddenly, as if he were an infant, he began to cry, leaning against her. She got him up. Still casting warning glances over her shoulder, she led him out of the room.

"I hope you're getting him a straightjacket!" Drew yelled, shaking now that it all seemed to be over.

"He's harmless!" Antoinette called back.

"Harmless!" Doug looked at the butcher's knife he was holding. He stared across the room at Grant, who appeared to be just as baffled.

"Are you both all right?" Grant asked.

"Yeah, thanks to your rather timely arrival," Drew said dryly. "Nice kick. A bit of Jackie Chan action, huh?"

"I was in a few kung fu movies," Grant explained briefly. "Doug—let's get you back into bed. Maybe this could cause a major setback for you."

"Are you kidding me? Back to bed—I've got to get the hell out of this loony bin!" Doug told him.

Grant didn't seem to hear. "Where are the doctors? Nurses, orderlies—anyone? What, is the staff around here nuts? What's going on? There's no one around? We heard you from the lobby!"

"Someone knocked over the blood bank this morning—the cops are talking to the staff," Drew explained.

"What?" Liz demanded sharply.

"Whatever supplies of blood were left are gone. Stolen. I didn't get what happened, either," Drew said, trying to make the story as short as possible.

"Please, while they're all tied up, can you get me the hell out of here before someone does kill me?" Doug pleaded.

"Doug, are you sure?" Stephanie asked anxiously.

"Please?" he repeated. "Come on, now. Before Attila-the-nurse comes back. Ask Drew—that guy nearly killed us!"

"But Doug . . . you were nearly dead!" Stephanie told him.

"I feel great," he assured her.

"I think we should get him out of here," Liz said.

"Yes, and quickly, please!" Doug urged.

Something had changed, suddenly and abruptly, in the night.

Lucien stood on the precipice, drawing pictures of the distant past in his mind.

This was where it had happened.

At that time, the outcropping of earth had gone much farther. That was the part that had broken cleanly from the cliff, tumbling downward in a rumble of the ground's power and fury.

If they wanted to find the remains of Conan de Burgh, they would be almost dead set below.

He shifted his gaze. There was a lot of activity in the camp, but around the sites where many of the men belonging to the ranks of both de Burgh and de Venue had fought and died, only a few workers were busy.

He closed his eyes, trying to see.

He felt the breeze, struggled to reach the plane where he could recall, and see with an ancient instinct and vision. For a moment, he could hear the clatter of armor, shouts and screams, the whinny of a horse, a howling sound . . . the world in his mind began to take shape out of the mist . . . he could see. Warriors with helmets and great shields, swords that glinted in the sun . . . swords, no longer glinting, for they were red with the blood of the fallen . . .

Then . . .

He lost it.

It was almost as if someone had stepped into his mind, and pulled a curtain.

He swore, and started the climb back down the cliff. Dusk was coming. It was important that he discover where the curtains were coming from, exactly what was happening here when the sun went down, here, where the core of it all existed, close, so close . . . just out of reach.

He needed to stay.

He couldn't stay.

Already, he sensed that there was trouble.

He had to get back.

But he would be going back with nothing! He still had no clues as to how to arrest the power that was different from his own.

He felt the wind again, and determined that he had to find some truth with which to fight.

Stephanie stayed behind when the group hurried through the lobby with Doug. She thanked God that he was all right, but it disturbed her that the old man who had attacked Doug was the same old man who had forced the cross on her the night before.

She felt around her neck, and remembered that she'd given the man's gift to Suzette. The old fellow was a jeweler.

It was unlikely he'd be making any sales that day.

She lagged behind the others, afraid that Grant would try to stop her if he knew that she wanted to stay behind, just for a few minutes. But though she thought it might not be a bad idea to get Doug out of the hospital now that he seemed to be so well, she couldn't forget the work that Dr. Antinella had done to save him. He had to be thanked.

She also wanted to do her best to talk to Merc and find out what he thought about the gentleman attacking Doug.

Did people around here really believe that legend? Why not—she was believing it! But she had some reason to do so now, while the average townsman or woman . . .

Lucretia Britto had severed her daughter's head.

This fellow had come to the room to decapitate Doug!

Thankfully, the hospital was small. It wasn't terribly difficult to find the corridor that led to the staff offices, and since there weren't many, she found the door with the plaque reading "Dr. Antinella" very easily.

She was afraid he'd still be involved with the police, or attending a patient in the hospital, or even out and about in the town, but to her relief, when she tapped at the door, he bid her to enter.

He looked at her suspiciously as she came in and sat down.

"*Buonasera,*" she told him.

He nodded.

"We've taken Doug out of the hospital," she said.

"I didn't release him."

She nodded. "I know, and that's why I've come to apologize. But, surely you're aware, the old man, the jeweler . . . he just tried to kill Doug."

Antinella sat back. He didn't reply.

"In the United States," she reminded him, "the man would have been arrested for attempted murder."

"This isn't the United States," he said, and she winced, thinking she had ruffled his feathers. Then he sighed. "Here, yes, usually, there would have been an arrest for attempted murder."

She hesitated, then said, "Dr. Antinella, did that man, Adalio Davanti, the jeweler, think that Doug had become a vampire? Did he believe he would be saving his entire community if he were to see to it that Doug was . . . beheaded? Is there a belief here that such things can happen? Is that why Maria Britto's mother severed her head, and . . . is that why you didn't perform an autopsy, and why she wasn't embalmed?"

He set his pen down on the charts on his desk, sat back, and stared at her.

"I don't know what Adalio thought he was doing, exactly," he said.

"But . . . there was no autopsy. You're a man of science. You said that Maria had been killed by animals. But then . . . Grant found an arm last night, so we can only assume that Gema is dead as well, and animals didn't bury Gema, nor did they leave the arm for Grant to find," Stephanie said.

Still, he paused. Then, at last, he said, "I am a man of science. Our police are men of the law. This is a fine community."

"It's a wonderful community," Stephanie assured him. "But . . . if there are things here that we should know . . ."

He looked at her angrily again. "There were not 'things,' as you say, until you arrived!"

"No!" she said, just an emphatically. "I am not the cause of any of this, nor is the theater, nor is Reggie . . . or any of us! This place has been filled with legends for centuries . . .

with stories about creatures ... devil dogs, demon dogs, witches. We didn't bring any of it here."

Antinella studied her again for a long moment, then sighed. "Every place has its history. Take your country. For years, they taught American school children that the cavalry defeated savage beasts, and they were talking about the Native Americans, the Indians, the indigenous tribes. Now, there is a fairer view—Europeans came and brought their civilizations, their gods, their guns, and their diseases. Yes, wars have raged across Europe. Every man thinks he is right. Countries have fought, barons have fought ... and here, yes, there was one fight that has stayed in local lore since it occurred. And," he added softly, "perhaps it has stayed for a reason. In essence, your country is new. In Europe, the Middle East, the Far East ... Africa, history is much older. Sometimes, yes, men were beasts. Then, there is the gray area. In mist-shrouded mountains everywhere, there are tales about creatures that aren't quite human. And here ... yes, again. You will find that many of the people have beliefs similar to those of Lucretia Britto—and Adalio Davanti."

Stephanie nodded, then persisted. "You were charged with the autopsy of Maria Britto. It wasn't done. Not at first, not when it should have been."

"No," he agreed.

"And it wasn't because you were afraid of hurting her mother any more than she had already been hurt. That was your official story, I believe."

He picked up his pen again, his fingers tightening around it. "Are you condemning me, Miss Cahill?"

"No. I'm just trying to find out if ..."

"If witches, vampires, and beasts exist?" he queried.

"You see," she explained, "I'm beginning to believe that they do. And I think you share many of the fears evidenced around here."

"What do you want from me, Miss Cahill? I am a medical doctor—I trained across the world. I am a man of science. I understand as well that the mind and the soul are greater factors in the human condition than we have ever imagined. Will I protect my community, my people? Yes. Science isn't always in books—and there are hundreds of mysteries that we haven't answered, or even begun to explore. Where there is knowledge sometimes, there is ignorance. Where there are miracles . . . there is also the frightening and the eerie. Simply, where there is good, there is evil. You have taken your friend from the hospital. We saved his life. Now, it is for you to protect what we have given you. And may I suggest that . . . you protect yourself as well."

She stood up, aware that he was dismissing her, and aware that he didn't intend to give her anything else.

"The evil seems to come from the excavations," she said, standing.

"Yes," he agreed. "I'm very busy, you know."

"One last question. What are the demon dogs?"

He shook his head. "I don't know. I wish I did."

"Thank you," she told him.

He nodded, and stared back at his charts. She knew he wasn't really reading them at all.

Out on the streets, they came across the funeral procession for Maria Britto.

Here, the local hearse was a Victorian horse-drawn vehicle. One giant roan pulled it.

Grant was stock-still as it passed them by. The sides of the hearse were etched glass. There was also a glass window on the coffin, and Maria's face was clearly discernable.

Now, her rich, dark hair was drawn around her neck.

Her head had been sewn back on her body by the coroner.

"Jesu!" Drew whispered, crossing himself.

They had all stopped, since the road ran between the hospital and the parking lot that serviced it. Lined up on the street, they listened to the sad toll of the violin being played by a man who followed directly behind Lucretia Britto. The priest walked with her, and behind him, scores of townspeople.

"They're headed to the cemetery," Liz murmured.

"Yes, I would think," Grant said.

The procession continued. At the end, Drew said, "I'm tempted to follow."

"Me, too," Grant said.

Doug groaned. "I'm tempted to go back to the resort, find my bed, and crawl into it."

Grant ignored him. He started after the last man trailing in the procession, and the others fell in line behind him.

Carlo Ponti stood in the center of the excavations with Heinrich, reading from transcripts he had received via the Internet just the night before.

"'And was thus, on the night of Our Lord, on the eighteenth of August, in the year 1215, that the great battle took place. The dead arose from their graves, as summoned by the devil's own bride, and there ensued a battle so fierce that the slain lay in greater numbers than the flies. Those who rode forth with the great knight fell in vast numbers, and in the end, found triumph, but through great loss, for their leader did not see all that was truth, and so, gave of his own blood. The ruins were searched, but the surviving were forced to flee, for in the end, God roared above all, and his earth created the grave, and where the fallen had not breathed their last, God commanded that the ground itself and the silver relics of the good be a tomb to hold them evermore,'" he read.

Heinrich, great white bushy brows knitting, shook his head. "Carlo, there is nothing new here. We know for certain the battle took place. We know about the fallen, and the earthquake. And we have unearthed a number of the dead." He shivered suddenly and fiercely. "These mountain breezes! One minute, it is the beautiful warmth of the summer, and the next . . . didn't you feel that snap of cold?"

Carlo waved a hand in the air. He wasn't interested in the weather. "My friend, did you hear the date?"

"Yes?"

"This was written by the old calendar!" Carlo pronounced. "We are standing here, centuries later, but on the exact date of the battle when you figure in the change!"

Heinrich smiled, amused by his friend and colleague's enthusiasm. "So, this will be a very good thing when the television stations arrive to do their documentaries. A hook to our story."

Carlo was very still. Then he shivered, too. "Dusk is coming. That is why it's suddenly so cold. This is wonderful," he said, shaking his paper. Then he sighed. "It was written by a monk in 1225, ten years after the battle, but my researchers believe that the monk, a Brother Marcus, was here at the time of the battle. I think his words mean so much more. If I can only fathom what he has written between the lines!"

Heinrich sighed. "I don't think there is anything written between the lines. It is all as it was recorded historically, and that was actually in line with the legends. There was a great battle, between a man kind and decent to the peasants, and a man who broke their backs and thought of human life as a very cheap commodity."

Carlo shook his head. "There's more. Listen. 'Let us, in the wake of this, know that the ways of goodness must be upheld. Ever present lurks the danger that the earth shall shift again, and let us forget that evil must be conquered, and the mistakes of the past never again relived.'"

"I'd say it was a big mistake for that many people to die," Heinrich said lightly. But he shivered again. Suddenly, he was very uneasy where he stood. Nonsense! He was a scientist. He studied the dead. He slept with old bones in his house upon occasion!

And yet . . .

He felt a presence. And Carlo's words were getting to him. *Evil.* It existed here.

"Let's get back to the camp—we'll reread all this tomorrow and look for what Brother Marcus is saying between the lines, eh? We'll work when the sun is up, and our vision is much better." He clapped a hand on Carlo's shoulder. "A monk must write such words, you know. All that about goodness and evil."

Carlo spoke again, very excited. "'When the moon rises, full upon us, there is danger. For the past never lies truly buried, and only as it is rectified as it was, can we look for the light.'"

Heinrich thought that he saw the great shadow of a monstrous bird's wings sweep around them, bringing an ever greater chill to his bones. Then, he realized that goose bumps had broken out over his flesh, and though he was cold, he was sweating.

His breathing was labored. His heart hammered too quickly.

He was afraid.

"Carlo! We will read this in the morning!" he insisted, and leaving his associate behind, he hurried along the trail to the camp, and the place where the lights burned.

Stephanie was baffled. She had assumed that they would reach Grant's car, realize that she wasn't with them, and wait.

Or come after her, one or the other. She had even expected Grant to be angry, but she had intended to deal with that—it had seemed very important to her to speak with Dr. Antinella.

But they were nowhere to be seen, and Grant's car was still in the parking lot.

She hesitated, then remembered her cell phone, pulled it out, and dialed Grant's number. She got his answering machine. She hung up.

The resort was a short drive, and no more than a twenty-minute walk. With nothing left to do at the hospital, she decided that she might as well head back. She'd find Lena and Suzette.

As she walked, she mused that Jade had told them that they should continue to refer to her and Lucien as Liz and Clay. Now, Stephanie wasn't sure that was such a good idea. Too many things seemed to be happening too quickly. At least, among the group of them, she thought that the truth should be out. If it *was* truth . . .

There she went again! Did she really believe all this?

She quickened her pace, noticing that the afternoon was already waning. She suddenly decided that it was imperative to reach the other girls before dusk.

The streets seemed to be oddly deserted. She remembered that today was Maria Britto's funeral, and thought that most of the people in the town would be attending it.

At last, she saw the resort ahead of her. She exhaled a sigh of relief. She hadn't realized just how uneasy she had gotten, following the road back toward the beach and the resort.

She walked through the reception area. It was empty. She exited the rear, and then paused.

There was already a wind blowing. Clouds were beginning to obscure what was left of the sun.

There was no one on the beach.

She started along the path that would bring her to Lena's cottage. As she walked along, she was startled when Giovanni suddenly came around from one of the other little places.

"Miss Cahill!" he said, pleased. "I've been looking for you."

"Oh? Why? What's up?"

"Reggie is here—she wants to see you," he told her.

Instantly, she felt a guard rise around her. She shook her head. "Giovanni, I spoke with Reggie just a few hours ago. She was in Belgium, and she said she still had some business to attend to."

"You have a cell phone?" he said. "Call her. She is here."

"If she's here, why doesn't she just come to me?" Stephanie said.

He sighed. "I told her that you would not believe me. Please, call her. She is here."

"She got a plane out of Belgium and got here this quickly?" Stephanie said. She felt a growing unease. But it was still daytime—surely that meant something. And they were out in the open—even if it seemed that no one was about. But he had to be lying about Reggie.

"Call her, please." He sighed, then lifted his hands and grinned. "I just work for Reggie," he said. He gave her a rueful, charming smile, and brushed a curl of dark hair from his forehead. The he lifted his shoulders in a shrug. "I will just tell her that you won't come. It's all right. She'll have to come to you."

"Yes, she'll have to," Stephanie said.

With another shrug, he started to walk off.

"Wait. I'll call her."

Stephanie pulled out her phone and dialed Reggie's number. Reggie answered instantly. "Stephanie?"

"Yes. Reggie, what's going on here? Giovanni is telling me you want to see me. I told him you were in Belgium."

"Oh, Stephanie, I lied. I'm here, I've been here. After we hung up, I knew I just couldn't lie to you anymore. But there are so many awful things being said about me . . . I've been keeping a low profile. I feel I have to see you and explain. I'm so sorry. Will you come to me? I don't want others to know I'm here—not until they can get some answers to the terrible things that are happening!"

It was definitely Reggie. And she sounded so upset.

"Where are you?"

"Giovanni can bring you to me," Reggie said.

Stephanie reminded herself that she had known Reggie for years, that she hadn't popped out of the ground at any dig. Still, she intended to be careful.

"Reggie, try to understand. No one in the theater group is angry with you. I was just going to stop in and see Lena and Suzette. Why don't you meet me there?"

"No, Stephanie," Reggie protested. "Just—"

"That's where I'll be, Reggie," Stephanie said firmly.

She looked at Giovanni, who just shrugged. "I have done my job," he said, and giving her a wave, he started walking toward the resort.

Stephanie hurried to Lena's cottage.

When she got there and knocked on the door, she was startled as it opened when she rapped.

Opened . . .

Creaked inward.

Cautiously, she stuck her head in. "Lena? Suzette?"

"Steph!" Lena called. "Come in."

She did.

It was dark inside. She blinked against the change of light.

Then she saw the two of them—and the scene in the living room area.

She stopped dead still in horror

She started to back away.

But behind her, the doorway was now blocked.

"Oh, no, Stephanie. You're staying!" she was told.

She recognized the voice, but turning back to the light,

she was blinded. There was a tall, large form there, hands on hips.

Then she knew.

"What are you doing?" she cried.

"It's time," he said simply.

Chapter 17

Maria Britto was laid to rest with a great deal of ceremony.

As they stood in the background, Arturo came around behind Grant and spoke softly. "Here, you see, she is in the hallowed ground. Beyond there . . . the small stone fence, there is where those who have died outside the church have gone. The priest has sprinkled holy water around the entire circumference of the grave, and before the dirt is thrown over the coffin, the great cross there will go over the length of it."

"I see, thank you," Grant whispered in return.

He noted that, bit by bit, most of the town had arrived. Merc and Franco had apparently ended their questioning of hospital employees, because they were there, together as usual, more like an eternal pair of twins rather than a father and son.

Dr. Antinella had arrived as well. Grant recognized people from the cafés, the shops, the hospital, and even the dig. Carlo Ponti was there, along with two of his closest associates, the German forensic anthropologist Heinrich Gutten and the French historian Jacques Perdot.

The person who was not with them, he realized suddenly, was Stephanie.

He backed up to where Jade was standing. "Where's Steph?"

Jade turned around, looking through the crowd. "I don't know," she admitted.

"Doug, Drew," Grant said, looking back, behind Jade. Drew was there; Doug was not. "Where's Stephanie—and Doug?"

"Doug . . . I don't know!" Drew said, looking around, frowning. "He was with me until we reached the gates . . . and Steph . . . she was with us when we were leaving the hospital."

Grant backed away, a feeling of urgency coming over him as he searched the crowd anxiously.

She definitely wasn't with him.

"I have to find Stephanie," he said to Drew. Turning quickly, he started to head out the cemetery gates.

Jade ran after him. "She must be back at the hospital."

"Why? Even Antinella, the cops, and the hospital staff are here," he said, his concern growing.

With Jade and Drew following behind him, Grant hurried on with long strides. But at the cemetery gates, he stopped.

The old man was standing there. Now, he was carrying a huge sword. It was a double-handed battle sword.

Grant thought the man intended to swing it.

But the fellow looked at him and began speaking earnestly. He didn't appear to be insane, nor was he as wild as he had been before, in Doug's hospital room.

He offered the sword to Grant, his words rapid, intent, and insistent.

"He wants you to take it. He says that you're going to need it," Jade said.

"I can't take that from him!" Grant protested. "It looks . . . if it's not original, it's a damned good copy."

"*Grazie, grazie, ma no!*" Grant said to the man.

The old fellow shook his head, and blocked the exit again.

"Take it from him!" Jade advised.

Unless he wanted to knock the man out of the way—or risk his temper and cause him to use it—Grant could see no alternative. He looked back. Many at the funeral were now watching him. They didn't seem to think it odd that the man was offering him a sword. They looked on with mild interest.

The man said something in Italian that Grant couldn't catch.

"He says that the time has come," Jade translated softly.

"What time?"

"The time when you're going to need the sword, I believe," she said.

Grant accepted the blade, thanking the old man again. The fellow stepped out of his way, nodding gravely.

The funeral-goers turned back to heed the words of the priest.

The entire area suddenly seemed to darken. Grant looked at the sky. It was growing late. Dusk was coming. And quickly.

He started to run toward the hospital.

"Grant, wait!" Jade called.

Irritated, he looked back.

"It's . . . too late. Can't you see, can't you tell?" She shook her head, indicating the sky. "He has her," she said softly.

Suspicion raged in him. *Who* had her? Had Jade been dogging him to keep him from realizing that Lucien was the real threat?

"What the hell are you talking about?" he demanded raggedly. "*Who has her*? Your so-called vampire husband?"

She shook her head. "No. François has her. François de Venue," she told him. "And that's why you're going to need the sword."

*   *   *

Stephanie was afraid she was going to pass out. She could smell the blood from the living room floor where Lena and Suzette were still strewn on the floor, naked and supine, and crawling over the body of one of the maids, tearing at her with their nails and teeth, as if they were canines or hyenas, starved for a meal.

And there was Doug, just staring at her.

"It's time for what?" she demanded. "Doug, you've got to let me by. We have to get help, and quickly."

"No. It's time to go, Stephanie."

"Where, Doug?" she asked. She tried to keep her voice level and calm, stalling for time. Reggie was on her way . . . except that Reggie could just become part of this travesty.

She hadn't really looked around the room—there hadn't been time, and she'd been too stunned. She hadn't seen any weapons. That thought made her feel weaker. Suzette and Lena had apparently attacked the woman with their bare hands—and teeth. And what they had done . . .

She didn't dare think about it. She had to keep her wits together. Terror was filling her. At any minute, they could turn on her.

"It's time to go," Doug repeated again.

She kept staring at him, wishing they had thought to ask so many more questions when they were with Lucien and Jade. *Was Doug a vampire now? Was he just under some kind of influence or unholy power?*

And what about the girls? Oh, God, just looking at them now . . .

"Tell me, Doug. Where do you want me to go?"

"With me."

"Doug, we need help here," she said very softly.

For a moment, she thought that something registered in his eyes. A form of humanity . . . as if in him, somewhere, he saw what the girls were doing, and knew that the women needed help.

No, that they *all* needed help.

But the look was quickly gone. "You must come, Stephanie. I don't want to hurt you."

"If you don't want to—don't!" she told him.

"You have to come."

"Doug . . . look ! For the love of God, look at Suzette and Lena!"

He did. Once again, for split seconds, she thought she had him.

But then he shrugged, and a strange, eerie smile parted his lips. "They're hungry," he said, and it sounded as if he was nothing more than amused.

Desperately, and quickly, she assessed her situation.

Lena and Suzette—suddenly turned into bloodied, murderous, scavenging maniacs—were intent in their unholy pursuit on the living room floor. Doug blocked the main entrance.

The back. She had to get out the back. Vampires couldn't abide seawater. She remembered Lucien's arm, the way it had looked.

"All right, Doug. Just one minute," she said.

He stood there. She turned and walked slowly, as if she was intent on seeing what the girls were doing.

Her stomach flipped.

She moved past the girls.

Only then did she run, clicking the lock on the back door, sliding the glass with a slam, and running out with the speed of the wind.

She heard him behind her. Heard him roaring out a command to Suzette and Lena that they must stop her.

She didn't dare look back.

She ran for the sea. Plunging in, she swam out.

As she had hoped, Doug stopped at the shore. He couldn't come any farther. All she had to do was stand in the surf, and he couldn't reach her. Help would come.

Soon, she prayed.

But from where he stood, Doug lifted a hand, and swept it toward the sea. Lena and Suzette, absurdly naked and bloodied, bounded in after her.

She could outswim the two, she was certain. In a parallel line, she crawled hard, diving under, swerving, trying to lose them.

They were coming after her like a pair of sharks, drawn to the scent of blood.

The salt water was stinging her eyes. At her speed, her muscles were flagging quickly.

"Stephanie!"

She heard her name called. Blinking, she tried to see to the shore. There was someone there . . . help!

If she'd listened in the first place . . .

She kicked with all her strength, trying to get in ahead of her maniacal one-time friends. Her feet hit the sand, and she started racing in, toward the man who had come to save her.

Yet . . .

As she reached him, she knew.

She saw the amusement in his eyes.

It was the man she had known.

And it wasn't.

He had changed. Eyes that had always been light with laughter were now that strange yellow-red that had struck her as being so unusual in Lucien's striking features. He seemed to have grown. His shoulders were broader, and the amusement in his features was touched with contempt and an air of superiority. He was simply larger.

"Ah, poor Stephanie! You had no idea. You would be thinking that such a powerful man as François de Venue would walk about as a leader of men, now as before. But you must understand. I knew that there would be someone to come and challenge my power. So . . . to stay close, what else would one do? I had to do what I did to avoid those I did not want to see, and yet so easily have invitations to enter where I wished to go! Of course, come in, please . . .there I was, invited! And now . . ."

He raised his arms. It seemed that a huge black cloud rose all around her.

She started to scream.

The water! She had to get back to the water.

But the girls were coming for her now, lethal sirens as they rose from the surf. She dodged, trying to seek another line of escape.

There was Doug. He walked straight up to her as she nearly plowed into him, and his hand flew hard across the back of her neck.

Stars appeared before her. She began to stagger.

Arms, draped in black, swept around her.

She heard a strange, sizzling sound. Someone . . . cursing. "Damned seawater!" came a growl of rage. And then, "Ah, but such a small price to pay. You are what I have been waiting for . . . you are what will make it complete!" she heard

She fought for consciousness in the smothering folds of darkness.

It was a losing battle.

"What do you mean, it's too late? Nothing is ever too late—it can't be too late!" Grant shouted, gripping Jade by the shoulders.

"What I mean is that you won't find her at the hospital, and we won't find her at the resort. What we have to do is find out how to get her back and why François wants her so much," Jade told him.

"What are you two talking about?" Drew demanded. But looking from one to the other, he groaned. "Something is really going on here—more than even I know."

"I'm going to the dig," Grant said.

"It may not be that simple—" Jade began.

"I'm going to the dig! She's there. I just—I just know she's there."

"All right, all right, but . . . you have to go prepared," Jade said. "Let's get back to Lucien's cottage—I have a few things that might help you."

"Is anyone actually going to explain this to me?" Drew pleaded.

They both looked at him, mouths opening.

"No," they said in unison.

"The explanation is too long, and you won't believe me, anyway. If anyone tries to bite you, stab at them with this!" Jade pulled the cross she was wearing from beneath her sweater and put it over his head. "Head for seawater, if you can; but just come with us now!"

"What?" Drew gasped. "Seawater?"

"It can kill a vampire. By the way, my real name is Jade. My husband is Lucien. He's a vampire, too, but a good one."

"What? Wait!"

But Grant and Jade were already running. He had to follow. They made it back to Grant's car. He tossed the heavy sword in back as they piled into the front. In seconds, they were back at the cottages.

The lobby was empty as they hurried through it. "I'm going to get Lena and Suzette," Drew said.

"Do it, but watch out. And if you see Doug . . . holler for help. If anyone gives you any trouble, just start screaming," Grant said, shouting over his shoulder as he followed Jade, right behind her as she hurried ahead to Lucien's cottage. Bursting in, she called her husband's name. There was no answer.

"Upstairs!" she said to Grant.

He followed her. She'd thrown open a suitcase on the bed.

It was filled with small vials of water, heavy silver crosses, and neatly aligned wooden stakes.

Staring at it, Grant shook his head. "But I thought your husband *was* a vampire," he said.

She shrugged dryly. "Takes one to kill one, sometimes. Get over here, stock up." As he neared her, she drew out a large silver medallion on a heavy chain. She slipped it over his neck. "Fill your pockets with the vials. Oh, and this!"

To his amazement, she handed him a kid's squirt gun. He stared at her.

"Works wonders," she told him. "I've got to try to find out exactly what powers Valeria has, and how they can be stopped. Lucien should have been able to *see* a resurrected vampire. He's been blinded by Valeria's power, and there has to be a way to defeat her—and you've got to be so careful. We still don't know *who* we're up against! I'll find you as quickly as I can," Jade assured him.

He nodded, feeling desperate—and ridiculous. He felt a terrible urgency to get back to the site of the dig—after that, he didn't know. All he knew was that he had to get there.

As he started down the stairs, there was a tapping at the door. He paused, looking back at Jade, who shrugged.

One of the stakes firmly gripped in his hands, he opened the door.

Reggie was standing there. "Grant!" she exclaimed. "Oh, Grant! Thank God. I was afraid . . . I was trying to get to Stephanie . . . and I'm afraid it's too late! You've got to go for her, help her!"

"How did you know where to find me? And what the hell are you talking about?" Grant demanded.

"I saw you walk in here, but Grant! Damn it, that doesn't matter! We've got to get to Stephanie."

He stood stiffly. "You lured her here, didn't you, Reggie?" he asked coldly. "Why?"

"Because," Jade said softly from behind him, "she *is* Valeria."

"Lena? Suzette?"

The door to Lena's cottage was standing open.

Tentatively, he pushed it open. The place was dark. He heard a giggle.

"Drew!" Suzette said from the darkness.

"Drew's come to play!" Lena said, her voice husky, sultry.

"Hey, come on, turn a light on in here," Drew said. He wasn't going in. Already, it seemed that the hair at the back of his neck was rising. He could smell . . .

Blood.

And it looked as if there was a body on the floor.

"Drew!"

Suddenly, Suzette was in front of him. Stark naked. Wet. Hair slicked back. Eyes glazed.

She reached for him. Somehow, he knew to step back. It was her eyes.

And, of course, the fact that she was naked.

"No, no! Come in!" the blonde urged.

"We can play!" Lena, every bit as sleek and sultry and bare, was right behind her. She licked her lips slowly as she looked at him.

Scream. Grant had said that he should scream.

He did.

"No fun, no fair!" Lena howled.

He turned and ran. Seawater. Liz had said to head for seawater.

Drew headed for the beach and plowed in. He stopped, turning back. They had paused on the beach. Lena giggled.

Then they started coming for him.

"Shit!"

He let out a scream again. The two girls were several feet into the water, about to plunge beneath it.

He heard a sharp command snapped out from the beach. "Stop!"

Suzette and Lena both froze.

Staring toward the sand, Drew saw Clay Barton. *Lucien, my husband's name is Lucien,* the woman he had known as Liz, now Jade, had told him. *He's a good vampire.*

A good vampire?

But both Suzette and Lena slowly turned. They walked like docile little lambs to stand about five feet in front of the man. Drew emerged from the water slowly and carefully, making sure that the *good* vampire was between him and the girls.

Once situated behind the man, Drew was tempted to make a face at the girls. Now, their faces were just blank. It was really a bizarre sight, the two of them, the blond angel and sultry Lena, buck naked in the breeze, staring at the man as if he were their puppeteer.

"We're going to need to restrain them," Lucien said. "Let's go."

"Let's go! They've become . . . harpies. There's . . . there's someone dead in their cottage!" Drew said. "And you're walking away and they're free, coming right behind me!"

"They'll follow," Lucien said, taking the path toward his cottage. "Hey, please, try not to drip on me, huh?"

"Don't drip on you—but they walked right into the water!" Drew said.

"They haven't turned—they're just under the influence," Lucien said.

"Under the influence, huh? I couldn't just have friends who got drunk or did drugs, noooo, my friends have to turn into half-vampires!"

Lucien cast him a quick gaze. "You want to turn into one

yourself? I didn't think so. So come along, and pay sharp attention."

Drew took a glance behind him at the women. He hurried along at Lucien's side.

"You bet!" he vowed nervously.

Stephanie awoke feeling the cold. She wasn't in pain, she was simply cold through and through.

Instinct warned her that she was in danger.

She opened her eyes slowly and carefully.

At first, she saw only the gray-toned slab of rock. Puzzled, she shifted her gaze. Despite her resolve, her eyes widened.

She was in a cave. That much was easily surmised.

She was on a bed in a cave, but quite a bed—heavy wood, antique carved. It was covered with a massive, arched canopy, and to one side, a heavy tapestry was hung. It should have given her some warmth. It did not. The fire that burned in an iron grate in the center of the area should have provided warmth as well. There was a massive, planked table not far from the fire; huge carved chairs surrounded it.

She tried to move. She was easily able to do so. Again, she found herself perplexed, for she was no longer wearing the jeans and shirt she had soaked in the ocean. She was in a long, medieval gown that felt like some kind of velvet. It was black; even the lace that edged the hem of the skirt and sleeves was black.

"So, you are back with us!"

She jumped, and turned.

Against the wall of the cave behind her was another massive medieval chair. The man sitting in it appeared to be something of a giant, for he was wearing a huge, sweeping black mantle that gave bulk to his shoulders.

She closed her eyes for a minute, accepting that none of

this was a dream. She knew him, yes, had known him . . . and thought so very little about him. He had just been there. And he was so different now. Gone was the lightness of features and manner that were usually his. The man's eyes blazed; his hair seemed like ebony, and there wasn't the least hint of laughter about his striking face.

"Giovanni," she said dryly.

He waved a hand in the air impatiently. "François, Comte François de Venue, if you care to be formal. But I will let you call me François."

She swung her legs to the side of the bed and sat primly, folding her hands in her lap. She was aware then of the slight pounding at her temples and the strange crick in her neck.

"I see," she murmured, wondering whether to believe in the impossible again, or deny that any of it could be. Maybe it was a dream, and she simply couldn't awaken. "So . . . you are a long-dead warlord. You know, kidnapping me is not going to be helpful if you really decide that you want to be in the theater."

He smiled and rose. She thought she would jump up— jump out of her skin. But all he did was look at her, and she realized she was spellbound by the fire that seemed to burn in his eyes. She sat where she was, feeling as if there were chains about her.

"Ah, yes, the theater. I rather think I've outshone all the others you consider to be such good actors. Perhaps, well, later. None of that is for tonight."

She didn't want to ask, but had to. "And what is tonight?"

"Tonight, I end it—for the next several centuries, at any rate."

"And what does that mean?"

"Why, we fight again."

"Who fights again?"

"Why, myself, with you at my side, against Conan de Burgh."

She shook her head. "Conan de Burgh died the night he sent you to hell."

François de Venue smiled, and it was a rake's easy smile, as if he chatted with her, drinking wine as they sat in an ancient castle. "As you see—I was not sent to hell."

"All right. I'll play along. Who is Conan de Burgh?"

"Come, come! Smart girl that you are. The fool who would follow you anywhere in the world. As he followed Valeria, centuries ago."

"Ah. You mean Grant."

"*Voila*, she is intelligent after all!" he mocked.

She shook her head. "I'm not Valeria, and he's not Conan. I know my personal history, and I wasn't dug out of the ground here. Neither was Grant. He's been working for a number of years, so I'm afraid that you're mistaken."

"Of course you are not Valeria. At this moment Valeria is with your friends."

Stephanie felt ill. Had Reggie lured her here? And if so— why? "Reggie?"

"Ah, yes, Reggie! Now, there you have the lucky one, but it's time for her to pay as well. Your Reggie—Valeria—has been living very well all this time, enjoying the luxury of life, hopping from decade to decade—century to century— by bouncing back and forth around the world. She has lived long and well—with the power I gave her."

"And that power is?" Stephanie asked.

"Obviously, that of the true vampire."

There was something in his words that was so simple and arrogant that she felt a chill even deeper than the cold that already seemed to lock her bones.

"I don't understand. Legend had it that Valeria was the one with the power," she said.

"Oh, yes. She has power. But she will always be subservient to me."

"And why is that?"

"Valeria had only the strength of a sorceress, something that was her right from birth, inherited from the time of the great Roman empire, when Egyptians were brought back to Italy as slaves. She, as her mother before her, was a direct descendent of a cult that honored a certain goddess, and through their training, they learned to use the amazing strength in their minds. Perhaps—I've learned so much about the new world in the past months—perhaps it is even genetic, as scientists believe today. Naturally, she honed her ability to an art, a craft of unimaginable strength. I studied a great deal when I went to battle. Amazingly, my own life was changed by a meeting in the great desert when I was seeking triumph and glory in the Holy Lands. It was rather ironic, actually. Men fell at my feet. I am extremely talented with a sword. But the spoils of war have always gone to the victor. There was a woman . . . when I finished with her, I discovered that she had not finished with me. Yet by day, my men found her in her weakness, and she has long since perished. They intended to take me home for burial, but . . . well, I didn't need to be buried. The closest I came to a real extinction was when I went to battle with Conan de Burgh. The injuries he inflicted healed so slowly while I lay buried beneath the rubble. And then . . . well, you know the rest. The earth shifted again. And I am free."

He sat down at her side. He stroked her face. Revulsion brought a tremor snaking through her. He saw it, and was amused. He was repulsive to her, and yet she had no power to move away from him, and he was very aware of it.

"I'm still very confused. Even you have said that Conan de Burgh was killed."

"Yes."

"Then . . ."

"He is back. His soul is returned in the form of your Grant Peterson. I knew, from the minute I opened my eyes from my long sleep, that he was in the world again. And, of course, it was fate that you two should meet. It was luck that you should have been so . . . enamored by him."

"So . . ." She managed to moisten her lips. He was close, and staring at her with such sensual interest—and amusement. She thought he was like a cat, playing with a mouse. He could end it with her whenever he chose.

Yet, if he'd wanted to kill her right away, he'd have done so already.

There was probably so much that he could do to her before she died!

"So, Grant is a reincarnation of Conan de Burgh. You are François de Venue. Reggie is Valeria . . . where do I fit in?"

"You still don't know?"

"Forgive me for being so slow," she murmured sarcastically.

"There was a daughter," he said.

"A daughter?"

"And her daughter had a daughter, and her daughter had a daughter, and . . . well, you surely understand my direction."

"I'm . . . Valeria's descendent?" she asked.

"There—you are speeding up. You see, when I first came upon Valeria, she knew she must obey me, or else . . . despite the life she has led, she did not want to be cursed as a vampire. She did not want it for her daughter. So, you see, she did as I commanded. Because I swore that the child would not be touched. I am a powerful creature, you know. Even without her at my side."

"If that's so . . . why are you threatening me now? You still have Valeria. She tricked me, and I came here. Why? Did you think Grant would follow me? That's a real irony— he came here on his own."

"Yes, I know. We could say that you're insurance. But then, that wouldn't be true."

"Why am I here?"

"This time, he will have to make a choice again."

"And that will be?"

"His life for yours."

Grant had just grabbed Reggie by the arm and dragged her into the entry when Lucien came through the front door.

"This is Reggie," Grant said raggedly. "I have to find out what she knows—and get to the site. Jade has said that she's Valeria. Is that true?"

"So, Valeria, you are here," Lucien said softly. "We do need to talk, don't we?"

"We can't talk long," Grant said. "I have to go now. I have to get to Stephanie."

"You have to wait," Lucien said firmly.

"I can't wait long," Grant said, then fell silent, staring in amazement. In Lucien's wake, Drew, soaked to the bone, walked in. And behind him, Suzette and Lena. They were both naked, and their eyes were like saucers. They seemed to be entirely unaware of their state of undress, or anything else, for that matter.

"What the hell?" Grant said, looking at Lucien.

"They're tainted, under the power of François," he said.

Something tightened in Grant's gut. "Then . . . do we . . . cut their heads off?" He didn't know what was really going on here, what was in the mind, what was real. The concept of murder, however, was a terrible one to him. Somewhere, it all had to end.

It was going to end with him in an Italian prison, he was afraid, or facing execution under Italian law.

Not even that mattered now. Stephanie mattered now.

"They don't need to die—I don't think," Lucien said. He glanced past Grant to his wife. "Jade?"

"I'm on it," she murmured, heading up the stairs.

Grant turned back to Reggie. Lucien and Drew were staring at her as well. "So, you're—Reggie?" Drew said.

"Yes, how do you do."

"Great. Thanks for the job here. I think," Drew said awkwardly. He seemed in a real state of hell, and surely thought himself in the worst nightmare. The girls, naked and dazed as zombies, were there, dripping on the carpet. Reggie wasn't noticing them, and both Grant and Lucien seemed to be taking the moment in stride.

"You lured Stephanie here. On purpose," Grant accused her.

"That's a lie!" Reggie protested. "I wanted to open the theater here. It all came about before the wretched dig that set François free. Don't be idiots, either of you. I came here, I tried to get Stephanie to come to me. I—I even used François. If I could have spoken to her and to him at the same time, well, I . . . I believe I could have gotten her out of here!"

"François is . . ." Drew asked.

"Giovanni," Reggie said absently.

"The baggage boy!" Drew said, astounded.

"Have you known who I am?" Lucien asked her.

"Recently, yes, but only recently. I could feel that one of your particular breed was here . . . and I'd heard of you, throughout the centuries, of course . . . but you have your own strength, don't you?" she asked.

Jade came back down the stairs. She seemed to be carrying handfuls of silver bracelets. Grant was baffled, wondering what good they were going to do.

Tension ripped through him with a jolt of deep agony. He was standing around here, watching this ridiculous Q and A, while Stephanie . . .

A cold sweat broke out on his hands.

"I have to get there!" he repeated vehemently, turning to Lucien.

Lucien placed a hand on his arm. "No. The time isn't

right yet. I know it's hard. You must wait, you must listen to me, and we must play by the rules."

"The rules?" Grant demanded.

Lucien looked at Reggie. "Yes, the rules of destiny," he murmured.

"I can't wait for the rules," Grant said, fighting down the frantic need for action that was tearing at him, muscle and gut.

"It's the only way to win. The only way to get her back alive," Lucien said.

Jade stepped up to the girls. As Grant watched, she began to wind the silver bracelets around Suzette's wrists, and then Lena's.

"Blessed silver," Lucien informed Grant.

Reggie stepped away from them both. She stared at Lucien. "All right, yes, obviously, I knew when François awoke. But this was all already under way. At first . . . at first he said he would spare the populace here, if I would just bring Conan back. I had already arranged for Stephanie to come because . . . because she needed a job! You don't understand, either. I couldn't just leave her in the United States. He would have found her. Without me there to protect her. She had no intention of telling Grant . . . but it didn't matter. He'd already felt the draw. It had to happen; he had to come here. So . . . I'm not evil! François lied to me, and used me . . . and all he wanted was Stephanie. I can help you, don't you understand? I know him, I know what he's doing!"

"So do I," Lucien said softly. He turned to Grant. "You have to beat him again. And this time, you have to destroy him. Yourself."

By that time, Jade had led Suzette and Lena to the sofa, and seated them. "They really need . . . clothing," she murmured.

"Well, get some blankets. Jade, don't forget their ankles.

And make sure you have them down with crosses on their chests. I don't want to have to kill them. God knows how many he will have in his little army he's been tainting when we get there, so they must be secured here." He paused, staring hard at Drew and Grant. "You will have to be careful of everyone. Some will be with us. Some will pretend to be with us—and turn on us. When we ride to battle."

"We're riding to battle?" Drew said, his voice weak.

"And Valeria," he said, looking at her.

Reggie had always been a beautiful woman, Grant thought. And she was never more so than now, standing at her full height, her chin high. A strand of dark hair fell over one eye, lips trembled. Her near-violet gaze was steady. "I'm trying to help you!" she told him passionately.

She ran to Grant suddenly, seizing his arm. "You know how long I have been dear to Stephanie! Yes, I have been caught up in this, but only because . . . Grant, I am so sorry! But I thought that if François could just . . . well, if he could kill you, then his hatreds would be at an end. He would learn the simple survival that can be for us, without bloodshed and harm to others."

She was so sincere! As he looked at her, Grant found himself believing her.

"Ah, but, Valeria!" Lucien said softly. "You've been shielding François from me. It's your powers of protection that have blinded me for so long."

"I didn't know who you were!" she swore, turning from Grant to Lucien, then back to Grant. "Please, you may not be able to save her without me!"

Grant looked at Lucien. "Is that true?"

Lucien was steady, but shrugged. "She is a sorceress of the oldest variety. She can protect them, or she can protect us."

"Which will she do?" Drew interjected.

"I don't know," Lucien admitted.

Grant shook off Reggie's—or Valeria's—touch. "We have to find them. Now. I feel it. Darkness has fallen, and the moon will be rising."

"The full moon," Lucien murmured. "Yes, it's time. Valeria, wear a cross, if you would ride with us."

She balked. "Wait . . . I haven't spent all these centuries being an angel."

There was a sudden banging at the door. Even Lucien seemed startled, but then he strode to it.

Grant followed quickly behind him.

And when they opened the door, he was amazed.

He felt as if he had walked into an old Hammer film, and Vincent Price or Bela Lugosi would appear at any minute.

Beyond the cottage door, night had fallen. But it was illuminated. There were dozens . . . maybe a hundred people out there. Some were carrying torches. Some were armed with pitchforks, some with kitchen knives . . . some with medieval weapons, apparently looted from a museum.

It wasn't Bela Lugosi or Vincent Price at the head of the crowd.

It was the old man. Adalio. Slim and fragile, yet he carried a heavy battle ax.

"It's time!" he announced loudly and clearly, his English accented but sure.

Grant looked behind him. There were a number of people on horseback. He recognized some of them. Both policemen were there, Merc and Franco. There were a number of waiters from the clubs, and from the local restaurants. There were hospital employees, shopkeepers, and local farmers.

Lucien turned to Grant. "Tonight, I am your squire," he said. He looked back to his wife. "Jade . . . ?"

"They're secure," she told him.

"Come on—they're prepared for you."

"The sword is in the car," Grant said.

"I'm sure that someone has gotten it for you," Lucien said.

They walked out. The crowd parted for Grant. Someone came forward with armor. He stood still, letting the villagers heft the plates on him, buckling the leather straps and fasteners. He heard the clank of metal as Lucien and Drew were likewise attired.

Merc came forward with the sword.

As Grant stood there, he was startled to hear a whisper in his ear. Reggie's voice. "I'm with you all, fighting for goodness and life, I swear it!"

Startled, he swung around. Reggie was nowhere near him.

"Where is she?" he demanded, staring at Lucien.

"Gone."

"I heard her—she said that she is with us," Grant said.

"She's a sorceress," Lucien reminded him dryly. "For good, or bad, she is part of this battle, and in the end, we'll know the truth."

"In the end?" Drew said weakly.

Grant saw the horse that had been brought for him. He thought it was the same huge black that had drawn the hearse that afternoon.

He mounted with ease—thanks to a life in theater and film. He turned the horse, ready to start for the hills.

"Wait, wait!" Drew called out. Grant looked back. Drew was pale, and hobbling along as he tried to mount up, weighed down by the armor. "Ah, come on! I've been in improv . . . and comedy. I never worked for a horse farm, I wasn't a stuntman . . . and I don't know a damned thing about medieval armor!"

Amazingly, Grant realized that he could smile. He turned to Lucien. "Is he going to be all right?"

"I think so," Lucien said, watching Drew and nodding

slowly. "It's what's inside the man that matters," he told Grant.

"It's time!" the old man shouted, his English fine.

It was then that they heard the first howling.

A sound that was unearthly, as if all the demons of hell had awakened.

"The devil dogs," Lucien said.

Every hair on Grant's body seemed to stand up. The sound was bone-chilling, horrible in its eeriness.

He spurred his horse.

Stephanie was up there, somewhere in the hills.

Chapter 18

"Kill me now," Stephanie said. She stared coolly at François, since it seemed she had control of her own eyes, and no more.

He smiled. "Kill you now? Are you mad, dear girl? Kill you . . . oh, I would not. You are not Valeria, you know. I control you completely."

"Why? Have I died already?"

He shook his head, smiling, amused, and lifted her hair from her shoulders. She couldn't pull away when he pressed his lips to her neck. She felt the slide of his tongue . . . his breath.

The rasp of his teeth against her flesh.

To her horror, she felt a faint stirring of . . .

Excitement.

He whispered against her flesh. "I've had just the most gentle of a lover's game with you . . . I enjoy my meals when they're awake, you see. Ah, poor child, but you're a great deal like Valeria was . . . once. I teased you in your dreams with the form of your lover cast over my own being, and yet . . . you knew, I think, that it was me."

Grant.

She closed her eyes. And she could see him. Grant, as he was in her dreams. Larger than life. And she saw him as he was. His smile. The darkness in his eyes, when they filled with passion. The way he walked to her, so aggressive in his confidence, beautiful in his nakedness, supple in movement. She was in love with him, had been, always would be . . .

"Rather," she murmured, ignoring his touch, "I think you tried to enter my dreams, but could not, because I will always see him," she said softly.

She felt a rip against her flesh.

"You are mine," he told her. "I haven't taken your petty mortal life as yet. But I've taken enough of your life's blood to see that you will obey me. Now . . . the devil dogs. You will raise them now."

"The devil dogs? I don't even know what they are."

He rose, irritated. He looked around the cave.

Someone entered—Doug. He looked at Stephanie, and smiled slowly. Perhaps something in his glance annoyed François, because he snapped out, "Has she come?"

"Not yet, my lord."

"My lord!" Stephanie echoed.

"It is what you will call me, too," he informed her.

In a sudden fury, he came to her, wrenching her to her feet. Her limbs felt like lead. She couldn't resist him, couldn't fight.

"The devil dogs! It's in your power. Raise them, now! All of them. I've heard the cries of the wolves, so the time is right. Now. Think of them . . . think of the corpses out there, rotting in the ground. Those that came before, you will make them come again!"

His grip on her arm was punishing. Yet . . .

She willed herself to ignore it.

"It's time—oh, I have waited, anticipated this day!" François said. "The horses, now!" he commanded Doug.

And Doug turned without question to obey, just as he had been ordered.

François stared at her, let out a cry of rage, and walked to her, falling on his knees before her. "Do you know what I can do to you? Do you know I can begin to make you suffer? The devil dogs. I need them now!"

It was as he had dreamed.

And, he began to believe, as it had been before.

They had ridden a distance from the seaside when another group, some mounted, some on foot, came to join them.

And there, at their head, was the priest. The same man who had so recently read the rites for Maria Britto.

Grant urged his horse close, and he bowed his head while the man said prayers in Latin. He came forward; Grant knew he would offer him a cross, but he wore one already. The priest did bear a cross, but a huge one on a large chain. He set it around the horse's neck, and Grant readjusted the reins, thanking him.

Then, they were both sprinkled with holy water, and more prayers in Latin rose to the heavens.

The demon dogs howled again.

They rode.

The moon sat high and full above them; a strange, cold wind whipped at them.

Lucien rode closer to his side. "I believe that the devil dogs are the corpses of the dead who have died on the side of evil—murderers, rapists . . . destroyers."

Grant glanced at him quickly.

"You must sever their heads," Lucien said.

"I . . . knew that," Grant murmured.

They rode hard, the hordes on foot following behind them. They neared the site.

As they rode, the wind whipped higher, cold and strange, for there was a fog upon the ground, and the wind did not disperse it. They could hear screams and cries, and still, that unearthly howling sound.

The encampment was under attack, Grant realized.

Reaching the higher ground at last.

They saw the troops of François de Venue emerging through the fog, making a line before them. They were made up of others of the townsfolk. Grant could see Doug was at his right-hand side. There was the pretty nurse from the hospital . . .

Arturo. Men he had met at the dig.

They were, indeed, an army.

François led.

Stephanie was at his side.

Her dark hair billowing down her shoulders . . .

Her eyes, so deep and magnetic a blue they were almost violet, dazed. And yet . . .

There was a glow about them. A glow like . . . tears.

"Let her go!" Conan roared. "She isn't really a part of this."

"If you would have her, you'll have to die."

"She is no part of it! I will face you gladly—you don't need to hold her."

François rose in his shadow. "Before, Conan, I let you live. Tonight, by all the fires of hell, you will perish, and no power will ever bring you back!"

The dark, handsome face of François de Venue, the man he had once know as Giovanni, darkened into a scowl of fury. "Tonight is the night you die!"

"We shall meet in hell, then, François. Indeed, if need be, we will meet in hell!"

"Now!" François roared to Stephanie.

"Stephanie!" Grant called to her, his voice rising above the howl of the dogs.

The wind began to whip anew in an eerie, dark swirl of fog and night. The baying increased.

And then the demon dogs came rushing through the throngs of horsemen and foot soldiers that flanked François and his troops.

And Stephanie.

The first animal leapt upon him. His horse staggered. Grant looked at the thing in amazement. It was a dog, and not a dog, huge in size . . . but not a wolf. Its teeth were those of a great cat, a tiger in the night.

It was a corpse. Not dog, wolf, or great cat. It was a corpse, summoned from the grave with the unholy power of a sorceress . . .

Stephanie?

No!

Corpse or not, it was vicious and powerful. Its shoulder muscles were gigantic, and its massive paws held great, tearing, catlike claws. The sheer power and size of it was so great that it knocked over his horse, and unseated him.

The head! Sever the head!

With a massive blow, he did so.

But looking up, he saw that they were coming in waves.

Near his side, Lucien was slashing away at the creatures with a practiced fury. Lucien glanced at him.

"Call out to her—call out to Stephanie! She can order them back to hell."

"Stephanie didn't call these foul beasts from the dead!" Grant shouted back.

"Whether she did or didn't, she can send them back to hell!"

He paused, shouting as loudly as he could, "Stephanie! Stephanie, for the love of God, you can do it! Send them back!"

Screams rose around Grant. But it seemed that they were pushing forward. He went to swipe at the head of a devil dog and then froze where he stood.

He never slashed into the neck. The thing, just suddenly,

in mid-leap, turned into a pack of dust and bones and fell harmlessly to the earth.

"Forward!" He heard himself rage out the command.

He turned back to see his haphazard army ready to obey. There . . . just feet from him, locked in battle, he saw Drew and Doug.

"Ah, come on, buddy, put down the sword!" Drew pleaded.

Grant saw the fierce twist of Doug's lips as he formed them into a snarl. Doug raised his massive, blood-drenched sword, ready to strike with a vengeance.

"Shit!" Drew cried.

And he rose, with tears in his eyes, and made a clean swipe with his weapon that sliced right through Doug.

He fell.

Someone lunged against Grant's back. Someone in full armor. He nearly fell, then staggered, gained his balance, and turned back. His opponent was fierce, driving him to defensive measures as onslaught after onslaught came his way.

He swung the great, double-handed blade with all his strength and agility, catching his opponent just under the neck.

The helmet flew from the fighter.

And he paused.

Catching at her throat, trying to stanch the flow of blood, was Valeria.

And for a moment, past images flooded into his vision. Valeria . . . beautiful, laughing at his side, long ago . . .

When she had been young.

Innocent . . .

And he hesitated.

She'd had a daughter. She'd ridden with François . . . because he had threatened the girl. The daughter had lived . . . and the centuries had gone by . . .

And now, she screamed in rage, rising, catching her

sword from the ground, and flying after him again. Her sword caught him such a blow against the chest that he went down.

Her arms stretched out to the heavens. Lightning cracked against the sky. The wind roared, and he heard again the baying of the demon dogs . . .

"No!" he roared.

He grabbed the cross he wore around his neck, rolled when her sword would have rent him into pieces. Staggering, he found his feet again. He didn't try to collect his weapon, but charged at her with the huge cross held high in his hands. He slammed against her, pressing the cross hard to her forehead and face.

She screamed with rage and pain that rose above the howling.

She fell to her knees.

Looked up at him . . .

And he knew. He saw her just as he had seen her centuries ago. He saw the snarl of triumph, the vicious snarl she had given him before . . .

François had not been all that had driven her to evil. She had found power, and she had loved it. And he had saved her life long enough for the earth to tear and crumble . . .

And crush all her enemies beneath it. And since then, she had been waiting.

He caught up his sword, and prepared to deal the death blow.

"*Conan!*"

The cry caused him to pause. Then, he saw again the change begin to take place in her eyes, in her features . . .

A smile . . .

That faded.

He heard the *whoosh* of the sword. For a moment, Valeria remained, frozen in time with that smile on her face.

Then . . . her head fell to her side.

"Move! He went to Valeria to fight his arm-to-arm combat this time!" Lucien told him. And he pointed.

The precipice was not what it had been before. It barely jutted from the cliff. But François had dragged Stephanie there. She was openly fighting him now, but he had her by the hair.

And there was Arturo, ready to help him, dragging Stephanie down, down by the shoulders, forcing her to her knees.

"No!"

Again, his cry rose to the night sky, to the darkness, to heaven, and beyond. He bounded upward, catching tree limbs, branches, anything to hurry his assent.

"She is Valeria!" Someone shouted. "She is the evil!"

They were mad; they were insane. They had ridden with him, and they knew . . .

Or did they? *They only knew that evil had been dug from the past, from the ground, and that it was living among them again.*

Above the roar, he could hear the rise of François's laughter.

With a desperate, mighty push, he thrust himself from the trail, jumping up on the edge where too many people struggled desperately.

He caught Arturo first, sending the man over the edge with a massive right to the jaw. Freed, Stephanie leapt up.

"Get behind me!" he ordered her.

"Grant! He's a vampire. You . . . you . . . haven't . . ."

Grant swung the sword. He knew he had a perfect and sure shot at the man's neck.

But François disappeared, and all he could hear was laughter.

"Stephanie, get away!" he urged her. He couldn't fight François, and hold off the people who were slowly but steadily making their way up the trail.

"I can't . . . I can make you see him. Grant!"

He turned just in time. Leering, furious, all but frothing at the mouth, François was at him again. Grant deflected the blow, and started to swing.

Again, the man started to disappear.

"No!" Stephanie shouted.

The image of the man wavered, but remained.

Grant swung.

The head of the man went flying.

Stephanie fell, first to her knees . . . and then, to the earth.

The wind ceased instantly.

The clang of steel was hushed.

The baying of the demon dogs had long since quieted.

"Stephanie!"

Grant screamed her name, falling down beside her.

And then, the noise began. A trembling that shook the earth. It was deep, horrible, a rumble that seemed to shake all the world . . .

From below, someone, it sounded like Carlo Ponti, shouted, "Quake!"

Stephanie was out cold. He could barely reach her, the earth was so volatile. He stretched out his arms . . . caught her, drew her to him.

It was going to go. The little piece of precipice that remained. He was bogged down in armor, so heavy laden. Still, he got her into his arms . . . he began to run.

Behind each footstep, more of the earth gave.

He hit the trail.

The ground jolted.

He fell himself . . . fell . . . flew.

They rolled . . .

Downward, downward, downward . . .

And the world was black.

* * *

The quake that struck the area was not nearly as bad as several that had devastated the region before.

Sadly, there was a death toll.

These were things Grant learned when he awakened, days later.

He woke feeling strange. Very strange. He'd been . . . out . . . for several days. But he awoke with a savage hunger, and a strange sense of power.

He awoke, in Stephanie's bed, at the resort.

And when he started to rise, he felt her at his side.

He stared at her a long moment. Her eyes were on his, more violet than ever. Her hair was like a cloak around her . . .

She was naked. And she smiled as he looked at her.

"Hello."

"Hello."

"How do you feel?"

"As if I could eat an entire cow."

Her smile deepened. "But . . . what do you remember?" she asked him.

"Everything," he told her solemnly. "And everything is vivid, except . . ."

"Except?"

"When we fell, when you were in my arms . . . there was a tremendous flash of . . . light. And you were with me, and it was as if we were floating, rising. Rising above all of it, and then . . . I felt the strangest stab of pain, and then . . ."

"And then?"

"I woke up."

"I had the dream, too," she said very softly.

"The same?"

"The light . . . the rising . . . floating, in clouds. I woke earlier than you."

He nodded, looked around.

"Valeria—Reggie—is dead."

"Sadly, yes. And Arturo, too. And François. Destroyed, forever."

"Why do I feel this way?" he asked her. "We should have been in a hospital or something. And instead, I feel as if I could take on the whole world."

"I'm not sure," she said hesitantly.

"But you think you know."

"Well, fate brought us here, you know."

"Yes?"

"I think we were supposed to . . . be buried with the quake."

"But we weren't?" he whispered.

She shook her head.

"Fate, as Lucien told me, can be changed."

"And what does that mean?"

"François had a chance to rise again. So many more would have perished. But we triumphed."

"I still don't understand what you're saying."

"We have some friends who are . . . different," she told him.

"Yes?"

"Could we be different now, too?"

He stared at her hard. "Jesu!" he breathed.

"There is good and evil in all existence!" she told him.

"You don't mean—"

She shook her head, rising.

As always, she was the most beautiful creature in the world to him. She might have been descended from the sorceress, and God knew, apparently, she even had some of her power. But she had used that power for good.

Her hair was a cascade of dark silk down her back. Her eyes . . . held just the slightest glistening.

And she moved toward him. She crawled atop him, straddling him.

He felt a rise like nothing he had ever known before. His muscles tensed, his being quickened.

She leaned against him. "Are you very, very hungry?" she whispered.

He nodded. "Starving."

She sighed, lowering her head. He reached out, lifting her chin. He drew her to him then, finding her lips, savoring them, wondering how one could awaken from a near-grave, and feel such a desperate burst of sexual urgency.

It was Stephanie . . .

Always Stephanie.

Always had been Stephanie.

"Food can wait," he told her huskily.

He kissed her again. And again. And then he rose against her, and rolled her to his side, and kissed every inch of her.

He reveled as he never had before in the scent and taste of her. She was lithe and sinuous, she moved like magic and liquid against him.

He needed her like air, like water . . .

More than either.

They made love. And he knew that he was fierce. And they made love again, and he knew that he was tender.

Later, they rose, showered, and dressed. And then walked to the cottage where they hoped to find Lucien and Jade.

Jade ushered them in, assuring him that Drew, Lena, and Suzette were all fine, and all—including Drew—thought that they'd just been part of the great quake that had struck the area.

Giovanni was dead, caught in the quake, but Merc and Franco had reported that they had forensic evidence that he'd been the killer, and so, despite the havoc, the region could rest in peace once again.

There was more, much more, of course. But . . . there was time now, too.

Lucien poured wine; Jade had made dinner in the cottage.

They sat down together, and at last, Stephanie said, "There's something . . . strange."

"Oh?" Lucien said.

Grant cleared his throat. "Well, I was half dead. And I awoke feeling like . . . well, feeling like the greatest damned sexual tiger in the world. I was dying of thirst, starving . . . and I looked at Stephanie, and I . . . I wanted her more than anything." He looked from Stephanie's huge and luminous eyes to Lucien. "Does that mean . . . ?"

Lucien smiled, glancing at his wife. "I think that means that you love her more than anything in the world. And you'd probably better ask her to marry you quickly. Before something else comes up."

Grant arched a brow. "Is something else going to come up?"

Jade let out a sigh of exasperation. "Grant. You idiot! Didn't you listen? You're in love!"

He turned to Stephanie. "I'm in love. I need you more than water, food, air to breathe—even life. Will you marry me?"

And she smiled. "In a heartbeat," she told him.

And he didn't care that others were there.

He kissed her.

That, he decided, was fate.

Embrace the Romance of
Shannon Drake

By Best-selling Author
Fern Michaels

__About Face	0-8217-7020-9	$7.99US/$10.99CAN
__Kentucky Sunrise	0-8217-7462-X	$7.99US/$10.99CAN
__Kentucky Rich	0-8217-7234-1	$7.99US/$10.99CAN
__Kentucky Heat	0-8217-7368-2	$7.99US/$10.99CAN
__Plain Jane	0-8217-6927-8	$7.99US/$10.99CAN
__Wish List	0-8217-7363-1	$7.50US/$10.50CAN
__Yesterday	0-8217-6785-2	$7.50US/$10.50CAN
__The Guest List	0-8217-6657-0	$7.50US/$10.50CAN
__Finders Keepers	0-8217-7364-X	$7.50US/$10.50CAN
__Annie's Rainbow	0-8217-7366-6	$7.50US/$10.50CAN
__Dear Emily	0-8217-7316-X	$7.50US/$10.50CAN
__Sara's Song	0-8217-7480-8	$7.50US/$10.50CAN
__Celebration	0-8217-7434-4	$7.50US/$10.50CAN
__Vegas Heat	0-8217-7207-4	$7.50US/$10.50CAN
__Vegas Rich	0-8217-7206-6	$7.50US/$10.50CAN
__Vegas Sunrise	0-8217-7208-2	$7.50US/$10.50CAN
__What You Wish For	0-8217-6828-X	$7.99US/$10.99CAN
__Charming Lily	0-8217-7019-5	$7.99US/$10.99CAN

Available Wherever Books Are Sold!

Visit our website at **www.kensingtonbooks.com.**

Romantic Suspense from
Lisa Jackson